Schüler-Lernkrimi Englisch

Teen Crime Club

Tatort Schließfach

Ultimatum per SMS

Eiskalte Rache

compact

In der Reihe Compact Lernkrimi Classic sind erschienen:
- Englisch, Französisch, Italienisch, Spanisch: B1, B2, C1
- Englisch GB/US, Business English: B1, B2
- Deutsch: B1
- Sammelband Lernkrimi Englisch, Französisch, Italienisch, Spanisch: B1/B2

In der Reihe Compact Lernkrimi Kurzkrimis sind erschienen:
- Englisch, Französisch, Italienisch, Spanisch: A2, B1, Deutsch: A2

In der Reihe Compact Lernkrimi Rätselblock sind erschienen:
- Englisch, Französisch, Italienisch, Spanisch: A2

In der Reihe Compact Lernkrimi Hörbuch sind erschienen:
- Englisch: A2, B1, B2, Business English: B2
- Französisch, Italienisch, Spanisch: A2, B1

In der Reihe Compact Lernkrimi Audio-Learning sind erschienen:
- Englisch: A2, B1, Französisch, Spanisch, Italienisch: B1

In der Reihe Compact Lernkrimi Sprachkurs sind erschienen:
- Englisch, Spanisch: A1/A2

Lernziele:
- Grundwortschatz, Grammatik (A2, B1)
- Aufbauwortschatz, Konversation (B2, C1)

In der Reihe Compact Schüler-Lernkrimi sind erschienen:
- Englisch, Französisch, Spanisch, Latein, Deutsch, Mathematik, Physik, Chemie
- Sammelband Schüler-Lernkrimi Englisch

Weitere Titel sind in Vorbereitung.

Chefredaktion: Evelyn Boos
Redaktion: Helga Aichele
Fachkorrektur: Fiona Cain
Produktion: Johannes Buchmann
Lernkrimi-Logo: Carsten Abelbeck
Illustrationen: Sonja Heller
Titelillustration: Karl Knospe
Typografischer Entwurf: Maria Seidel
Umschlaggestaltung: EKH Werbeagentur, Hartmut Baier

ISBN 978-3-8174-7899-6
7278991/2

www.compactverlag.de, www.lernkrimi.de

Vorwort

Mit dem neuen, spannenden Compact Schüler-Lernkrimi-Sammelband könnt ihr eure Englischkenntnisse auf schnelle und einfache Weise vertiefen, auffrischen und überprüfen.
In diesem Band sind Schüler die Helden. Begleite sie bei ihren abenteuerlichen Erlebnissen und verbessere dein Englisch – ganz nebenbei.
Jeder Krimi wird durch abwechslungsreiche und kurzweilige Übungen ergänzt, die das Lernen unterhaltsam und spannend machen.
Prüfe dein Englisch in Lückentexten, Zuordnungs- und Übersetzungsaufgaben, in Buchstabenspielen und Kreuzworträtseln!
Dieses umfassende Sprachtraining zum englischen Grund- und Aufbauwortschatz sowie zur englischen Grammatik bietet die ideale Trainingsmöglichkeit für zwischendurch.
Schreibe die Lösungen einfach ins Buch!
Die richtigen Antworten sind in einem eigenen Lösungsteil am Ende des Buches zu finden.
Das ausführliche Glossar im Anhang erleichtert das Verständnis der Krimis. Es umfasst die schwierigsten Wörter, die im Text kursiv markiert sind.

Und nun kann die Spannung beginnen ...

Viel Spaß und Erfolg!

Schüler-Lernkrimi Englisch Sammelband

Inhalt

Schüler-Lernkrimi
Englisch

Crime Scene: Locker Room

Woods Delaney

Inhalt

Story

Endlich Ferien! Sarah, Kevin, Simon und Julia sind glücklich: bei strahlendem Sonnenschein können sie nun sechs herrliche Wochen ihre Freizeit genießen. Der beste Treffpunkt dafür ist natürlich das Freibad.
Doch plötzlich verschwinden auf rätselhafte Weise Dinge aus den Schließfächern. Als auch noch Kevins nagelneuer CD-Player gestohlen wird, ist er außer sich. Die Polizei nimmt die Anzeige auf, kann aber keine Verdächtigen ermitteln. So versucht Kevin auf eigene Faust, die Täter zu finden. Wer ist für die Diebstähle verantwortlich? Und wie werden die Schließfächer ausgeraubt, obwohl die Türen nie aufgebrochen sind? Für Kevin steht fest, wer die Diebe sind. Auf abenteuerliche Weise verfolgt er ihre Spur, um sie zu überführen. Aber seine Freunde haben einen ganz anderen Verdacht.
Werden sie es schaffen, die wahren Diebe zu stellen?

Chapter 1: Holidays at Last!

"School is finally over. I thought the summer holidays would never come," said Simon.
"I didn't think I would survive another day of school," said Sarah, "not with the *beady eyes* of Mr Jones watching my every move."
Sarah liked most of the teachers, but Mr Jones, the school headmaster, was not a favourite. "He's really *creepy* sometimes."
"He's all right," said Simon. "I'm sure he's as happy about the summer holidays as we are."
The two were standing directly in front of the school. It was the end of July, and there was no more school until the beginning of September.

Übung 1: Unterstreiche die zehn Wörter, die falsch geschrieben sind, und verbessere sie!

! ÜBUNG 1

They felt free but didn't know what to do with their fredom.
Simon was *handsome* and *shy*, and though Sarah was not exactly pritty, she was interesting and *outgoing*. Usually her hair was pink, but sometimes she *dyed* it green or some other strange colour. Her noise ring had been a bit of a shock at first. There was no written school rule that said you couldn't get your nose pierced, but everyone knew that you couldn't. And then Sarah had got her nose pierced. In the meantime many boys and girls were whering such rings – and getting their eyebrows, their lips, their tongues pierced as well. Sarah was moar than a hair colour or a piercing, though. She had personality, charm – "*that certain something*," as thay say in Hollywood. They might have made a good cupple, but whenever they were together Simon could think of nothing werth talking

about. Every thought that came into his head seemed stuppid, so he hated the idea of being alone with Sarah. She had no idea how to read Simon's silences. Was he uninterested, boared or was he simply comfortable with the silence?

______________________ ______________________

______________________ ______________________

______________________ ______________________

______________________ ______________________

______________________ ______________________

"Hey, Simon, what are you doing?" Kevin, Simon's best friend, was calling to him from across a busy street. Over his clothes he was wearing *kneepads* and *elbow pads* and he was holding his skateboard under his arm. Kevin was a skateboard *freak*. There were only two places he didn't bring his skateboard – in the shower and in bed. His skateboard was a bit *battered*, but Kevin loved it.

ÜBUNG 2 !

Übung 2: Setze die Verben ins Simple Past!

"I don't know," Simon (1. to answer) ____________, looking at Sarah helplessly. "And you?"

"I've got to go home," Kevin (2. to say) ____________. "I promised my mum I'd help her with the *spring cleaning*."

"A bit late for that, isn't it?"

"Yeah. She wants to throw a lot of *stuff* away, and I've got to make sure she doesn't throw anything of mine away. I've got lots of CDs she'd just love to *get rid of*."

"If the weather's nice tomorrow, we could meet at the pool," Simon (3. to suggest) ____________.

"I'll see if I can get away. I do need to work on my *suntan*." Kevin (4. to set) ____________ his skateboard down, put his *headphones* on and pressed the play *button* on his CD player, got on the skateboard and (5. to skate) ____________ away down the *pavement* and out of sight.

Simon and Sarah (6. to look) ____________ at each other. The silence between them (7. to be) ____________ *uncomfortable* for both and becoming *unbearable*. Sarah finally broke the silence.

"So, do you *fancy* going to a music shop and having a look around?"

"Um, yes, er, no, I mean, um, why not?"

Sarah smiled at him, but there was a little bitterness in her smile.

"You don't have to come, Simon. You can do what you like."

"No, I do want to come, I do. It's just that …"

"What?"

"Nothing."

"I feel *like* I'm *pulling teeth*."

"No, it's not that. Sometimes I just can't tell what I'm in the *mood* for. But looking through CDs would be just the thing."

"Let's go, then," Sarah said, walking away from the school.

Simon followed her. After looking through CDs for more than an hour, they sat at a café and had a cup of tea.

"I don't think we have the same taste in music," Simon said.

"I never thought we did. But that doesn't really matter, does it? I mean you can introduce me to things that you like and I can tell you about things I like. We can bring new ideas into our band." They were members of a band called The Sneakers. Simon played guitar, Sarah played drums and Kevin played bass. Other friends played saxophone and *keyboards*. They were taking the summer off, though, since they would all be going away with their parents on holiday at different times.

"Well, I must be off," Sarah said, "let's pay."

Outside the café, Sarah said, "Bye, Simon."

"Bye, Sarah." They looked at each other a moment. They both wanted to get away but were not sure if they had said goodbye in an *appropriate* way. "Maybe we'll see each other at the pool."

"Pools are not exactly my thing," Sarah said. "They aren't punk rock." Her nose ring sparkled in the sunlight.

Neither am I, thought Simon, but he said, "I suppose not. But I'll be spending a lot of time there just the same."

"Maybe I'll see you there then."

"Kevin will be there too."

"Bye," Sarah said and walked away.

ÜBUNG 3 !

Übung 3: Setze das richtige Fragewort ein!

1. __________ are you doing tomorrow?

2. __________ did you go last night?

3. __________ did you turn the television off?

4. ____________ is your favourite actress?

5. ____________ old is your father?

6. ____________ is the name of the French president?

7. ____________ movie do you want to watch – this one or that one?

8. ____________ has the best CD collection?

9. ____________ do you want to meet tomorrow? After lunch?

The next day was beautiful. Usually it rains on the first day of the summer holidays – which is the price one has to pay for nearly six *glorious* weeks of no school. No one in the city expected such a beautiful day. The *lifeguards* were ready, though. They knew the city pool was going to be *overcrowded*. There had been few bathers the past few weeks, mainly tourists and people on holiday. Now, with the start of the school holidays, the summer would really begin at last.

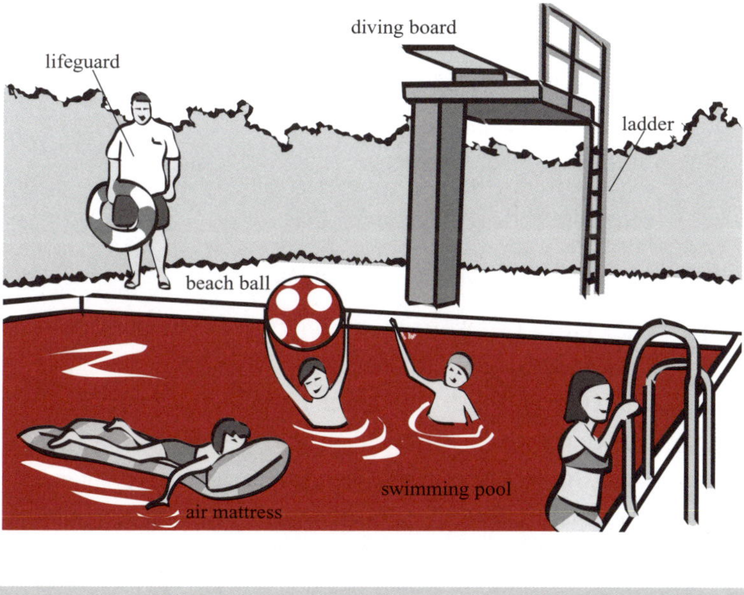

Simon got to the pool around 11 am. He paid the *entry fee* to the *lifeguard* at the entrance, changed in the *locker room* and then walked out to the poolside. He put his towel and a shirt across two white plastic *deckchairs* to save them before walking up to the pool and looking at all the people. There were little boys running around and screaming, pushing each other into the pool, jumping off the *diving boards* and going feet-first into the water. There were girls who joined the boys in their rough games and girls who swam around together like little schools of laughing fish. It was chaos. Simon was a good swimmer, but with so many people in the water there would be no swimming.

ÜBUNG 4 !

Übung 4: Vervollständige die Sätze mit ***a, an*** *oder* ***the****!*

1. Sarah has ______ nose ring.
2. ______ nose ring was a real shock.
3. Simon likes going to ______ pool.
4. Did you have ______ chance to read that book?
5. Kevin rides ______ skateboard.
6. ______ blue skateboard is Kevin's.
7. I'll have ______ apple and ______ banana.
8. Has ______ post come yet?

He *dived* into the cold water and came up for air gasping. The first shock of the cold water was more than he expected. It's always best just to *dive* in, he thought, so you get used to the water. The longer it takes you to get in, the more you *suffer*. Just *dive* in.

Simon swam over to the side of the pool and *grabbed hold of* the rail. No more school for almost two months, he thought. My summer: It will be nothing but relaxing and lying in the sun, playing guitar in the morning and evenings. His thoughts then turned to Sarah, but he didn't know what to think about her – so he preferred not to think about her. He swam to the *deep end* of the pool then went underwater and swam along the bottom of the pool. He did *somersaults* and blew air out his nose until his lungs were empty, then he swam to the surface. He looked around at the *crowd* and decided to get out. He swam over to a ladder, climbed out of the pool and walked back to the *deckchairs*.

Übung 5: Übersetze die Verben und enträtsele das Lösungswort!

ÜBUNG 5 !

1. schwimmen ☐ _ _ _
2. springen _ ☐ _ _
3. treffen ☐ _ _ _
4. hochsteigen _ _ _ ☐ _
5. Kopfsprung machen _ _ _ ☐
6. laufen ☐ _ _

Lösung: _ _ _ _ _ _

"Do you have any *sunscreen*?"
Kevin was standing over Simon, blocking the sun.
"Yes I do," Simon said, picking up his backpack and reaching inside. "I saved this *deckchair* for you."
"Thanks," Kevin said, throwing his bag down on the chair and putting his skateboard underneath it.
Simon finally found his *sunscreen*. "Here," he said to Kevin.

"Thanks, *mate*," Kevin said, "but you're the one who needs it. You're going to be as red as a *lobster* if you don't put some on straight away."

Simon started putting on the *sunscreen*. "My mum always throws it in," he said, "but I always forget to put it on."

"So how are things going with Sarah?" Kevin asked.

"About as well as with Susie," Simon answered.

"You're *snogging* now?"

Both boys knew that the other was hopeless with girls. They liked girls and girls liked them – but something kept everything from working out. There was a simple explanation, however. Simon was *shy* and there was only room for one on Kevin's skateboard. The girls who interested them were simply not the type to just follow them around.

ÜBUNG 6 !

Übung 6: Setze das Gegenteil der Wörter in Klammern ein!

The two lay back on the *deckchairs* and (1. opened) __________ their eyes. They talked about music and politics and what their *fellow students* were doing during the holidays. There were (2. short) __________ silences too. After a while, they both became very hot.

"I've got to jump in," Kevin said. "Are you coming?"

"Yes, I'm (3. cold) __________ too."

They walked up to the pool. Little kids were running around and jumping in.

"Adult swim," Kevin (4. *whispered*) __________ but no one

stopped doing anything. "It was worth a try," Kevin said and *dived* into the pool.

Simon (5. led) __________ him. They hung on the side of the pool and looked around. They saw some people from school, but didn't want to speak to them. Simon swam out to the *deep end* and Kevin followed, though he wasn't as (6. bad) __________ a swimmer as Simon.

"What do you call that?" Simon asked, referring to Kevin's swimming *stroke*.
"*Freestyle*."
"That was not *freestyle*, Kev. It looked like a cross between *freestyle* and butterfly, and they don't go together well."
Kevin put his hands on Simon's shoulders and *dunked* him. Being the better swimmer, though, Simon *grabbed hold of* Kevin's hands and pulled him farther down and then swam away. Simon reached the surface first and watched as Kevin came up and breathed in deeply, before smiling at Simon.
"Are you two trying to *drown* each other?"
They looked up at a girl with brown hair. She had been a quiet girl at the beginning of school last year but had become a bit more *outgoing recently* – perhaps because she was playing saxophone in their band, The Sneakers.
"Hello Julia," Simon said.
"Hey, Jules," Kevin said, playfully changing her name.
"Where's Susie?"
"Painting."
"What's she painting?"

"How should I know? She doesn't tell me anything."
"Are you going to stand there all day, Julia, or are you coming in?" Simon asked.
"I'll help you in," Kevin said, pulling himself up on the side of the pool and reaching for her *ankle*.
Julia stepped back, quickly *pinched* her nose shut and jumped over Kevin and into the water before he could *grab hold of* her. They swam around together and then got out of the pool. Julia followed the boys over to their *deckchairs*.
"Where's your towel?" Simon asked.
"My things are over there," she said, *pointing* a short distance away.
"I could bring your *deckchair* over here, if you want," Simon suggested.
"I can do it," she answered.
"No, I'll do it," he said, walking away. "This one?" he called.
Julia nodded her head to say 'yes' and Simon carried the *deckchair* back.

ÜBUNG 7 !

Übung 7: Welches Wort ist das „schwarze Schaf"? Unterstreiche das nicht in die Reihe passende Wort!

1. classroom, teacher, study, student
2. floor, room, wall, door
3. cough, swim, jump, dive
4. okay, good, fine, great
5. broken, sad, happy, tired
6. bicycle, skateboard, train, car
7. sunny, happy, rainy, windy
8. freestyle, butterfly, dive, backstroke

They spent the rest of the afternoon sitting on the *deckchairs* and cooling off in the pool, though Simon covered himself up.
"Should we go have a tea somewhere?" Simon suggested. The other two agreed, so he added, "We'll meet you outside in fifteen minutes."
The two boys went into the *locker room* to shower and change. As they entered, they saw a tall young man look at them and then leave the men's *locker room*. It was Mick, one of the *lifeguards*.
"Why didn't he say 'hello'?" Kevin wondered aloud.
"Might be busy."
Their *lockers* were in different parts of the *locker room*, so they talked over the *lockers* while they dressed.
"Doesn't your skateboard fit in the *lockers*?" Simon asked.
"No. Besides, I don't like to have it so far away from me."
"You're not going to *ride* it at the pool, Kev."
"Why not? I go down stairs on my skateboard. Maybe one of these days I'll go off the *diving board* on it when the *lifeguards* aren't looking."
"The low board or the high board?"
"The high board, naturally."

Übung 8: Unterstreiche im folgenden Textabschnitt alle Verben im Simple Past!

ÜBUNG 8 !

They walked out and waited for Julia near where the *lifeguards'* office was. Here the *lifeguards* took their breaks, ate lunch, and waited to be called. They worked an hour in the sun, an hour at the door collecting *entry fees*, an hour in the sun and then got an hour off.

"Hey Simon, hey Kev."
"Hey Mick," Kevin said.

"How was university last year, Mick?" Simon asked.
"Don't ask. Are you thinking about going?"
"I don't know."
"Take my advice, don't! There's got to be a better way to get an education."
"Who's here from last year?"
"Just about everyone. Rob's back managing the pool and there's Annie, Lori, Bill, Chris – Mary didn't come back. She got married in June. There's a new *guy*, David, who took her place. He's a bit *thick*, but he's all right. You're a bit *thick*, right Dave?"
"What?" a voice from within asked.
"See? The pay is bad here, so they can't expect everyone they *hire* to be Albert Einstein. I should have taken a job waiting tables, but I'd rather *hang out* with *mates* in the evening than work in a restaurant."
Julia walked out and the three left for a café.

ÜBUNG 9 !

Übung 9: In diesen Sätzen sind die Wörter durcheinander gekommen. Wie lauten die Sätze richtig? Trage sie mit Satzzeichen und richtiger Groß- und Kleinschreibung ein!

1. man young simon shy is a

Simon is a shy young man.

2. hair sarah pink has

....

3. rides everywhere kevin skateboard his

....

4. hot day was it a pool at the very

5. running the pool crowded children was with

6. café do go to you want to a

Chapter 2: Theft at the Locker Room

The next few days passed much the same way. A group of ten or fifteen people, a large circle of friends, met at the pool when the weather was nice. They swam, talked and lay in the sun.

One morning the following week, Simon *showed up* at the pool about *noon*, immediately jumped into the pool and then lay on the *deckchair*. He was getting a nice tan.
"You look like you've been to Ibiza," a girl's voice said.
Simon immediately sat up. "Sarah. I didn't think you'd ever come round here."
"Do you want some company?"
"Pull up a *deckchair*."
"What have you been up to?" Sarah asked, once she was settled on the *deckchair*.
"You're looking at it."
"Have you been playing guitar at all?"
"Yes," Simon answered. He had been practising but felt that the more he practised the worse he became. It wasn't a topic he wanted to discuss. "Have you been practising?" he asked her.

"Yes, but my mum always asks why I didn't take up the flute. Can you imagine me playing the flute?"
Both were happy when Kevin arrived.
"What are you doing here, Pinkie?" Kevin asked. "I thought you punk rock *chicks* were vampires – you only come out at night."
"Kev, *put a sock in it*," she answered.

ÜBUNG 10 !

Übung 10: Beantworte die Fragen zum Text!

1. How long are the summer holidays?

2. What month does the story begin in?

3. What colour is Sarah's hair?

4. Which two characters are best friends?

5. Do Sarah and Simon listen to the same music?

Kevin left and got a *deckchair*. He returned and they had a pleasant conversation. Simon and Sarah spoke to each other while speaking to Kevin. If only it was always so easy.
"I left my CD player in my *locker*," Sarah said and left to *retrieve* it. When she came back she put some music on that Kevin and Simon recognised as punk rock.

Sarah was playing it so loudly they could hear it *blasting* through the *headphones*.
Kevin leaned towards Sarah, pulled one of the *headphones* away from her ear and asked, "What's the difference between punk and heavy metal?"
"*Attitude*," she answered, taking her headphone from his hand and closing her eyes.

Übung 11: Welche der Erklärungen stimmt? Kreuze die richtige Lösung an!

1. Do you fancy a cup of tea?
   a) ☐ Do you like tea?
   b) ☐ Would you like a cup of tea?
   c) ☐ Did you have a cup of tea?

2. Talking to you is like pulling teeth!
   a) ☐ It is difficult to talk to you!
   b) ☐ It is painful to talk to you!
   c) ☐ It is easy to talk to you!

3. I don't think we have the same taste in music.
   a) ☐ We like different music at restaurants.
   b) ☐ We like different kinds of music.
   c) ☐ We like the same kind of music.

4. I must be off!
   a) ☐ I must be crazy!
   b) ☐ I must go now!
   c) ☐ I must be sure!

5. Pools are not exactly my thing.
   a) ☐ I don't know how to build pools.
   b) ☐ I don't really like pools.
   c) ☐ I don't know much about pools.

"The sausages are almost finished, Simon. Did you hear that several *lockers* were *burgled* at the pool?"
Simon's mum was preparing breakfast before she left for work. She had warmed up some baked beans and had set some toast out.
"No, mum. Probably someone who was bored," he answered, sitting down at the table and *grabbing* a piece of toast.
"Do you keep your *belongings* in a *locker*?"
"Of course, mum. I don't want to leave my *wallet* and things on a *deckchair* when I go for a swim."
"Where do you hide your *wallet*?"
"In my shoe."
"Nobody would ever think to look there," she said sarcastically.
"Well, what should I do?"
"Mind that you don't take anything *valuable* with you. Don't take much money with you – just enough for a drink or a snack. And don't forget your *sunscreen*."
"Oh, mum."
"You're *fair-skinned*, Simon. If you get too much sun at your age, you might regret it later – you might get *skin cancer* when you're my age or your grandparents' age."
"Isn't it time you were off to work?"
"Yes, I'm *running late*," she said, throwing off her *apron*. "Clean the kitchen before you go anywhere."
"You have a good day too," he said, with sarcasm in his voice.
Simon looked around the kitchen. There were plates and glasses and pots and pans *stacked* everywhere.

Übung 12: Ordne den passenden zweiten Teil jedes Wortes zu! Trage die richtige Nummer in das Kästchen ein!

1. swim-	☐ -guards
2. deck-	☐ -phones
3. sun-	☐ -suit
4. head-	☐ -style
5. skate-	☐ -chair
6. life-	☐ -screen
7. free-	☐ -board

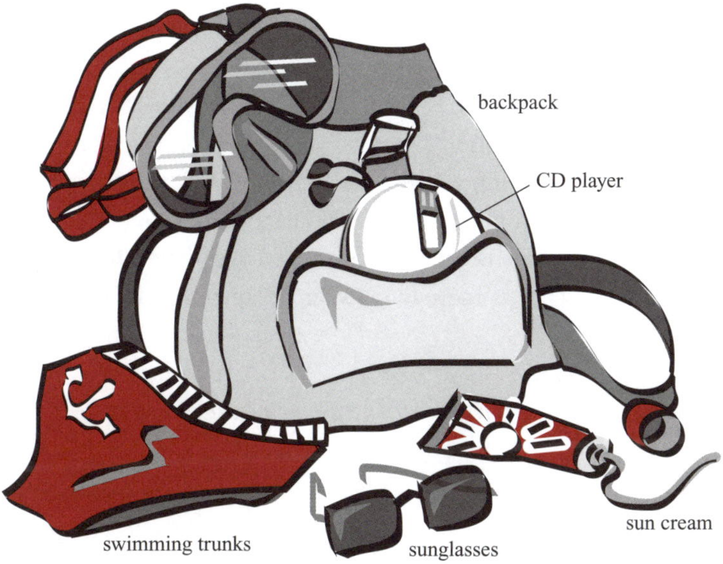

It was early afternoon when Simon got to the pool.
"Your *mates* are already here, Simon," Mick said as he collected the *entry fee* from Simon and noted down his *locker* number.
"I heard about the *burglaries*."

"It was a real drama. Some woman had her watch stolen and some boys lost a few things – I don't know what it was, but I *reckon* it was money."

Simon changed into his swimsuit, *locked* his *belongings* in a *locker* and joined his friends.

"Where have you been?" Kevin asked. "We thought you'd be here early to collect the *deckchairs*. That's your job."

"Yeah, right. Push over; I'm going to put my *deckchair* right there."

The group of young people all pushed their *deckchairs* and towels in different directions to make *space* for Simon.

"Simon, *check this out*. I've got a new CD player. It's really cool! You can hear the bass as if it's right there in your fingers. It's absolutely *amazing*. It vibrates right through your body. Riding my skateboard is going to be a whole new experience."

Simon put on the new CD player and listened for a little bit, then passed it back to Kevin.

"What's wrong?" Kevin asked. "It's *fabulous*."

"It sounds good, but that's not my kind of music."

"That music is cool. Besides, you can't always listen to the same kind of music. There's more than Oasis or Blur or Coldplay."

! ÜBUNG 13

Übung 13: Ordne die Buchstaben zu einem sinnvollen Wort!

Simon lay (1. kcab) ______________ on the *deckchair* and the others carried on their conversations or sunned themselves quietly. After a (2. eliwh) ________________, Simon got up to go for a (3. misw) ______________ and Kevin and a few of the others followed him.

"Did you (4. rahe) __________ about the *robbery* at the pool yesterday?" Simon (5. saked) __________ Kevin.

"No, I didn't hear anything."

"Hey, Lori, what's the (6. swen) __________ on the *robbery*?"

"Do you (7. wokn) __________ who did it?"

She was a dark-haired young woman, about nineteen years old, but seemed much older to the two boys. She looked at them through her sunglasses a moment without saying anything.
"That wasn't a trick question," Kevin said.
"How would I know who did it? All I know is that three *lockers* were broken into," Lori said, as if bored with the question.
"Did they break the *locks* on the *lockers*?" Simon asked, looking at the key to his *locker*, which was *tied around* his *wrist*.
"No," she said coolly.
"The *lockers* weren't damaged?" Kevin asked, surprised.
"Do I have to repeat myself?" she asked.
The two boys walked away.
"What's the matter with her?" Kevin wondered.
"Probably missing her boyfriend," Simon guessed.
"I hope she sees him again soon."

"Who's that over there, Simon?"
"Where?"
"Over there, at the *deep end* – those two men."
"I don't know. Looks like they're checking the *chlorine* and the pH levels of the water. They must be the pool *maintenance men*."
"What do you mean '*maintenance men*'?"
"Someone has to make sure the water's safe to swim in and to clean

the filters and check the water pumps. Someone has to make sure everything is functioning correctly. The sun affects the water. People jump in the water after lying in the sun, and they're covered with *sweat* and *sunscreen*. Keeping this water safe is a full-time job."

"Hmmm. Have you ever *noticed* them before?"

"Not them. Last year there were different people. That one *guy's* nearly two metres tall. He looks like a heavyweight boxer."

ÜBUNG 14 !

Übung 14: Bilde Sätze mit dem Komparativ!

1. bicycle/skateboard (few wheels)

A bicycle has fewer wheels than a skateboard.

2. July/April (hot)

____

3. desert/pool (dry)

____

4. children's swimsuits/men's swimsuits (small)

____

5. Chinese/English (difficult)

____

6. ice cream/water (cold)

____

7. pool/bathtub (big)

____

8. hip-hop/punk rock (funky)

....

After swimming around a bit they returned to their *deckchairs*. Sarah was there once again.
"Hello, Pinkie," Kevin sang.
"You're so original," Sarah said *scornfully*.
"Pinkie, do you want to hear my new CD player?"
"No, and if you call me 'Pinkie' one more time, I'm going to hurt you!"
Kevin leaned back in his *deckchair*, pulled the *headphones* over his head and started tapping his foot to the music.

Übung 15: Wähle das passende Wort für jeden Satz aus und unterstreiche es!

ÜBUNG 15 !

1. The sun effects/affects the water.
2. I want to hear/listen the new song.
3. They returned to there/their deckchairs.
4. He looks like/shines a boxer.
5. I'm covered with water/sweat.
6. Do you see/think they were here last year?
7. She took away/off the headphones.
8. We made place/space for Simon.

Later in the afternoon, the group of young people left the pool. After changing, Simon and Kevin looked into the *lifeguards'* office.
"Hey, Mick," Kevin said, "what do you know about those two maintenance *guys*?"

"Nothing."
"Do you know where they're from?"
"One is from Russia, but I don't know anything about the other one. What's it to you where they're from?"
"I was just wondering. Listen to my new CD player. It's got a great sound. It's the best thing on the market at the moment."
"How'd you get it, Kevin? Did you *nick* it?"
"No, I have a part-time job."
"What – skateboarding? That's not a job."
"I help one of my *neighbours* every morning. He's old and needs help around the house, so I do things for him."
Kevin handed the CD player *headphones* to Mick and pressed 'play'. Mick nodded his head and then looked really impressed.
"That has a really good sound," Mick said, "handing it back to Kevin. How much did it cost?"
"Over £200."
"You rich boys. I *bet* mummy or daddy bought that for you. Little Kevvy's birthday yesterday?"
Kevin made a questioning look at Simon.
"Let's go," Simon said.
"What's with Mick today?" Kevin asked.
"Maybe he didn't like your question about the *maintenance men*."
"I didn't mean anything by it."

! ÜBUNG 16

Übung 16: Vervollständige die Sätze mit ***my, your, his, her, their*** *oder* ***our****!*

1. Kevin really likes ______ skateboard.
2. Sarah has ______ nose pierced.

3. They like ______ chips with lots of salt.

4. I ride ______ bicycle to the pool every day.

5. The British like ______ tea!

6. "Excuse me, is that ______ towel?"

7. "We were wondering if you had seen ______ dog anywhere."

8. Sarah and I have ______ bicycles locked together.

Chapter 3: The Stolen CD Player

The next two days it rained all over England. Rain clouds seemed to be anchored over the UK and Ireland. Simon stayed at home and practised guitar and Kevin played his bass, while the other friends read, played games, shopped, and did whatever it is that people do to pass time on holiday when they can't do what they really want to do. The *lifeguards showed up* for work both mornings, but the pool closed once it was clear that the rain was not going to stop. The *maintenance men* checked the *chlorine* and pH levels and left.

The following day *dawned* dark but by 11 am, the sun had come out and by 1 pm Simon and some of his friends were once again at the pool. The sun had dried the *deckchairs*, although there were small *puddles* of water here and there on the poolside. By 2 pm, the temperature had gone up so high that the *puddles* of water had *evaporated* and the pool was once again crowded. The depressing atmosphere of the past two days was gone. The friends talked and played and pushed and swam and *dunked* each other. Some held hands and others flirted.

The afternoon passed in joking and laughter – and in serious conversations. For one afternoon, summer seemed like it might last forever: *eternal* summer and *eternal* youth. Sarah was not there from the group of friends, but so many other people were there that only Simon *noticed* her absence.

ÜBUNG 17

Übung 17: Ordne den Substantiven die in Klammern stehenden Verben richtig zu! Verwende jedes Verb zweimal!
(blows, falls, shines)

1. The wind ______________.

2. The sun ______________.

3. The rain ______________.

4. Light ______________.

5. A whistle ______________.

6. Snow ______________.

"Anyone know what time it is?" Kevin asked.
"Ten to six," one of the young people answered.
"Oh no! I've got to get home. My mum will *have a fit*." He picked up his skateboard and left.
A few minutes later he returned, still in his swimsuit, his towel over his shoulder, looking *upset*.
"What's the matter with you?" Simon asked. "I thought you were leaving."
"Did I bring my CD player out here?"
"I don't think so," Simon answered, and then looked around on the ground. "I don't see it anywhere."
"I don't see it either. In fact, I don't remember seeing it."
"Me neither."
"Damn! I knew I didn't bring it out," Kevin said, sitting down on the *edge* of a *deckchair*, "but I hoped that I had and I had just forgotten. Someone broke into my *locker* and stole my CD player," he said quietly. "I remember laying it on my *trainers* and wrapping the *cord* around the *headphones* before I closed the *locker* door."
"Did you unlock your *locker* or was it already open?"
"It was *locked*. I had to use my key to open it."
"You've got to report it to the pool manager straight away," Simon said.
"That will do me a lot of good," Kevin said sarcastically.
"I know it's useless, but you have to do it just the same."

"Whoever took it is probably long gone by now. Did you *notice* those *maintenance men* today?"
"I never saw them," Julia answered, "but they have to come every day. Even when the pool isn't open they come, so I'm sure they were here today. We were just so busy having fun that we never *noticed* them."
"Damn!" Kevin said again, and walked away from the group and towards the *lifeguards'* office. Simon ran after his friend to see if he could be of any help.
"I want to speak to the manager," Kevin said, at the doorway to the office.
"What do you want with him?" Lori asked.
"Someone stole my CD player," Kevin answered.
"You should have left it in your *locker*," she said.
"It was in my *locker*," he responded.

ÜBUNG 18

Übung 18: Welches Wort ist das „schwarze Schaf"? Unterstreiche das Wort, dessen Aussprache nicht zu den anderen Wörtern der Reihe passt!

1. cow, bow, know
2. let, ballet, get
3. speak, weak, break
4. Moscow, row (a boat), row (a fight)
5. blind, wind (weather), mind
6. wear, bear, tear (crying)
7. where, here, there

A young man of 23 walked over to them. Rob, the pool manager, was tall, had black hair and a broad nose. Simon and Kevin had seen him walking around, speaking with the *lifeguards*. He wasn't as friendly as the other *lifeguards*.

"*What's up*, Lori?"

"This is Kevin. He says someone stole something from his *locker*."

"Not just 'something'," Kevin said, angrily. "It was a new CD player that *cost me a fortune*."

"You shouldn't be bringing things like that to the pool," the manager answered. "You should leave really *valuable* things at home."

"What's the point of having *lockers* if people can break into them without any problem?" Kevin shouted. "If you don't call the police, I will. That CD player cost me more than £200."

Übung 19: Schreibe die Wörter in Großbuchstaben um!

1. Change a letter in COOL to make a word for a place where you cool off. ____________________
2. Change a letter in SWEET to make a word for what you do when you exercise. ____________________
3. Change a letter in FALL to make a word that describes someone over two metres in height. ____________________
4. Change a letter in COOK to make a word for something that has many words in it. ____________________
5. Change a letter in PRIME to make a word that describes an action that is against the law. ____________________

6. Change a letter in TELL to make a word for what you do if you work in a shop. ________________

The manager walked away and phoned the police. In a short while a tall policeman appeared and started asking the pool manager and Kevin some questions.
Together the three of them went to the *locker* where Kevin's *belongings* were still waiting for him.
"Are you sure you *locked* the door?"
"Of course. You can't take the key out of the door without *locking* it – you turn the key, pull it out and the *locker* is *locked*."
"And you're sure you brought it with you? Your expensive, new CD player isn't sitting at home somewhere just waiting for you?"
"I'm *positive*. I had my *headphones* on while riding my skateboard to the pool and I remember putting the player right there on my *trainers*," he added, *pointing to* the *trainers* sitting at the bottom of his *locker*.
"I'll have to write a report on this. You do know, by the way, that riding a skateboard on the street with *headphones* on is not only dangerous but illegal, don't you?"
"It's not like I'll be able to do it anymore anyway," Kevin said sadly.
The policeman asked Kevin for the *brand*, model and colour of the CD player and whether he still had the *receipt* for it.
"Yes, it's with the guarantee," he said. "I was going to send in the form for the guarantee, but the day turned out so nice that I decided to go to the pool instead."
"You know, there's little hope of getting it back," the policeman said.
"I know. But my CD player isn't the first thing that was stolen here."
"Is that right?" the policeman asked the manager.
"Several days ago, a few other things were stolen."

"What was taken?"
"A woman's watch and a couple of *wallets* were emptied. The watch was only worth about £85."
"Was it just like this – things taken from *locked lockers*?"
"I'm afraid so."
"Was a police report filed?"
"Yes – for the woman's watch. The boys each lost £20 or £25."
"Were there any *witnesses*?"
"No."
"Is there a *pass key* that works for all these *lockers*?"
"Yes, but I don't have one. I'm responsible only for the *lifeguards*, and none of us has a *pass key*."
"Who does have a *pass key*, then?"
"The *maintenance men*," Rob answered. "They have to clean the *lockers* occasionally, so they have to be able to open them and get inside."
"Do you have the names of the *maintenance men*? The *constable* is going to want to speak with them if this continues."
"I can get their names and phone numbers for you."
"They're foreigners," Kevin said.
"Is that right? Since when is that a crime?" the policeman asked.
"Foreigners are always committing crimes. They come over here and start breaking our laws."
"Do they?" the policeman asked. "And you haven't broken any laws?"
"Kevin, *shut up*," Simon said.
"I want my *blooming* CD player back," Kevin responded, furious again.
"I'm afraid the chances of that are not very good," the policeman repeated, "and *blaming* foreigners is stupid. There's no one group of people who steals. The main difference is how people steal."
"We'll see," Kevin said.

ÜBUNG 20 !

Übung 20: Beantworte die Fragen zum Text!

1. Do Simon and his friends know the *lifeguards*?

2. Where do the friends keep their clothes while they're at the pool?

3. What does Kevin always have with him?

4. How much did Kevin's new CD player cost?

5. Did the maintenance men work at the pool last year?

6. What is the pool manager's name?

7. Who does Kevin think stole his CD player?

8. How does the thief seem to have got in the locker?

The policeman had the information he needed from Kevin so Kevin and Simon left. A great day had suddenly turned sour.

"I'm going to be very late," Kevin said.

"I think once you tell your parents what happened, they'll understand."

"They don't know about the new CD player," Kevin said quietly. "My parents don't *notice* things like that. They would be very *upset* with me if they knew that I had bought another CD player. But the bass just sounded so good on it that I had to get it. And now it's gone."

"What are you going to tell your parents, then?"

"I don't know. I'll think of something. I'll probably just tell them I was at the pool. They'll be happy I was at the pool. They're more worried about girls these days."

"My mother too. Well, I'm really sorry about your CD player. I guess you won't feel like coming to the pool anymore."

"I don't really. But I want to find out who stole my player, so I'll be back tomorrow, if the weather is as nice as it was today."

Simon began the walk home, and Kevin got on his skateboard and, a little less joyfully, began the ride home. Simon watched his friend disappear into the distance. I've got to help him find out who stole his CD player, he said to himself. Even if we don't get it back, we have to stop whoever is stealing things at the pool.

Julia ran up behind Simon.

"Oh Simon," she said, "I can't believe it. Someone stole the £20 I had in my *purse*. I just can't believe it. You can't bring anything here anymore. That money was supposed to last me a week. It's only Tuesday, and my parents won't give me any money until next Sunday. What am I going to do? I can't even pay to get into the pool now."

Simon almost made a joke about Kevin paying for her, but then he thought about Kevin's trouble and kept the joke to himself.

"Are you sure your money was in your *purse*?"

"Of course, Simon. Where else am I supposed to keep it? Besides, my *purse* wasn't where I'd left it. It was *jammed* in one of my shoes."

"That's where I keep my *wallet*," Simon said quietly and quickly pulled out his *wallet*. He opened his *wallet* and saw that his money was still there.
"Well, you're lucky, but I wouldn't leave it there anymore," Julia warned.
"I guess not."
They both shrugged their shoulders.
"Here," Simon said, handing her some money. "For tomorrow."
"I can't take your money, Simon. I'll see if I can get a little bit of money from my Dad. I'll tell him what happened."
They said goodbye. A *glorious* summer now seemed about to become a different kind of summer, a dark summer. Years from now when they looked back on this summer, the friends would only remember being *robbed*. Not exactly a pleasant memory, thought Simon.

Übung 21: Welche der Erklärungen stimmt? Kreuze die richtige Lösung an!

1. "I'm running late."
   a) ☐ I am late.
   b) ☐ I am running slowly.

2. "Check this out."
   a) ☐ Put a mark on this.
   b) ☐ Look at this.

3. "Did you nick this?"
   a) ☐ Did you steal this?
   b) ☐ Did you touch this?

4. Sarah showed up at the party.
   a) ☐ Sarah looked at the party.
   b) ☐ Sarah went to the party.

5. “My mother will have a fit.”
   a) ☐ My mother will be tired.
   b) ☐ My mother will be angry.

Chapter 4: The Suspicious Maintenance Men

At home, Kevin *put up a brave front*. Inside, though, he was miserable and furious. He had spent money, which he had been saving for university, on something that had been stolen. I know it was those *maintenance men*, he said to himself, I’m sure of it. Even the pool manager said that they had a master key. They have easy access to everybody’s *locker*. They can take anything they want any time they want.

“Hello, Pinkie,” Kevin said, but not as energetically as usual.
“Hello, Skateboy,” Sarah answered. “One of these days, Kevin, you’re going to say the wrong thing at the wrong time.”
“Get off it, Pinkie. Why do you have to be so serious all the time?”
“Why are you so miserable, Skateboy?”
“Someone stole his new CD player yesterday.”
“That’s terrible!”
“Well, I’m going to find out who stole it and even if I can’t get it back I’m going to make sure everyone knows who stole it.”
“Who do you think stole it?”
“The *maintenance men*.”

"Come on, Kevin, why would they steal something from you?"
"They're foreigners. They're always stealing things."
"Come on, Kevin. That's such a stupid thing to say."
"They're going to learn that it's a stupid thing to steal from Kevin Jones."
"Okay, Skateboy. Go ahead and make a fool of yourself."

! ÜBUNG 22

Übung 22: Setze die richtigen Präpositionen ein!
(in, to, for, from)

"Rob," Kevin said, "where are those *maintenance men* 1. ______?"

"I don't know. I didn't *hire* them."

"Well, if you didn't, then who did?"

"The city owns the pool, so someone 2. ______ the city government, I *reckon*. Why? What's it 3. ______ you where they're 4. ______?"

"I'm just curious. People 5. ______ some of those eastern European countries have a *reputation* 6. ______ stealing."

"Do you think you're some young Sherlock Holmes?"
Kevin walked away from the pool manager. He didn't like the *scorn*, and he was powerless again him. But I know they stole my player, he thought, and I'm going to *prove* it.

"Annie," Simon said to a young woman walking along the *edge* of the pool, swinging a silver *whistle* at the end of a long string, "have you heard anything about who might have stolen that woman's watch the other day?"

"No, I haven't heard anything. Hey you, quit running and pushing! I only know that it happened."
"Whoever it is probably took Kevin's CD player as well."
"That's awful," she said. "Hey, I said quit running and I meant it!"
"He thinks the *maintenance men* stole it," Simon said once she was listening to him again.
"That's absurd. They're nice *guys*. They've only ever been helpful to me."
"You're a woman."
"If that's the case, then why would they steal a woman's watch?" she asked, looking at the watch on her *wrist*.

"I don't think they did it. At least I don't *assume* they did it. I just wanted to know what you knew about them."

"As I said, they've only ever been helpful to me."
"Do you know where they're from?"
"The tall blond one is Russian. I think his name is Boris. But I'd watch out, Hercule Poirot, they may not like being *accused* of being thieves."
"I'm not *accusing* anyone."

ÜBUNG 23 !

Übung 23: Trage die fehlenden Buchstaben des beschriebenen Körperteils in die Lücken ein!

1. Below your shoulders is your ___ a ___ k.
2. You can bend your leg using your k ___ ___ ___.
3. Your n ___ ___ k holds your head up.
4. You can bend your arm using your e ___ b ___ w.
5. Your w ___ ___ st connects your hand and your arm.
6. Your ___ nk ___ ___ connects your foot and your leg.
7. You can nod your h ___ ___ d to say 'yes'.

"Were you speaking to Annie earlier?" Sarah asked, walking up to Simon. Her hair was no longer pink. She had just *dyed* it a dark green.
"Yes."
"She said I was a young Miss Marple and that you were an English Hercule Poirot. What's that supposed to mean?"
"I don't know," Simon said.
"They're detectives in Agatha Christie's crime novels. You two should read more," one of their friends said.

"There they are," said Kevin.
"There 'who' are?" asked Sarah.
"The *maintenance men*, Greenie."
"I'm really going to *clout* you one of these days, Kevin."
"Simon, let's go over and see what we can hear from Vladimir and his friend."
"Who's Vladimir?"
"That's one of the *maintenance men*, the tall one."
"Annie said his name was 'Boris'," Simon corrected.
"Boris or Vladimir, it doesn't matter to me. He stole my CD player and that's the only thing that matters at the moment."
"You don't know that he stole it," Sarah said.
"Yes, I do."
They began walking in the direction of the *maintenance men*. One was *sweeping* the poolside, and the other was sitting in a white plastic chair, leaning back with his face in the sun.
"I say we just sit near them," Simon said. "I don't want to walk up to them and call them thieves."
"I'm not as stupid as all that," Kevin said. "I just want to listen to them, see if they talk about anything that might be of interest to me."
The two boys sat down very close to the two *maintenance men*. They listened for some time, staring up at the blue sky. Finally, they looked directly at each other.
"Well, it certainly isn't German," said Simon.
"And it isn't Spanish," Kevin said.
"I *reckon* it's Russian. Most of the people in Eastern Europe learned Russian, so they're probably speaking Russian."
"But they live in England, so they have to speak some English at least. I mean, they couldn't have got their jobs, could they, without speaking some English?"
"They probably speak some English," Simon agreed.

"I don't care if they speak Swahili, though. I just want either my CD player back or my £220. Nothing else matters to me."

They listened again to the men speaking. They heard one of the men say 'Boris' occasionally, so they knew Boris really was the name of one of the men. They could also hear English words – or words they thought were English – *scattered* throughout the conversation. They heard 'club' and 'table' and '*pawn*.'

"Did you hear that, Simon?"

"I don't know. What did you hear?"

"He said, '*pawn*.'"

"Are you sure it was '*pawn*'?"

"What do you think he said?"

"I'm just not sure it was '*pawn*.'"

"He said '*pawn*,'" Kevin repeated, this time more sure of himself, "and I'm sure they mean *pawnshops*. Thieves are always stealing things and then taking it to *pawnshops*. I *bet* they're talking about what they're doing with the *stuff* they're stealing. They might be making plans as we speak."

"They wouldn't do it here," Simon argued.

"Why not? Who speaks Russian here?"

The shorter man left for a moment and the Russian man they thought was named Boris remained. Suddenly, Boris stood, "Zoltan, Zoltan," he shouted. The boys watched as the shorter man, who had almost reached the *storage area*, turned around. "Zoltan … " The rest of what the Russian man said was in whatever language the two men were speaking, but it ended in 'cigarettes.'

"Zoltan must be his name," Simon theorised.

"Good job, Sherlock," Kevin said sarcastically.

When Zoltan returned, he was carrying a small *boombox*, an *extension cord*, and a package of cigarettes, which he threw at Boris. Boris lit a cigarette, while the other man set up the *boombox*.

"What a smelly cigarette!" Kevin said.
"I think all cigarettes are smelly. Imagine kissing someone who smokes: it must be like kissing an *ashtray*."
"I wonder what kind of music they're going to play," said Kevin.
"Probably some Russian music."

Übung 24: In diesem Gitternetz sind sechs Sprachen versteckt. Findest du sie alle?

ÜBUNG 24 !

S	P	A	N	I	S	H	G
F	A	B	T	L	E	F	E
R	D	U	T	C	H	A	R
E	N	G	L	I	S	H	M
N	F	K	M	L	D	E	A
C	P	Z	L	B	A	R	N
H	R	U	S	S	I	A	N

....
....
....
....
....
....

A look of surprise crossed Kevin's face as he heard 'The Payback' by James Brown start to blast out of the *boombox*. The hard, *insistent* bass supported the song alongside the drummer.
"You look surprised," Simon said.
"Well, aren't you?"
"Hey, it's James Brown."
"I know. I love James Brown. How many times have I tried to get you interested in this CD? So much hip-hop music today *borrows* directly from James Brown or from Parliament-Funkadelic."
"Russians listen to the Beatles and the Rolling Stones and Oasis –

why not James Brown? There's German Rap and French Rap, why not Russian Rap?"
"I'll *bet* they don't listen to that in Moscow."
"Don't be *thick*, Kevin. Of course they listen to that in Moscow and St. Petersburg and other cities in Russia. They may not play it in the countryside, but in the cities there must be people who listen to it."
"Well, just because they listen to music I like doesn't mean that they didn't steal my CD player."
The two boys sat there a while, listening to the music. The two men talked and laughed, and Simon and Kevin couldn't *make head or tail* of their conversation.
"They should be speaking in English," Kevin said.
"Right, and you would speak only French in France!" Simon answered.
"Okay," Kevin said. "But I think we should follow them around and see where they go."
"They probably go to other pools and work there, too."
"And steal there, too," Kevin added.
"We should see if there have been reports of *thefts* at other pools. But Julia lost £20 yesterday and didn't report it to the police, so police reports won't tell us everything we need to know."
"What are you two doing here?" Sarah asked, sitting down with them. "Are you listening to the music or *spying* on the *maintenance men*?"
"We aren't *spying*," Kevin said. "We're *investigating*."
Sarah listened for a moment. "It appears they're speaking a language none of us knows – probably Russian, I guess. And they're playing funk music – "
"James Brown" – Kevin put in.
" – which I expect you like."
"That may be," Kevin agreed, "but I don't like people who steal from me."

Übung 25: Sind die folgenden Aussagen richtig? Markiere mit richtig ✔ oder falsch –!

1. If a person is fit, he or she is in good physical condition. ☐
2. If you can't make head or tail of something, then you don't understand it. ☐
3. If there's an entrance fee, you get in for free. ☐
4. Kissing an ashtray is a pleasant cxperience. ☐
5. Burglary, robbery and theft have a similar meaning. ☐
6. A thick person is very intelligent. ☐

Sarah was angry with both boys, though more with Kevin than with Simon. This fear and hatred of foreigners is so stupid, she thought. If you hate foreigners then you don't have to try to change other things in the world, which are usually the real problem. She had *recently* been to a protest march against globalisation and against political movements that were anti-foreigner.
"Just make sure you're certain you know who *nicked* your CD player before you start *accusing* people."
"They did it all right," Kevin said.
"How do you know?" Sarah asked.
"Who else could have done it?"
"Any number of people," Sarah said.
"Come on, Greenie, they have a *pass key*. A *pass key*, Greenie. You know what a *pass key* is? It's one key that opens all locks. Not one *locker* but all."
"I know what a *pass key* is, Kev. *Spare me* the sarcasm."
"I think these people should be sent back to their own countries."
"So you're a skinhead, Kevin?"
"I like music made by black people. How can I be a skinhead?"
"You talk just like a skinhead, Kevin. Shame on you."

"I don't go out beating people up just because they're black or brown or look like Indians or Asians," Kevin said, defending himself.

"No, you don't. You just want to send them back 'to their own countries.' One day you're talking like that; soon you start to take action. You don't know where they were born. Plenty of people speak another language even though they were born right here in England."

"They should speak English if they live in England. And I *still* say that the *maintenance men* stole my CD player. I'll believe that until you can *prove* me wrong."

"Clearly," she said, shaking her head.

"I don't need this," Kevin said, standing up. Sarah and Simon watched Kevin walk away towards the pool and *dive* into the water.

Übung 26: Setze das passende Wort ein!
(stole, answer, mean, intelligent, mad, friends)

"He doesn't 1.____________ it," Simon said.

"How do you know?"

"I know him. We've been 2.____________ since we were three. We've been in school together just about our whole lives. He's only 3. ____________ because he lost his CD player."

"Because somebody 4.____________ his CD player," Sarah corrected.

"Right. But if the *maintenance men* didn't do it, who did?"

"That's an 5.__________ question, and that's the question we have to find an 6.__________ to."

"Do you have any ideas?"
"We know that there have been at least two *robberies* here, probably more, right?"
"Right."
"So that means that it isn't someone who just came here once. It's someone who comes occasionally."
"Or regularly," Simon suggested.
"A regular," Sarah agreed. "It could be a regular."
"Someone who comes to the pool regularly. Like us."
"But we don't have access to a *pass key*."
"There are other people who come here every day or almost every day."
"We should start looking at the people who come each day and start trying to remember them. Can you think of anyone who comes regularly?"
They looked around at the people lying out on the *deckchairs*, people sitting on chairs at tables, people lying on the poolside, people running around at the side of the pool and people swimming in the pool.
"There's got to be more than a hundred people here," Simon said.
"More than two hundred on some days," Sarah added.
Kevin, wet, walked up to them.
"We should follow them," he said.
"Who?" Sarah asked.
"Who do you think?"
"Don't be *daft*," Sarah said, almost laughing at him.
"You think we should follow the *maintenance men*?" Simon asked.

"Right."
"And how should we do that?" Sarah asked. "We're just going to jump into our Rover and drive off right behind them?"
"I can follow them on my skateboard," he said.
"Your skateboard goes 40 or 50 miles per hour?"
"Downhill."
"There aren't enough hills around here," Simon said.
"Whose side are you on?" Kevin asked. "Hers or mine?"
"It's not a question of sides," Simon answered.
"It's a question of finding out who really *nicked* your CD player," Sarah declared.

! ÜBUNG 27

Übung 27: Welcher Satzteil enthält die richtige Redewendung? Kreuze die richtige Lösung an!

1. I'm right,
   a) ☐ ain't I?
   b) ☐ aren't I?

2. You know where you are,
   a) ☐ you don't?
   b) ☐ don't you?

3. She doesn't know me,
   a) ☐ does she?
   b) ☐ do she?

4. We're not late,
   a) ☐ we are?
   b) ☐ are we?

5. The movie is over,
   a) ☐ isn't it?
   b) ☐ ain't it?

Chapter 5: A Dangerous Search

The three looked over at Boris and Zoltan. They were still sitting and listening to the music that Kevin liked, moving their heads and their feet to the music. Not four metres away, they were the topic of a warm discussion. Suddenly, Boris looked at his watch and said something that must have been an order. Zoltan turned off the *boombox* and unplugged it. He carried it back to the *storage area* and rolled up the *extension cord* as well.

"They're leaving," Kevin said.

Boris got up and followed Zoltan into the *storage area*. A few minutes later, they walked along the side of the pool and walked out the exit.

"They're gone," Kevin said.

"Thank you for the report," Sarah said.

"Let's go over and see if we can see anything in their *storage area*. If you *noticed*, they didn't *lock* it."

"Why do you want to look in there?"

"I just want to see what we can see in there. Maybe they're storing things they steal in there."

"Don't you think they would *lock* it if there were something to hide?" Sarah asked.

"I think you're being a bit *daft* as well," Simon agreed. "You don't really expect to find your CD player sitting on a *shelf* in there, do you?"

"Maybe there's another room inside where they can store things." Kevin walked over to the *storage area* and Simon followed, mechanically.

"I really don't think this is a good idea," he said.

"You don't have to come along," Kevin reminded him.

Übung 28: Setze das Gegenteil der Wörter in Klammern ein!

They (1. ran) ____________ to the *storage area* but could see almost (2. everything) ____________ inside. The day was so (3. dark) ____________ and the interior so dark that looking inside was like looking into a (4. white) ____________ hole that *swallowed* all light. Kevin turned to look at the pool, saw that all the *lifeguards* were focused on the people in it and (5. slowly) ____________ stepped into the *storage area*. Simon was thinking of joining him when one of the *lifeguards* called to him.

"Hey you, away from there."

"The pool's over here, *mate*," another *lifeguard* called.

"I was just wondering what's (6. out) ____________ there," Simon said, walking to the pool.

Inside, the air was cool and it took Kevin's eyes a few moments to adjust to the darkness. He *stubbed his toes* a couple of times and had to bite his lip to keep from crying out.

There were hoses and plastic containers of *chlorine* as well as other equipment used to clean and maintain pools – a large underwater *vacuum cleaner* with an extension pole attached to it and soap for cleaning the pool walls along the waterline. As his eyes got used to the darkness, he moved to the back of the *storage area*. It was rather bigger than he had expected. He looked back towards the entrance to see if anyone was coming in. No one was, so he moved farther in. There was a work area, with many tools, and behind that a closed door. Kevin immediately made for the closed door. He stopped and listened to hear if anyone was coming. He heard nothing, so he put his hand on the *doorknob*, thought of his CD player to give him *courage*, and then twisted the knob. The door was *locked*. What's behind there, he wondered. What are they hiding in there?

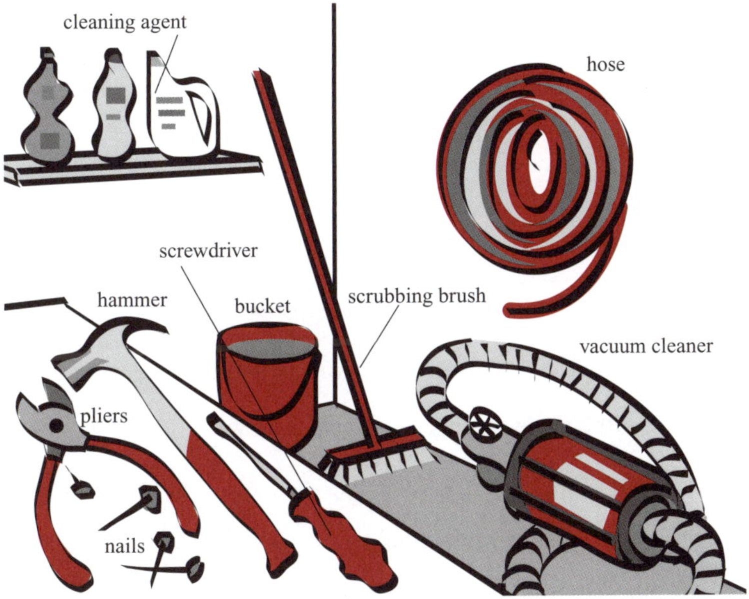

Kevin walked out quickly and went back towards the pool area. People were going about their business outside. Nobody had seen him go in, and he did not see Boris or Zoltan anywhere. It seemed that Simon had *abandoned* him. Well, Simon hadn't had a CD player stolen. He'd be thinking differently, Kevin said to himself, if he had lost something really *valuable*. Sure that his absence had gone unnoticed, he went back to the *locked* door.

ÜBUNG 29

Übung 29: Finde für das Wort in Klammern ein Reimwort, das in den Zusammenhang passt!

He began (1. cooking) ____________ around for something to use to break in. Wooden *shelves* next to the *locked* (2. floor) ____________ contained *screwdrivers*, hammers and many – as it turned out – *locked drawers*. Trying to pull himself up to (3. free) ____________ what was on one of the *shelves*, Kevin discovered a (4. tree) ____________. One couldn't see it unless one was quite tall or (5. true) ____________ that the key was there. He put the key to the (6. shock) ____________, and it fit. Kevin opened the door and walked in. The dry smell of *chlorine* nearly knocked him out. Several large windows lit the room. A short distance away were two large, circular metal containers – two (7. carry) ____________ large containers. Water was pumped from the pool to these (8. thanks) ____________, passing through filters, to be cleaned. On the other side of these tanks, Kevin realised, must be the pool. To his left, along a (9. fall) __________, were more *shelves*, filled with an assortment of things – towels, baskets, *lane lines* for swimming *competitions* and the *boombox*. He didn't see his CD player, however.

"I should take their *boombox*," he said quietly, "as *revenge*."

"Where's Kevin?" Sarah asked.
"Yes, where is Kevin?" Julia asked, looking at Sarah.
"He'll be right back," Simon said to Julia and then leaned over and *whispered*, "He went into the *storage area*."
"And you didn't go in with your best friend?"
"I wanted to, but one of the *lifeguards* saw me so I couldn't follow him."
"Lucky you."
"What do you mean? He's my *mate*. I try to keep him from doing *mad* things, but he has to make his own decisions."
"Look who's coming back," Sarah said.
Simon followed her finger and saw the two *maintenance men* returning. He looked towards the *storage area*, then to the table where he and Kevin and Sarah had been sitting but saw no sign of Kevin. Kevin, he realized, was still inside looking around. Simon stood up.
"What are you going to do?" Sarah asked.
"I don't know, but if they find him, who knows what they might do?"
"They might turn him over to the police."
"Or they might do something worse."
"You don't think you could fight them, do you? The tall one would break you and Kevin in two just like matchsticks."

"No," Simon said, looking shyly at Sarah. "I know I'm no fighter, but I can't just sit here either."

"Choose your *evil*," Sarah said. They watched the two men enter the *storage area*.

Simon walked up to the pool and then towards the *storage area*. He sat down on the hot white *concrete* poolside, close enough, he thought, that he could hear if there was any sort of *punch-up*.

ÜBUNG 30 !

Übung 30: Vervollständige die Sätze mit ***his, him, she*** *oder* ***her****!*

1. Sarah spoke with Kevin but she couldn't understand ____________.

2. Kevin jokes with Sarah about ____________ hair.

3. The maintenance men are not friends of (Kevin's) ____________.

4. She doesn't know what ____________ can do.

5. Give (Kevin) ____________ back ____________ CD player!

Kevin was examining the shelves, looking for his CD player. Suddenly he heard the sound of footsteps. The *maintenance men* were returning. They seemed to be walking quickly. Did they know he was in there? The *shelves* in front of Kevin appeared to contain lost and found items from years past. Everything on the *shelves* was useless or cheap or needed to be repaired. There were also a few tools, but most of the items on the *shelves* were just rubbish.

Hearing the voices, Kevin looked around for a place to hide. The door to the pump room was open and the key was still in the door. It was too late for him to run out of the room and out of the *storage area*. He looked at the tanks and ran towards them. Running around behind the farthest one, he discovered a ladder on it. He immediately climbed to the top. Carefully he looked over the *edge*, expecting to see a head at any moment. He was not long in waiting. Boris came in and *glanced* around the room. He walked in and started looking around. "Hello?" he called. Kevin could only hear the sound of Boris' shoes. Suddenly he *noticed* the footsteps were coming right for him. He heard the sound of a ring against the ladder. Oh, no! If he comes up here, I'll knock the ladder down and run out, Kevin thought. Then he saw the ladder go up in the air and against the wall. Boris wasn't coming up. Though Kevin couldn't understand a word, it was clear that he was *telling* Zoltan *off*. Zoltan followed him in. Zoltan, stretching out his arms and raising his shoulders, must have been saying, "I don't know why the door is open." Boris looked around carefully one more time, looked along the floor, but never looked up and saw Kevin. Satisfied that the room was empty, Zoltan walked out first and Boris followed him.

Übung 31: Setze die Verben in der richtigen Zeitform ein!

The door (1. to close) ________________ and Kevin (2. to hear) __________ the lock go into place. He waited what seemed an eternity before he (3. to come) __________ down from the tank, which was harder since the ladder was gone, and walked over to the door. He (4. to press) __________ his ear to the door but couldn't (5. to hear) __________ anything. He (6. to put) __________ his hand to the *doorknob* and (7. to try) __________ to turn it, but it would not turn. When he (8. to look) __________ at the knob to see if it was possible to unlock it from within, he saw there was simply another keyhole on the inside. He (9. to feel) __________ along each of the *shelves* next to the door but did not find a key.

"Now you (10. to get) __________ yourself into it," he said.

Simon watched the two men leave the pool area again. He watched the *lifeguards* as well. For whatever reason, he felt that they were watching him. Sarah walked up and sat down next to him.

"Are you going to go in?" she asked.

"Yes, if Kev doesn't come out soon."

"Did you hear anything?"

"I could hear one of them shouting, but I never heard Kevin's voice, so I *assume* he wasn't shouting at Kevin."

"That's good."

Simon and Sarah waited a while, but Kevin still did not reappear.

"I've got to get in," Simon said, "and see if anything happened."

Sarah stood and jumped in the water. She swam towards the middle of the pool and came up behind a student a year ahead of them. Robin Parker was known as being tough, although Sarah *claimed* he was only a talker and that he wasn't tough at all. She climbed on his back and *dunked* him. He came up and started *yelling at* her. At that moment, with all the *lifeguards* looking at Sarah and Robin Parker, Simon slipped into the *storage area*.

"Kevin," he called quietly. "Kevin."

He wandered around but did not see any signs of Kevin. Finally, he *noticed* the door. Simon walked to the door, tried the *doorknob*, but discovered that the door was *locked*. He tried the door several times and then gave up. What's in there? he wondered. He turned around several times, looking around, but also listening for the return of

Boris and Zoltan. There must be some other way out of here, he said to himself. He turned to the door, one more time, and tried the handle one last time. It still didn't turn. What did you expect? he asked himself. As he started to walk away he heard a voice behind the door.

"Simon? Is that you, Simon?" The voice was quiet: almost too quiet for someone on the other side of the door to hear it.

"Yes, it's me. Is that you, Kevin?"

"Of course it is," Kevin answered.

"Well, the door is *locked*," Simon said.

"I know it is," Kevin answered, frustration in his voice.

"What do you want me to do, then?"

"Do you see the *shelves* on your right?"

"Yes."

"Can you reach the top *shelf*? The key should be lying there."

Simon reached his hand up but felt only dirt and dust. "I don't feel it," he said to Kevin.

"Quick," Kevin said, "you have to find it before they come back."

Simon kept trying to find the key. He moved his hand around a bit more and felt the cold metal key on the *shelf*. "I've got it," he said to Kevin.

"Quickly, now," Kevin said.

In a moment he had the door open and Kevin *bounded* out of the room.

"What's in there?" Simon asked, starting to walk in the room.

"It's the pump room," Kevin answered.

Simon *glanced* in, but Kevin pulled him back. He closed the door and removed the key and put it back on the *shelf*. The two boys walked back quickly towards the entrance, listening for the *maintenance men* the whole way. Kevin watched from inside until he saw an opportunity – the *lifeguards* were rotating stations – and said,

"Now, Simon," and pulled him out by the shoulder. Outside, the light was blinding. Kevin ran towards the pool and jumped into the water. Following his lead, Simon ran behind him and *dived* into the water. When they came up for air, the boys looked around at the *lifeguards* to see if their actions had been *noticed* but no one seemed to be paying them any special *attention*.

! ÜBUNG 32

Übung 32: Finde im folgenden Textabschnitt die sechs Adjektive und unterstreiche sie!

"Did you find anything?" Simon asked.
"Not really. There are dirty *shelves* filled with things people have lost over the years, but nothing they've lost *recently* – and nothing that looked worth stealing. I'm sure that if they wanted to they could find plenty of good hiding places in that *storage area*. And the pump room would be a perfect place to keep things safe and secure. They don't have the best hiding place for the key, but I discovered it purely by accident."

"So, did you find what you were looking for?" Sarah asked as the two boys returned to their *deckchairs*.
Kevin didn't answer, so Simon did, "Not really."
"Not yet," Kevin corrected.
"You think they have your CD player somewhere in there?" Sarah asked.
"They might. They might have other things as well."
"Isn't that the policeman from yesterday?" Simon was *pointing* across the pool *towards* the *lifeguards'* office.
"It *blooming* well is," Kevin said and walked off in the policeman's direction.

"You'd better go with him, Simon," Sarah *advised*. "You never know what he might say to the policeman."
Simon ran to *catch up with* his friend.
"Have you interviewed the *maintenance men*?" Kevin was asking just as Simon *approached*.
"Are you still talking about them?" the policeman asked.
"Well, of course."
"No, I haven't spoken to them. What do you think they're going to say? – Naturally, we stole the CD player? Do you really expect that?"
"I don't know what I expect them to say, but I expect someone to ask them questions."
"Look, I called the person who *hired* them and they have to go through a complete *background check* so I think they're okay. In any case, I have no reason to think they're not."
"I'll *bet* it was all fake – their *papers*. How can they be okay and have stolen my CD player?"
"Have there been any *thefts* at the other pools?" Simon asked before the policeman could answer Kevin's question.
"No, the *thefts* have all been here."
"So what are you doing here? Are you here to do some work or just to look at the girls in bikinis?"
"Okay, Kev," Simon said, *grabbing hold of* Kevin's arm, "I think it's time to go."
At that moment, Rob, the pool manager, appeared. He walked over to the policeman. "She's right in here," he said, directing the policeman into the *lifeguards'* office.
Kevin followed, pulling Simon with him, but waited just outside the door.
"Someone stole £70 from me," a *weeping* young woman said.
"You had it in your *locker*?"

"Yes."

"Why did you bring so much money with you?"

"I was planning on going out this evening, after swimming. I guess I'll just be going home now."

"Do you hear that?" Kevin asked Simon. "She lost a lot of money. I wonder when she was *robbed*. I'll *bet* that they were *robbing* her while I was in the *storage area* or when I was *locked* in the pump room."

"You mean the *maintenance men*? Didn't we see them leave?"

"We thought so, but we were mistaken unless they came right back."

"I suppose we could have been mistaken," Simon agreed, "but I really thought I saw them leave."

"Stop thinking so much," Kevin said. "They somehow *managed* to get into the women's *changing room* and steal money."

"But how did they *manage* to find her *locker* and get her money? There are hundreds of *lockers* and they found hers?"

"I don't know how they *managed* it. Perhaps it was just *dumb luck*."

"If so, I'd like some *dumb luck* right about now."

"You're not a foreigner," Kevin said.

"Don't start that again," Simon said. "I'm really sick of this anti-foreigner *attitude* of yours."

"It's not my fault that they're foreigners."

"Be reasonable, Kevin. They may be foreigners, but we don't know that they stole anything. You'd better get that into your *thick* head before you do something stupid."

"Now you're sounding like Greenie. Is she going to be the next girl you almost *go out with*?"

"Very funny. I suppose that would be just like you and Susie."

"Susie and I aren't together and never will be as far as I can see. And I won't be playing my new CD player anymore either."

Übung 33: Schreibe die Zahlen aus!

1. 17 ______________________________
2. 75 ______________________________
3. 2nd ______________________________
4. $^{1}/_{4}$ ______________________________
5. 1,400 ______________________________
6. 1,000,000 ______________________________
7. 25th ______________________________

Chapter 6: Looking for Proof

"They're back," Sarah sang out. "Kevin! Wake up! Your criminals have returned."

Kevin opened his eyes and watched the two *maintenance men* walk over to the *storage area*. They entered and a few minutes later walked out, closing and *locking* the door.

"Do they always do that?" Kevin asked.

"I don't know," Sarah answered.

"I never *noticed* before," Simon added. "They probably do it each afternoon when they're finished for the day."

Kevin got up from the *deckchair*, slipped on his flip-flops and walked quickly to the pool entrance. The *lifeguard* there stamped his hand and he walked outside. He looked to his left and right – and saw the two *maintenance men* walking down the street. He followed them a short distance. They stopped next to a rather old green *van*. Kevin watched them drive away slowly.

ÜBUNG 34 !

Übung 34: Unterstreiche im folgenden Textabschnitt die Synonyme für die Wörter in Klammern!
(1. find out, 2. go behind, 3. believed, 4. pinched, 5. softly, 6. nice)

"So, what did you learn?" Simon asked.
"I know what kind of car they drive. It's a green *van*. It moves slowly. Between that and all the stop signs around town, I should be able to follow it on my skateboard."
"You're dreaming," Simon said.
"You're *daft*, you are," Sarah laughed, leaning forward to look at Kevin. "You don't really think you can follow a car on your skateboard, do you? I thought we talked you out of that yesterday."
"You can't talk me out of anything, Greenie. They stole my CD player and I'm going to *prove* it – one way or another."
"You have the right to make a fool of yourself, I *reckon*," Sarah said, lying back. "And apparently I can't talk you out of that either."
"You'll see," Kevin said quietly. "I have nothing against foreigners until they steal something from me."
Kevin walked away from his friends and up to the pool. A blond *lifeguard* stood near him. It was Chris.
"What do you know about the *maintenance men*?"
"They're new here. They worked somewhere else before coming here."
That's helpful, Kevin thought.
"They have several jobs," she added. I think they fill *vending machines* and I don't know what else they do. They always seem to be off to one place or another."
"Are they friendly?"
"Yes. To me and Lori and Annie. I think they're friendly to all the *lifeguards*, really. Why?"
"No reason. Well, actually, I just can't remember who did it last year."
"I don't remember either."

"So, are you coming to the pool tomorrow?" Simon asked Sarah.
"Probably. Something interesting is going on, and I don't want to miss out on it."
They stood looking at each other silently.
Kevin's right, Simon thought, she'll just be another woman I almost date.
Simon doesn't have enough *courage*, Sarah said to herself. He stands on the *edge* waiting to be pushed. Kevin may be wrong about a lot of things, but at least he has the drive to do something.
"How are you getting home? Are your parents picking you up?"
"I don't have a *mobile phone*, so my parents wouldn't know when to pick me up."
"Why don't you get a *mobile phone* then?"
"Because they aren't – "
"Let me guess," Simon *interrupted*, " – they aren't punk rock."
"Exactly."
"That's rather silly, isn't it?"
"I don't want my parents to be able to call me at any time."
"Good point. So, how are you getting home?"
"I'm walking."
"Would you like some company?" Simon asked, his face turning red in the process.
"Sure. But it'll be a long walk for you. You live in the other direction."

Übung 35: Wähle das passende Wort für jeden Satz aus und unterstreiche es!

ÜBUNG 35 !

1. Sarah likes/wants to go to the pool tomorrow.
2. They like their/there pool.

3. Someone has stole/stolen money.
4. I become/get money from my parents.
5. Rob is Mick's chef/boss.
6. Sarah dived/pushed into the water.
7. Sarah doesn't have/has a mobile phone.
8. "I must be of/off."
9. Kevin lost/losed his CD player.

They started walking. At first they were quiet, but then they started talking about the series of *robberies* at the pool over the previous few days.

"Who do you think is doing it?" Simon asked. "It seems to be someone who is at the pool quite often."

"Good point," Sarah said, suddenly sounding bored of the topic.

"The problem is that we can't really tell who comes regularly and who doesn't. And even if we could, they're probably mostly people like us who would have no way of getting into the *lockers*."

"Who else comes every day?" Sarah asked.

"I don't know. The *maintenance men*."

"And?"

"I don't know."

They kept walking in silence. "You really don't know?" Sarah asked.

"I really don't know," Simon answered.

"You can't think of anyone else who comes every day – or at least nearly every day?"

"I *give up*, Sarah. I can't read your mind."

"You don't have to read my mind, Simon. It should be obvious. It's the *lifeguards*," she said quietly.

"I suppose that was rather obvious," he *admitted*.

"It was just *staring you in the face*."

Actually, Simon thought, Kevin was wrong. She won't even be someone I almost dated.

"If it is one of the *lifeguards*," Simon said after a while, "then which one?"

"I don't know. But when you pay your *entrance fee*, you have to sign in and your *locker* number is written down next to your name so whoever takes your money that day is probably the one who would know if you had something to steal."

"When did you *figure all this out*?"

"This morning. When I signed in and watched Lori write the *locker* number next to my name."

Simon smiled at Sarah.

"So, I'm not Miss Marple."

"And I'm not Hercule Poirot."

Übung 36: Welche der Erklärungen stimmt? Kreuze die richtige Lösung an!

ÜBUNG 36 !

1. This music is terrible!
   a) ☐ This music is bad.
   b) ☐ This music is excellent.

2. He found out about the concert too late.
   a) ☐ He heard about the concert at 10 pm.
   b) ☐ All the tickets for the concert had already been sold when he heard about it.

3. She couldn't talk him out of ordering a pizza.
   a) ☐ She couldn't talk about anything but pizza.
   b) ☐ She tried to get him to order something else besides pizza.

4. The truth is staring you in the face!
   a) ☐ The truth is obvious.
   b) ☐ The truth is friendly.

5. Could you give me a hand?
   a) ☐ Could you help me?
   b) ☐ Could you give me money?

The next day was rainy, so no one went to the pool. Simon called Kevin to tell him what he and Sarah had discussed on their walk home.

"You think one of the *lifeguards* is breaking into the *lockers* and stealing from pool customers?"

"I don't know if I think that's what is happening," Simon answered. "I'm only saying that's one possibility we hadn't thought of. Actually, it was Sarah's idea."

"I should have known. Well, I don't think the chances of that being the case are very good. The *lifeguards* are all friends of ours."

"They're not really friends of ours," Simon corrected him. "You and I are friends, but we're not really friends with the *lifeguards*. We're friendly to them and they're friendly to us, but we're not really anything more than *acquaintances*."

"We went to that party at Mick's last summer," Kevin challenged.

"*Still*, we don't really know him."

"I don't care. The *maintenance men* stole my CD player and they've been stealing money from everyone else. Nothing you can say will *convince* me that I'm wrong."

"Okay," Simon said, *giving up*. "See you at the pool tomorrow, if the weather's nice."

"Actually," Kevin said quickly, "I was going to ring you up to see if you wanted to go with me to the *pawnshops* today."

Later that day, the two met and went around to many of the *pawnshops*. They saw lots of CD players but none were new and none were the model that Kevin had just bought days earlier.
"They've still got it," Kevin decided.
"Maybe it's already been sold."
"I doubt it. It would have been pretty expensive. Who shops in these places? It isn't rich people."
"So, you think they still have it?"
"They have to have it."
The two boys gave up their search of the *pawnshops* and went back to Kevin's house to listen to music.

Übung 37: Unterstreiche die vier Sätze, die inhaltlich nicht zum Text passen!

ÜBUNG 37

The sun shone down on the sunbathers and the bathers. The *lifeguards* were covered in a thick layer of *sunscreen*. In the air was the smell of perfume. Heat *rose* from the poolside in waves. Everybody was drinking cold drinks or diving into the pool to cool off. Every twenty minutes, one of the *lifeguards* taking a break went around to the other *lifeguards* to let them jump into the water to cool off. Clouds crossed the sky, blocking the sun completely.
Having finished off the big bottle of water he'd brought with him, Simon walked into the *locker room* to get his money from his *wallet*. It was dry everywhere. He opened his *locker* and pulled his *wallet* from the hiding place he had made for it: attaching it to the hanger on which his shirt hung with the aid of a rubber band. He opened his *wallet* and it was empty. There was lots of money inside. I thought I had £5 there. When I paid my entry, I used pound *coins* and loose change, but I thought I still had another £5.

"Sarah, could you lend me enough money for a bottle of water?"
"Sure," she answered, reaching into a little brown leather *purse* she carried around. "Would you put some *sunscreen* on my back, Simon?"
"I could have sworn I had £5 this morning when I got here," he said while spreading the *sunscreen* all the way down her back, "but my *wallet*'s empty now."
"Who would steal just £5?" she asked, handing Simon two pound *coins*.
"I don't know."
"Is £2 enough?"
"Yeah. I'll pay you back tomorrow."
"It's only £2, Simon. You can buy me a cup of tea sometime."
"By the way, Sarah. For a punk rocker, you do seem to be getting a bit of a tan."
"It's not illegal, Simon."
"No, but it is unusual."

Kevin and Simon got out of the pool.
"I've got to go to the toilet," Simon said.
"Me too."
The two boys walked into the *locker room* silently. The giant *fan* blowing fresh air in the *locker room* washed over any sound they might have made. They had almost reached the toilets when suddenly Kevin looked to the right. A young boy was trying to open a *locker* with a *screwdriver*.
"Hey, what are you doing?" Kevin shouted and jumped at the boy.
The boy turned and backed away from the *locker*. He held the *screwdriver* up for a moment and all three froze. Suddenly, the boy ran towards the main entrance. Kevin looked at Simon and then ran after the young boy. Simon ran behind his friend.

Crash!! Simon turned the corner to the door, and there lay Kevin on the floor.
"Are you all right?" Simon shouted.
"I'm fine," Kevin said, getting to his feet.
"What happened?"
"I hit my head on the door," he said quickly, then opened the door and ran out.
"What's going on?" shouted Annie.
The two boys ran by without answering. Out on the *pavement*, they looked in both directions, but the boy was gone. They turned around and looked back at the pool entrance, looked left and right again and then stopped.
"Goodness!" Kevin said. "We should have got him. How did he get away?"
"Little kids are sometimes faster than they look."
Annie walked outside to them. "What's going on?" she asked again.
"We *caught* that boy breaking into a *locker*," Kevin shouted.
"Don't shout at me," she answered.
"I'm sorry," Kevin said. "I haven't been myself lately."
"I'll say," Simon agreed.
"Do you think that boy stole all those things?" Julia asked.
"I don't know," Kevin answered. "I'm not going to *give up* on Boris just yet. I've got something planned for tonight."

Übung 38: Setze die richtigen Präpositionen ein!
(to, on, in, of)

ÜBUNG 38 !

Kevin had dressed and was waiting with his friends. He watched as the tall, blond *maintenance man locked* the *storage area*. Today, only Boris was working. Kevin followed him out 1. ______ the pool area with his skateboard under his arm and all his *belongings* 2. ______ his shoulder 3. ______ his backpack.

"Wish me luck," he said 4. ______ the gang as he walked away.

"You're going to need luck," Sarah said, "keeping up with him and keeping out 5. ______ trouble."

"I have a plan," Kevin said *confidently*, and walked away quickly.

"He's going 6. ______ get himself into trouble," Sarah predicted.

"I can't help him," Simon said. "I can't follow him 7. ______ his skateboard, and he didn't *let me in on* his plan."

"He's 8. ______ his own. He's a big boy."

Kevin followed Boris to the *van*. Earlier he had looked to see where the *van* was parked, and it was still parked in almost the same place. Clearly, they drove to different pools around the city or had some other business that *required* a vehicle. Kevin put his skateboard down, got on it and slowly skated around, waiting for the right moment. As Boris closed the door to the *van*, Kevin quickly skated over to the back of the *van*, *squatted*, and grabbed the handle of the back door.

I hope I don't see any police, he thought. He had done this three or four, maybe five times. One time he had held onto the back of a friend's car, but usually he had *ridden* on the back of a car driven by someone he didn't know. People always told stories of *mates* who had been badly hurt or even killed doing what Kevin liked to call 'road surfing' – but he had no other way of keeping up with Boris.

It was 5.30 pm and he wanted to see where Boris went after work. Kevin didn't know what he expected to learn, but he felt he had nothing to lose. Suddenly loud music began to *pulse* from the *van*. It was someone playing a cover version of a Sly and the Family Stone song.

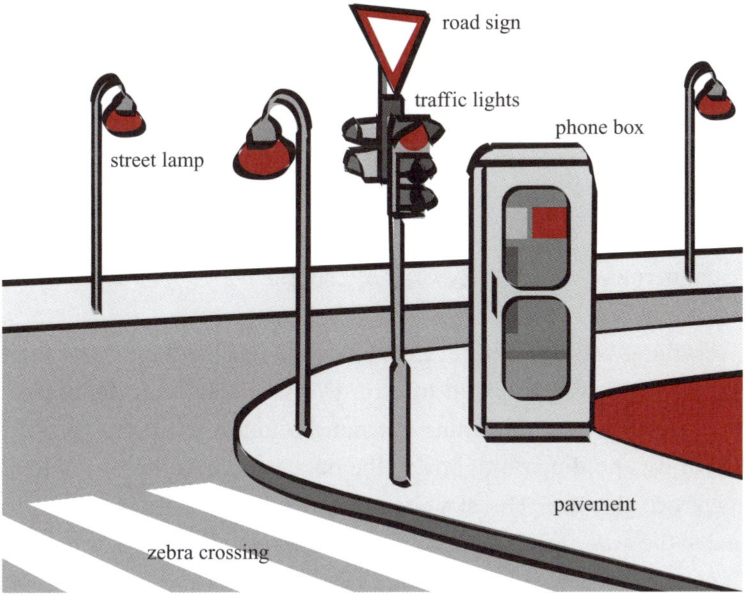

The *van* pulled out onto the road and picked up speed slowly. It was easy for Kevin to hold on and stay out of sight of the driver. Kevin watched houses and terraced houses and shops pass by. People on the *pavement* shouted to the driver that someone was on the back of his *van*, but because of the music Boris never heard. Drivers behind the *van* leaned their heads out of their windows to shout at Kevin, but he simply ignored them.

"Are you trying to kill yourself?" someone *yelled at* him.

Yes, of course, he wanted to *yell* back. Instead, he said nothing, for fear of making Boris aware of him.

Übung 39: Welche Gegenteile gehören zusammen? Trage die richtige Nummer in das Kästchen ein!

1. tall	☐ dry
2. difficult	☐ narrow
3. large	☐ safe
4. wide	☐ tiny
5. sweaty	☐ short
6. dangerous	☐ simple

Everything was going fine. Kevin saw the left-hand indicator light go on, so he was prepared to turn. Boris suddenly hit the brakes, however, when an oncoming car ran through a red light. Luckily, Kevin was holding on tightly to the door handle, so he was able to stay with the *van*. His skateboard, however, went flying forward under the *van* and straight down the street – also through the red light.

"You idiot!" Boris *yelled at* the driver, and then made his left turn. Kevin dropped safely from the back of the *van* and ran to collect his skateboard. Once he had it, he ran back to the street to follow the *van*. Far in the distance he *spotted* the vehicle sitting at a light that had just turned green. Kevin pushed the skateboard as hard as he could along the side of the road. Passing drivers *yelled*, but he ignored them. He was focused on one thing: the green *van*. Try as he might, it was slowly moving out of view, even though there were stop signs about every fifty metres and cars had to wait their turn

going through the crossroads. Kevin's hair was wet, his face was covered with *sweat* and his shirt was beginning to *stick* to his skin. He kept going straight ahead and at each crossroads looked in both directions for the green *van*. Finally, he saw it parked in front of a nightclub, The *Prawn*.
That's not a very promising name for a club, he thought. Then he realised it was familiar and that he had heard older people talking about the club. It was a hangout for fans of hip-hop music. He was too young to get in the club, however. No doorman would let him in unless he was *outrageously* dressed. It's just six o'clock now, he thought. I *bet* I can get in without any problem.

Übung 40: Unterstreiche die zehn Wörter, die falsch geschrieben sind, und verbessere sie!

! ÜBUNG 40

Kevin tryed the door and it opened. He walked into the cool darknesse and stood just inside the club. After a moment, he moved a little farther in and saw a large dance flur. It was dark to. Behind the dance floor was a smell stage and there stood Boris. On stage with Boris was a large sound systum with a set of *speakers*. Boris put on a vinyl LP and stood listening a moment, nodding his hed to the music. Kevin didn't recognize the sing, but he liked the music.
"More bass," someone shouted.
"Okay," Boris answurd, and began turning knobs.
Kevin looked for the person who had spoken to Boris. A short distance from the dance floor was a bar he hadn't *noticed*. There was a young man with dreadlocks standing in frunt of the bar.

"More!" the young man shouted again.
"That's all there is!" Boris shouted back.
"The club's not open."
Kevin turned to face Zoltan.
"It doesn't open until 9 pm."
Kevin turned round and ran out of the club as fast as he could.

Kevin rang Simon later that night.
"I followed him to a club," he reported.
"That doesn't help you, does it?"
"There's an expensive sound system there. I'll *bet* they bought it with money they stole from people at the pool. And I'm sure they want to buy more equipment."
"*Give it up*, Kevin. You followed him to a club. People pay to get in and that's how they finance the place. Besides, we found that boy trying to break in the *locker*."
"Maybe. I don't know. Let's talk about this tomorrow. I'm too tired to think about this at the moment."

ÜBUNG 41 !

Übung 41: Bilde das Simple Past dieser Verben!

1. stand ______
2. take ______
3. rub ______

4. go ____________________

5. study ____________________

6. give ____________________

7. steal ____________________

8. fly ____________________

Chapter 7: On the Right Track?

The next day was just as hot as the previous one. The group of friends sat at a table with a large multi-coloured parasol on it for a change. The heat was heavy like a blanket.

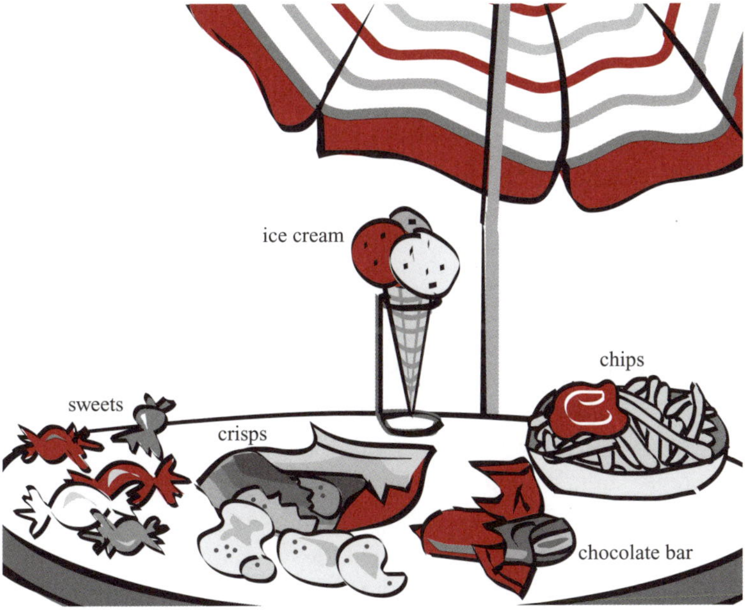

"So you made it on the back of the *van*?" Sarah asked.

"Not really."

"Not really?"

Kevin explained how he had gone quite a way before Boris had suddenly braked and sent his skateboard flying straight ahead, across the crossroads and down the road.

"You were lucky," Simon said.

"I know. And it wasn't easy jumping off the *van*. Luckily, it's rather slow. Anyway, I *managed* to follow him or at least to find him."

"So where did you follow him to?"

"To a club called The *Prawn*."

"Oh that place," Sarah said. "That's for people who like – who like the same kind of music as you like."

"I went in and saw Boris standing behind a sound system. And he was speaking English and setting it up."

"Did he see you?"

"No. But Zoltan did. He came up behind me and *threw me out* of the club – in English, too. He told me to come back after 9 pm. I don't think he recognised me from the pool though."

"The *Prawn*," said Sarah. "What word was it you heard the other day?"

"*Pawn*," Kevin and Simon answered together.

They looked at each other.

"You don't think they were saying '*Prawn*' now do you? I know there's only one letter difference, but there's a world of difference between '*pawn*' and '*prawn*.'"

"There is," Julia agreed, "but not in how the two words sound."

"Think of it," Sarah added, "they aren't *native speakers*, so maybe they say the word just a little differently."

"It can't be that big a difference," Kevin said.

"Are you sure, Kevin?" Sarah asked. "Are you so sure of yourself?"
"If I didn't know better, I'd swear you were all working with them."
"But you do know better," Julia jumped in.
"You haven't *convinced* me," Kevin said *stubbornly*. "You haven't *convinced* me that they didn't steal my CD player. Not yet."
"*What about* the boy we saw breaking into the *locker* yesterday?" Simon asked.
"I didn't hear about that," Sarah said. "What happened?"
Kevin explained that he and Simon had seen a boy trying to break into a *locker* with a *screwdriver*. They had stopped him and then had run after him – but he had got away.
"He can't be the one," Sarah said. "Whoever is doing this has a key of some kind. A *screwdriver* would leave marks on the *lockers*."
"You're right," Simon said. "So we're back at the beginning."
"No, we're not," Kevin disagreed. "I know who did it."

Übung 42: Trage die fehlenden Buchstaben des beschriebenen Substantivs in die Lücken ein!

1. Something you carry when it rains. _ m b _ _ l _ _
2. You wear it in the pool. _ _ _ m s _ i _
3. It's cold and comes in many flavours. _ c _ c _ _ _ _
4. Drinks come in this. b _ _ t _ _
5. You dry off with this. _ o _ _ l
6. This keeps your skin from burning. _ _ n _ _ r _ _ n
7. You keep your belongings in this. _ _ c _ _ r

Later that day, Sarah leaned over Simon and *whispered* in his ear.
"The next time you walk into the *locker room*, look up at the *ceiling*."
"Why?"
"Just do it. I want to see if you think the same thing I thought when I looked up there."
Simon felt Sarah was just playing a game with him, so he didn't *rush* to the *locker room*. He wasn't interested in mysteries. If she had something to tell him, then she should tell him straight away. Only later, while he was changing his clothes, did he remember their *whispered* conversation and looked up.
The *ceiling* was not a normal *plaster* one, like in his house. It was see-through. Well, see-through, he decided, was not quite the right word. You could see *pipes* and *ventilator shafts*. Below that was an iron *grate*. Between the *pipes* there was plenty of *space* to *crawl* around.
Simon walked around the *locker room* looking for a way to get up into the *crawl space*. First I should find out if the *grate* is strong enough to hold someone, he said to himself.
With some difficulty, he climbed up on top of a row of *lockers* and put his fingers through the *grating*. He pushed up and pulled down on the *grate* but could not move it. That can hold me, he thought. How do I get up there, though? He walked all over the *locker room* but saw no place in the *ceiling* where he could make his way into the *crawl space*.

"Bye-bye," Simon said to Mick, as he left the pool.
"Bye-bye," Mick answered. "Having a nice lazy summer?"
Something in Mick's voice made Simon think the *lifeguard* was not being entirely friendly, but Mick was probably just having a bad day.

Übung 43: Finde für die britischen Begriffe auf der linken Seite das amerikanische Gegenstück! Trage die richtige Nummer in das Kästchen ein!

1. autumn	☐ trashcan
2. biscuit	☐ sidewalk
3. dustbin	☐ gasoline
4. pavement	☐ fall
5. queue	☐ cookie
6. petrol	☐ line

Simon walked home and thought no more about the pool or the *ceiling* in the men's *locker room*. He thought no more about the money that had been stolen, the CD player or the woman's watch. Forget it, he thought. It's my summer after all. If someone stole £5 from me, then I should be happy it was only £5.

Sarah, however, was thinking that if someone was to take a more aggressive *approach*, they might actually find out who was responsible for the *thefts*. As far as the police were concerned, apparently, the *thefts* were not really worthy of *investigation*. They were simply isolated incidents. The pool was not a bank or a shop but items and money seemed to be disappearing left and right. It seemed like every other day they heard someone complaining that something was missing from their *locker*. If you can't change the world, she had once been told, then at least you had to try to change your part of it – whether it was your *neighbourhood*, your village or city, or your country. Perhaps, she thought, I'll just try to solve one little problem at a swimming pool.

Kevin, naturally, was still trying to *figure out* how he could *prove* that the *maintenance men* had stolen his CD player. It was eating at him – a £220 CD player was gone one day after he *purchased* it. You could just never tell, he thought, about people. We're all part of Western culture, but even among Europeans there are differences. The French are different from the Germans who are different from the Swiss and the Spanish. It's a shame, he thought, because under other circumstances we might have become friends. Though we're different we have music in common.

ÜBUNG 44 !

Übung 44: Beantworte die Fragen zum Text!

1. How does Kevin follow Boris?

2. Where does Kevin look for his CD player?

3. Who lets Kevin out of the locked room?

4. What kind of club does Boris work in?

"Did you have a look at the *ceiling* yesterday like I asked you to?" Sarah asked, while she and Simon walked up to the pool.
"Naturally," he answered, putting his toes in the water.
"What did you think?"
"That's a nice *ceiling*," he answered sarcastically.
Sarah looked at him, *puzzled*. What had got into him? This whole business was making everybody a little bit crazy. It had to end – and soon.

"Okay," Simon continued, "I think I understand what you're thinking. We should hide up there and wait to see who steals money."
"Right."
"The only problem is that whoever is stealing from the *lockers* does not steal every day. We could spend a day or days up there waiting for someone to steal something. We'd be like monkeys who live in trees, *hanging around*, waiting for who-knows-what."
"Okay," Sarah *admitted*, "that's a weakness to the plan."
"I'd call that a serious weakness," Simon added.
"Well, if you're so clever, why don't you come up with a better idea?"
"Perhaps we should just let the police do their job."
"That's up to you. I've only become involved because you are – you and Kevin and Julia," she added quickly. "If you don't care, then I don't care. These *thefts* are meaningless to the police. They won't worry unless it's more than a few hundred pounds. One of these days, Kevin's going to make a mistake and go after the *maintenance men*. Do you want to keep him from doing something *foolish*?"
"How do we know they didn't steal it?"
"We don't know for sure that they didn't, but it does seem a bit too obvious, doesn't it? Just because they have a key doesn't mean they did it. It just may be that other people have a key."
"And we're supposed to *hang around*, up there in that *crawl space*, waiting?"
"I have a theory, Simon," Sarah said.
Just then, Kevin walked up behind them.
"What are you two lovebirds up to?"
Sarah pushed Kevin in the pool and then *dived* in after him. Simon watched for a moment, but the two were off in their own underwater world. He felt strange standing there just looking at them. He almost decided to join them, but then decided to go back to the *deckchair*.

"Where's Kevin?" asked Julia.
"He's in the pool. With Sarah."
Julia looked at Simon a moment, surprised.
"I thought you two were together."
"No," Simon said after a moment, "we're just friends."

! ÜBUNG 45

Übung 45: Welches Wort ist das „schwarze Schaf"?

1. ceiling, floor, table, wall
2. village, town, city, neighbourhood
3. cup, plate, knife, chair
4. efficient, handsome, pretty, good-looking
5. bicycle, van, scooter, motorcycle
6. programme, favour, color, honour

"Remember what I said the other day?" Sarah and Simon were sitting at a table in the shade of an umbrella. "We were walking home and discussing who might be stealing from the *lockers*."
"Yes. You said that it might be one of the *lifeguards*. But who could it be? It can't be Rob or Mick or Lori or Annie or Bill or Chris. Last year they invited us to several of their parties. They wouldn't steal from Kevin."
"Have they invited you to any parties this year?"
"No, but that doesn't matter. Dave's the only person we don't know and he's the new *guy*. Last year we didn't have this problem. Maybe he's the one who's breaking into the *lockers* and stealing things."
"Simon, you're thinking just like Kevin: Dave isn't Russian; he's only new. If he's new, that's a good enough reason to make him the next *suspect*. He's also got his eyebrow pierced, that's a good enough reason, isn't it? *What about* Rob, does he speak to anyone?

No. Maybe he's the one breaking into the *lockers*."

"Who do you think it is?"

"I have some ideas."

"Are you going to share them?"

"No, I'm not, Simon."

"Do you mind explaining why you're going to *keep me in the dark*?"

"I just want to keep it to myself. I want to see if you come to the same *conclusions* that I have."

"I *reckon* you're telling everything to Kevin, so I'll just ask him. He's my friend, too."

"He still thinks Boris and Zoltan did it. He wants to believe they did it. He needs to believe they did it. If he stops thinking they did it, he won't know who to be *mad* at. Right now, he needs someone to be *mad* at. You should just be glad he's not *mad* at you."

Übung 46: Formuliere die Sätze im Passiv!

ÜBUNG 46 !

1. Boris drove the van.

The van was driven by Boris.

2. Simon did not steal the CD player.

....

3. Simon freed Kevin from the room.

....

4. Simon disappointed Sarah.

....

5. My parents drove me to the airport.

6. Simon and Sarah suspected one of the lifeguards.

Kevin was riding his skateboard to the pool when he saw the green *van*. He stopped and *glanced* inside. The passenger side door is unlocked. I'll be right back, he thought and got back on his skateboard.

"Julia, I need your help for a few minutes."

Kevin walked away from the group of friends towards the pool entrance. He was fully dressed and carrying his skateboard. Julia followed him.

"What do you want?"

"I want you to sit here and watch for Boris and Zoltan or whatever their names are."

"What are you going to do?"

"That's not important."

"You're not going to tell me? Well, okay. If I see them, what should I do?"

"Just walk to the entrance and call my name as loud as you can."

"I don't like this, Kevin."

Kevin walked away, away from the pool and out of view. He walked down the *pavement* until he came to the green *van*. He knew the chances of finding the CD player in the *van* were about as good as winning the lottery – and one always heard that one had a better chance of *getting struck by lightning* than winning the lottery. So, he thought, I have a better chance of *getting struck by lightning* than finding my CD player in this *van*, but I have to look.

Übung 47: Setze das Gegenteil der Wörter in Klammern ein!

Since the *van* was open, getting inside wouldn't be (1. easy) d__________. With any luck, he would only be in the *van* for (2. more) l__________ than a minute or two. Kevin (3. slowly) q__________ looked in both directions. He could almost see the table at the pool entrance where he paid his *entry fee* each day. (4. Unfortunately) L__________, the *lifeguards* couldn't see him. He knew, however, that many other people could: the *van* was parked in front of a store, so he had to be fast. Setting his skateboard on its side, he opened the door and climbed inside. He started looking around in the front before moving to the back of the *van*. He moved tools and other equipment lying about, in order to see if the CD player were there. He looked (5. nowhere) e__________, but it was clear that his CD player was not in the *van.* He pulled a box out from under the back seat but it contained nothing of interest so he (6. opened) s__________ it. He looked (7. away from) t__________ the pool but saw no sign of Julia. Suddenly, there was a knock on the *van* window. Kevin turned to look and there was a man of about forty, with a thick black *moustache*, looking at him.

"Get out!" The man reached into the *van*, unlocked the side door, opened it and pulled Kevin out.

Kevin was so surprised he didn't even *struggle*. The man pulled him into his shop, which was dark and sold books and magazines and drinks and ice cream. "What were you doing?" Kevin didn't answer. "Say nothing, that's fine." The man pulled out a *mobile phone* and dialled a number. Kevin was starting to wake up, to think about to how to get out of this mess when he heard the man say, "Hello, Boris, this is Ray. I found someone going through your *van*."

At that very moment, Kevin pushed the man, who fell over a box and landed on the floor. In a second, Kevin was outside, and on the skateboard that still lay in front of the *van*. He pushed off away from the swimming pool. He went around the corner as fast as he could. I can't keep going straight on this road, he thought, it'll be too easy for him to follow me. So he turned at the next corner and made a big circle so that he came back to the pool from the other side. Before he got to the pool, though, he put his skateboard under his back-pack. He saw Boris speaking to Ray for just a moment as he entered the pool. They were looking in the *van*, though, so they didn't see him.

"Thanks, Julia," he said.

"What were you doing?"

"Nothing."

"Don't tell me 'nothing'. You're *sweating*. You've done something."

"Sorry, but that's my answer."

"Well, the next time you want my help you know my answer, too."

Julia walked off angrily.

"Hey, Mick."

"Hey, Kevin. How's it going?"

"All right, and you?"

"Same thing, different day."

Simon and Sarah were in the pool, hanging onto the side, talking of the coming school year. They still had nearly three weeks before school started again, but the summer was passing fast.

"Julia's really *cheesed off* with Kevin," Sarah reported. "He asked her to watch for the *maintenance men* while he did something outside the pool."

"I'll *bet* he broke into their *van*," Simon *whispered*.

"That would be *foolish*."

"That doesn't mean he didn't do it."

"It means he probably did do it. If he's breaking into cars now, Simon, he's getting really serious. I think it's time we took action – we'd better do something before he gets himself into trouble."

"What can we do?"

"We need to get into that *crawl space* and watch what happens."

"I thought we already agreed that that wasn't the best plan. We could be waiting up there until Christmas."

"I don't think so," Sarah said *confidently*. "I think there's some intelligence behind all this."

"What are you thinking?"

"Do you have a digital camera?"

"Me? Of course not. My Dad has one, but I don't."

"Could you use it?"

"I'd probably have to ask, but I *reckon* he'd let me. I'd have to promise to be careful and all that, but he trusts me. I think he does, anyway."

"I have one that I can use too. We also need a *mobile phone*."

"We can use mine, but why do we need a *mobile phone*?"

"To call the police. First, we take pictures of the person opening a *locker* and then going through it. Finally, we call the police. We'll let the police *do the dirty work*. That's what they're paid for."

"You finally found a use for a *mobile phone*."

"Well, I don't plan on calling the police very often."
"I know – the police aren't really punk rock."
"They aren't punk rock at all, Simon."

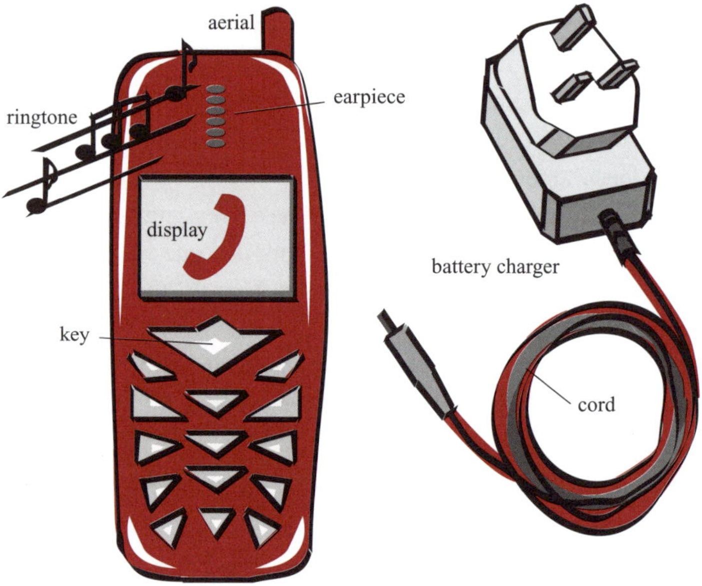

"Have you *figured out* how we can get up there? I walked all over the boys' *locker room* and couldn't find any way up."
"Then you'll just have to come over into the girls' *locker room*. On one side, there's a *space* where you can climb in, if you're careful. I *reckon* they left it open on the girls' side because they thought we wouldn't be climbing up there all the time. Boys are always doing something *daft*."
"I still don't want to just sit up there all day."
"We won't have to. We'll come in around *noon*."
"How does that help us?"

"They're going to steal from us."
"From us? I already lost £5. I don't want to lose more."
"You want a picture of someone stealing your money, don't you?"
"Not exactly."
"It might help the police find out who stole Kevin's CD player."
"Okay, I'll risk £10, but that's all. I'm sorry that someone stole Kevin's CD player, but life's hard."
"*You're all heart*."
"You have to be practical sometimes."
Sarah studied Simon's face a moment and then said, "I'll call you tomorrow morning so we can meet before coming to the pool."

Übung 48: Schreibe die Wörter in Großbuchstaben um!

ÜBUNG 48 !

1. Take away a letter from SUITE to make a word for what you wear at a pool. ____________
2. Change a letter from FOUR to make a word for something that has sixty minutes. ____________
3. Change a letter in JEANS to make the second word in a kind of food – baked ____________
4. Change a letter in TRY to make a word for something people do when they're sad. ____________
5. Change a letter in BLOCK to make a word for something that tells you what time it is. ____________

6. Change a letter in HONEY to make a word for coins and notes.

____

7. Change a letter in SHORT to make a word for something you wear. ________

Four of the friends left together that day – Sarah, Julia, Simon and Kevin. As they passed the *lifeguards'* office, Dave and Chris both said "Goodbye."

"Goodbye," Simon said, a little uncomfortably.

"See you tomorrow," Sarah said.

"Not me," Dave said, "I have the day off. You'll have to put up with Mick."

"Hmmm," Sarah said.

"What are you up to tonight?" Simon asked Kevin.

"I'm going to the *Prawn*."

"Doing some *investigating*?"

"No. I'm just going to see if I can get in. Zoltan said that I could come in after 9 pm, so I'm going to see if I really can."

"Will your parents allow you out?" Julia asked.

"Of course not, but I'm not going to ask them. I'm just going to leave quietly a short time after nine o'clock. I'll tell them I'm tired after a day in the sun at the pool. They'll just be glad for a bit of peace and quiet. They're not always happy that I play bass. 'That's not a *profession*,' my father is always telling me. My mother is always asking me if we play nice songs. They'll be glad for a bit of peace, and I'll be out of the house."

"Your life sounds so tragic," Julia said. "You poor baby."

"Okay ladies," Kevin said, setting his skateboard on the ground, "I'll see you tomorrow. Simon – *behave* yourself."

"You do the same, *mate*."

Übung 49: In jedem Satz steht ein Wort an der falschen Stelle. Verschiebe es mit einem Pfeil an die richtige Stelle!

ÜBUNG 49 !

1. Kevin saw yesterday where Boris works.

2. Sarah spoke about to Simon the problem.

3. Why Kevin did go into the storage area?

4. Who the deckchairs moved?

5. Julia said, "I'll never again help you."

The three friends watched Kevin *ride* away and then each went home. Sarah said something to Simon but he couldn't hear a word. When she repeated herself, he read her lips – "I'll call you tomorrow morning."

Chapter 8: A Detailed Plan

"Simon, telephone."
He walked down the stairs, *rubbing* his eyes.
"You need to change your boxer shorts," his mother said.
Simon picked up the telephone and said, "Hello."
"Simon, are you wearing dirty underwear?" Sarah asked.
"Mum," Simon said. "Hello, Sarah."
"What Simon?" his mother asked.
"She heard you."
"Stop *whinging*. Was that just something between you and your mother?" Sarah laughed.
"Could we get on with it?" Simon asked. "I'm tired. I was reading till late last night, so I'm not in the best *mood*."

"Okay, here's the plan. Let's meet at the Rockin' Café at half past eleven and we'll see who's on duty at the entrance."

"Who are we looking for?"

"Mick."

"Why Mick?"

"Think about it."

"What?"

"Think about it. I'll meet you in a bit, Simon. Put on something clean."

ÜBUNG 50 !

Übung 50: Setze das passende Wort ein!
(broke, desk, entrance, wallet, tomorrow, collecting, reason)

Sarah and Simon stood not far from the 1.______________ to the pool. They each had a drink in their hands, and they were looking to see who was 2. ______________ the *entry fee*. Their plan was to go in once Mick was at the 3. ____________ with the sign-in sheet.

"How much money do you have in your 4. ______________?" Sarah asked.

"£10."

Sarah *frowned* at him. "I have some money that looks real, if he only *glances* at it quickly. £20 notes. We have to give him some 5. ____________ to want to *rob* you. I'm going to bring in a digital camera that my father 6. __________ last Christmas. Since the two of us will look like we have something to steal, chances are better that he'll go after one of us. If it isn't him, then we'll try someone else 7. ______________."

"That's just what I was afraid of. I don't want to spend the rest of my summer up there in the *ceiling*."
"Relax, Simon."
They waited until they saw Mick take a seat behind the desk, and then they walked up to the pool entrance.
Simon pulled out his *wallet* and opened it wide. There appeared to be a lot of money in it. Simon pulled out a £5 note and paid his *entry fee*. Sarah pulled out a digital camera and took a picture of Simon.
"You shouldn't take that camera out in the sun," Simon warned. "It's not good to cook cameras."
"Don't worry. I'm not taking it out."
They signed in and went to their *lockers* and then met out in the pool area. They got their *deckchairs* and turned them around so they faced away from the pool. No one in the *lifeguards'* office would be able to see if they were there or not. "We'll be back in a little while."
Simon returned to his *locker*, got a shirt, his digital camera and his *mobile phone*. The previous evening, he had programmed the police phone number into this phone. He walked back to the entrance to the boys' *locker room*, which wasn't far from the front entrance. He walked out quietly, saw Mick's back and quickly ran into the girls' room. Just inside Sarah met him.
"Wait a moment," she *whispered*. "There's a woman in the toilets."
They waited silently. Finally, they heard the toilet *flush* and after that feet walking towards the pool area.
"Come, quickly," Sarah *whispered*.

Übung 51: Übersetze die Wörter und trage sie in das Kreuzworträtsel ein!

HORIZONTAL
1. sicher
5. Schließfach
6. Decke

VERTIKAL
1. Lager
2. Brieftasche
3. Geld
4. stehlen

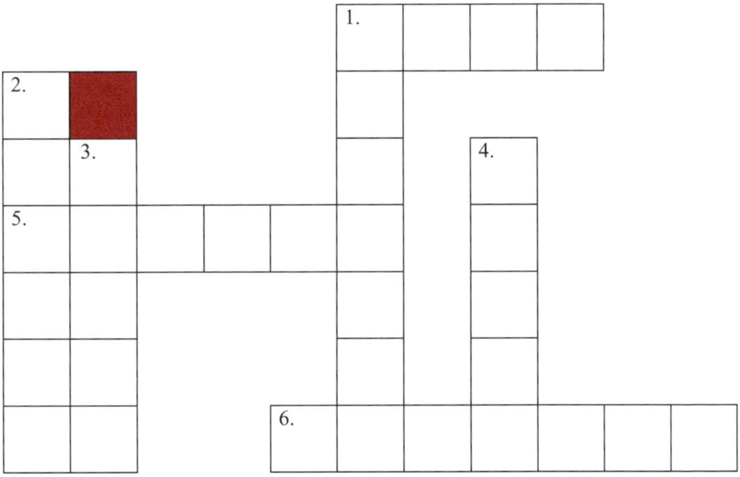

They ran to the area with the toilets and sinks.

"There it is," she *pointed*. "We can get in there."

Simon stepped on the back of the toilet, pulled himself up the wall separating the toilets and *managed* to get up into the *crawl space* over the *locker room*.

"Do you think it'll support both of us?"

"Both of us?" Simon asked.

"Yes, you're watching in the boys' room and I'm in the girls' room."

"I *reckon* it will. If it doesn't, we'll be in big trouble."
Simon helped Sarah climb up, as much as he could. Both could nearly sit up in the *crawl space*. With Sarah leading, they *crawled* over to the wall dividing the boys' and girls' *locker room*. The wall didn't go up into the *ceiling*.
"This is comfortable," Simon said ironically.
They found that from the middle they each had a good view of their *locker room*. Each could find a comfortable position.
"I hope this holds us," Simon said.
"If one of the *lifeguards* comes in," Sarah said, "we should *crawl*, as quietly as possible, to a place where we can get good pictures. The *fans* in the *locker rooms* will hide some of the sound, but if you aren't careful they might *still* hear us."
Simon *crawled* around a bit to get used to moving about – quietly – on the *ceiling*. Then they sat together, waiting.
"Did Kevin go out last night?" Simon *whispered*.
"Yeah. He said the club is cool, even if the name is boring."

Übung 52: Welche Wörter gehören zusammen? Trage die richtige Nummer in das Kästchen ein!

ÜBUNG 52 !

1. to make	☐ a van
2. to ride	☐ a cold
3. to drive	☐ a mistake
4. to do	☐ a picture
5. to catch	☐ an idea
6. to get	☐ a promise
7. to break	☐ homework
8. to take	☐ a bike

They waited one hour and then two hours. People came in, changed from their street clothes to their swimsuits and left. Up in the *crawl space*, the two young people began to feel a bit warm.

"I'm not sure this was a good idea," Simon said.

"Stop *whinging*. Mick saw that digital camera and he thinks you have lots of money in your *wallet*. He'll be coming."

A while later, Simon looked at his watch. "It's half past two. He's not coming."

"You have to be patient, Simon. By the way, remember not to let the flash go when you take a picture. It'll give us away."

"That probably won't be a problem."

They waited.

And waited.

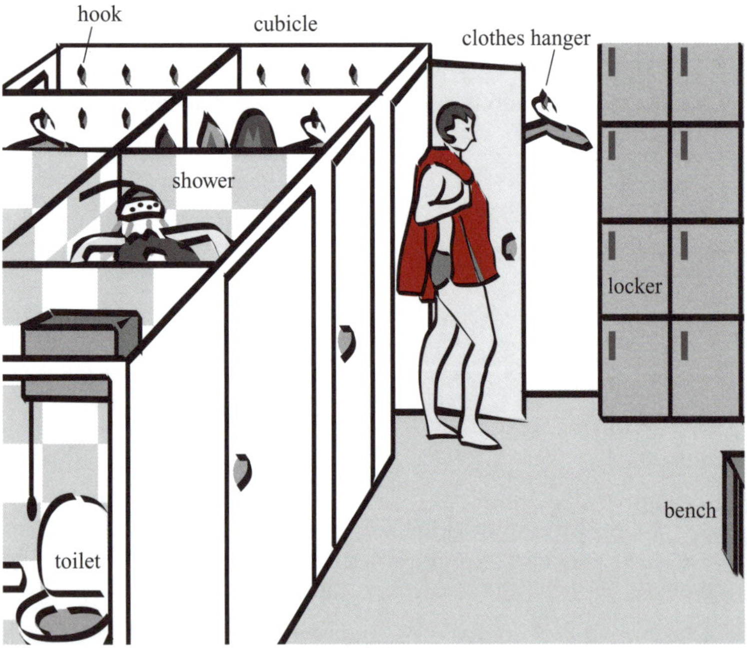

"Who's that?" Sarah asked.
Simon leaned forward.
"That's only Lori," he said, and leaned back.
Sarah watched the *lifeguard* walk over to the toilets and enter one of them. A minute later, she walked out and went into the *cupboard* where the *cleaners* kept their supplies. She took out a sign that warned those who wanted to come in to wait ten minutes: the *locker rooms* were being cleaned. She carried it over to the pool entrance to the *locker room*. You could not see the sign from the pool; you would only be able to see it if you tried to get in. Lori walked over to Sarah's *locker* and put a key in the *locker*. While watching the *lifeguard*, Sarah had been getting into position. She snapped a picture of the *lifeguard* at the *locker*, another of her opening the *locker*, another reaching around in the *locker*, another with the digital camera in her hand and a last one of her closing the *locker*. They watched Lori leave the *locker room*.
Sarah *crawled* back to Simon, a big smile on her face. "Can you believe it?" she almost laughed. "My plan worked."
"What do we do now?"
"Wait."
"We should call the police straight away."
"Just wait," Sarah repeated.
Lori returned shortly and put the cleaning sign back in the cleaners' *cupboard*.
When she was gone, Simon asked, "What are we waiting for?"
"Simon, there's a lot of money in your *wallet*. Let's see what happens."
"It's 2.57," Simon told her. "We can't wait till the pool closes."
"Don't worry, Simon. I really don't think we'll have to wait that long. Lots of people come around 3.30. I'm sure she'll be back before then."

Übung 53: Sind die folgenden Aussagen richtig? Markiere mit richtig ✔ oder falsch –!

ÜBUNG 53 !

1. Simon changed his mind about Boris stealing Kevin's CD player. ☐
2. Julia believes Kevin is right. ☐
3. Sarah is going to the pool because she wants to find out who is stealing things from the lockers. ☐
4. The lifeguards are friends of Simon, Kevin, Sarah and Julia. ☐
5. Simon has a plan to figure out who is responsible for the thefts. ☐
6. Simon has courage. ☐
7. Boris and Zoltan know that Kevin believes they stole the CD player. ☐
8. Lori stole Sarah's camera. ☐

Outside, among the group of friends, Simon and Sarah's absence was becoming strange.
"Where could they be?"
"They're in love," Kevin answered.
"I'm not sure about that," Julia said. "Sarah has her eyes on someone else, I think."
"I wonder what they're doing."
"Are they in the pool?"
"For more than two hours? Sarah doesn't like the pool that much."
"Maybe they're having a heart-to-heart talk."
"As I said," Julia said, "I don't think they're in love."
"It may be better to have such talks with someone you don't love."

In the *locker room*, Simon had decided he would sit up there until 3.30 – but not a moment longer. Once he had set an end-time, he

was able to be patient. The two sat quietly – *whispering* occasionally, but saying nothing important or meaningful.
"There's Kevin," Simon *whispered*. They watched him walk into the *locker room*. He looked around a minute or two and then went back outside. "I wonder if he was looking for me."
"He can't think you're just *hanging out* in here."
Rob walked into the *locker room*. Just like Lori, he made sure the *locker room* was empty and then put the sign at the pool entrance to the *locker room*, closing it. At the same time, Simon turned on his digital camera and made sure the flash would not go off. Rob went directly to Simon's *locker*, put a key in and opened it. He quickly found Simon's *wallet*, opened it and took out the money and then closed the *locker*. He put the money in a pocket in his swimsuit. Simon took five pictures of Rob going through the *locker* and then shutting it.

Übung 54: Welche der Erklärungen stimmt? Kreuze die richtige Lösung an!

1. Let me in on your plan!
   a) ☐ Tell me what you're going to do.
   b) ☐ I don't want to help you.

2. Zoltan threw him out of the club.
   a) ☐ Zoltan had a party for him.
   b) ☐ Zoltan made him leave.

3. Shall I fetch you a towel?
   a) ☐ Shall I get your towel?
   b) ☐ Shall I take your towel?

4. He's keeping me in the dark.
   a) ☐ I'm locked in a room.
   b) ☐ There's something he's not telling me.

5. You're all heart.
   a) ☐ You're a nice person. (Ironic)
   b) ☐ You cry all the time.

6. Stop whinging!
   a) ☐ Stop complaining!
   b) ☐ Stop crying!

Sarah and Simon watched the door close behind Rob. "We should get out straight away," Simon said.
"Naturally. First, though, let's call the police."
Simon made the call and then they *crawled* over to the women's toilets. As they were making their way over, the *grating* they were on fell away from the *ceiling*. At the same time, a woman in her forties was walking into the *locker room*.
"What's going on?" she screamed.
"Quickly," Sarah *whispered*.
"Move," Simon agreed.
They *crawled* as fast as they could and were getting down onto the toilets when Annie walked in.
"What are you doing?" she demanded.
"Nothing."
"Simon!"
"Hello – er, uh."
"What were you taking pictures of?"
"We were taking pictures," Sarah said, "but it's not what you think."
"Who are you?"

"The police are on their way here," Sarah said, hiding her camera as best she could in her hand.
Rob *showed up* a moment later in the *locker room*.
"What are you doing in the women's toilets?" he asked Simon.
"It was just a *prank*," he explained, hiding his camera in the *palm* of his hand.
"This had better be good," Rob warned. "Come with me."

Übung 55: Setze die Verben in der richtigen Zeitform in die Lücken ein!

Simon (1. to *notice*) ______________ that Rob (2. not look) ______________ especially comfortable. Perhaps he (3. to see) __________ the camera. In any case, he (4. to hold) __________ onto Simon's arm, leading him out of the girls' *locker room*.

Sarah (5. to follow) __________ with Annie. As they walked out of the *locker room*, she hoped to see a policeman walking in. Instead, she (6. to see) __________ that Mick (7. to be) __________ once again at the desk.

Mick looked at Rob. "What (8. to go) __________ on?"

"I (9. not know) __________. But I (10. to expect) __________ to find out very soon."

Rob led the two into the *lifeguards'* office, followed by Annie. Mick closed the door behind them.

"What exactly were you doing in the girls' *locker room*?"
Sarah and Simon looked at each other but said nothing.
"They were up in the *ceiling*," Annie explained.
"Where?" Mick asked.
"In the *ceiling*. There's a *crawl space* up there."
"What were you doing up in the *ceiling*?"
"We weren't doing anything," Sarah said at last. "I was just showing him you could get up there."
"That's a lie," Annie said. "What's with the cameras?"
"I want the truth, Simon, and fast," Mick said.
Rob stood next to him silently.

ÜBUNG 56

Übung 56: Lies weiter und setze die richtigen Präpositionen in die Lücken ein!

There was a knock 1. __________ the door. Every one turned towards it.

"Open it," Rob said 2. __________ Annie.

A policeman stood 3. __________ the other side.

"How convenient," Annie said. "Officer, we found these two *crawling* around 4. __________ the *ceiling* of the girls' *locker room* – and they damaged it."

"Someone called the police," the policeman answered.

"Someone called you?" Rob asked.

"Yes," Sarah *interrupted*. "Simon called."

"Why?" Rob asked.

"I'll take over, if you don't mind," the policeman said.

"We have some pictures 5. __________ you," Sarah said.

"Yes," Simon said, handing his digital camera 6. __________ the police officer.

Though the pictures were a little small, he looked 7. __________ Rob and back 8. ______________ the camera. Then he looked 9. __________ Sarah's pictures. After looking 10. __________ Annie, he said, "Who's this?"

"It's Lori, another of the *lifeguards*," Sarah answered.
"Please could you fetch this 'Lori'," the policeman said to Annie.
The policeman called his office and asked for another officer to come.
"What was taken?" the policeman asked Simon.
"A digital camera and some money," Simon answered.
"Money, that's hard to *prove*. Where did the money come from?"
"My *locker*," Simon said.
"Come with me," the policeman said. "You and you," he *pointed* at Rob and Lori who had just come in.
"Excuse me," Sarah said to the policeman and *whispered* into his ear.
"You too," the policeman said, *pointing to* Mick.
The three *lifeguards*, the policeman, Simon and Sarah all walked into the boys' *locker room*. Simon led them to his *locker*, opened it with the key on his *wrist*, and pulled out his *wallet*. Opening it, he saw that there was still money in the *wallet*. A £10 note was gone but a few of the fake £20 notes were still there. Simon looked at Sarah helplessly.

Übung 57: Finde für das Wort in Klammern ein Reimwort, das in den Zusammenhang passt!

ÜBUNG 57

"How many are (1. air) ______________?" she asked.

"Three."

"There were (2. heaven) ______________ in your wallet, weren't there?"

"So where are the (3. best) ______________?" the policeman asked.

Simon looked from the policeman to Rob and (4. track) ______________. "Right there," he said, "*pointing to* the bulge on the (5. wide) ______________ of Rob's swimsuit."

"What's in your pocket, (6. cheese) ______________?" the policeman asked.

"Nothing."

"(7. Wood) ______________, then open it."

Rob opened the pocket unhappily. Inside was a roll with several fake £20 notes and one real £10 note.
"Let's go back into your office," the policeman said.
As they walked back into the office, the second policeman came in. This was the policeman Simon and Sarah had seen before.
"What's going on?" Kevin called, from the other side of the *lifeguards'* office.

"We found out who's been stealing things from people's *lockers*," Simon explained.
A look of surprise crossed Kevin's face.
"We're going to have a quick look around to see if we can find the digital camera," the first policeman said. He looked around the office but found nothing. "Let's see what's in your *locker*, please," the policeman said to Lori.
She opened the *locker*. The policeman found her clothes, some make-up and some *sunscreen* but no digital camera.
"If I might suggest," Sarah began, "you might want to look in Mick's *locker*. He was on duty when we paid our *entry fees* and he saw Simon's money and my digital camera.
"If you please," the policeman said to Mick.
"No," Mick answered.
"We can open it now or we can go down to the station, get permission and then come back. In either case, you're staying with me."

Übung 58: Unterstreiche im folgenden Textabschnitt die Gegenteile der vorgegebenen Wörter!
(1. running, 2. leaned forward, 3. pushed, 4. whispered, 5. speaking, 6. something, 7. smaller)

! ÜBUNG 58

Mick stared at the policeman and then at Simon and Sarah before walking over to the *locker*. He opened it and then stood back. The policeman looked around a moment, found a sock and pulled the digital camera from it.
"Unbelievable!" Kevin shouted. "He must have my CD player!"
"That's long gone," Mick said, unable to remain silent.
Kevin turned red, but there was nothing he could do. Mick was bigger and the police were there to make sure nothing happened.

"Did you hear that?" Kevin asked at last.

"Yes."

Suddenly, Rob punched Simon in the back of the head.

"Rich boy!"

Simon quickly turned around, but a policeman came between the two.

"That's enough, you," he said to Rob. "You're in enough trouble, don't you think? Let's get them down to the station. I'll call a *van*."

Soon after, the two policemen led the group to the *constable's* office.

"Now that I think of it," Kevin began, "I remember the way Mick looked at the CD player and how he was a bit strange to us much of the time. If only I had seen that earlier."

"You decided the *maintenance men* were responsible and looked no farther," Sarah said. "You just stopped thinking."

"Okay, I was stupid. I don't dislike Russians or any group of people. I like meeting people from other countries and cultures. I was just so angry that I stopped thinking, like Sarah said."

"It's good you have friends who'll think for you when you stop thinking," Simon said. "You said just about every stupid thing someone can say, Kevin. I really couldn't believe it was you."

Sarah *shook* her head. "You surprised me. It was just one cliché after another about foreigners."

"But I don't think that way, Sarah. I don't – do I, Simon? Tell her."

"I told Sarah you weren't really like that, but you kept on saying the same stupid things, so it was hard to *prove* that you're an open, intelligent person."

"Okay, okay. I'm not prejudiced, though. I know it. Or maybe there's a part of myself I never knew existed before. I'm not like that, though. At least, I don't want to be like that."

Übung 59: In diesen Sätzen sind die Wörter durcheinander gekommen. Wie lauten die Sätze richtig? Trage sie mit Satzzeichen und richtiger Groß- und Kleinschreibung ein!

1. had idea a sarah great

2. locker hot in the were two very the room

3. doing ceiling what you are the in

4. the police was very angry with mick

5. kevin admit did his mistake

6. the rob thieves mick lori and were

ÜBUNG 59 !

Simon tried to call Kevin and then tried to call Sarah but neither of them was at home. He got on his bike and cycled into the city. I don't want to go to the pool, he thought. Maybe I'll go and look at some CDs. The best store for CDs was down in the city centre, so he *pointed* his bike in that direction. It was a pleasant ride. He had spent so much time at the pool *recently* that he had forgotten about his bicycle. He got to the store, *locked* up his bike and wandered in.

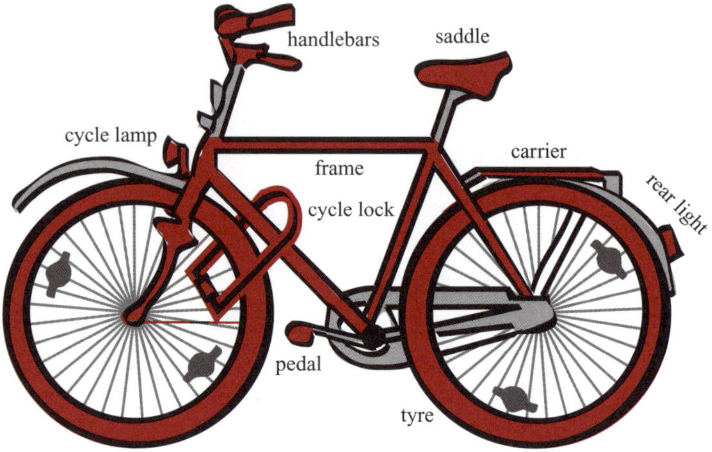

"Hey, Simon."

"Hey, Kev. Oh, hello Sarah."

"Hi, Simon."

"You just looking around?" Kevin asked. "Or are you looking for something?"

"I just thought I'd look around. I didn't know what else to do."

"I'm sick of the pool, myself," Kevin said.

"I think we all are," Sarah agreed.

"What are you up to?" Simon asked.

"We're off for some lunch. Do you want to join us?"

They looked at each other a moment. It was becoming *awkward*. Simon didn't feel like being on his own, but he knew that *hanging out* with Kevin and Sarah was not possible.

"No," Simon answered. He could see they were *relieved*. "I think I'm just going to cycle around. Is there any news on your CD player?"

"They found the woman's watch at Mick's house but, like Mick said, my CD player is long gone. I think they usually stole money."

"I'm sorry."
"Yeah, well, *life goes on*."

Übung 60: Ergänze die Begriffe!

ÜBUNG 60 !

1. to _ _ ke a walk
2. C _ _ c _ it out!
3. _ _ d _ my bike!
4. to _ r _ v _ a car
5. to c _ _ c _ a thief
6. C _ _ e with me!

"Simon, did you read the article in the newspaper about the pool?"
"No, mum."
"The three have been charged with stealing, but there is not much evidence of what they stole. Many people are now saying they lost money at the pool, but the police can't *prove* anything. It looks like they'll get charged with stealing the woman's watch, Kevin's CD player, the digital camera and the money found on the pool manager."
"At least that's something."
"Do you know why they were stealing from people's *lockers*?"
"No. I guess it doesn't say in the article."
"No. How did they get in?"
"They had a copy of a *pass key*. No one knows how they got it and Mick's not explaining anything."
"Where are you going?"
"Upstairs – to play guitar."
"You're not going to the pool?"
"I've had enough of the pool for one summer!"

THE END

Abschlusstest

Übung 1: Welches Wort ist das „schwarze Schaf"?

1. lifeguard, policeman, sunbather, swimmer
2. teacher, board, headmaster, student
3. steal, burglary, daft, theft
4. ceiling, house, wall, floor
5. dive, swim, sunbathe, jump
6. hip-hop, song, pop, punk

Übung 2: Setze die richtigen Präpositionen ein!

1. Sarah wanted ___________ help Simon and Kevin.
2. Where are you ___________ ? (Where were you born?)
3. Simon was worried ___________ Kevin.
4. Simon flirted ___________ Sarah.
5. I want to go ___________ the pool today.
6. She looked ___________ him while she spoke with Simon.
7. What are you up ___________?

Übung 3: Ordne die Buchstaben zu einem sinnvollen Wort!

1. At a pool you can (miws) ___________.

2. Lifeguards make sure the people in the pool are (aesf) __________.

3. According to Sarah, (basuthngni) __________ is not punk rock.

4. At the pool, you can put your belongings in a (krecol) __________.

5. To get in, you have to pay an (ytern efe) __________.

6. You dry off with a (lewto) __________ when you get out of the pool.

Übung 4: Wähle das passende Wort für jeden Satz aus und unterstreiche es!

1. Each morning I listen to/hear the radio.
2. Sarah likes/wants to go to the pool tomorrow.
3. The friends made place/space for Simon.
4. He looks like/shines a boxer.
5. Do you think/mean Sarah had a good idea?
6. I become/get £250 a week for working in a restaurant.
7. Rob is Annie, Lori and Mick's chef/boss.
8. They moved their/there deckchairs closer together.

Übung 5: Setze die Verben ins Simple Past!

1. Yesterday, I (to swim) __________ at the pool.

2. Simon (to run) __________ to get Kevin.

3. Sarah (to take) ____________ a bus to school.

4. Lori (to answer) ____________ all the questions.

5. We (to meet) ____________ at the café last night.

6. Where (to be) ____________ you on holiday last summer?

7. She (to go) ____________ to Bath.

Übung 6: In diesen Sätzen sind die Wörter durcheinander gekommen. Wie lauten die Sätze richtig? Trage sie mit Satzzeichen und richtiger Groß- und Kleinschreibung ein!

1. skateboard his takes kevin everywhere almost

____

2. punk listens music sarah to rock

____

3. his simon riding bicycle enjoys

____

4. player kevin's stole who cd

____

5. russian english speaks and boris

____

6. into jumped julia water the

____

Übung 7: Ergänze die Begriffe!

1. To go into water feet-first is to _ u _ p.
2. When you go into water head-first you _ i _ e.
3. Paper money is also called a n _ _ e.
4. Lifeguards don't like it when children are _ u _ n i _ _.
5. To move on your hands and knees is to c _ a _ _.
6. When your skin is brown because of the sun you have a _ _ n t _ _.
7. The clothing you wear in a swimming pool is your s _ _ _ s _ _ t.
8. The room where you change is called a _ o _ _ _ r room.

Übung 8: Setze die Verben in der richtigen Zeitform ein!

1. Simon (to think) ____________ the summer would be quiet.
2. He (not know) ______________________ how exciting it would be.
3. Kevin (to enjoy) ____________ his summer until someone (to steal) ____________ his CD player.
4. Simon and Kevin (to be) ______________ friends since they were little boys.
5. Sarah (to have) ____________ her nose pierced.
6. She (to be) ____________ the first to have her nose pierced.

Schüler-Lernkrimi Englisch

Ultimatum by SMS

John William Holway

Inhalt

Story

Nach einem Hockeyspiel in der Schule ist plötzlich Susans Medaillon aus der Umkleidekabine verschwunden. Susan ist außer sich, denn das Medaillon ist ein Erbstück ihrer Großmutter, das ihr sehr viel bedeutet. Kurz darauf bekommt sie eine mysteriöse SMS mit der Forderung, bis Ende der Woche £200 zu zahlen und niemandem davon zu erzählen. Falls sie sich nicht an die Abmachung halten sollte, würde sie ihr Medaillon nie wieder sehen.
Wer steckt hinter dem Diebstahl? Und aus welchem Grund? Susan hat eine Vermutung. Gemeinsam mit ihren Freunden Tracey, Heather, George und Arthur versucht sie den Dieb zu fassen – eine mehr als abenteuerliche Aufgabe.
Wird es ihnen gelingen den wahren Dieb zu stellen?

Chapter 1: The Winning Shot

Holding her stick firmly in both hands, Susan raced down the side of the hockey field. She was determined to reach the goal *at all costs*. Faster and faster she ran and her heart beat wildly. It was a *glorious* day at St. Mary's and the sun shone brightly from a cloudless sky. Her friends *cheered* from the sidelines "Susan, Susan" and she felt *pride rise up* in her *chest.* Although she was only 15, Susan was the captain of the senior hockey team at St. Mary's High School and hockey was her greatest love. Today was the final match of the season against their *local* rivals Merrywood School and there was *still* no score.

There were only five minutes left to play and Susan felt that she just had to make it all the way to the goal. Her parents had also come to watch today and she knew they simply had to win. She felt that everything depended on her. All eyes were now on her as she quickly *steered* the hockey ball down the side of the hockey field towards the goal. Over her shoulder one of the Merrywood *defenders* raced to try to *catch* Susan, but Susan was much faster.

Then suddenly in front of her came the final Merrywood *defender*, a big blonde girl built like an *ox*. The girl was *convinced* she would block Susan, but Susan had other ideas. Quickly she moved to the right, then back to the left and in an instant she was past the *defender* with only the *goalkeeper* to beat.

With a *keen* eye she focused on the goal, then she swung back her stick and with a *whack* sound the stick crashed against the leather of the ball. The ball *sailed* high and into the top right-hand corner of the net. Cheers went up from around the ground:

"Goal, goal, goal! Hooray, hooray, hooray," but Susan let out a scream of pain and fell to the grass.

"Agh, my leg, my leg," she cried.

ÜBUNG 1

Übung 1: Unterstreiche die sechs Wörter, die falsch geschrieben sind, und verbessere sie!

In her efforts to *score* the gole she had stretched aut her leg too far and *torn* a *muscle* in her rite leg. A fire burnt in the *calf* of her leg and she rolled in paine on the ground. Susan was a brave fighter, but she fellt the emotions *well up* inside of her and teers of pain rolled down her cheeks.

1. ____________________ 4. ____________________

2. ____________________ 5. ____________________

3. ____________________ 6. ____________________

Quickly she tried to *fight off* the tears and *wiped* her streaming eyes with her *muddy* hands.

The team coach Mrs Hiller made her way through the *crowd* that was now *gathering* around Susan.

"Let me through, out of the way," she cried as she pushed the players to the side and *knelt* down beside Susan.

"Where does it hurt? Are you alright, Susan?" she asked in a *compassionate* voice.

In Susan's mind there was only one question:

"Did I *score*? Did I get the goal?"

"Yes, yes," replied Mrs Hiller. "Super goal, well done, my dear, you won the match. Now about your leg, where does it hurt?"

In her moment of triumph Susan had completely forgotten about the pain: she had won the match! Her shot had *scored* a goal and St. Mary's had won! As she looked up she saw a sea of faces around her. Her own *team mates* and even some of the Merrywood girls were *gazing* down at her.

"Give the girl some *space*!" shouted Mrs Hiller. "She needs to breathe and get some fresh air."

Übung 2: Lies weiter und ordne die Buchstaben zu einem sinnvollen Wort!

ÜBUNG 2 !

By now (1. eth) ____________ *referee* and several parents had arrived to push back the *onlookers* and to (2. kame) ____________ *space* for Susan to be treated.

"It's my right leg," said Susan. "I think I (3. veha) ____________ *torn* the *calf muscle*."

"Let me see," said Mrs Hiller as she gently (4. tlef) ____________ the muscles in Susan's right (5. gel) ____________.

"Ooh, ahh," cried Susan as she felt the (6. aipn) ____________ shoot through her leg.

"Give me the *sponge*," said Mrs Hiller and *squeezed* cold (7. awter) ____________ over the back of Susan's leg.

Immediately Susan felt *relief* as the cold water *eased the pain*. Again Mrs Hiller gently pressed on the *calf* muscle before announcing:
"Yes, it is definitely the *calf* muscle. You will have to go off, my dear. There is no way you can continue to play with this injury."
Then Mrs Hiller turned to two of the girls standing nearby and said:
"Heather and Tracey, help her to get up and take her back to the *changing rooms*, please".

Heather and Tracey were actually Susan's best friends and so it was not by chance that they were standing nearby.

"Here, let me!" said a deep voice as her father stepped forward from the *crowd*, determined to help.

"It's okay, dad. We can *manage*," said Susan.

It was just too *embarrassing* to let her dad help her off the *pitch* with all her friends standing around and watching.

Mrs Hiller and the girls slowly *helped* Susan *to her feet*. She put her arms around Tracey and Heather, while Heather carried her stick. She then slowly *limped* from the field, trying to put all her weight on her left leg. The *crowd* from St. Mary's *clapped* and *cheered*, giving her a hero's reception as she was led off the *pitch*. After a *stern* look from their trainer, some of the Merrywood girls began to *clap* as well as they watched Susan being helped away. From a

distance a small *crowd* of boys had also *gathered* to watch.
"Poor Susan," said Arthur. He had *fancied* Susan for a long time, but was too *shy* to *ask her out*.
"I hope she isn't hurt too bad! It looked really terrible when she crashed to the grass like that!"
"Don't worry," said George, the boy standing next to him. "She will be fine. She is a tough fighter, your Susan!" Arthur's face turned bright red. "What do you mean?" he asked.
"You know just what I mean!" said George in a firm voice. Meanwhile further back in the *crowd* there was a small group of *guys* who seemed very pleased with what they had seen.
"Serves her right!" said the tall *guy* in the old school blazer. "She's a real little *witch* that girl. She is so *stuck-up*, too."
"Yeah," said another.
"Come one, let's go. This match is boring anyway." Two of the gang *turned on their heels* and *headed back* to the main school exit, unnoticed by the rest of the *crowd*. In the distance the *whistle* blew as the hockey match restarted for the final minutes. Mrs Hiller had sent on three *substitutes* to cover for the missing girls. Susan and her friends had finally reached the girls' *changing rooms*. Heather and Tracey guided Susan to the *bench* where she had hung up all her clothes. She sat down *exhausted*.
"I don't think I can *face* the shower," she said. "I will just have to go home dirty and shower there. Anyway, my parents are waiting outside, so I want to be as quick as possible."

ÜBUNG 3 !

Übung 3: Übersetze die Verben und enträtsele das Lösungswort!

1. halten ☐ _ _ _
2. spielen _ _ ☐ _

3. helfen _ _ _ ☐
4. erscheinen _ ☐ _ _ _ _
5. versuchen _ _ ☐

Lösung: _ _ _ _ _

Heather and Tracey helped Susan into her school uniform. Putting on her socks was the most difficult and they decided to leave one knee sock off, *due to* the pain in her leg.
"Here," said Tracey. "Let me carry your shoe and your sock." "Thanks!" said Susan. "I don't know what I would do without friends like you!"
Despite the obvious pain she was in, she smiled and looked up at Heather and Tracey, who were standing by to help. She pulled on her school blazer and then felt into the right-hand pocket for her *locket*. At that moment a look of shock and horror came over her face.
"My *locket*!" she cried. "It's gone!"

Chapter 2: Blackmail by Text Message

"Are you sure you had your *locket* with you?" asked Tracey.
"Of course," answered Susan. "I always wear my *locket*, you know that."
"Look in the other pockets," said Heather, trying to sound optimistic. Susan quickly checked through all her pockets, but there was no sign of the missing *locket*. In a state of panic she even picked up the blazer and *shook* it upside down. All the contents of the pockets fell out. Handkerchiefs, a *comb*, a chocolate bar, several hair bands, some *coins*, a few old toffees and even some pens fell to the floor, but no *locket*.

"I can't believe it!" she cried. "It's gone! It's gone! It's gone! Someone has been in here and stolen my *locket*."
"Calm down," said Heather. "There has to be an explanation. We have to find out who took it and how to get it back. Hold on, I will just go outside and tell your parents."
"No!" cried Susan. "Don't tell my parents. They mustn't know. They will kill me if they find out I left my *locket* in my blazer in the *changing rooms*. They are always telling me to take better care of my *stuff*. If they find out that I left the *locket* in my blazer I will get into big trouble."

Übung 4: Welches Wort ist das „schwarze Schaf"? Unterstreiche das nicht in die Reihe passende Wort!

ÜBUNG 4 !

1. breathe, eat, apple, sleep
2. win, stick, ball, goal
3. happy, anger, sad, hopeful
4. cry, tear, sad, left
5. terrible, wonderful, pleased, satisfied
6. tall, fat, short, shoe
7. always, often, never, new

"But your parents are sure to find out," said Heather. "How can you keep this a secret?"
"You must promise me not to tell anyone," said Susan. "We must keep this a secret."
"Okay, I swear," said Heather.
"Me too," said Tracey.
"The *locket* was a present from my grandmother," said Susan. "It is a family *heirloom* and my gran gave it to me before she died."

Heather and Tracey knew the *locket* well because Susan always wore it. The *locket* had a long gold chain and was oval in shape. It opened and had two photos inside, one of Susan's parents and the other of her grandparents. It was Susan's most precious possession and she *was* very *attached to* it.

"I am just so stupid," cried Susan. "Why didn't I put it in the bag with the *valuables* that the coach collected? I have to get it back. Who could have taken it?"

"Don't worry!" said Heather. "We will get it back for you. Maybe someone just took it for a practical joke. I mean they can't really sell it, can they? Not with your photos fixed in it."

"They can always take out the photos," said Susan. "But no, I don't think someone took it for the money. I think someone was trying to *get at* me. It just isn't fair! What have I ever done to hurt anyone?"

ÜBUNG 5 !

Übung 5: Lies weiter und setze die Verben in Klammern ins Simple Past!

With that, she (1. sit) __________ down on the *bench* and (2. cry) __________ again, tears streaming down her cheeks. Heather and Tracey both (3. put) __________ their arms around her shoulders and (4. try) __________ to *comfort* her.

"Don't cry," they (5. say) __________. "We will get it back for you, we promise. Now come on, let's get outside and get you to your parents. They will be wondering what is going on."

"Okay," said Susan, drying her eyes. "But remember, not a word about the *locket*."

"Alright!" said Heather. "Don't worry, we will keep this secret. We won't tell anyone, we promise."

"Yes, you can trust us," said Tracey.

Heather (6. help) __________ Susan put her blazer over her shoulders and the two girls helped her *limp* out of the *changing rooms*.

Her parents (7. be) __________ waiting outside.

Susan's mum and dad came *rushing* across when they saw her coming out.
"Susan, *darling*!" said her mum. "Are you alright? That was a terrible fall you had."
Susan's mum was always worrying about her and it was *embarrassing* sometimes, but today Susan felt so awful that she just fell into the arms of her mum and *wept* and *wept*.
"There, there my love," said her dad, as caring as always. "Let's get you home and put your leg up. Thank goodness it was not broken. That was a great goal you *scored*, well done!"
Susan looked across at her dad and *managed a smile*. Dear old dad, he was always good at *cheering* her *up*.

Susan said goodbye to her friends. Secretly, she decided to make a plan to get back the *locket* and she was sure that she would need their help.
"Come and see me tomorrow!" she said.
Then her parents helped her into the car and they drove carefully to 12 Featherwood Street. As they arrived Susan was delighted to see their little house. Her dad helped her up into her bedroom and asked if she wanted anything.
"No," said Susan. "I just need some *rest*, thanks."

ÜBUNG 6 !

Übung 6: Beantworte die Fragen zum Text!

1. Which school does Susan go to?

2. Who are her best friends?

3. What is her father like?

4. Who gave Susan the locket?

5. What did Mrs Hiller blow?

Susan fell into her bed and once her dad had gone she started crying again. What was she going to do? She just couldn't tell them about her *locket*. Would she ever get it back, she wondered? Tracey and Heather would be sure to help. She just had to find a solution.

She lay on the bed and *stared* at the *ceiling*. Sleep seemed impossible. Then suddenly she heard a familiar sound. 'Deedle do da da, deedle do da da': her *mobile phone* was ringing. Quickly she rolled over and picked it up from her bedside table.
"You have a message," said the display. She pressed the *button* and read the words "*r u* missing something?"
What? she thought. Who could this possibly be? She did not know the person sending the message, as her phone said 'Number not

recognized'. Typical, she thought. Someone is just *winding me up*.

Susan loved her *mobile phone*. In fact you could say she was really *addicted to* her phone. She was always *texting* her friends and even slept with the *mobile* by her bedside. Any time of day the phone went she would always jump to answer it. Whenever she heard the ringing tone 'deedle do da da, deedle do da da', she knew she had a message and dropped everything to get to the phone. This time however, it was different. Who was the mystery person who had sent her a message? It must be the person who had taken her *locket*, she thought.

She grabbed the phone, typed in the reply "Who *r u*?" and then pressed the 'Send' *button*. It seemed like forever as she waited for the reply and then came the sound 'deedle do da da, deedle do da da'. Her fingers were trembling as she pressed the 'Read' *button*.

"*u r 2 nosy*! Do *u* want *yr locket* back?"

Susan was tempted to scream and shout out:

"Of course I do, you idiot," but she did not want to alarm her parents, so she *managed* to control her temper, putting her hand over her mouth.

"Of course I do!" she then typed back. "Who *r u*?" she typed in once more, desperate to know who had her precious possession.

"*u* will never know!" came the immediate reply. "Just do as I say or *u* will never *c yr locket* again! Tell *no1*" said the message. "Get us £200 by Friday or *u* will never *c yr locket* again!" wrote the mystery caller.

What? thought Susan. Two hundred pounds? How can I get such a lot of money? I only have 20 *quid* in savings. He was crazy! She was being *blackmailed*.

Susan took a deep breath and thought, calm down, girl, think what to do next. How could she get so much money? Her first thought was to play for more time. “Friday is *2* short notice. I need more time *pls*,” she *texted* back.

ÜBUNG 7

Übung 7: Vervollständige die Sätze mit ***my, your, his (2x), her (2x), their*** *und* ***our****!*

1. Susan said: “Where is ___________ locket?”

2. Heather and Tracey like ___________ school.

3. Susan said: “Someone has stolen ___________ locket.”

4. Susan told me that a thief had stolen ___________ locket.

5. Arthur looked at ___________ friend.

6. We have lost ___________ money.

7. Susan got the locket from ___________ gran.

8. Susan’s father loves ___________ daughter.

But the answer was short and final.
“Get the money by Friday or *u* will never *c yr locket* again! Do not *txt bk* and tell NO-ONE!!!” came back the demand. It was clear that it was impossible to discuss the matter with this person. Then came another short message a few seconds later: “*u* will hear from us again!”
Us, thought Susan. So, was there more than one person? Was there a whole gang in on this? Or was someone trying to *fool* her?
She crashed on the bed and *pounded* the pillows with her *fists*.
“It just isn’t fair!” she cried. “It just isn’t fair!”

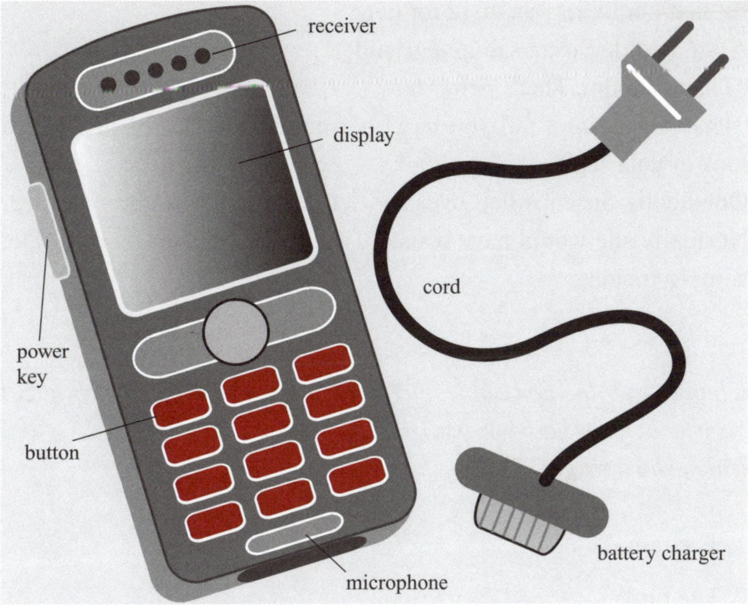

At that moment came a loud knock on the door.
"Are you alright, dear?" came the caring voice of her mother.
In her desperation she had forgotten all about being calm. Quickly she *rubbed* her eyes and blew her nose.
"Can I come in?" asked her mother, sounding rather anxious.
"Yes, just a minute, mum," came the reply.
Susan put her *mobile* in the *drawer* of the *bedside cabinet* and closed it before shouting:
"Okay, you can come in now."
The door opened and her mum entered the room.
"Oh my poor dear," she said with a soft voice. "Have you been crying?"
For the second time that day Susan *flung* her arms around her mum and *sobbed* her heart out. It was all just too stressful. She was grate-

ful that her mum was there for her.
After a while Susan sat up and said:
"Thanks, mum. That's better now."
"That was quite a fall you had," her mum said. "Can I just take a look at your leg?"
Obediently Susan rolled over and let her mother examine her leg. Normally she would have resisted, but today she was happy to get some sympathy.

! ÜBUNG 8

Übung 8: Ordne den Substantiven die folgenden Verben richtig zu! Verwende jedes Verb zweimal.
(falls, runs, sings)

1. The rain ....
2. The bird ....
3. The rabbit ....
4. The train ....
5. The apple ....
6. The girl ....

"I think we will have to take you to the doctor's with this," her mother said.
"No, it's okay, mum. I'll be fine, and anyway it's Friday and the doctor's will be closed. I definitely don't need to go to hospital either, it's not that bad."
"Well, if you're sure. I will just quickly get some *ointment* and *rub* it *in*."
Susan allowed her mum to *rub in* the *ointment* and then said:

"Thanks, mum, but I need a bit of *space* now. I just need to *chill* for a while. Could you leave me alone, please?"
In fact she could not wait to *text* her friends the news of the *blackmail*, but there was no way she would tell her mum. The message had said 'tell NO-ONE' but she knew she could trust Heather and Tracey.
As soon as her mum was gone she opened the *drawer* of her *bedside cabinet* and took out her phone. She had to talk to Tracey to tell her the news. At first she wanted to ring her, but then she *hesitated*. What if her parents overheard her? It was just too risky to call and so she decided to *text* her instead. She knew that her parents would not let her out of the house today. There was no school tomorrow, so she decided to meet Tracey in the park nearby.

Übung 9: Bilde Sätze mit dem Komparativ!

1. June/January (hot)

June is hotter than January.

2. running/walking (fast)

---

3. Russian/English (difficult)

---

4. hockey stick/tennis racquet (long)

---

5. house/flat (big)

---

6. grandmother/mother (old)

The girls spent a lot of time *hanging out* in the park. It was one of the few places they could meet without being disturbed by grown-ups. Susan quickly typed in the message.

"I need *yr* help. Meet me in the park *2moro* @ 9," it said, then she pressed the 'Send' *button* and scrolled down the menu until she got to the name Tracey in her address book. Then she thought again. She would need a lot of help and she decided to *text* Heather as well. It was a good idea to get her involved as well and she was at the *changing rooms* when the *theft* of the *locket* was discovered. Tracey was really her best friend, but she could trust Heather as well. After she had sent the second message she sat back on the bed *racking her brains*.

Who could have taken the *locket*? It must be someone who knew her well enough to get hold of her *mobile* number. Was it someone on the hockey team? There were one or two girls who did not like her. Amanda Jones had been really *nasty* to her since she had started *going out with* Giles. She *claimed* that Susan had stolen Giles from her, because Amanda and Giles had been *going out* together for six months, but later Giles had *split up* with Amanda shortly before he met Susan. And there was also Beverly Little who could not stand the sight of her. Beverly was jealous of Susan and Susan was *convinced* that this was because she attracted boys easily and Beverly had never had a boyfriend, as far as Susan knew. Well, was that her fault?

Susan looked in the mirror at her long blonde hair. Yes, many boys did find her attractive, but she could not help her good looks and that was no reason for Beverly to be so *nasty* to her.

Yes, maybe Beverly could have taken the *locket*, she thought.

Then she remembered that Amanda and Beverly had been on the *substitutes' bench*. They could easily have slipped into the *changing rooms* to get the *locket* while no-one was looking. Maybe they had planned this before the game?

Übung 10: Wähle das passende Wort für jeden Satz aus und unterstreiche es!

ÜBUNG 10 !

1. Susan hit/hurt her leg.
2. Arthur means/thinks Susan is very attractive.
3. The handy/mobile was ringing.
4. She cleaned/blew her nose.
5. Tracey looked/watched in the mirror.
6. It was too much/many money.

Susan used to be friends with Amanda before she had started *dating* Giles, and so she would *still* have her *mobile* number as well. It had to be someone who knew she always wore the *locket* and how much it meant to her. Then in a flash another idea came to her. Perhaps it was Giles, her ex-boyfriend? He had been really horrible to her when they had *split up*. He also swore that he would *get his revenge*. Yes, suddenly she was certain it was him. She decided she was going to make him pay for what he had done. Her first thought was to call him *right away* and ask him to tell her the truth, but she thought he would be sure to *deny* it over the phone.
Then at that moment she received a text message on her *mobile*. Tracey confirmed that she would be at the park tomorrow, and shortly afterwards Heather responded, too, saying she would also be there.
It was now 10 p.m. and Susan realized just how *exhausted* she was.

Übung 11: Lies weiter und ordne die Buchstaben zu einem sinnvollen Wort!

After the hockey (1. hamtc) __________, the accident and then the *blackmail* shock she had lost all sense of time. She *yawned* and then stretched her (2. mars) __________ high. I should try to get some sleep, she thought. After much struggling she *managed* to get into her pyjamas. Again she did not (3. anwt) __________ to ask for help and *despite* her sore (4. gle) __________ she *managed* to get ready for bed, *crawled* (5. derun) __________ her *duvet* and then switched off the bedside light. A few minutes later came a knock at the (6. rood) __________.

"Are you okay? Can I (7. meco) __________ in?" asked her mum.

"Yes, mum," (8. aisd) __________ Susan.

Normally Susan could be very *grumpy* and she often drove her parents crazy, but after the shock things were different. There was no way she wanted to tell her mum what was going on. But her mum just quickly wished her a good night and left the room again.

The next morning Susan woke early. She looked over at the electric alarm clock, which said 5:30 a.m. She could not believe that it was so early. Usually she woke up at around 7 a.m., but last night she had slept very badly and had had a *nightmare* with dark figures reaching around her neck.

The loss of her *locket* had *shaken* her badly and she had no idea how she was going to *raise* so much money. Two hundred pounds was a huge sum. She rolled over and tried to go back to sleep, but the thoughts kept going round in her mind. Yesterday she thought that Giles had taken her *locket*, but now she wasn't so sure any more. Would he really have *crept* into the *changing rooms* and gone through her things? Did he hate her so much? She had *been* very *fond of* Giles and had *dated* him for over eight months, but the *break-up* had been hard for him.
Towards the end of their relationship they had nothing to talk about any more and she just could not *cope with* the long silences.

Übung 12: Ordne jedem Wortanfang den passenden zweiten Teil zu und trage die richtige Nummer in das Kästchen ein!

ÜBUNG 12 !

1. ☐ changing	a) mother
2. ☐ black	b) hear
3. ☐ heir	c) room
4. ☐ goal	d) mail
5. ☐ grand	e) keeper
6. ☐ over	f) loom

At around 8:45 a.m. Susan *limped* downstairs to find her dad reading the paper and her mum busy hoovering the lounge. She had arranged to meet Tracey and Heather in the park at 9 a.m. and knew it would take her a bit longer than usual to get there.
"My leg is much better now, mum," she said. Normally she hated lying, but this was an *emergency*. "Look, I can walk on it well." She *clenched her teeth together* and was able to walk on her leg across the lounge without showing any pain.

"Well, if you're really sure," said her mum.
"Be careful," said her dad. "I don't want you to have any more accidents."
"Okay," said Susan. "I will be really careful, I promise. You don't need to worry."
She moved slowly and carefully to the front door. Once she had closed it behind her, she breathed a sigh of *relief*.

ÜBUNG 13

Übung 13: Welche der Erklärungen stimmt? Kreuze die richtige Antwort an!

1. She was determined to reach the goal.
   - a) ☐ She was very short.
   - b) ☐ She wanted to score a goal.
   - c) ☐ She put out her arms to touch the goal.

2. She tried to fight off tears.
   - a) ☐ She punched someone with her fists.
   - b) ☐ She tried not to cry.
   - c) ☐ She was very afraid.

3. Susan was attached to her locket.
   - a) ☐ It was tied around her neck.
   - b) ☐ She could not let go of it.
   - c) ☐ She liked it very much.

4. Her dad cheered her up.
   - a) ☐ He made her feel better.
   - b) ☐ He shouted hooray.
   - c) ☐ He told her she was pretty.

5. She racked her brains.

a) ☐ She asked for help.
b) ☐ She scratched her head.
c) ☐ She thought it over.

The park was roughly five minutes' walk away, but today it took much longer *due to* Susan's bad leg. She entered the park through the main gate and could see her two friends Heather and Tracey waiting for her at their usual meeting spot over by the *swings*. When they saw her they both got up from the park *bench* where they had been waiting and ran towards her.

"Hey Susan!" *yelled* Tracey. "Great to see you! I was really worried about you yesterday. *What's up?*"

"Yes, you must tell us everything!" said Heather. "We are dying to know what is going on."
"Well," began Susan. "Just after I got home last night I got this, you see. Some *jerk* has stolen my *locket* and wants me to pay him or her two hundred pounds to hand it back! I mean – can you believe it? Two hundred *quid* just to get back my *locket*!"
"Do you have any idea who it could be?" asked Heather, anxious to know the identity of the thief.
"The message said 'Number not recognized'. I tried to *text* back and get the sender to give his or her name, but of course they did not want to, did they?"
"Yes, I guess a *blackmailer* would be really stupid to tell you their name," said Tracey.

ÜBUNG 14 !

Übung 14: Sind die folgenden Aussagen richtig? Markiere mit richtig ✔ oder falsch – !

1. Susan missed the goal. ☐
2. Hot water eases pain. ☐
3. Arthur fancies Susan. ☐
4. Giles was blackmailed. ☐
5. Susan's father is reading. ☐
6. Giles is Susan's boyfriend. ☐
7. Susan was often grumpy. ☐

"You must have some idea who has taken the *locket*," continued Heather. "I mean – who would want to steal from you? It must be someone who knows what that *locket* means to you and someone who has got access to your *mobile phone* number. So it must be someone you know."

"Well, I do have a few ideas," said Susan. "First I thought of Amanda Jones. I mean, she has been really *mad* at me since I started *going out with* Giles. And then of course there is Beverly Little who has never really liked me and is always making *nasty* remarks. Both of them were not playing in the team on Friday, so they could easily have gone back to the *changing rooms* without being *noticed* by anyone.

Maybe they even did it together. Of course it could possibly have been Giles. He has been so *mad* at me ever since we *split up*."

"What?" said Tracey. "Do you really think Giles would do this to you? Was he that *mad*?"

"We have to treat him as the *prime suspect*," said Susan.

"Is there anyone else who comes to mind?" asked Heather. "I mean, you really seem to have a lot of enemies!"

"It's not my fault!" cried Susan. "I always try to be nice to people, it's just that some people don't appreciate how hard I try. I really do!"

At this point Susan looked as if she was about to cry, so Tracey quickly stepped in to calm her down:

"Hey, keep cool, just relax," said Tracey. "Don't get *upset* again, that won't help at all. Here, have a tissue and dry your eyes."

"Yeah, sorry," said Heather. "I didn't mean to *get at* you. I just was a bit surprised that there are so many people, who *are*, shall we say, *out to get* you."

"Okay," said Tracey. "Let's get down to business. We have three possible *suspects*. How are we going to find out who took the *locket* and what are we going to do about the money? I mean two hundred *quid* is a lot of cash to *raise*."

Heather looked at Tracey.

"Maybe we should get some help with this," said Heather. "I mean, have you thought about *contacting* the police?"

ÜBUNG 15 !

Übung 15: Lies weiter und setze die richtigen Präpositionen ein! ***(for, to, out)***

"No!" replied Susan. "There's no way can we *contact* them. The message said 'tell no-one' and my parents are sure (1.) ________ find (2.) ________ if we *contact* the police. I trust you two, but we can't tell anyone else. We have (3.) ________ solve this ourselves. If the thief finds (4.) ________ we have told anyone the *locket* may be gone (5.) ________ ever. I'm sure he or she would just *dump* it somewhere and that would be the last I would see of it. I just can't *take* that *risk*. That *locket* really means a lot (6.) ________ me!"

"We will have to look (7.) ________ the *locket* ourselves," agreed Tracey.

"Alright, alright," said Heather. "We won't go to the police and we won't tell anyone. Do you agree, Tracey?"
"That's cool with me!" said Tracey.
"Well, let's work out a plan of action then," said Heather.
Heather turned to Susan and said:
"Well, Susan, let's look at this logically. Who is your *prime suspect*? Who do you think is most likely to have taken the *locket*?"
"I really can't say," said Susan. "As I told you, Giles, Amanda or Beverly could all have taken it, or somebody else. I am really not sure who it was."
"Well," said Heather, "we have to start investigating each *suspect* then. Who do we start with?"

"I only see Amanda or Beverly at school and so we can't *check on* them until Monday."
"Okay," said Heather. "Let's start with Giles then. Where does he normally *hang out* on Saturday mornings?"
"That's easy," said Susan. "He's always over at the shopping centre on Derby Road with his little gang. They always *hang out* at the billiard café there. But I really don't know if I can *face* him alone. I mean, I haven't spoken to him since we *split up* six months ago."
"Keep cool," said Heather. "We will be with you all the way!"
"Yeah, that's what friends are for!" continued Tracey.
"Thanks, girls," said Susan, *giving* them both *a* quick *hug*. "I don't know what I would do without you two!"
The three girls then made their way towards the shopping centre on Derby Road. It was a brand new shopping centre with three floors. In the girls' opinion it was the best thing that had happened to Middlesex for ages. It had *loads of* trendy outlet stores selling clothes, fashion jewellery and music. Normally the three girls loved going there and trying on the latest fashions, but today was different. Today they had a mission.

Übung 16: Beantworte die Fragen zum Text!

1. Where did Susan keep her mobile?

....

2. Why did the three girls go to the shopping centre?

....

3. What did Susan do with her pillows?

....

4. What did Susan's mum rub on her leg?

5. What colour is Susan's hair?

6. Did Giles finish with Susan?

Chapter 3: Showdown at the Shopping Centre

The shopping centre was just a short bus ride away. They often walked, but because of Susan's sore leg the girls decided to *catch the bus*. They entered the centre on the ground floor and wandered around for a short time.

"Normally Giles and his gang always *hang out* in the billiard café on the top floor," said Susan. "Let's see if he and his friends are here today."

The three friends went up the escalators to the top floor of the centre and slowly made their way to the billiard café at the end of the row of shops. As they got closer, Susan started to realize just how nervous she was about *facing* Giles. When they had *split up* she had been very *bold* and just told him that she did not want to *go out with* him anymore. However, she had not anticipated his reaction. He was furious, had called her a stupid *stuck-up* cow and marched away.

Since that day Susan had always *avoided* him. She had seen him around, but had not spoken one word to him. For a long time she had told herself she was 'over him'. However, now that she was about to speak to him face to face, she realized just how nervous she was. In fact she felt herself shaking a bit as she thought of meeting him again. She told herself it was probably just the shock of the accident yesterday, but when she got within sight of the door of the café she panicked and turned around, quickly walking in the other direction.

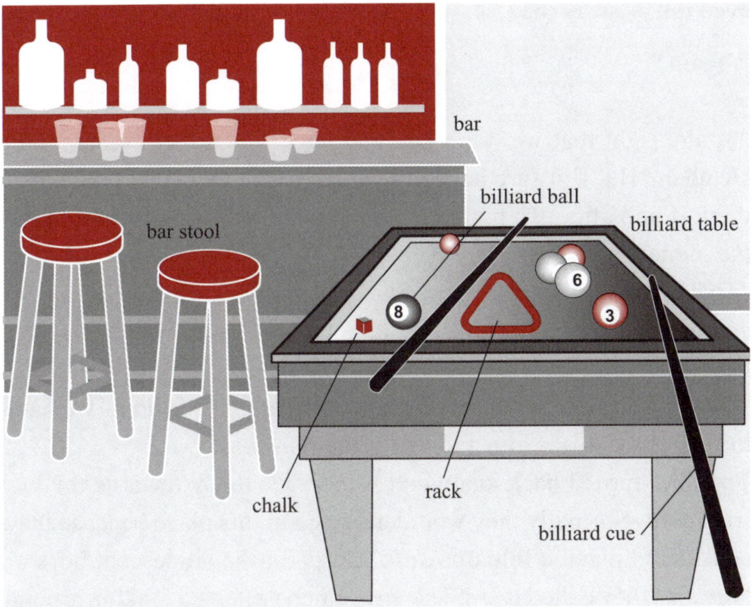

Übung 17: Lies weiter und setze das passende Wort ein!
(time, locket, feet, explode, thing)

ÜBUNG 17

"Hey Susan!" Tracey grabbed her arm and came alongside her. "*What's up?*"

"I just…, I'm just not sure if this is the right (1.) __________ to do," said Susan, trying to sound convincing.

"Have you got cold (2.) ______________?" asked Heather.

"No, no," replied Susan, playing for (3.) ______________. "It's just that I'm worried what he might do if I confront him face to face. I mean, he might (4.) ______________ and go for me. He might even throw away the (5.) ______________ and I would never see it again."

"You're right that we don't know exactly how he will react," said Heather. "But I'm sure he won't *get rid of* the *locket* that quickly. I think if he's after two hundred *quid* then he will want to wait to get the money."
"That's true," replied Susan. She was slowly trying to pluck up *courage* to *face* him again and did not want to show her fear to her friends.
"Okay!" she said finally, taking a deep breath. "Let's do it. We have to find out if it was him and this is the only way."
The girls turned back again and wandered slowly towards the billiard café. Normally they would never go in this place because they considered playing billiards *daft*. It was for the adolescent boys or '*yobs*' as they called them. The girls much preferred looking around the shops for trendy clothes, but this was the only way to get to Giles.
They entered the door and slowly moved among the tables looking for Giles. Suddenly Heather pulled Susan's arm.
"Look, there he is! Over there by the corner table!" she said.
"Where?" replied Susan. She looked over to where Heather was *pointing*, but she didn't see him.
"Behind the big *guy* with the black leather jacket," said Heather.
"Oh! I see him now," said Susan.

Susan knew the *guy* in the leather jacket only too well. It was Adrian Cholerton. He was Giles's best *mate* and the two went everywhere together. Susan had never liked him and he *gave* her *the creeps*. But now was not the time for hesitation. Susan turned to her friends and said:
"Come on, girls, let's make our move."

Übung 18: Lies weiter und setze das Gegenteil der Wörter in Klammern ein!

The three girls walked (1. quickly) s__________ between the billiard tables towards Giles and his *mates*. He was actually with Adrian and two other *guys* who Susan knew by sight, but she did not know their names.
Susan had really hoped that Giles would be alone, but now it would be (2. easy) d__________ with all his *mates* around him. Nevertheless she was determined to *approach* him. As she moved (3. further) c__________ to the table where he was standing, Adrian stopped in the middle of his shot and looked up. Instantly he recognized the (4. big) s__________ gang of girls and his eyes *narrowed*.
"Oh, look who we have here!" said Adrian in a sarcastic voice. "If it isn't Goldilocks and her two bears!" he continued, referring to Susan's (5. short) l__________ blonde hair.

Just a short distance behind him, Giles looked up and his eyes met Susan's. For a moment Susan thought she saw a look of compassion on his face. Perhaps he *still* felt something for her after all. Perhaps she was wrong in *suspecting* him and he had nothing to do with this whole business.

She just had to find out. She had to be sure if he had stolen the *locket* or not.

"Someone to see you, I think," continued Adrian. He stood aside to let Susan *approach* Giles. This was exactly what she had wanted to *avoid*, a *showdown* in public, with all his *mates* standing around.

She opened her mouth to speak.

"Giles, I just, I just wanted to know…"

! ÜBUNG 19

Übung 19: Lies weiter und setze die Verben in der richtigen Zeitform ein!

"What!" snapped Giles back quickly. "Have you come to *ask me out* again?"

His friends (1. laugh) ______________; he (2. be) ______________ feeling really strong now. Since Susan had finished with him he had been very miserable and now he (3. feel) ______________ his anger *rising up*.

"Yeah – you tell her!" joined in one of the other boys standing nearby.

"Got something on your mind?" (4. continue) ______________ Giles in an abrupt tone.

"I (5. be) ______________ just wondering if you…"

Susan could not finish her sentence before Giles *interrupted*:

"If I what? If I want to *go out with* you again? You *have a nerve*, coming here and *crawling* back to me after how you treated me!"

The blood (6. rise) ________________ to Susan's cheeks and she *struggled* to speak. She had (7. lose) ______________ her nerve.

Smelling fear the other boys turned on her quickly:
"*What's up?* Lost your tongue now, have you? Is Goldilocks going to cry now, is she?" they *piled on the pressure*.
"Just leave her alone!" shouted Tracey, trying to defend her friend and to show the boys that they were not going to be *bullied*. She realized it was useless to ask about the *locket* now. They had really *blown* it.
The tears were now streaming down Susan's cheeks. She did not know if it was the pain of rejection or the shooting pain in her leg that hurt the most. She just wanted to get out of this place as soon as possible. She felt *humiliated*. How stupid she had been confronting Giles on his home territory!

Übung 20: Setze die richtigen Präpositionen ein!

ÜBUNG 20 !

In front (1.) __________ his gang Giles was playing the strong man role, but secretly he *was still sweet on* Susan. His *pride* had been hurt when she had finished with him though and he certainly was not going (2.) __________ *admit* to his friends that he *still had a soft spot for* her.

Meanwhile Susan had now made it (3.) __________ of the café with Tracey and Heather (4.) __________ either side of her. She did not look back. She definitely did not want the *guys* to see that she had been crying.

"Come on," said Tracey. "Let's get you home. *No point in* getting *upset* (5.) __________ those losers."

"Yeah," said Heather. "Nothing more we can do here. There is no way they are going to talk to us now."
"Sorry," said Susan. "I really messed that up, didn't I?"
"We have to *trap* them somehow," said Heather.
"Yes, but how?" asked Tracey.
"There must be someone else who we could get them to talk to," said Heather.
"Look, girls," said Susan. "I've really had enough now, I'm *done in*. Can't we leave it for now and get on home? It's almost lunchtime and my parents will wonder where I have been if I get back too late."
"Alright," said Tracey. "Let's get you home and perhaps we can meet again after lunch."
The girls went back down the escalators towards the main exit of the shopping centre.
Down below two young boys had been *hanging around* outside the ice cream stand. They had a good view of the top floor of the shopping centre and had seen Susan and her friends come out of the café in a hurry and travel down the escalators. They were the same boys who had seen Susan get injured during the hockey match. George and Arthur were both members of the chess club, where Susan

played as well. Arthur had *fancied* Susan for a long time. When he saw her coming out of the café with her two friends he realized that something must be going on, because Susan and her friends never went near the billiard café normally.
Arthur plucked up *courage*. This was his chance to make a move.

Übung 21: Trage die fehlenden Buchstaben in die Lücken ein!

1. A part of the school uniform is a b _ _ z _ _.
2. A replacement player is a s _ b _ _ it _ _ e.
3. Another word for 'very tired' is e _ h _ _ _ _ e _.
4. Something of value is something p _ _ ci _ _ _.
5. When you are very worried you are a _ _ i _ _ _.
6. When you break up with someone you s _ li _ up.
7. When you are tired you _ aw _.

He stepped out from behind the ice cream stand just as Susan, Heather and Tracey came down the escalator.
"Hi, Susan!" he said, his heart *pounding* as he spoke. Then he saw her red eyes and *noticed* she had obviously been crying. It was too late to stop now.
"Are you alright?" he continued. He felt stupid saying that, but the words just slipped out before he could stop himself. As soon as he had spoken he felt the blood *rush* to his cheeks.
However, before he had a chance to continue, Heather stepped in: "Sorry, Arthur, we have to leave, we don't have time to stop and chat. Excuse us please."

And with that the girls disappeared out of the main door, leaving Arthur and George standing.
"What was that all about?" asked George.
"I don't know," replied Arthur. "But I am going to find out. Come on, let's go up to the café and see who's in there. Susan was crying when she came out, so somebody must have been pretty *mean* to her. I have a good idea who it was, but let's go and make sure."
The two boys ran up the escalators and then made their way to the café. They had often been there, so it did not look *suspicious* when they went inside. Casually they walked over to the bar and ordered two cokes. They sat and drank them while looking around to see who was in.

ÜBUNG 22 !

Übung 22: Welche Gegenteile gehören zusammen? Ordne zu!

1. ☐	tall	a) happy
2. ☐	first	b) down
3. ☐	further	c) nearer
4. ☐	up	d) short
5. ☐	quickly	e) last
6. ☐	sad	f) slowly

Sure enough, over in the corner were Giles and Adrian, together with two other *lads* who they did not know. They were happily playing billiards and seemed very pleased with themselves. Arthur tried to get a bit closer so that he could hear what they were saying. He wanted to find out if they were talking about Susan.
He got an angry look from Adrian as he got closer. One of those looks that said: "Don't even think about speaking to me".
Arthur and George quickly they finished their cokes and left.

"Well, what do you make of that?" said Arthur. "Do you think they could have been *bothering* Susan?"
"I don't see who else it could have been," said George. "There was no-one else in the place that I recognized."
"But what was Susan doing there?" said Arthur with a *puzzled* look on his face. "I mean, she finished with Giles ages ago. They never even speak to each other normally."
"Well, she certainly wanted something from him today," said George.
"And it was obviously something she did not get!" replied Arthur. "I simply must find out what is going on."
"Not today, you won't," answered George. "You saw the look Heather gave you. I would leave it until you see her at school next week."
Reluctantly Arthur agreed. He was burning to know what was going on and hoped that in some way he could *find favour with* Susan. He *had* a really big *crush on* her and wanted to help her.
Meanwhile Susan, Tracey and Heather had reached the bus stop to *catch the bus* back home. They sat downstairs as Susan's leg was hurting badly now and they did not want to put her through any more pain.

Übung 23: Lies weiter und unterstreiche die sechs Wörter, die falsch geschrieben sind. Verbessere sie anschließend!

ÜBUNG 23 !

When Susan got home her dad was waiting for her.
"I thaught I told you to take it easy," said her dad, sounding very *cross*. "Yesterday you could hardly walk *due to* the pain and today you are runing around all over the place."
"I'm fin, dad, really. You don't need to worry."

In reality she was feeling really *lousy*, but she did not want her parents to kno this. They were certain to make her stay in if they knew how she really felt. Her dad was always easier to *fool* than her mum. She had got very good at *twisting* him *around her little finger*. She looked her dad straight in the eyes and said in a soft voice:
"I really am fine, my leg is a lot better now."
Her dad looked at her *suspiciously*, not shure if she was *pretending* to be well and trying to *fool* him. He *hesitated* before answering:
"Well, I want you to stay in for the rest of the day and that is final!"
Susan realized that this tim he meant what he said and there would be no way to persuade him to let her go out again.

1. ______________________ 4. ______________________

2. ______________________ 5. ______________________

3. ______________________ 6. ______________________

Susan sighed and went up to her room. A short while later she suddenly heard the ringing tone of her *mobile*. It made her jump. She sat up on the *edge* of the bed.
"You have a message," said the words in the display. Quickly she pressed the *button* marked 'Read'.
"I said tell *no1*! Do *u want 2* lose the *locket*?"
Susan *stared* at the phone, totally shocked. How had they found out that she had spoken to someone? It must have been Giles after all, she thought! She must have really *shaken* him by *approaching* him in the shopping centre like that. Now she was certain it was him and she would *get revenge* for sure. Quickly she dried her red eyes and blew her nose.
Now what should she write back? She was sure of herself now and in the *mood* for *revenge*. How could Giles be so *mean*?

Übung 24: Setze die Aussagen ins Simple Past!

ÜBUNG 24 !

1. The team beats us every time. ....

2. The sun shines. ....

3. He is suspicious. ....

4. They are annoyed. ....

5. He comes to the park every week. ....

6. We have a message. ....

7. They win the match. ....

She typed a reply message into her phone:
"I told nobody," she wrote. Then she thought for a moment. Was it a good idea to *deny* having told anybody? Surely the *blackmailer* must have seen her talking to somebody about the *locket*? But then she had not even mentioned the *locket* when she *approached* Giles. How could he have known that she had spoken to anyone? Unless he had just *assumed* by her reaction that she was planning a counter attack with her friends.
She pressed the 'Delete' key and decided to write a new message. It would be better to *admit* that she had asked for help and that she needed help to *raise* the money. That would be more likely to keep the *blackmailer* from getting angry. She typed in the new message:
"I need help *2* get the money," she wrote, hoping that this would calm the person sending the message.
She waited anxiously for the reply. When it finally came the text read:
"no more chances. Do as I say or *u* will never *c yr locket* again! – Get me £200 *b4* Friday."

Well, that was clear. She wondered if she should answer, but decided to keep the reply short. She did not want to annoy the caller: "Ok, I promise," she typed and pressed the 'Send' *button*.

ÜBUNG 25

Übung 25: Lies weiter und setze die Verben ins Simple Past!

She (1. sit) __________ quietly for a while and (2. think) __________ about the message. In future she had to be more careful about who she (3. speak) __________ to. After a while she remembered that she had promised to *text* Heather and Tracey. After the shock of the last message she could not wait to tell her friends.

"can *u* come *2* my house now?" she typed in and (4. send) __________ the text to Tracey.

"sorry, not til 3," (5. come) __________ back the reply.

"ok, *c u l8r @* 3," she typed back.

Susan then *texted* Heather to get her over as well. But the reply came back:

"sorry, i can't come *2day*. have to go *2* shops with mum."

What! thought Susan. Just when I need her she has to go shopping! Angrily she (6. grab) __________ her *mobile* and typed in the reply.

"I need *u* here! Can't *yr* mum shop alone?"
"Sorry, I promised her. Will *c u 2moro*!" came the answer.

"Oh shit!" screamed Susan, crashing onto her bed. "This is so unfair." She punched the bed with her *fists*. What was she to do until three o'clock? Then she remembered the money. Two hundred *quid*, how could she get that much money by Friday? She opened her desk and took out her post office *savings book*. Seventy-five pounds and fifteen pence. Well, that was a nice surprise! She had a lot more money than she thought she had. Maybe she would be able to get the two hundred pounds after all, but then did she want to just hand over the cash without first trying to *catch* the *blackmailer*? It was all very risky. She lay on the bed and tried to sleep. The clock seemed to go around very slowly, but after a while she was awakened by a knock on the door.
"Susan, are you asleep? There's someone here to see you, it's Tracey," said her mum.
"Okay, I'm coming!" answered Susan. She got up and straightened her dress. When she opened the door Tracey was already standing outside and waiting.
"Hi Tracey!" said Susan. "Good to see you, come on in. Unfortunately, Heather can't come."
Tracey came into the bedroom and Susan closed the door behind her. She pressed it hard to make sure it was shut *tight* and no-one could hear them from outside.
"So," said Tracey. "*What's up?*"

*Übung 26: Vervollständige die Sätze mit **a, an** oder **the**!*

1. Susan is ______ hockey player.

2. ______ apple is a fruit.

3. She wants to score ______ goal.

4. The girls helped her off ______ field.

5. It was ______ sad day for Susan.

6. Mrs Hiller pressed gently on ______ calf muscle.

7. Susan had ______ excellent eye for the ball.

8. Susan closed ______ door behind her.

9. She has to get ______ money by Friday.

Susan explained how she had received another text message from the *blackmailer* and that she was sure it was Giles. Tracey was of a different opinion.

"Why would Giles *text* you so soon after you confronted him?" she asked. "It just doesn't make sense. If he did have the *locket* he would not want to *arouse suspicion* by *contacting* you again so soon after your meeting."

Susan had to agree that Tracey *had a point*. Maybe it was not Giles after all. Surely he would not be so stupid as to *text* her and complain that she had told someone about the *locket*. Then she would know for sure it was him who took it.

"But it must have been somebody who knows that you and Heather are helping me find the *locket*," said Susan. "There must be someone who saw us together in the shopping centre and who *suspects* we were trying to find the *locket*. Who else did we see in there? Can you remember?"

"It was pretty busy," said Tracey. "Lots of people could have seen us. It is easy to follow someone in that place."

She paused, and then suddenly she shouted, "of course, Arthur! He was *hanging around* with that boy George. Maybe the two of them did this as a practical joke to get your *attention*. You know he has been *chasing* you for ages!"

Chapter 4: The Secret Admirer

On Sunday morning Susan awoke at around 9 a.m. She felt much better after her long sleep. As soon as she got out of bed, she pulled back the curtains and saw that the sun was shining. Well, thank goodness it's stopped raining, she thought. It seemed to have been raining for days. She bent down and examined her leg. The swelling had gone down a lot. It was badly *bruised* and *still* stiff, but it did not hurt as much as before. When she got up, she saw that the bathroom was free and she decided to have a long bath. She called downstairs:

"I'm just running a bath, okay?"

There was no answer from below, so she went to the top of the stairs and shouted again:

"Mum, dad… I'm having a bath, is that okay?"

Finally her mother's voice answered from below:

"Yes, dear, that's fine. How are you feeling today?"

"Good, thanks. I just need to relax a little."

Normally, whenever she ran a bath somebody decided they needed to use the toilet. It was a real *nuisance* that they only had one toilet in the house. She often wished her parents were rich like Tracey's. Tracey had her own bathroom and toilet. Her house had four bedrooms and they had three bathrooms, one for her parents and even one just for guests. It was just not fair that Susan's parents were poor. Her dad worked in the post office as a chief inspector, while Tracey's dad was some manager of an oil company or something. At Christmas time Tracey always got *loads of* presents and for her birthday too. Susan *was* often *fed up* of being in a middle-class family and dreamed of living a life of luxury like Tracey. Her other friend Heather was more 'normal' however. She was *better-off* than Susan, but her family was not as wealthy as Tracey's.

ÜBUNG 27 !

Übung 27: In den folgenden Sätzen sind die Wörter durcheinander geraten. Bringe sie in die richtige Reihenfolge und beachte dabei die Satzzeichen und Groß- und Kleinschreibung!

1. arms of she her mum fell into the

She fell into the arms of her mum.

2. by mobile her was bedside the

____

3. in you can come now

____

4. message the sent who

____

5. of now space need bit I a

____

6. anyone tell not do

____

7. was she get annoyed starting to

____

Also, Heather was very *down-to-earth* and practical. Sometimes Tracey could be quite a *snob* and she really *got on* Susan's *nerves*. *Still*, they had been friends ever since they started school at St. Mary's and all three of them were in Year 10 together. Next year they would be taking their *GCSEs* so they had to do a lot of revision. Tracey was very clever at maths (one of Susan's worst subjects), while Susan was much better at French. Heather was more interested in art and spent most of her free time painting or making models out of *clay*. Apart from schoolwork and hockey, Susan also played chess, but found it quite difficult. She was on the chess team at school and they played every Wednesday afternoon. When she thought of chess she remembered Arthur. Tracey had said he had been *chasing* her for ages.

Arthur was a tall *lad* with brown curly hair. He wore glasses and Susan had always thought of him as a bit of a *swot*. He was only in Year 9, but because he was very good at chess, he played on the same team as her. Of course she had *noticed* that he often seemed to be *hanging around* when she was playing chess, but he had never really spoken much to Susan. He was always talking and trying to be funny with the other players. He liked trying to attract *attention* to himself. There was no way she would even consider *going out with* someone in Year 9 and he was really not her type at all. Really she had tried to ignore him, but when Tracey said he had been *chasing* her, it rung a bell for Susan. Did Arthur really think he had a chance with her? Could he really have taken her *locket*? Susan found that hard to believe, but it seemed very *suspicious* that he had been *hanging around* in the shopping centre and just happened to be there when she was walking out. What if he had planned the whole thing with that friend of his? What was his name again? George, that was it. Maybe the two of them had planned this together to attract Susan's *attention*.

Übung 28: Was gehört zusammen? Ordne zu!

ÜBUNG 28 !

1. ☐ to ring a) a bus
2. ☐ to catch b) a text message

3. ☐ to find c) a job
4. ☐ to send d) a bell
5. ☐ to score e) a game
6. ☐ to play f) a goal
7. ☐ to answer g) a book
8. ☐ to run h) a question
9. ☐ to read i) a bath

Perhaps they had intended to *put the blame on* Giles and his friends. Then when the *locket* turned up again they could claim to be heroes for *recovering* the stolen *locket*! It was a complicated theory, but it was possible that Arthur could have planned this whole thing just to win over Susan. How stupid some boys could be!

Susan was used to boys *chasing* her at school. Her long blonde hair and her good figure meant that she found it easy to attract them. However, the idea that some boy could steal her property and then try to *put the blame on* her ex-boyfriend Giles made Susan really *mad*.

She decided that she would march up to Arthur at school tomorrow and tell him she had uncovered his plan. Maybe she should *text* him now and tell him to bring back her *locket* at once.

The sound of running water *interrupted* Susan's daydreaming. The bath was running over and she *rushed* to turn off the water. The bathroom floor was flooded with water and it took her a while and a number of towels to mop it all up. She would have to be more careful next time.

For a long time she lay in the bath enjoying the feeling of the warm water and lots of bubbles. It was a great way to relax. Normally nothing much happened on Sundays in the Wilson household. If there was no hockey match to play, Susan often found the day quite boring, but today she was happy just to have a *rest*.

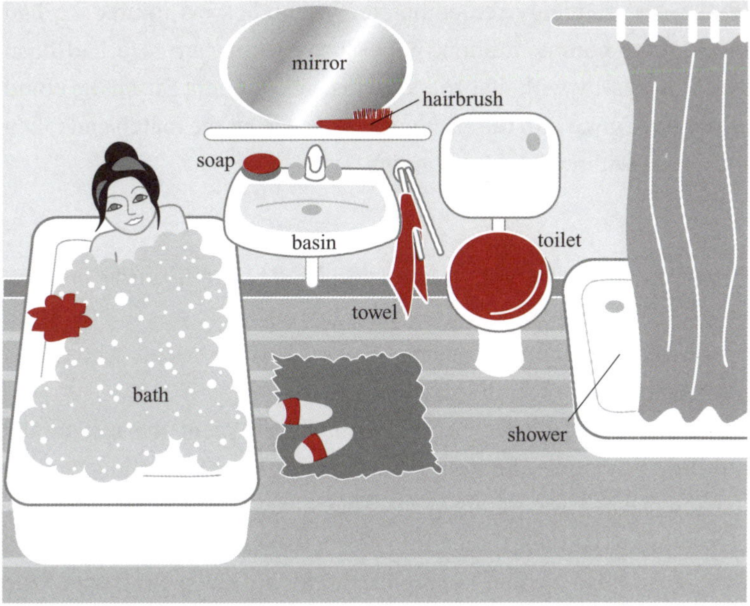

As she lay in the bath, her mind went over the events of the last two days. *Scoring* the goal during the hockey match had been a great triumph. Tracey had told her that the St. Mary's team went on to win the match after she had left the hockey field. Her goal had won the match and she was delighted with that. However, the *theft* of her precious *locket* had really upset her. First she had cried and now she was angry that someone had *dared* to steal her property. At first she had wrongly thought it was Giles, but after the second text message and the conversation with Tracey she was sure that it could not have been him. He would not have given himself away so easily. Now that Arthur's name had been mentioned she could see how he could have been behind the *theft*.

The more she thought about it, the more she was *convinced* that he was guilty. Her thoughts went back to the hockey match. Yes, that was it, she suddenly remembered. When she was injured he had made some comment about poor Susan being hurt. He had been standing nearby with that friend of his. Yes, thought Susan, he could easily have gone into the *changing room* during the match and taken the *locket* without anyone *noticing*.

ÜBUNG 29 !

Übung 29: Lies weiter und unterstreiche die acht Adjektive im Text!

Some admirer, thought Susan. A *would-be* boyfriend who steals your property in order to play the hero!
When she had finished her hot bath Susan spent the rest of the morning tidying her bedroom. She went downstairs for lunch. Sunday lunch was always a big event. They always had a roast for lunch. Her father would not eat anything else, so Susan's mum always had to work in their kitchen to prepare the food. Dad spent most of the morning reading the Sunday paper. They were a very traditional family. Today it was roast beef and Yorkshire pudding. Susan's mum was a great cook and always made her own Yorkshire puddings, small round ones that tasted very good with *gravy*.

After lunch she went back up to her room and *texted* her friends.
As the weather was so nice they decided to meet in the park by the *swings* at three o'clock. Heather arrived first, closely followed by Tracey.
"Did anyone follow you?" Susan asked Tracey.
"No," answered Tracey.
"Are you sure?" continued Susan, anxious to know if the boys were *still* watching them.
"Well, I didn't *notice* anyone," said Tracey.
"And you, Heather?" asked Susan.

"Well, to be honest I didn't really look behind me, sorry," came the reply.
"Listen," said Susan, "in future we have to be more careful and always check that nobody is following us."
She turned to Heather and said: "I got another text message yesterday. Tracey knows as we met when you were out shopping with your mum," she continued in a sarcastic tone.

Übung 30: Schreibe die Zahlen aus!

ÜBUNG 30 !

1. 16 ________________
2. 69 ________________
3. 1/3 ________________
4. 1,500 ________________
5. 2,000,000 ________________
6. 4th ________________
7. 110 ________________
8. 80 ________________
9. 53 ________________
10. 46 ________________

"Okay," said Heather. "No need for you to be so *mean*. I do have a family as well, you know. I am not your personal servant!"
"Alright, alright," said Susan in a soft voice. "I'm sorry, it has all just been so stressful *recently* and I overreacted."
"Well, what was the message?" asked Heather finally.

Susan explained how the sender knew she had told someone about the *blackmail* as he or she had seen her with her friends. Heather agreed that they could now rule out Giles as he would not send a message so soon after she had spoken to him in the café. That would just be too obvious.

"So who do you think it is now? Who is the main *suspect*?" asked Heather.

"It was Tracey who gave me the idea," said Susan. "I am *convinced* now that it was Arthur. He and his friend George were at the hockey match and they were *spying on* us in the shopping centre. I'm sure it was him."

Heather also knew that Arthur was often hanging around Susan. She also agreed that he had a good reason to take the *locket* in order to make Giles look bad. His behaviour certainly looked *suspicious*. She remembered that she had seen Giles and Arthur fighting in the *playground* a while back; they were definitely not the best of friends.

"So what do we do now?" asked Heather.

"Well," said Susan. "We cannot *approach* Arthur until school tomorrow. If he really is behind this it will be no problem to get my *locket* off him. I mean he is not angry at me, he is trying to get a date with me after all!"

"True," said Heather. "We can certainly *tackle* him easily. I think we should get him alone in the *playground* and make him tell us everything. Girlpower – that's what we need!" They all laughed together.

It was good to laugh after what they had been through over the last few days. Things had been very tense. The idea that they might be able to solve the mystery together really *cheered* them *up*.

"We will certainly make him *suffer* for all this!" said Tracey. "I mean, *what a cheek* stealing your *locket* just to get a date!"

Übung 31: Lies weiter und unterstreiche im folgenden Textabschnitt die Synonyme der Wörter in Klammern!
(1. saw, 2. shouted, 3. certainly, 4. usually, 5. stood up, 6. discover)

Suddenly Susan looked up and *noticed* two figures coming into the park.
"Oh no, look who's coming!" she cried out.
Heather and Tracey looked across and saw two girls walking up the hill and towards the *bench* where they were sitting.
"It's Amanda and Beverly," said Susan.
"What are they doing here?" said Tracey.
"I think they've seen us," said Heather.
At that moment the two girls, Amanda and Beverly, stopped and looked across to where the three friends were sitting. They had definitely been *spotted*.
"Do you think they have been *spying on* us?" said Heather. "They normally never come in the park. What are they doing here today?"
Susan got up and said:
"Come on, I'm going to find out what they want."

Susan started walking *boldly* across the grass to where the other girls were standing.
"No, wait!" said Heather, pulling Susan's *sleeve*. "Look, they are leaving already!"
The two girls had obviously changed their minds and were now *heading* down the bank.
"Very strange," said Heather. "What are they up to now?"
"I don't know, but I'm not waiting around here to find out," said Susan. "Come on, let's *catch them up*."
This time Heather followed Susan obediently. She saw that Susan was determined to follow the girls. She turned to Tracey and said:

"Come on, you come, too. We have to stay together."

As fast as they could, the three girls made their way down the bank towards the bottom of the park.

"Hey!" shouted Susan. "What are you doing, *spying on* us?"

Now Beverly turned. She realized that she had been *spotted* and there was no longer the chance to get away unnoticed.

"What's it got to do with you?" she said in an angry voice.

She moved closer to her friend Amanda for support. Although she was taller than Susan she saw that Susan had her two friends with her and she did not like *being outnumbered*. However, she was confident that she could beat Susan one on one and so she decided to go for the attack:

"You don't own this park. Anyone can come here!" she said in a really sarcastic voice. She walked towards Susan until they were *facing* each other *eyeball to eyeball.*

Susan was now really frightened. She was *convinced* that Beverly and Amanda had been *spying on* her. Susan bit her lip, put her hands on her hips and took a deep breath.

"What is it you want, Beverly Little? Why are you coming here and *spying on* us?"

Suddenly Beverly's face went red and in a rage she ran towards Susan. She realized that Susan had discovered her *spying*. Her *fists* were *clenched* and she was on the attack.

"You little *bitch*!" she screamed.

In a flash she was on top of Susan and the two of them were *scratching* and pulling each other's hair. A real *fight* had started. Susan *struggled* to defend herself, but she *was* no *match for* Beverly.

"Stop!" cried Heather. She fell to the floor and tried to pull the two girls apart. Tracey stood back horrified and did not know what to do. She had seen girls *fight* before and it was not a pretty sight. She wanted to *dive* in to help Susan, but fear kept her from moving.

She couldn't feel her legs and couldn't move.
Meanwhile Amanda had joined in and was now *helping* Beverly *to her feet*. Beverly's face was *bleeding* where Susan had *scratched* her. Susan was *rubbing* her sore head, and she had been *scratched* on the face as well.

Übung 32: Welche Ergänzung ist die richtige? Kreuze an!

ÜBUNG 32 !

1. Susan is a good hockey player,
   a) ☐ doesn't she?
   b) ☐ isn't she?

2. Arthur likes Susan,
   a) ☐ doesn't he?
   b) ☐ do he?

3. The locket was stolen,
   a) ☐ ain't it?
   b) ☐ wasn't it?

4. They met in the park,
   a) ☐ didn't they?
   b) ☐ weren't they?

5. You know the answer,
   a) ☐ aren't you?
   b) ☐ don't you?

Beverly was shaking. She was furious.
"You haven't heard the last of this, Susan Wilson!" she screamed.

"Just wait! I will *get my revenge*! You will be so sorry that you ever touched me! I will make you pay for this!"

The two girls then turned and disappeared from the park.

Tracey now came over to Susan.

"Sorry, sorry Susan," she stammered. "I just froze. I couldn't move. I don't know what came over me."

"She is a really *mean bitch*!" said Heather. "She came at you like an angry bull. Are you sure you're okay?"

Susan sat up and *rubbed* her head again.

"I'm okay, nothing broken. Just a bit of shock, that's all," she said.

Her friends *helped* her *to her feet* and they went over and sat on the *bench* again. Heather and Tracey wanted to take her to the hospital, but Susan said they were overreacting. She just wanted to sit for a while and get her breath back.

"Don't tell my parents about this, will you?" she said to her two friends. "I have to keep all this quiet until I know for sure who has got the *locket*."

ÜBUNG 33 !

Übung 33: Beantworte die Fragen zum Text!

1. What did Tracey do while Susan was fighting with Beverly?

....

2. Where on her body was Susan hurt?

....

3. Where did Heather and Tracey want to go with Susan?

....

4. Who is Beverly's friend?

5. Does Susan want to tell her parents about the fight?

"Well, those two certainly *have it in for* you," said Heather. "Beverly especially seems to *hate your guts*!"
"Yes," said Susan. "She obviously came here looking for trouble. I have never liked that girl and I'm certainly glad to *see the back of* her."
"In future maybe we shouldn't *hang around* in the park," said Heather. "They could come back with more friends next time. We don't want any more trouble."
"Agreed," replied Susan. "We need to find a safer place to meet. Can we go over to your place, Tracey?" she asked.
Tracey agreed and the three friends then walked over to Tracey's house. Luckily her parents had gone out so they had the place to themselves.
"That's cool," said Susan. "Let's agree a plan of action for tomorrow. Where does Arthur *hang out* in the first break?"
"He's always by the ping-pong tables," said Tracey.
"Okay then," said Susan. "Let's meet in the first break and get him on his own. The three of us will soon find out what he is hiding."
"But if he does have the *locket* he is not going to *admit* it," said Heather.
"Don't worry. I will make sure he *confesses*," said Susan. "If we all *stick together*," she added, glancing across at Tracey, "he *isn't a match for* us, believe me!"
The three girls spent the rest of the afternoon chatting and playing CDs. They discussed various ways to get the truth out of Arthur. They were sure that the three of them would be able to *pressure* him

into telling the truth. If he had taken the *locket*, then they would force it out of him. They thought that surprise was the best option.

Chapter 5: Unexpected Help

Normally Susan hated Monday mornings and going back to school, but today was different. She just could not wait to get to school. At last she had the chance to confront Arthur. She had to find out if he was behind all this. Quickly she ate her cornflakes and drank her orange juice before *catching the bus* to school. Tracey was on the same bus and Susan was really pleased to see her. When they arrived at St. Mary's they went to the *playground* and met up with Heather.

"Has anyone seen Arthur yet?" asked Susan.

"Yes, I saw him arrive with his *mate* George earlier," said Heather.

"Good, well done," said Susan. "Right, don't forget. We meet at first break by the canteen exit."

The first two lessons were double biology. Susan spent a lot of her time staring out of the window. She could just not concentrate. At one point the teacher, Mrs Henderson, asked her a question about the reproduction organs of eagles. Susan had awoken with a jump and the whole class had laughed at her. Normally that would have *bothered* her, but today she had only one thought in mind: to get hold of Arthur.

! ÜBUNG 34

Übung 34: Welche Gegenteile gehören zusammen? Ordne zu!

1. ☐ excited	a) different
2. ☐ quickly	b) difficult

3. □ same c) find
4. □ far d) slowly
5. □ hide e) wrong
6. □ easy f) bored
7. □ right g) near

When the bell rang for first break, Susan packed up her things and left the class as soon as possible. Tracey and Heather were in a different class for biology so she met them in the *playground*.
"So, are we all ready?" asked Susan in an excited voice.
"Sure thing," said Tracey.
"Me too," said Heather.
"Let's go and find him then," replied Susan.
The three girls *set off* for the table tennis area. They moved slowly as they wanted to see Arthur before he saw them. It was important to get him alone.
"Look!" cried Heather. "There he is, over by the second table."
Sure enough Arthur has *hanging around* chatting to some friends by the tables.
"Right," said Susan. "This is what I suggest: Tracey, you go over and tell him that you need to talk to him in private. Get him to follow you over to the trees in the far corner of the *playground*. Heather and I can hide behind the *dustbins* and when you get there we can surprise him. Is that agreed?"
"Yeah, good idea," said Tracey. "It will be best to get him on his own. I will make up some story to get his interest. It will be easy, just watch me!"
Heather agreed and she went with Susan to hide behind the school *dustbins*. They were a bit smelly, but it was a great place to hide as no-one ever went there and there was a *courtyard* where they could *trap* Arthur. They could then question him without being disturbed.

As soon as they were out of sight, Tracey slowly walked over towards the ping-pong tables. She waited for a while until Arthur had finished talking to his friends and then quickly made a move from behind. She tapped him on the shoulder and said:
"Excuse me, Arthur, I need to talk to you."
"Eh, what?" exclaimed Arthur, very surprised that someone should be talking to him. A girl even! And a pretty one, too. He was both delighted and shocked at the same time. In fact he was speechless. Tracey took the initiative and continued speaking.
"In private. I really need to talk to you in private."
"About what?" said Arthur, now he had found his voice again.
"I can't mention it here. It is something very personal," said Tracey. She looked him straight in the eyes and tried to look as loving as possible. Arthur was totally shocked and when she put her arm in his, he happily gave in and followed her across the *playground*.
Was this really happening to him? He could hardly believe it. He felt he should speak and say something clever or impressive, but nothing came to mind. At one point when he tried to speak, Tracey turned to him with a finger on her lips and said:
"Shush, not here, wait!"
So he did not say a word and allowed Tracey to lead him across the *playground*. He had no idea what she wanted from him and he was anxious to find out. Tracey turned the corner by the tree and as she did so Susan and Heather jumped out from their hiding place.
"Hi, Arthur," said Susan in very *stern* voice. "We have something we want to speak with you about!"
Suddenly Arthur realized that he was surrounded by three girls. Was he dreaming or was this an *ambush*? Before he had a chance to speak, Susan stepped out and said:
"We need to talk, Arthur!"
She led him into the corner behind the *dustbins* and Arthur realized

he was *trapped*. His first thought was to push past the three girls and to run away, but then he thought: I haven't done anything wrong. Why should I have to run away? It would be better to stay and *face* them.

"What's going on?" he cried. "Is this some kind of *ambush* or what?"

Susan looked him straight in the eyes. She was not going to *back down* now and she was determined to make him tell the truth.

"Something of mine has gone missing!" she said and waited for his reaction. Arthur looked *puzzled*.

"Something of mine that is very precious has been taken and I want to know if you took it," she said. "Do you know what I am talking about, Arthur? Someone has been sending me messages and I need to know who it is."

Übung 35: Lies weiter und unterstreiche die acht Wörter, die falsch geschrieben sind. Verbessere sie anschließend!

Arthur *stared* at Susan with a blank expression on his face. He had no idea what she was tolking about and actually he was getting quite frightened now. Susan to was surprised at his reaction and started to wonder if he wos perhaps *innocent* after all. He made no effort to defend himself and really seemed to have no idea what she was talking about. Susan decided to continue to make sure.
"Someone has stealed my *locket* and is *blackmailing* me," she sad.
"And you think I had something to do with this?" said Arthur with a look of *amazement* on his face. "I sware I had no idea your *locket* had been stolen, or that you were being *blackmailed*. Really, you have to beleive me, Susan. I would never do anything to hurt you."
Susan saw that tears were beginning to *rise up* in Arthur's eyes. He really did seem to be telling the truth.
"But what were you doing in the shopping centre? Why where you following us?" said Susan.

1. ______________	5. ______________
2. ______________	6. ______________
3. ______________	7. ______________
4. ______________	8. ______________

"We were just there by chance," said Arthur. "George and I often go there. When we saw you coming out of the billiard café looking so sad I just wondered what was up. That's all. I'm telling the truth, Susan, honestly."
"I have an idea," *interrupted* Tracey. "We should check his *mobile*

number. That way we can know if he sent the messages."
"Great idea, Tracey, good thinking," said Susan.
"Come on then, Arthur, show us your *mobile*," she continued.
"Sure," said Arthur. "Anything to show that I am *innocent*."
Obediently Arthur took out his *mobile*. Susan then took out hers and opened the messages section.
"Now if I reply to the *blackmail* message we will know for sure if you sent it!" said Susan triumphantly.
"But then if it's not Arthur, the *blackmailer* will get the message instead," said Tracey.
"Good point," said Susan. "Okay, we have to make it a serious message then. What shall I write?" she asked.
"Hmm, let me think a bit," said Heather. "How about – I know who you are!"
"No way," said Susan. "That might *scare* him *off* and I would never see the *locket* again."
"Well, write something about the money then," said Tracey. "How about – I need more time to get the money."
"Just a moment," said Susan. "He said not to *contact* him, so that might cause more trouble. Not a very good idea."
Then suddenly Susan had another idea.
"I don't need to write a proper message, you know. I could just type in a few letters and press send. You know, *pretend* it was sent by mistake. That way the *blackmailer* would not know what was going on and would just think it was a technical fault."
"Great idea!" said Heather. "That way he cannot *suspect* anything."
So Susan took the phone and typed 'ntee'. Then she pressed the 'Send' *button*. At the same time she held Arthur's *mobile* in her other hand. She waited and waited, but no sound came from the phone at all.
"Well," said Susan and she turned to look at Arthur. "It does seem

that you are telling the truth after all."

"Look, Susan, maybe I can help," said Arthur. He was now beginning to feel confident again. Actually, he would do anything for Susan and saw his chance to win her friendship.

"Has someone really stolen your *locket*? Are you really being *blackmailed*?" he said in a very concerned voice.

Susan thought for a moment. Arthur now knew what was going on anyway. There was *no point in denying* it and maybe he might even be able to help them.

"Look, Arthur," said Susan, now much calmer. "I'm really sorry we *accused* you. I see now that you had nothing to do with all this."

"It's okay," said Arthur. "No bad feelings. I just want to help, that's all."

Susan looked at Tracey, then Heather. They both nodded their heads in agreement.

"Well," began Susan. "It was like this…"

She then continued to tell the story of how the *locket* was stolen and about the ultimatum that came by text message. Next she told him about the *showdown* with Giles and then the *fight* with Beverly.

"But that's awful!" exclaimed Arthur when she had finished. "No wonder you were *upset*. Look, I really think I can help you with this. Don't you think it would be good to have a *guy* on your side?"

Susan and Heather laughed. Was Arthur trying to play the Romeo now?

ÜBUNG 36 !

Übung 36: Bilde das Simple Past dieser Verben!

1. to go ____________

2. to find ____________

3. to see ____________

4. to tell ____________

5. to lose ____________

6. to do ____________

7. to say ____________

8. to know ____________

"Well," said Susan after a while. "It would be good to have some help. We *still* have to find a way to *raise* two hundred *quid* by Friday!"

Susan told her friends that she had seventy-five pounds in her post office savings account. That was all the savings she had. She did not want to lose the money, but saw no other way.

Arthur felt pleased now he saw that he would be able to join in the little gang. He would do anything for Susan and he intended to get back her *locket at all costs*.

"We have to work together to get the *blackmail* money. That is certain," he said. "Otherwise your *locket* will be gone, Susan. The *blackmailer* is certain to destroy the *locket* or *get rid of* it somehow if he doesn't get the money."

"No! No!" said Susan, now sounding very scared. "I must get that *locket* back; it means the world to me!"

"Now, now," said Arthur. "Calm down. There may be another way. Maybe when we hand over the cash we can somehow *catch* the *blackmailers*. They will be expecting you to come alone. However, if we have enough people to help us, then perhaps we can jump on them when they pick up the cash."

Susan started to feel a *glimmer of hope*.

"But who would you get to help?" she asked.

"And we are not supposed to tell anyone, remember!" remarked Tracey.

"Well, you've already told me now, haven't you," said Arthur. "And the *blackmailer* knows about Tracey and Heather, too. I would just suggest we include my *mate* George. He is a big strong *lad* and would come in very useful."

"Well," said Susan. "I can *see* your *point*. A bit of muscle power would be a good idea. What do you think, girls?" she said, turning to the other two.

! ÜBUNG 37

Übung 37: In diesen Sätzen sind die Wörter durcheinander geraten. Bringe sie in die richtige Reihenfolge und beachte dabei auch Satzzeichen und Groß- und Kleinschreibung!

1. friend is Heather good of Susan's a

   ....

2. locket someone stolen the has

   ....

3. scored a goal Susan

   ....

4. felt rise Susan hope

   ....

5. toffees floor the on fell the

   ....

6. is Tracey who

....

7. to there explanation has be an

....

8. message she text a sent

....

"What have we got to lose?" asked Heather.

Tracey was not so sure at first. She was worried about too many people being involved. Also she seemed mistrustful of Arthur, but eventually the other two girls persuaded her and she agreed to ask George for help.

"But he doesn't need to know all the details," she said. "Arthur, can't you tell him you need him for a mission on Friday, without telling him any more details? Just make up some story. We can't risk involving too many people," said Tracey.

"Yes, you *have a point*, Tracey," said Susan. "It would be good to keep this to ourselves until the last minute."

"Sure," said Arthur. "I can *manage* that. I will tell him we have some business to take care of on Friday and I will give him the full details later. You can *rely on* me. I will keep your secret."

Susan looked at Arthur as he spoke. She realized that she had been wrong about him. A short while ago she had *ambushed* him and was questioning him. Now here he was offering to help and to get his friend to assist, too. Maybe he was not such a loser after all. It was *amazing* that help often came from the most unlikely places.

"Thanks, Arthur," said Susan. "You really are a big help. I'm really sorry for how I treated you. I was wrong to *suspect* you and I apologize. I feel really bad."

Arthur started to *blush*. Susan's kind words and soft tone of voice had made him quite *embarrassed*.

"No problem," he replied quickly. He tried hard to hide his embarrassment. Then he changed the subject to *divert attention*.

"Now *what about* the money? How are we going to *raise* two hundred *quid* in cash by Friday? Susan has seventy-five pounds, *what about* the rest of you?" said Arthur.

"Well, I don't have much savings," said Heather. "Not more than fifty pounds, I would say."

"Thanks, Heather," said Susan. "That's *real nice* of you, but I couldn't possibly take all your savings from you."

"Look, Susan, you're not taking anything. It's just a *loan*, that's all. I'm getting the money back, aren't I? I mean, we are all getting our money back. That's the idea, isn't it?" She looked across at Arthur for confirmation.

"Yes, certainly!" replied Arthur. "If our plan works, sorry, I mean, when our plan works, we will all get our money back."

"Your money, too?" snapped Tracey. "Are you also willing to put up some cash?"

"Well, I haven't got much, but I could *manage* say about twenty *quid*," Arthur replied.

"Is that all?" said Tracey sarcastically. "Do you think you can buy Susan's friendship with only twenty pounds?" she continued.

"Now hold on, Tracey!" *interrupted* Susan. "No need to be so *mean* to Arthur. I am grateful for all the help I can get. What were you thinking of contributing anyway?"

Susan looked at Tracey. She knew that Tracey had *loads of* money. At school she always wore the latest fashions and her parents lived in that big *mansion*-style house.

"Well," said Tracey, calming down a little. "I'm sure I can *manage* fifty pounds as well."

Übung 38: Welche der Erklärungen stimmt? Kreuze die richtige Lösung an!

1. I couldn't possibly take them.
   a) ☐ I don't want to take them.
   b) ☐ Maybe I'll take them.

2. Are you also willing to put up some cash?
   a) ☐ Will you steal some money?
   b) ☐ Will you give us some money?

3. I could manage twenty quid.
   a) ☐ I could provide twenty pounds.
   b) ☐ I could earn twenty pounds.

4. How much were you thinking to contribute?
   a) ☐ Have you any good ideas?
   b) ☐ What will you give?

"Great!" said Susan. "That makes one hundred and ninety-five pounds in total. I can easily *borrow* another five pounds from my dad and then we will have all the money we need."
Tracey was now having doubts about handing over the cash. Although Susan was her best friend, Tracey was always a bit *tight* with spending money. She did not want to appear *mean* in front of Arthur, but she really did not want to part with the money. Then she had an idea.
"How about using false notes?" she said. "My dad has a really super copier. We could copy some twenty pound notes and mix them in with the real ones," she said.
"No," said Arthur. "That would not work. They are sure to *notice*. I

mean, we are not professional *forgers*. The banknotes we make would not be good enough to *fool* them."

"Nice idea though!" added Susan, trying to save the situation. "Well, can you all check that you do have those amounts and let's meet back here again tomorrow. Shall we say at 10.30 a.m. here again?"

"Yes, that's cool with me," said Tracey.

"Me too," said Heather.

"Yes, I can make it as well," said Arthur. "No problem."

"Look, Arthur," said Susan. "Maybe you had better go back into the *playground* alone. I think it's best if we are not seen together to *avoid suspicion*."

Arthur was disappointed. He had rather hoped he could *hang around* with Susan and spend more time with her. But he realized that what she said made sense.

"Okay," he replied. "I will *head* on back to my *mates* and will meet you here tomorrow. See you then," he said. Then he turned and made his way back to the *playground*.

"Are you sure we can trust him?" said Tracey, as soon as he was out of sight.

"He seems *genuine* to me," said Susan.

"Me too," said Heather. "I mean, he didn't have to offer to help us. After the way we treated him he had every right to be angry with us."

"I have a good feeling about Arthur," replied Susan. "I am *convinced* he is going to be a great help to us and we definitely need help if we are going to *recover* my *locket* safely."

"Well, I *still* think we should keep a close eye on him," said Tracey, sounding very doubtful.

"Don't worry," said Susan. "We will watch him closely and make sure he does exactly what we ask him to. Now come on, it's time to get back inside or we will be late."

The three friends left their hiding place behind the *dustbins* and walked back across the *playground*. In the distance Susan saw the familiar figures of Beverly and Amanda. She slowed her *pace*; she did not want to *face* them again today. However, it was only a question of time before she would have to confront them. The school was only a small place and she could not *avoid* them forever. The rest of the day passed without event. Susan felt as if she was in a dream.

Übung 39: Finde die neuen Wörter!

ÜBUNG 39 !

1. Change a letter in LOOK to prepare a meal. COOK
2. Change a letter in BARK to find a place to meet. ____________
3. Change a letter in ROCKET to make an item of jewellery. ____________
4. Change a letter in RIGHT to make it dark. ____________
5. Change a letter in ROUND to make English money. ____________
6. Change a letter in BAD to make an item of furniture. ____________

Susan could not concentrate during the lessons and in maths Mrs Fisher *told* her *off* twice for not paying *attention*. At lunchtime she sat with Heather and Tracey as usual, but she did not finish her lunch and did not feel hungry. If Arthur was *innocent* who else could have taken her *locket*, she thought. Giles too had been excluded *due to* the timing of the text message after their *show-*

down. So that only left Beverly and Amanda. The *fight* in the park had *shaken* her and at the time she had forgotten about the *locket*. But now she thought about it, she realized that the two of them could easily have taken her *locket* and sent the text messages. But how could she *prove* it? She certainly could not *approach* them directly – she needed someone else to help. Her thoughts were *interrupted* suddenly:

"Hey Susan!" said Heather. "Are you falling asleep over your pie and chips?"

"Eh, what, oh sorry!" said Susan.

"You seem to be far away," said Heather.

"I was just thinking about who else could have taken the *locket*."

"And who do you think?"

Übung 40: Sind die folgenden Aussagen richtig? Markiere mit richtig ✔ oder falsch – !

ÜBUNG 40 !

1. If something is not difficult, you can do it easily. ☐
2. If you seem to be far away, you aren't concentrating. ☐
3. A teacher likes pupils who don't pay attention. ☐
4. Innocent is the opposite of guilty. ☐
5. Agreeing on something means being of a different opinion. ☐
6. If you are shaken by something, you are brave. ☐

"I can only think of Beverly and Amanda, they certainly acted very strangely in the park."
The other two agreed.
"We have to work out a plan how to find out if they stole the *locket*," said Heather. "And we need someone who knows them to help us."
"I know. How about asking Arthur? They won't *suspect* him."
Heather agreed that it was a good idea. Tracey was not sure at first, but eventually agreed that it was the best idea.
"In the meantime we have to work on getting the money together," said Susan. "Don't forget: we're meeting tomorrow to *sort out* the money."
They all nodded and went back to their afternoon classes.

Chapter 6: Beg, Borrow or Steal

Later that day after her evening meal at around 6 p.m., Tracey went up to her room. She had a secret hiding place where she kept all her banknotes. It was in a pink *pouch* at the bottom of her *wardrobe*. After a few minutes she found the *pouch* and took it out. She sat on

the bed and counted her savings. She had thirty-five pounds and twenty pence.
Oh dear, she thought. I told Susan I would give her fifty pounds. What am I going to do now? She knew that Susan would be disappointed if she could not lend her the amount she promised. There had to be a way to *borrow* the money. And who could she ask? Her dad was always the best option. She just had to think of an excuse why she needed the money.
She had often *borrowed* money in the past from her dad, sometimes for clothes, for trips to the cinema and for other essential items like shoes, handbags and make-up. Being a teenager was an expensive business and her monthly *pocket money* of fifty pounds just never seemed to last until the end of the month.

! ÜBUNG 41

Übung 41: Trage die fehlenden Buchstaben ein!

1. You play h _ _ k _ _ with a stick.
2. A lot of people is a cr _ _ d.
3. Your arm is attached to your sh _ _ _ d _ r.
4. Susan was bl _ _ km _ _ _ _ d.
5. The locket was a pr _ _ _ _ t from her grandmother.
6. Pupils in England wear a school u _ _ f _ _ _.
7. Was the sender an _ ny _ _ _ s?
8. She was tired and y _ _ n _ _.

She looked at herself in the mirror. In her old sweatshirt and jogging trousers she did not look her best. To get her dad's *attention* she had

better smarten up a bit. She looked through her *wardrobe* and took out her favourite pink blouse; her dad always liked her in that. Next she put on her black jeans. She had already learned various tricks for persuading her dad when she wanted something. She looked in the mirror one last time and walked slowly down the stairs.
Her father was sitting on the sofa watching football on TV. Luckily her mum was in the kitchen washing the dishes and so she could speak to him alone.
"Hi dad!" she said in her sweetest voice and sat down beside him. He continued to watch the TV and just *mumbled*.
"Hi."
Tracey was not going to *give up* easily.
"Good game?" she asked, trying to show an interest in what he was watching.
"Er, what?" he replied.
"I said is it a good game?" asked Tracey patiently.
"Yeah, Chelsea are winning one nil," he answered.
Tracey was pleased. Her dad was a big Chelsea *fan* and if his team was winning then he was sure to be in a good *mood*.
"Dad," she said slowly, building up to the big question.
"What is it you want this time?" her father answered. He knew his only daughter well and knew when she wanted something.

Übung 42: Vervollständige die Sätze mit ***his, him, she*** *oder* ***her****!*

ÜBUNG 42 !

1. Susan was worried when ________ locket was stolen.

2. George was pleased to help ________ friend Arthur.

3. Susan's mum thought ________ should go to the doctor.

4. Giles was annoyed when Susan finished with ________.

5. Tracey tried to get money off ________ dad.

"The thing is I need a new pair of boots for hockey," said Tracey. Her boots were fine, but this was the best excuse she could think of to get some money from her dad. However, her father was not so easily *fooled*.

"Hockey boots?" he said. "What's wrong with your old boots? Didn't we buy you a new pair just a few months ago?"

Tracey had to think quickly: "Well, they are already really worn out and *scratched*. They are *uncomfortable*, too. I really need a new pair," she said. She was trying hard to think of a way to persuade her father to hand over the money.

"That's funny," said her father. "Have you only just realized they are *uncomfortable* after you have been wearing them for several months? Maybe I should have a look at them."

"Alright," said Tracey. She now realized that her father was not as easily *fooled* as she thought. Maybe she should tell the truth after all. But no, that would not work. *What about* her promise to Susan not to tell anyone? Could she trust her parents not to report this to the police? No, she thought. She could not *take* that *risk*; she would have to think of some other excuse for needing the money.

"You win!" she said *reluctantly*. "I don't really need new hockey boots. I just need some money."

"And why?" asked her father *expectantly*.

"Well, it's for Susan, you see." Tracey started talking and then she had a *brilliant* idea. She could mention the *locket*, but *pretend* that it was only broken and had to be repaired!

"Go on," said her father. He now seemed more interested. Usually his daughter asked for money to buy clothes, make-up or shoes.

This was the first time she was asking for money for somebody else.
"Susan has a big problem," said Tracey. "She has broken a really *valuable locket*. It was a present from her grandmother, a family *heirloom*. The chain snapped and it will cost a lot of money to repair it."
Tracey was really pleased with herself. This is a good story she thought, it is not all a lie and the money really is for Susan.
"Can't her parents pay for the repairs?" said her dad.
"No, that's just the problem. You see, she broke the chain in a *fight* with another girl. If her parents find out they will be really *cross* with her. They are very strict, you know." Again Tracey felt almost triumphant. This was a really good story she was making up.
Her father stopped watching the match and looked at her to see if she was telling the truth. His daughter had been friends with Susan for many years, ever since junior school in fact. So it did seem normal that she would want to help Susan. He also knew that Susan's parents were not *well-off* and so they might be very angry if she had damaged a *valuable* piece of jewellery.
"Wow, I'm really touched," said her dad. "That is really kind of you to help Susan to *raise* the money for the repair. Is anybody else helping?"
Tracey explained how Heather was also helping. She said that Heather had offered to lend Susan fifty pounds.
"Fifty pounds!" her father exclaimed. "How much does the repair cost?"
Tracey *hesitated* for a moment. If she said two hundred pounds her father would never believe her.
"About ninety pounds," she said quickly. She realized that she had made a big mistake by saying fifty. "You see, Susan is really *broke* and the most she can get is twenty pounds."

Übung 43: Setze das entsprechende Verb im Present Perfect ein!

1. *Has* she *found* the money? (find)
2. ________ you ______________ another jeweller? (try)
3. ________ they ______________ to the billiard café? (be)
4. ________ I ______________ the locket before? (see)
5. ________ it ______________ from your bag? (disappear)
6. ________ we ______________ the boy? (meet)
7. ________ she ______________ her parents? (tell)
8. ________ he ______________ a message? (receive)
9. ________ you ___________ a new pair of hockey boots? (buy)

"Have you asked around different jewellers to get the *locket* repaired?" her father said. "Maybe you can get it done cheaper somewhere else?"

"Yeah, great idea, dad," said Tracey quickly. "Why didn't we think of that? Tell you what: I will discuss it with the others tomorrow. But for now can you lend me twenty pounds?"

"Well, alright, I suppose so," her dad said. "But I am only lending it to you, remember. I will take it out of your *pocket money* for next month."

"Okay," said Tracey *reluctantly*. She had hoped he might just give her the money, but at least he was lending it to her. After all, she intended to get the money back from Susan anyway. It was only a *loan*, she told herself.

"Thanks, dad," she said and threw her arms around him. She *gave* him *a* big *hug* and a kiss. "You're the best!" she added. It was a bit *over the top* she thought, but at least she had got what she wanted.

Her dad took out his *wallet* and handed over a twenty-pound note. "Now," he said. "Maybe I can go back to watching the match again?"
"Yeah, sure, dad," said Tracey. "I'll just go back up to my room and watch *telly* for a bit."
With a feeling of delight Tracey turned around and raced up the stairs. She shut her bedroom door and crashed down on the bed.
She was so excited that she decided to *text* Susan straightaway.
Her phone was on her bedside table. She picked it up and pressed the key pad to type in her message: "have *yr* money – all of it! *c u 2moro, lol* tracey". Then she pressed the 'Send' *button*.
Meanwhile Susan was also in her bedroom trying to concentrate on the maths homework. When she heard the message tone she reached over and grabbed her phone. At first she thought it might be another message from the *blackmailers*. She was very *relieved* when she saw the name 'Tracey' in the display.
After reading her message she felt much happier. At last the money was being *gathered* together. Tomorrow she would take her post office *savings book* to school. Then she could go straight after school to the *local* post office and *withdraw* the money. Seventy-five pounds was a lot of money. Maybe she should take her friends with her to support her, especially if someone else might be watching her. She was *still* very worried that she might meet Beverly and Amanda alone somewhere.
She typed a message to Tracey: "*gr8*, *thx. c u* at school. *lol* susan". Then she pressed the 'Send' *button*.
She went back to her maths homework and now the sums seemed much easier. It would soon be bedtime and she wanted to get the calculations finished before she went to bed. At least Mrs Fisher would be happy if she got all these done, she thought. She did not want to cause any more trouble.

Übung 44: Setze das richtige Fragewort ein!

1. .... old are you?
2. .... took the locket?
3. .... one do you prefer?
4. .... much homework do we have?
5. .... did you lose it? During the game?
6. .... did you hide? In the bushes?
7. .... is the best thing to do?
8. .... hates me so much?

Heather, however, did not find it so easy to get her share of the money. When she got home she went straight to her room to check her *savings book*. She usually kept it in the *drawer* of her writing desk. It was not there. Where could it be? She searched through all four of the *drawers*, but could not find it anywhere. In her frustration she emptied the contents of all the *drawers* onto her bed. There were books, magazines, *stationery* and photo albums spread all over her bed. She even put them all into piles to try to *sort* them *out*, but she could not find her *savings book* anywhere.
Oh no, she thought. What have I done with it? And what do I tell Susan? She is depending on me. I suppose I will have to go to the bank and tell them I have lost my *savings book*, but it may take a while to get a new one. I really need to help Susan, but what can I do?
In desperation she sat down on the bed and cried. She felt so desperate. She did not want to let Susan down, but how could she get fifty pounds in such a short time?

Then an idea came to her.
Her dad had a secret hiding place for banknotes in his desk, she thought. Maybe she could *borrow* the money and put it back before he *noticed* it? It was not really stealing the money, was it? She was going to put it back and he would never know. It was a risky plan and if she got caught there would be trouble, but she could not think of a better way.
Her parents normally came up to say goodnight to her at around 9 p.m. When her mum came up she *pretended* to be asleep. The bedroom door was open. Her mum knocked gently and there was no answer. She put her head to the door and *whispered* "Goodnight, Heather", but Heather did not reply. Luckily her mother then closed the door quietly behind her.
Later Heather heard her parents going to bed. She looked at her alarm clock. It was 10.30 p.m. She had found it hard to stay awake and she had put a *torch* under her *duvet* to read with. First she had to be sure that they were asleep. Her father *snored* and usually this annoyed her, but tonight she was glad of it. It was one way to make sure he was sound asleep. She read some more of her book and then checked the clock. It was now 11 p.m.
"Here goes," she *whispered* to herself. It should be all quiet now, she thought.

Übung 45: Beantworte die Fragen zum Text!

1. What did the thief want from Susan?

2. When was the locket stolen?

3. Which boys helped Susan and her friends?

4. Who is Giles?

5. Who lends Tracey twenty pounds?

Heather opened her bedroom door and *tiptoed* along the *hallway* to her parents' room. The door was open and she could hear her dad *snoring*. But *what about* her mum? She put her head through the *gap* and *whispered*: "Mum? Mum? Are you awake?"

She waited, but no answer came.

After pausing for a few minutes she decided it was safe to go downstairs. She walked very slowly and carefully as the stairs sometimes *creaked*. She had to make as little noise as possible.

When she reached the bottom of the stairs she turned left and walked into her father's study. His writing desk was up against the wall to the left of the window. Heather moved slowly across the room and shone her *torch* on the desk. Fortunately it was unlocked. She had often seen her dad put banknotes in a tin in the top right-hand *drawer* of the desk. Her dad did not know that Heather had often watched him and she knew his hiding place. Her fingers now trembled as she searched for the container. It was an old cigar box. Carefully she placed it on the desk and opened it. Quickly she counted the banknotes inside – one hundred and twenty-five pounds.

Heather told herself that she was going to put it back, and her dad wouldn't *notice*. She counted up fifty pounds, two twenty-pound notes and one ten-pound note. It's for Susan, she told herself. My friend needs my help and I will not let her down.

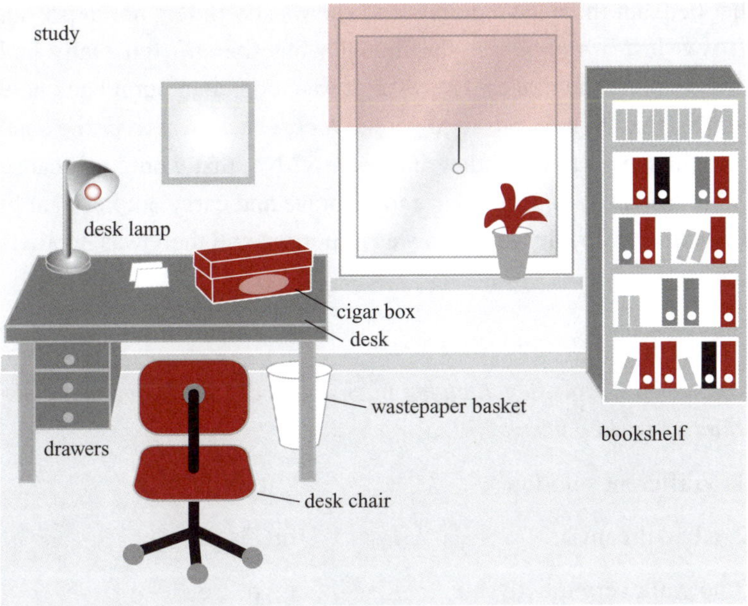

Once she had the cash safely in the pocket of her pyjamas, she *crept* back up the stairs. Her parents' room was *still* quiet, except for the sound of *snoring*. Poor mum, she thought, she must need *earplugs* to sleep with all that noise. She closed her bedroom door and then hid the money in her *purse* in the top *drawer* of her *chest of drawers*. Then she pulled back the *covers* from her bed and jumped in. In no time she was asleep, but she slept badly and had a *nightmare*. In her dream her father came into the room with a dark stranger and demanded her to return the money. It was a terrible *nightmare*. She felt so guilty for stealing the money, but she did not know how else she could help Susan.

Next morning Heather awoke with a shock. She had been *sweating* in the night and her pyjamas were wet with *sweat*. She looked under her bed, but there were no rats and she was definitely not in prison. It was just a *nightmare*, she thought, but she *still* felt really bad about taking the money. However, it was too late to put it back now and she had to help Susan to get her *locket* back, whatever the cost. Should she go to her father and *confess*? No, that would just cause more trouble. She would have to be brave and carry out her plan to the end. Her loyalty to Susan was important and there was no alternative.

ÜBUNG 46 !

Übung 46: Trage die fehlenden Buchstaben des beschriebenen Substantivs in die Lücken ein!

1. a different solution	_ lt _ _ n _ _ iv _
2. a bad dream	ni _ h _ m _ r _
3. to walk very quietly	t _ pt _ e
4. it covers you up at night	_ uv _ t
5. a kind of newspaper	_ a _ _ z _ n _
6. you keep your money in it	p _ _ s _
7. a light you hold in your hand	_ o _ c _
8. to make a loud noise when asleep	_ n _ r _

Because she slept badly Heather felt very tired. She decided to have a shower to freshen up. The warm water on her skin made her feel better and she dressed quickly for school. Her mum asked what she wanted for breakfast, but Heather was not hungry and said that she had a bad stomach ache.

“Maybe you should stay home today?” her mum asked. “Shall I write you a *sick note*?”

"Er, no, thanks. I'll be fine," said Heather. She simply had to get to school to tell Susan the news about the money.

As soon as she closed the front door she hurried along the road to *catch the bus* to school. As usual, Susan and Tracey were already on the bus and they all sat together. They talked about the weather, homework and what was on TV the night before, but they did not mention the money. They could not risk someone overhearing their conversation. At break time they all met behind the *dustbins* as agreed. Arthur was the last to arrive. Susan asked him to check that no-one was *spying on* them and reminded everybody to keep watch at all times.

"So, how did it go?" she asked. "Did you all get the money?"

"No problem!" said Tracey. "I had to *borrow* some from my dad. It wasn't easy at first, but I *managed* in the end."

"Thanks, Tracey, you are a real *mate*. I will pay you back when this is over. I promise!" said Susan.

Heather meanwhile was not looking so happy. She had been trying to smile and put on a brave face, but she felt so *exhausted*. She was not good at lying.

"*What's up*, Heather?" said Susan in a *compassionate* voice. She knew her friend well and felt something was wrong.

At that moment Heather *burst into tears*. Big hot tears rolled down her cheeks and she *sobbed* and *sobbed*. Susan put her arms around her and *hugged* her tight. Heather's body *shook* as she cried and it took a long while before she could speak.

ÜBUNG 47 !

Übung 47: Formuliere die folgenden Sätze im Passiv!

1. The blackmailer sent a text message.

A text message was sent by the blackmailer.

2. Heather stole the money.

---

3. Susan scored the goal.

---

4. Someone hated her.

---

5. Her parents looked after them.

---

6. The girls suspected Giles.

"I just can't do it!" she said and cried some more.
"What can't you do?" asked Susan.
"I can't keep on lying," she continued in a broken voice.
"About what?" said Susan.
"About the money," replied Heather. "I lost my *savings book* and I did not have any money so I took some from my dad's desk," she said. After she had told the truth she felt much better.
Now Tracey and Arthur also came over and both *comforted* Heather. She had a really bad conscience about taking the money.
"I think maybe I should put the money back."
The others agreed, and then Arthur came up with an offer of help.
"Don't worry," said Arthur. "We will *sort* this *out* somehow. You know I am sure that I can *borrow* some money from my parents like Tracey did. I can easily make up some story that I need to buy something. My dad is always generous."
He was not really sure if he could so easily *borrow* the money, but

he wanted to *reassure* Heather and to calm her down.
"Could you really?" said Heather. She was now much calmer. After she blew her nose she looked up at Arthur and said:
"Thanks! That would be really great!"
She *flung* her arms around Arthur and *gave* him *a* spontaneous *hug*. Arthur *blushed* and was very *embarrassed*.
"Sure!" he said. "No problem, I will get the money tomorrow!" Secretly he was not sure if he could get the fifty pounds, but he wanted to sound confident to impress Heather and above all to impress Susan.
"Wow, Arthur!" said Susan. "That is really *awesome!* If you can get the money that would solve the problem!"

Übung 48: Welches Wort ist das „schwarze Schaf"?

ÜBUNG 48 !

1. notice, see, observe, clock
2. school, playground, car, classroom
3. desk, quid, pounds, money
4. chest, drawers, shoulder, head
5. hockey, football, billiards, pitch
6. chocolate, sweets, teacher, ice cream
7. house, swing, mansion, flat

They agreed that Heather should return the money to her father's desk after school. He got home from work around 7 p.m., so she had lots of time to go into his study. It was important to do it when her mum was not looking, but that should be no problem. Susan agreed to go home with her and to distract her mum so Heather would be able to enter the study unnoticed.
Once that was agreed, the friends had to decide what to do next.

Susan felt that they should watch Amanda and Beverly. They were her two *prime suspects* and the others agreed. The only person who could *spy on* them easily was Arthur. After the *fight* between Susan and Beverly it was not easy for Susan and her friends to go near Beverly. Arthur, on the other hand, was not known to Beverly. It would not be difficult for him to secretly follow her and watch her movements. If she did have the *locket* she would maybe talk about it to her friends. If Arthur could somehow get near to them in the *playground* or in the school, perhaps he could get some useful information.

Arthur agreed. He was ready to help Susan in any way he could. He thought he would have no problem *spying on* Beverly. He had never really spoken to her and she would not *suspect* him. There was nothing to link him to Susan. They had been careful not to be seen together, so there was no reason for Beverly to be *suspicious* of him.

Chapter 7: Trouble in the Woods

When their meeting was over they all went back to their classes.

At lunchtime Arthur decided to eat with his friend George as usual. When he entered the canteen he *noticed* that Beverly, Amanda and some other girls were sitting over by the window. When he collected his lunch from the *serving hatch* he persuaded George to come and sit with him by the window. The table behind Beverly and Amanda was free! Nervously he sat down with his back to the girls. He did not want to attract *attention*. George was talking about the TV programme he watched last night – 'Eastenders'. It was a soap opera they both loved, but Arthur only half listened. He concentrated hard as he tried to hear the words spoken by the girls.

At one point he was sure he heard them say: "Stupid little *stuck-up*

bitch" and then "who does she think she is?"
It was not clear if they were talking about Susan, but there was obviously some girl at school that they *were out to get*.
After a while, George *noticed* that Arthur was not really paying *attention* to him and not eating his lunch.
"*What's up?*" he said.
"Oh, nothing," replied Arthur. "I was just dreaming, that's all."
He *still* tried to lean back and hear what the girls were saying from time to time, but it was too difficult.

Übung 49: Finde das gesuchte Wort!

1. a table at which you do your schoolwork ____________
2. He tries to stop the ball going in the net. ____________
3. the meal before you go to school ____________
4. You go there if you are injured. ____________
5. the day before today ____________
6. the opposite of interesting ____________

After lunch Arthur told George he had to meet up with the geography teacher. When George had left, Arthur followed Beverly out of the canteen. He kept a safe distance behind her as he did not want to be seen. He followed her down the corridor leading to the gym. That's funny, he thought. There were no gym lessons after lunch, so what was she doing down here? Beverly was acting very *suspiciously*. She looked around to check that no-one was following her. Luckily she had not *noticed* that Arthur was hiding behind a *pillar*.

All was quiet. Nobody was in the corridor.

Beverly took out her *mobile* and started typing in a message. Who was she *texting*, Arthur wondered, It was not allowed to use *mobile phones* on the school grounds, but many people *still* did anyway. However, most pupils used their *mobiles* in the *playground* away from the teachers and not indoors. Also why was Beverly on her own away from her friends? It all seemed very *suspicious*.

Arthur stood very still. Beverly was obviously waiting for a reply. She had stopped typing and was just staring at her *mobile*. Suddenly there was a 'peep peep' sound as a new message arrived on her *mobile*. Immediately she typed in a reply, then put the *mobile* back into her handbag.

He looked at his watch to check the time. It was 1.15 p.m. Beverly then hurried back down the corridor. As she passed, Arthur moved slowly around the other side of the *pillar* so as not to be *noticed*. Fortunately Beverly did not see him.

Susan had spent most of lunchtime *hanging around* in the *playground*. She had not gone into the canteen today and had just eaten some crisps from the snack bar instead. She sat on a *bench* with Tracey under the trees at the *edge* of the *playground*. From this spot she had a good view over the whole area. In the distance she *noticed* that Giles was playing football with his *mates*. He did not even see her and she was happy to keep out of his way.

Suddenly she heard the noise 'deedle do da da, deedle do da da': she had a new message on her *mobile*.

Quickly she took it out of her handbag and pressed the 'Read' *button*.

Tracey leant over to read what it said. The message was short and direct:

"Have *u* got the cash yet?"

Susan turned to Tracey and said:

"What shall I say? Shall I tell them I have it?"
"Sure," said Tracey. "No reason to wait. Let's see what they say."
Susan typed in a short "yes" and pressed the 'Send' *button*.
It seemed like ages until the answer came back:
"meet us *2nite* @ Bluebell Woods @ 7 p.m. @ picnic area. don't be *l8*! come alone!"
"So!" said Susan. "We have to do the *handover* tonight! At last I get my *locket* back!"
"And we will get the *blackmailers*, too!" said Tracey triumphantly. "They will pay for this!"
Susan typed in a quick message: "ok no *prob* i will be there" and pressed the 'Send' *button*.
Bluebell Woods was a short walk from the school. It was a popular place at the weekends, but was normally very empty during the day. Susan and her friends knew the area well. There was a big picnic site in the middle of the woods with a *playground*. They often went there to get away from the noise of the city.

Übung 50: Schreibe die Wörter in Großbuchstaben um!

ÜBUNG 50 !

1. Change a letter in CHEST to make a game you play on a board: ____________

2. Take a letter away from CLOSER to make someone who doesn't win: ____________

3. Change a letter from WOOD to make something you can eat: ____________

4. Add a letter to TREE to make a number: ____________

5. Change a letter in STOP to make a place where you can buy things: ______________

6. Find a word that rhymes with CHIPS to make part of your face: ______________

At that moment another text message came on Susan's phone: "Meet me by the bins now I have news." It was from Arthur.

Susan looked up and saw him standing over by the school exit. He did not wave to her, but started walking over to the bins. Obviously he did not want anyone to see him talking to them.

"Come on, Tracey," said Susan. "Let's see what he wants. And get Heather, too."

Tracey walked across the *playground* and found Heather. She told her what was going on and they all met behind the bins in their secret meeting place.

"So, *what's up?*" asked Susan.

Arthur explained how he had just seen Beverly sending a text message.

"And I have just received a message!" explained Susan. "So it must be Beverly who took the *locket*!"

"Just a moment," said Tracey. "What if Beverly is not working alone? I mean this is a big plan to carry out by herself. She is not that clever surely?"

"Yes, I *see* your *point*," said Susan. "Maybe we should hand over the money as planned and then we can see if she is working alone. If we *approach* her now maybe she will alarm the rest of her gang and the *locket* will be gone forever."

The others agreed.

"Well," said Arthur. "So what's the plan? How are we going to

arrange the *handover* and *catch* Beverly with her gang, if there is one?"
"They told me to go alone," said Susan. "But I really don't feel safe going there on my own."
"No way!" said Arthur. "It would be really *foolish* to go there alone."

Übung 51: Lies weiter und setze das Gegenteil der Wörter in Klammern ein!

ÜBUNG 51

"We will be with you all the way," said Tracey and Heather.
"And don't (1. remember) f_______________ George," said Arthur. "He is a really (2. weak) s_______________ *guy* and could be very useful if there is any trouble."
So the four friends agreed to meet at the back of Susan's house at 6 p.m. From there they could go on their bikes to Bluebell Woods. Each of them was to (3. take) b_______________ their share of the money in cash and Arthur said he would *borrow* the rest (4. to) f_______________ his dad. Susan would carry the money in a plastic *pouch*, which she could hang around her neck. After they had agreed the plan, they all (5. came) w_______________ separately across the *playground* and back to their classes.

It was raining when they all *gathered* around the back of Susan's house. They had all brought their waterproof jackets. *Despite* the weather they had no choice but to carry out their plan. By meeting around the back of the house they could *avoid* being seen from the main road. They agreed that Susan should leave first and the others would follow in pairs: Arthur with Heather and George with Tracey. Susan was very grateful to George for agreeing to help them. He was a tall strong *lad* and it felt good to have him with them.

When they were all ready, Susan *set off* on her bike towards Bluebell Woods. As soon as she was out of sight, Arthur followed with Heather. George and Tracey waited until they could no longer see the others and then they too jumped on their bikes and cycled towards the woods.

Susan felt very nervous as she *approached* the woods. It was good to know her friends were behind her, but it *still* felt strange as she could not see them. Although it was raining it was *still* light when she entered the woods. She *rode* up the hill that led towards the picnic spot. As she got towards the top of the woods she had to get off and push her bike, as it was very *steep*.

She kept looking around to see if anyone was watching her. A few times she thought she heard a noise in the trees nearby and turned around quickly, but she could not see anyone.

She stopped several times on her walk up the hill. She wanted to make sure that her friends had enough time to *catch up with her*.

The plan was that Arthur and Heather would hide their bikes at the *edge* of the woods and then walk up through the trees to the picnic site. By not using the path they hoped they would not be seen.

Tracey and George also walked up through the trees and used a route that came in from the other side.

Susan had to make sure that her friends were all in position before she arrived at the picnic spot. She did not know how many people

would be waiting for her. She was a little bit afraid.
Finally Susan reached the picnic spot. There was nobody there. Slowly she walked over to the table in the centre and walked around it casually. From the corner of her eye she looked into the trees around the picnic spot for signs of her friends. Suddenly she saw the familiar sight of Heather giving her a small wave from behind one of the trees. Then she saw that Tracey was also hiding on the other side of the picnic area.
She was scared when she suddenly heard the ring tone of her phone: 'deedle do da da, deedle do da da'.
"*r u* there?" came the message.
"Yes," Susan typed back.
"Wait!" came the reply.
She sat on the picnic table and waited. It was very hard to keep cool and be patient. What was going on? Where were the *blackmailers*?

Übung 52: Lies weiter und setze das passende Wort ein!
(towards, mopeds, impossible, loud, figures, run, braked, table)

A (1.) ______________ noise alarmed her and she jumped down from the (2.) ______________. The sound of engines roared through the trees. Then two (3.) ______________ with riders rode onto the grass in the picnic area. Normally mopeds were not allowed in the woods, but the two riders obviously did not care. They rode their mopeds straight towards Susan and (4.) ______________ in front of her. The two (5.) ______________ were wearing dark motorbike helmets with the *visors* down. It was (6.) ______________ to see who they were. They were also both wearing black leather jackets. With another loud roar two more mopeds rode into the picnic area from behind. The riders stopped the engines and walked over (7.) ______________ Susan. She was surrounded. She was very frightened, but had to be brave and not (8.) ______________ away.

"So, where is the cash?" said one of the figures. He was a young boy with a deep voice. Nobody she recognized. If she handed over the money they might just leave.
"Show me the *locket* first!" she said. "No *locket*, no cash."
"Sure, here it is!" said another of the figures. The figure unzipped the side pocket of his leather jacket and took out Susan's beloved

locket. She ran towards him and tried to grab it.
Another figure stepped in front of her and pushed her back.
"Now where is the cash?" he growled.
Susan's fingers trembled as she reached into her coat and took out the plastic *pouch*.
"Here, take it. It's all there," she said as she pushed the *pouch* towards the figure demanding the money. He grabbed the *pouch* and quickly counted the notes.
"Yep," he said. "All there! Okay *guys*, let's get out of here."
Suddenly Susan realized that they had no intention of returning her *locket*. She had been tricked! In her desperation she *dived* onto the *guy* holding the *pouch* and knocked it from his hands. He pushed her to the ground and as she fell she shouted out to her friends.
"Help! Help!"
At this signal her friends came running out of their hiding places in the trees.
"Attack, attack!" cried Arthur as he came *rushing* through the trees towards the *guy* who had held the *locket*. He pushed him with both hands and he fell to the ground. The *guy* next to him turned on Arthur and grabbed him around the neck. At that moment George came running from the other side. He grabbed the helmet of the *guy* holding Arthur and pulled him over backwards.
"Leave us alone!" screamed Susan. She had now got up again and joined in the *fight*, kicking and *pounding* her *fists* against the attackers.
The *guy* with the *locket* had *managed* to get to his feet. He jumped on his moped and wanted to ride off, but at that moment Tracey came running out of the trees and tried to block his way. He *swerved* to *avoid* her, but then with a *sickening thud* the moped crashed into Tracey, throwing her to the ground. She let out a scream of pain and then went silent. She lay *bleeding* on the ground.

Susan *rushed* over to where Tracey was lying.
"She's *unconscious*!" she cried. "Help, somebody help me!"
Heather and Arthur came running over to where Susan was *kneeling* beside Tracey.
George was *still* trying to *fight off* the other attackers, but he *was outnumbered*. They had knocked him to the ground and kicked him as he lay on the ground.

Übung 53: Welche Wörter gehören zusammen? Ordne zu!

1. ☐ to score	a) annoyed
2. ☐ to ease	b) a secret
3. ☐ to take	c) a goal
4. ☐ to be	d) care
5. ☐ to keep	e) sense
6. ☐ to ride	f) the pain
7. ☐ to get	g) a bicycle
8. ☐ to make	h) dressed

"Come on! Let's get out of here!" one of the voices said. The other figures got on their mopeds and rode off out of the woods.
Susan was in a state of shock and did not know what to do.
"We need to call an ambulance!" said Arthur. "We need to get help!"
Susan just nodded. She was shaking from shock.
"Give me your phone!" said Arthur. Quickly, he called an ambulance. Then he looked up and *noticed* that George was lying on the ground and *groaning*.
"Heather, go over and *check on* George!" he shouted.
Heather did as he said and ran over to where George was lying.
"He's hurt," she said. She leant over him and tried to *comfort* him.

"Help is coming," she said. "We have called for an ambulance!" Gently she *stroked* his head to *reassure* him. She took off her coat and put it over him to keep him warm and dry.

Übung 54: Lies weiter und unterstreiche die sieben Adjektive im Text!

Susan and Arthur had done the same for Tracey and had covered her with their coats. Arthur checked that she was breathing, but they were afraid to move her. They had both done first aid at school and remembered that it was not wise to move an injured body. There may be *internal injuries* or broken bones. Susan was shaking from shock and Arthur put his hand around her to *comfort* her. He called over to where Heather was and said:
"Help is on its way! The ambulance will be here very soon."
The ground was very *muddy* and Tracey looked badly hurt. She lay on her back in the grass. Arthur moved away the branches and made the *space* around her so that the ambulance men would be able to reach her better.

Susan *was overcome with tears*.
"It's all my fault!" she cried. "It's all my fault! If I had not got you all involved none of this would have happened. And now Tracey is badly hurt. She may even die!"
"Calm down!" said Arthur, taking control. "She is not going to die. She is just *unconscious*, that's all. Don't worry; help is on its way. And Susan – it isn't your fault! We all wanted to help you, remember? The only fault is with those cruel *guys* on the mopeds. Who were they? Did you recognize anybody?"
"No," replied Susan. "With those helmets and the black jackets it

was not possible. I didn't recognize any of their voices either."
"Well, the important thing is that we get Tracey to hospital as soon as possible. We can deal with the rest later," said Arthur.
Yes, thought Susan. All that mattered was that Tracey was all right. She could not even think about what she would do if anything happened to Tracey. She looked across at Heather. Heather was trying to be brave and not cry, but Susan could see that she was very shocked and *upset*. She called over to her:
"How is George doing?"
"He is conscious!" cried Heather. "But he is in a lot of pain. I think he may have broken his shoulder!"
"Oh no!" said Susan. "Those *guys* were really rough, weren't they?"
Her words were *interrupted* by the sound of a siren in the distance. Then they saw a blue flashing light as an ambulance drove slowly up the hill. It stopped at the *edge* of the picnic area. Three men got out and raced over to where Tracey was laying. Susan *pointed* across to where George was, as well. Two of them stayed with Tracey and the other ran over to *check on* George.
The ambulance men soon decided that both the injured teenagers would have to go to hospital. They *radioed* for another ambulance, which came shortly afterwards, followed by a police car.
Tracey had to be carried into the ambulance on a *stretcher*. They asked if Susan wanted to go with her and she agreed.

! ÜBUNG 55

Übung 55: Lies weiter und setze die Verben in der richtigen Zeitform ein!

Heather (1. stay) ____________ with George and rode in the ambulance with him, while Arthur (2. ride) ____________ in the police car.

He (3. want) ______________ to go to the hospital, too, but the policeman (4. say) ______________ it was better if they accompanied him. He (5. give) ______________ them the personal details of George and the phone numbers of their parents, too.

As the ambulance (6. drive) ________________ down the hill, Susan (7. sit) ______________ and (8. hold) ______________ Tracey's hand.

It had been an incredible evening. It had all gone so badly wrong. She did not *care about* her *locket* anymore. The only thing that she cared about was that Tracey should *recover*. She began to cry and the ambulance men *comforted* her.
"Don't worry," they said. "She will be fine."
They were giving Tracey oxygen and she was breathing slowly. It looked horrible to Susan, but the *paramedics* assured her that everything was okay and all her body functions were normal. They had cleaned up the cuts on her face and she looked a lot better.
For Arthur it was the first time he had been in a police car. In some ways he was actually quite excited, but he was worried about the others and kept asking the police questions. Eventually they agreed to take him to the hospital as well, but first they took him home to see his parents. His mum and dad were of course very shocked and had lots of questions, but the police were able to *reassure* them and to keep them calm.
When they finally got to the hospital Tracey had *regained consciousness*. She was sitting up in the bed with a bandage on her head and looked much better. Her parents were with her and Susan refused to leave her bedside. Susan's parents were waiting outside the room as it was too crowded inside.

Once Arthur was sure Tracey was okay, he went into the room next door where George was.

"How are you feeling?" he asked. George too was sitting up in bed and his shoulder was bandaged.

"It's just a bad *sprain*," he said. "Luckily it isn't broken. I have strong bones!"

"Man, you were great!" continued Arthur. "The way you *fought off* those *guys* was *awesome*!"

"Yes, but there were just too many of them. And then they got away with both the *locket* and the cash!" said George, disappointed. "We should have jumped on them sooner!"

"Don't worry," said Arthur. "The police are sure to *catch* them sooner or later."

The two of them sat chatting for another half hour until eventually the nurse said that Arthur would have to leave. He said goodnight to his friend and was driven home by Tracey's parents.

ÜBUNG 56 !

Übung 56: Wähle das passende Wort aus und unterstreiche es!

1. Arthur hid/slept in the bushes.
2. The blackmailer demanded/wished the money.
3. The phone called/rang.
4. Susan's friends hit/helped her.
5. The gang fought/spoke with George.
6. Chess is quick/quiet.
7. The four friends agreed/argued to meet at Susan's house.
8. Tracey had to be caught/carried into the ambulance on a stretcher.
9. It's all Susan's fault/fool.
10. Susan and her friends new/knew the area well.

Chapter 8: Justice is Done

Susan awoke early the next morning and lay in her bed thinking about everything that had happened the night before. It all seemed like a bad dream. But at least Tracey was being looked after now. Both Tracey and George had spent the night at the hospital under observation.

Übung 57: Lies weiter und ergänze den Text mit ***she, her, they*** *oder* ***them****.*

Her parents had said that Susan could stay home from school, so (1.) ________ did not have to get up early. (2.) ________ mum said that Susan should take a *rest* and that (3.) ________ would write (4.) ________ a *sick note*. They were very pleased that Susan was not injured. When she told (5.) ________ that her *locket* was stolen, she was very surprised that they did not even get angry. (6.) ________ were more concerned over the *blackmail* and the *fight* in Bluebell Woods. How silly she had been not to trust (7.) ________, she thought. (8.) ________ should have gone to (9.) ________ straight-away.

Halfway through breakfast, suddenly the doorbell rang and her mum was surprised and got up to answer it. She came back with a concerned look on her face. “It’s the police, dear,” she said. “They want to ask you a few questions.”

"No problem," said Susan *confidently*. "Show them in."
The police asked about how the *locket* had been stolen and then about the text messages that Susan had received. They said they would have to take her phone away with them and maybe they would be able to trace the sender of the messages. Good idea, thought Susan. That had not occurred to her. They wanted a full description of the *locket* and details of the moped riders.
"Thank you very much, you have been very helpful. You were very lucky that no-one else was hurt," they said. "In future, don't *take* such *risks* and *contact* the police straightaway."

ÜBUNG 58

Übung 58: Lies weiter und finde für jedes der Wörter in Klammern das passende Reimwort!

Susan agreed and promised that she would not (1. cry) ____________ to act without telling her parents next time. She hoped that there would never (2. tree) ____________ a next time! She did not want to go through such a *nightmare* ever again!
Once they (3. mad) ____________ finished interviewing Susan, the police *constables* visited the homes of all the (4. mother) ____________ teenagers, too. They were very serious in their *investigation* and (5. look) ____________ notes of everything that the five friends (6. hold) ____________ them. They also asked the parents questions, but of course they (7. hit) ____________ not know anything of what had happened and had been *left in the dark*.

Eventually when they had left, Susan caught the bus to the *local* hospital to visit Tracey.
When she arrived, Tracey was sitting up in bed reading a magazine.
"I'm bored!" she said. "When can I get out of here? The nurses are nice, but there's nothing to do really. And you can't even use your phone!"

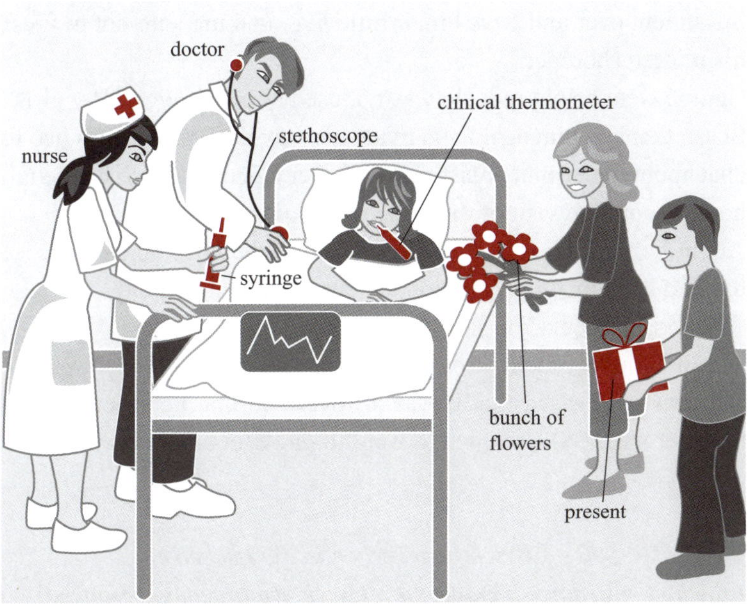

"Heather sends her love," said Susan. "She is sorry she is not able to come in today, but I think she is *still* in shock. Her mum rang me. She said Heather was sick in the night and has to stay in bed, poor thing."
After a while Susan felt that Tracey was obviously much better, so she went next door to visit George.
George looked up when Susan entered his room. What a pretty girl

she was! He could see now why Arthur was so *keen* on her.
Susan walked up to the side of his bed.
"Thank you for what you did!" she said, looking him straight in the eyes. "You were really brave yesterday. How can I ever repay you?"
"Oh, it was nothing," he answered with a big smile. "That's what friends are for. Arthur told me you were in trouble and I was only too glad to help."
Susan lent over and *gave* him *a* little *hug*, making sure not to press his injured shoulder.
George went bright red. He was not used to being *hugged* by girls.
Susan thanked him again and made her way back to Tracey's bed to chat about the events of last night all over again. She also had to tell her all about the visit of the police *constables*.
About half an hour later Arthur arrived at the hospital as well. He too had been given permission to stay off school that day.
"*Due to* the shock," he said and laughed.
"Thank you so much!" Susan said and *gave* Arthur *a* big *hug*, too. She was so pleased that it was all over and that her friends were together again. She seemed to want to *hug* everyone today.

! ÜBUNG 59

Übung 59: Setze die richtigen Verben in die Lücken ein!
(blushed, murmured, made, stay, check, wounded, go, enjoyed)

Arthur (1.) ______________, but secretly he (2.) ______________ being *hugged* by Susan. He hoped this would not be the last time either.
After a short time Arthur announced that he would (3.) ______________ next door to (4.) ______________ on George.
"I'm sure he's getting lonely!" he (5.) ______________. Really he

would rather have stayed with Susan, but he knew that it was more important to (6.) ______________ loyal to his friend. After all, he had been (7.) ______________ in action!

Later in the day the doctors (8.) ______________ their rounds and said that both Tracey and George could be *dismissed*.

The next day when they returned to school their *classmates* were *suspicious*. Why had they missed school, they all wanted to know? And why were all five off sick? And what had happened to Tracey, why was she wearing a *plaster* on her head? They had decided to say that Tracey had been involved in a bicycle accident and George in a *fight*. (Well, that was true anyway!)

Übung 60: Unterstreiche im folgenden Textabschnitt die Gegenteile der Wörter in Klammern!
(1. earlier, 2. started, 3. up, 4. bad, 5. short, 6. whispered)

ÜBUNG 60 !

Later that day Susan had invited her friends to have dinner with her at her house. Suddenly the doorbell rang and they all stopped talking.
Susan's mum led in two policemen and invited them to sit down.
"Well," they said. "We have some good news. We found the *locket* when we searched Giles' bedroom. We had to apply for a *search warrant*, that is why it took so long. We have *recovered* the cash as well."
"Giles! My ex-boyfriend!" shouted Susan angrily. "That can't be true! He was the one behind this after all? We thought it could not possibly be him!"

The policemen explained how Giles had been working together with a band of thieves. He was not the *ringleader*, but he had led them to Susan and told them about the *locket*. On the day of the hockey match two of the gang had been standing by the *pitch* in the *crowd*. The other two had gone into the *changing room* unnoticed and stolen the *locket*. Apparently Giles had persuaded Beverly to help them. He knew she hated Susan and he had promised her a share of the money as well. Beverly had showed the *guys* where Susan's clothes were hanging and made sure no-one saw them steal the *locket*. She also then helped sending the text messages. The police had traced the messages to her phone and she had *confessed* everything when they questioned her.

"So she was involved as well!" said Susan triumphantly.

"And here is your *locket*!" said the policeman.

He hung the *locket* around Susan's neck and Susan held it *tight*. She would not let it out of her sight for a long time. She turned to see her friends standing around her: Heather, Tracey, George and Arthur. She went to each of them and *gave* them *a* big *hug*, but Arthur got the longest one. In her joy she even gave him a kiss as well.

"Wow!" he smiled. "Well, that definitely makes my day!"

George turned to Heather, put his arm around her and said, "Mine too!"

"*What about* me?" asked Tracey and they all joined together in a big group hug. All their problems had now been solved and they were one happy band of five!

THE END

Abschlusstest

Übung 1: Wähle das passende Wort für jeden Satz aus und unterstreiche es!

1. She went/waited through the crowd.
2. I become/get my pocket money tomorrow.
3. Where/Were is he now?
4. Are/Our car is muddy.
5. There/Their she is at last.
6. Arthur is sweat/sweet on Susan.

Übung 2: Setze die Verben ins Simple Past!

1. She (ring) ______________ her mother.
2. We (bring) ______________ the money.
3. I (twist) ______________ him round my little finger.
4. They (sleep) ______________ very badly.
5. We (catch) ______________ the ball every time.
6. You (ride) ______________ your bike to the park.

Übung 3: Welches Wort ist das „schwarze Schaf"?

1. goalkeeper, referee, player, ball
2. ambush, blackmail, paramedic, theft
3. trap, limp, crawl, tiptoe

4. talk, speak, hear, mumble
5. sun, fall, rain, snow
6. locket, look, spot, see

Übung 4: Ordne die Buchstaben zu einem sinnvollen Wort!

1. Tracey (diel) ______________ to her father.

2. The shopping centre was full of (sposh) ______________.

3. (samth) ______________ is my favourite subject.

4. Her father (nosred) ______________ loudly every night.

5. She (sturb) ______________ into tears.

6. She ate in the school (teenanc) ______________________.

7. A school jacket is called a (rablze) ______________________.

Übung 5: Setze die richtigen Präpositionen ein!

1. We are meeting _______ the park.

2. She was the captain _______ the hockey team.

3. She was determined _______ score.

4. I had forgotten _______ the pain.

5. He had fancied her _______ a long time.

6. What is _______ telly?

7. She stared _______ the ceiling.

Übung 6: Ergänze die Begriffe!

1. If you have no money, you are _ r _ k _.

2. A _ o _ st _ _ l _ is a policeman.

3. You hang your clothes in a w _ r _ r _ b _.

4. A p _ u _ h is a kind of bag.

5. Part of a helmet is a _ i _ o _.

Übung 7: Finde für jedes Wort in Klammern das passende Reimwort!

1. He (look) ________________ the locket.

2. Her mother always (books) ________________ the breakfast.

3. He (kid) ________________ in the bushes.

4. (Man) ________________ you get the money?

5. She didn't know his (came) ________________.

6. (Think) ________________ your coke.

7. (Bell) ________________ done!

Übung 8: Sind die folgenden Aussagen wahr?
Markiere mit richtig ✔ oder falsch – !

1. Tracey thought Heather was a witch. ☐
2. Susan was a substitute at the hockey game. ☐

3. Giles was Susan's ex-boyfriend. ☐
4. You can have bath in your bed. ☐
5. Ambulances have stretchers in them. ☐
6. Susan met her friends in the park. ☐

Übung 9: Welche Wörter gehören in die Lücken?
(savings, park, escalators, mind, goal)

1. She scored a ________________.

2. ________________ are quicker than stairs.

3. Put the money in your ________________ book.

4. The swings are in the ________________.

5. I have changed my ________________.

Übung 10: Schreibe die Wörter in Großbuchstaben um!

1. Change a letter in RAIN to make something that hurts: __________
2. Add a letter to SORE to get a goal: ________________
3. Change a letter in MOVE to mean a larger amount: ____________
4. Take a letter away from FAST to mean not thin: ________________
5. Add a letter to CARE to mean frighten: ________________
6. Take a letter away from HEAR to make a possessive pronoun: ________________
7. Add a letter to SAD to mean spoken: ________________
8. Change a letter in FOOL to make a part of the body: ____________

Übung 11: Wie lauten die Wörter in der richtigen Reihenfolge? Bilde sinnvolle Sätze!

1. too stretched Susan had far and her torn out a leg muscle

2. cheeks down streaming tears the now Susan's were

3. savings out and she her desk took her opened book

4. a blank stared on with his Susan expression Arthur face at

5. band had working Giles with been a of thieves together

Schüler-Lernkrimi
Englisch

COLD REVENGE

Laura Montgomery

Inhalt

Story

Sarah, Justin, Kevin, Simon und Julia sind begeistert: Ihr Lieblingslehrer Mr Sharp wählt sie als Musiker für eine neue Band aus und sie werden an einem Bandwettbewerb teilnehmen! Der Spaß beim Komponieren des ersten eigenen Songs und bei den Proben schweißt die "Sneakers" zusammen.
Allerdings stehen ihnen unerwartete Komplikationen bevor: Ihr Song für den Wettbewerb muss brandneu sein – daher verpflichten sich die Bandmitglieder zu strengem Stillschweigen. Als ihr Lied "Secret" jedoch im Internet auftaucht und als Raubkopie in der Schule kursiert, ist die Aufregung groß – ihre Teilnahme am Bandwettbewerb ist gefährdet!
Wer hat eine der CDs mit dem geheimen Song geklaut und warum will der Täter den "Sneakers" schaden? Verdächtige gibt es jede Menge. Viele Mitschüler sind neidisch, weil sie selbst nicht für die Band ausgewählt wurden. Andere sind enttäuscht – Sarahs beste Freudin Karen ist sauer, weil Sarah ihre Zeit nur noch mit der Band verbringt. Auch Al, ein guter Freund von Mr Sharp, den sie bei den Aufnahmen im Tonstudio kennen gelernt haben, ist verdächtig: Er scheint sich allzu geschäftstüchtig um die Zukunft der Band zu kümmern ... Ob es den Sneakers bei ihren Nachforschungen gelingt, den Täter zu stellen und ihren Traum vom berühmten Song zu verwirklichen?

Chapter 1: The Band Competition

"Rrrrring!"

Simon jumped when he heard the school bell ring. The loud sound woke him up from a daydream he had been enjoying. Simon had been imagining himself on the stage at a rock concert. In his thoughts hundreds of people were watching him play his guitar. His girlfriend was standing in the first row and smiling at him. He was in the middle of his fantastic guitar solo when the bell brought him back to reality.

In that reality Simon was not a rock star. He was just a teenage school pupil who liked playing the guitar in his free time. And although he was one of the best-looking boys in school, he didn't really have a girlfriend. Instead, the reality was that Simon was late for music class.

"Oh no," he said to himself. "Another boring hour with Mrs Snood."

Suddenly he heard the voice of his best friend, Kevin, call to him, "Hey Simon! You're late!" Kevin was running past Simon to the front door of the school.

"I'm late?" Simon answered, as he followed his friend into the building. "You're late too! Old Mrs Snood is going to scream at both of us."

Übung 1: In diesem Textabschnitt sind die Adverbien durcheinander gekommen. Finde heraus, wohin die Adverbien tatsächlich gehören!

The two boys hurried and went (1. slowly) __________ up the stairs and down the corridor to room 363, where Mrs Snood was probably waiting with an angry look on her face. (2. immediately) ______________ and (3. quickly) ______________ they opened the door of the classroom, hoping that no one would see them walk in. But when they looked at the front of the classroom, they realized that they had been worried for no reason.

Mrs Snood wasn't there. In fact, there was no teacher there at all.

"Simon! Kevin! Come to the front of the room (4. loudly) ______________. You're both in very serious trouble!"

The two boys saw Sarah, one of their *classmates*, standing on Mrs Snood's desk. She was imitating their teacher's voice, speaking (5. quietly) ______________. Sarah's head, which was covered with short, bright pink hair, *shook* from side to side as she *pretended* to be very angry with the two late pupils.

"What? *What the heck* is going on here?!" said Kevin.

"It's great, *guys*," Sarah said. "You won't believe it. Mrs Snood is moving to Australia! She's never coming back. We're free!" She pulled a piece of *fabric* out of her pocket that had the symbol for anarchy on it. She held it above her head. Then she jumped off the desk and started running around the room.

"That girl has too much energy," Simon said to Kevin. "I don't …"

Suddenly the classroom door opened behind Simon. He turned around and saw the headmaster's small, black eyes looking at him angrily. Sarah stopped running. All the pupils went to their desks.

"All right, everyone, the party's over," Headmaster Jones said.

Übung 2: Setze die Verben ins Simple Past!

"I guess someone (1. to tell) ______________ you that Mrs Snood has decided to move to Australia to help her sister, who is ill," the headmaster (2. to say) ______________.

"Hooray," Sarah said quietly.

"I (3. to hear) ______________ that. Anyway, we're all very lucky because Mr Sharp has agreed to teach your music class for the rest of the year."

"Mr Sharp – who's that?" (4. to ask) ______________ Simon.

Headmaster Jones (5. to step) ______________ away from the door. Behind him stood a tall young man wearing jeans and a black jumper. His straight black hair, which normally (6. to come) ______________ down to his shoulders, was pulled back into a *ponytail*. He (7. to smile) ______________ at the teenagers in the room.

"This is Mr Sharp's first teaching job, so be nice," Headmaster Jones said. Then he looked at Mr Sharp and added, "They're all yours."

He walked out of the room and closed the door. Mr Sharp went to the front of the classroom. He looked at the pupils for a few seconds and said, "So, *what's up*?"

Before anyone could answer, the door opened again and a pretty blonde girl wearing a flowery dress *burst* into the room and started talking quickly.

"Mrs Snood, I've got a note from my mum that says I was … Wait. Where's Mrs Snood?" she asked. "And who's the *cute guy*? He's really *fit*."

"Janet," *whispered* Simon, "that '*cute guy*' is our new teacher, Mr Sharp. Now you'd better sit down and be quiet before he *punishes* us all."

"Oh, he wouldn't *punish* us – would you, Mr Sharp? You seem like you're too cool for the rules," said Janet.

"Well, there are some rules that you have to take very seriously," Mr Sharp said. The pupils *frowned*. "But," he added, "there are some rules that were made to be broken."

"*Damn*, this *guy* really is cool," Kevin said.

"Well … what's your name?"

"Kevin."

"Well, Kevin, I'm not so cool that I'll let you use words like that in my classroom. But I think you'll find that I'm much more *laid-back* than old Mrs Snood."

The pupils laughed. They spent the next thirty minutes telling Mr Sharp their names and talking about what they'd been doing in class for the past few months. They explained that each of the pupils played a different instrument. But *recently* Mrs Snood had been teaching them about classical music.

ÜBUNG 3 !

Übung 3: Übersetze die musikalischen Instrumente und enträtsele das Lösungswort!

1. Trompete _ _ _ _ ☐ _ _
2. Gitarre _ _ ☐ _ _ _

3. Saxophon _ ☐ _ _ _ _ _ _ _
4. Geige _ _ _ _ _ ☐
5. Orgel ☐ _ _ _ _

Lösung: _ _ _ _ _

“How boring!” said Sarah. “I kept waiting for the day when she’d stop talking about that stupid *stuff* and start talking about real music. You know, good *stuff* like punk and ska.”
“Yeah, but it could have been worse,” said Kevin. “Old Snood could have made us listen to jazz music.”
“Hey! Don’t say anything bad about jazz. Jazz is great. You’re just too *dumb* to understand it.”
Most of the pupils were surprised to hear the voice of Julia, a sweet but *shy* girl who didn’t talk much. Usually she sat low in her chair, silently looking at everyone through her glasses. But now she sat up straight and looked at Simon with a strong, angry expression on her face.
Julia played the saxophone and was a huge fan of jazz music.
“Just because you can sing and play a few simple songs on your silly guitar, you think you know everything about music,” Julia said to Simon.
Simon’s face turned red and he said nothing. Although everyone at school liked him, he was actually quite *insecure*. Yes, he was very good at sports and girls often flirted with him. But Simon often worried that he wasn’t very good at making the thing that was most important to him – music.
“Julia has a point,” said Mr Sharp. “No kind of music is better than the other. They’re just different. That’s why someone like Sarah might like punk, Julia might like jazz, or – Kevin, what kind of music do you like the most?”

ÜBUNG 4 !

Übung 4: Vervollständige die Sätze mit ***a, an*** *oder* ***the****!*

1. The instrument Simon plays is ______ guitar.

2. Would you like to hear ______ interesting song?

3. That's ______ best song I've ever heard!

4. Could you say that ______ bit slower, please?

5. Kevin is ______ very nice person.

6. I've been waiting here for ______ hour.

Kevin answered, "Oh, I like anything I can listen to while I'm skateboarding. Anything fast with a *wicked* bass, because I play the bass, and I …"

"I'm a singer," Janet *interrupted*. "I sing pop songs. That's my real talent. Mrs Snood always wanted me to play the *tambourine*, but the *tambourine* is the instrument that *backing singers* play. I was born to be a solo singing star!"

"That's good to know, Janet," Mr Sharp said with a smile. The school bell rang and the pupils began collecting their things. "Be ready to talk about classical music again in our next lesson, everyone!"

Simon said, "Oh, come on, Mr Sharp! You said you were going to be more fun than stupid old Mrs Snood!"

"Simon," he answered, "you can become a great musician only if you understand the masters who have come before you. But I promise that we'll have a lot of fun in other ways. See you on Thursday, everyone!"

Two days later, the pupils returned to room 363 for their second music lesson with their new teacher. Although they talked about

classical music during the 45-minute lesson, the pupils had a great time and laughed a lot. Somehow the subject seemed much more interesting when Mr Sharp talked about it.
"Have a good weekend," Mr Sharp said at the end of the lesson. "And don't forget – I'm going to have a nice surprise for you next week. Bye!"
As Simon walked out of the classroom, he *whispered* to Sarah, "I wonder what it will be!"
"*Chill out*, Simon," she said. "We'll find out soon enough."

On Tuesday morning the kids found out what Mr Sharp's surprise was. When they arrived at the entrance to their classroom they saw a big sign on the door:

WANTED:
Five *brilliant* musicians to form
the coolest band in the school!
Lots of hard work –
but you could become famous!
***Auditions* will be in room 363 this afternoon at 4.00 pm.**
Only the best five will be chosen.

Übung 5: Schreibe die Uhrzeiten in Zahlen!

ÜBUNG 5 !

1. quarter past ten in the morning — *10.15 am*
2. five minutes to nine in the afternoon ______
3. three twenty-seven in the afternoon ______
4. ten past eleven in the morning ______

5. noon ....

6. half past one in the afternoon ....

7. eight forty-three in the morning ....

"You want the best? Here I am," said Janet.
Sarah's nose piercing sparkled as she shouted, "Wow! I'll finally get a chance to show what a great drummer I am! Everyone *protect* your ears – it's going to get loud!"
Julia had a huge smile on her face but said nothing.
The kids ran into the classroom and formed a circle around Mr Sharp. Everyone shouted and asked questions at the same time.
"Which instruments will be in the band?"
"When will the band have *rehearsals*?"
"Are *auditions* only for the people in this class?"
"How will we become famous?"
Mr Sharp told the pupils to be quiet and then said, "The *auditions* are open to anyone in the school. Of course we'll need a guitarist and drummer, but the other instruments will depend on who the best musicians are. *Rehearsals* will be after school, because this is a special, extra project." He continued talking and explained that he wanted to form the band because there was a national teen band *competition*. Bands from around the country were invited to write a song, *record* it, and send it in for the *competition*. The band with the best song would win £5,000 and a chance to get a *recording contract* with a famous English record company.
"*I'm gonna be* a rock star, I just know it!" said Kevin.
"That's fantastic; that's my greatest dream," said Simon. "I would love to be in a recording studio, playing my guitar – and maybe even singing."
"We could sing a duet together, Simon," said Janet, flirting with

him. "Wouldn't that be romantic? You could come to my house and we could *rehearse* in my room."
Simon's face turned red. He knew that Janet liked him. But he had never felt attracted to her. He thought she needed too much *attention*. He wanted a girl who was happy with the way she was. But he said nothing, because he didn't want to hurt Janet's feelings.

Übung 6: In diesem Gitternetz sind fünf Farben versteckt. Findest du sie alle?

T	E	N	G	I	W
A	S	G	R	E	H
B	L	U	E	Z	I
M	O	R	E	D	T
O	R	A	N	G	E

Later that afternoon around 25 pupils from the school went to the band *auditions*. Each pupil had to go into room 363 alone and play a song for Mr Sharp. Some kids brought their own instruments. Others used the instruments in the music classroom.
While waiting for her chance to play a song on her saxophone, Julia saw a boy named Justin walk out of the *audition* room. She was surprised. Everyone at school knew that Justin was a computer *genius* – but no one had known that he was interested in music too.
"Hey, Justin," Julia said. "I thought you spent all your time playing with your computer and writing computer programs that do your homework for you. What instrument do you play?"

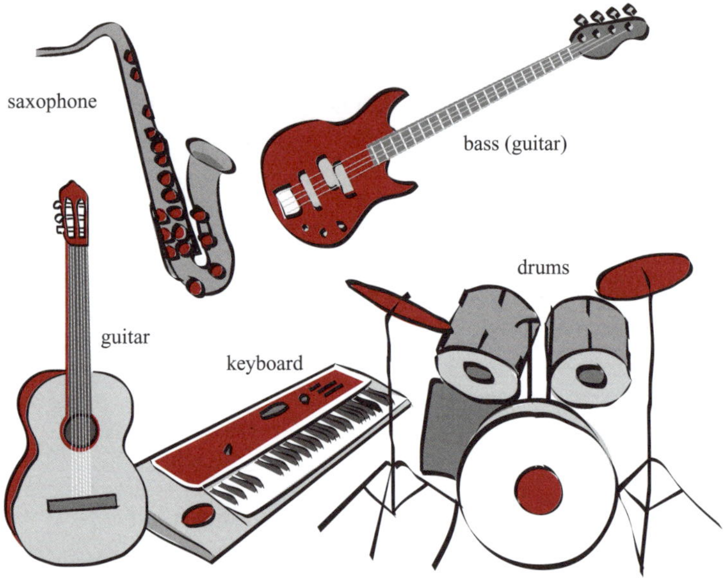

Justin answered, "Well, a computer *keyboard* isn't the only keyboard I like to play with. I've been taking piano lessons since I was four years old. So I decided to *audition* by playing the electric keyboard."

"Oh," Julia said, "so there's a secret side of Justin, is there?"

"I think we all have our own secret side – even you, Julia," Justin said. "Well, I have to go. Good luck!"

As Justin walked away Julia heard Mr Sharp call her name. She picked up her saxophone, took a deep breath, and walked into room 363 for her *audition*.

Two days later a small piece of paper hung on the door to Mr Sharp's classroom. On it was written: "Thank you to everyone who took part in the *auditions* on Tuesday. This school is filled with musical talent, and the final decision was very difficult." After that were listed five names:

Guitar and *vocals*: Simon Smith
Drums: Sarah Patton
Bass: Kevin Jones
Saxophone and *vocals*: Julia Monaghan
Keyboard: Justin Roe

The pupils formed a *crowd* around the door.
"Yes!" screamed Sarah. "I'm the drummer! I was so worried because my ex-boyfriend was at the *auditions* too. He's the person who taught me how to play the drums. But he's a perfect idiot about everything else. He'll be so angry that Mr Sharp chose me." She smiled.

Übung 7: Welches Wort ist das „schwarze Schaf"? Unterstreiche das nicht in die Reihe passende Wort!

1. table, chair, desk, room
2. piano, music, flute, violin
3. teacher, pupil, class, headmaster
4. big, huge, tall, thin
5. corridor, kitchen, bedroom, radio
6. lesson, hour, minute, second
7. sick, ill, flu, unwell
8. angry, mad, glad, annoyed

"I can't believe he chose me for *vocals*," said Simon.
"I can believe he chose you," Kevin said. "But I can't believe that he

wants Julia, the quietest girl in school, to sing." He *pointed to* Julia using the skateboard he was holding in his hands.

Simon said, "I heard Julia through the door when she *auditioned*. She's got a fantastic voice. You'll be surprised. And she's a great sax player too. I mean, I'm not a fan of jazz, but she really seems to know what she's doing."

Janet had been standing at the back of the *crowd*, smiling. She had simply *assumed* that Mr Sharp had chosen her to be the band's lead singer. But now that she heard Simon and Kevin talking, she pushed her way to the front of the *crowd* to see the list on the door.

"Wha... What? WHAT?! There must have been a mistake. Where is my name? I can't believe that! The list is supposed to say 'Lead *vocals*: Janet Starr'. Where's Mr Sharp? I want an explanation!" she screamed.

"I can give you an explanation," Sarah said sarcastically. "Your voice stinks, *darling*. I heard you sing a version of some pop song for your *audition*. But I didn't even know what song it was, because you were so terrible."

Janet ran towards Sarah, "Take that back! I was born to be a star!" She stopped and turned towards the others. "But instead, stupid Julia and that computer *geek*, Justin, stole my place. *What about* our beautiful duet, Simon?"

Simon looked at the floor and said nothing.

"I understand now, Simon! You're one of the singers. You're probably happy that you get to sing and I don't!"

Janet *shook* her blonde hair dramatically and covered her face with her hands. Suddenly she pulled her hands away and ran down the corridor. The other pupils in the *crowd*, the ones who hadn't been chosen to be in the band, started walking away too. A boy and a girl stood in front of the door for a few more moments. They both looked very shocked and sad. But finally they left too.

Übung 8: Setze das richtige Fragewort ein!

ÜBUNG 8 !

1. ________________ are you doing this afternoon?
2. ________________ do you enjoy more – swimming or running?
3. ________________ does the film start? I don't want to be late!
4. ________________ is she? I've never met her before.
5. ________________ big is your family's new house?

Chapter 2: Choosing a Band Name!

Soon Simon, Kevin, Sarah, Julia and Justin were alone. Kevin was standing in front of the door to room 363 and he jumped when he heard a noise behind him. He turned around and saw Mr Sharp's left eye looking at him through a small opening in the door.

"Is the storm finished yet?" Mr Sharp asked. He opened the door wider. "I wanted to wait until all the other pupils left. I didn't want to *embarrass* the rest of you." He opened the door completely and took a step backwards. "Come inside. We have a lot to talk about."

The five chosen teenagers walked into the room and Mr Sharp closed the door behind him. "Starting now," he said, "everything that we talk about in this room is *top secret*. Of course, not the things we talk about during our regular music lessons. I mean anything that we talk about in the afternoons after school – during our band meetings and *rehearsals*. Do you understand?"

Everyone nodded. But then Simon looked at Sarah and said, "Hey, did you hear that, *big mouth*? Secret. Do you really understand what that means?"

"*Shut up*, Si-monster," Sarah said. "I might be loud, but that doesn't mean that I can't keep my mouth shut about things that are really important."

Mr Sharp continued. "There's a reason for making everything such a big secret."

Although they knew that the other pupils in the school had already gone home, Justin, Sarah, Simon, Kevin and Julia moved closer to Mr Sharp. Their teacher also started speaking more quietly.

"As I explained a few days ago there's a national teen band *competition*. It's being organized by a famous English record company. They're looking for the best new, young band in England. To take part in the *competition*, each band has to write an original song. So we can't simply play our own version of a song that someone else wrote. But there's a special rule that every band has to follow. The song for the *competition* has to be brand new. That means the song can't be *released* before the *competition*. The people at the record company want to be sure that they have exclusive rights to the song. That's why I think we should keep everything a secret. I think you *guys* are really talented. And I don't want anything to destroy your chances of success."

ÜBUNG 9 !

Übung 9: Welche der Übersetzungen stimmt? Kreuze die richtige Lösung an!

1. Es gibt bestimmte Regeln.
   a) ☐ There are certain rules.
   b) ☐ It gives certain rules.

2. Die Band hat eine Chance bekommen.
   a) ☐ The band got a chance.
   b) ☐ The band became a chance.

3. Sie will am Wettbewerb teilnehmen.
   a) ☐ She will take part in the competition.
   b) ☐ She wants to take part in the competition.

4. Sie sind sehr an Musik interessiert.
   a) ☐ They are very interesting in music.
   b) ☐ They are very interested in music.

5. Justin spielt seit 12 Jahren Klavier.
   a) ☐ Justin has played the piano since 12 years.
   b) ☐ Justin has played the piano for 12 years.

"I agree," said Kevin. "I don't want anything to come between me and five thousand pounds!"
"You mean one thousand pounds," said Justin. "If we win, we each get part of the prize money."
"Okay," Mr Sharp said. "Now that you all understand what's happening, I'll leave the five of you alone for a while."
"Why?" asked Julia. "Do we have to start writing the song now?"
Mr Sharp answered, "No, Julia, not yet. But you do have to do something almost as important. You have to choose a band name! Good luck! I'll see you all tomorrow." He walked out.
As soon as Mr Sharp closed the door, Simon said, "Let's try to do this quickly."
"Yeah, I have to meet some friends in the park to go skateboarding," said Kevin.
"And I have to meet my best friend, Karen. We're going to a punk concert this evening," Sarah said. "I think we should call ourselves The Anarchists!"
Justin said, "But I'm not an anarchist. I always follow the rules."
"You're so boring, Justin!" Sarah said.

"I am not! I think The *Fabulous* Five sounds better," Justin said.
"I like the name The Winners," said Simon. He looked around at the others to see if they agreed. "With a name like that, there's no way we can lose the *competition*!"
"The Winners? You loser. That's a stupid name," Sarah laughed.
They were quiet for a while and tried to think of a good name. Kevin *scratched* his head. Sarah bit her fingernails.

ÜBUNG 10

Übung 10: Beantworte die Fragen zum Text!

1. What subject does Mr Sharp teach?

____

2. What instrument does Kevin play?

____

3. How much money could the band win?

____

4. What kind of music does Julia like?

____

5. What band name does Justin like?

____

"I have an idea," said Julia. "Mr Sharp said we have to keep this project a secret. So why don't we call ourselves The Sneakers?"
"That sounds cool," said Justin. "It combines the verb *'to sneak'* and the American word for *trainers – sneakers*."
"Yeah, cool," said Simon.

Kevin and Sarah agreed too. The five teenagers picked up their rucksacks and walked out of the classroom. When they reached the front door, Sarah said to the others, “See you tomorrow, Sneakers!”

“Careful – don’t say that so loud!” Justin said. “Everthing about our band is supposed to be a secret, remember?”

The Sneakers said goodbye to each other and walked away in different directions.

The next day Justin arrived at school very early in the morning. Mr Sharp found him waiting in front of the door to his classroom. There were no other pupils in the school yet. Justin seemed a bit nervous.

“Good morning, Justin,” Mr Sharp said. “Is something wrong? You seem to be worried about something.”

“Well, Mr Sharp,” Justin answered, “I wanted to know if you might be able to do something for me.”

“What is it?”

“You see, I would like to know if I could transfer into your music class. I mean, everyone else in the band is in the class, and I don’t want to miss anything just because I’m not there. I know our *rehearsals* are after school. But I’m worried that I will be left out if I’m not in the class too.”

Mr Sharp thought for a moment. “I understand how you feel, Justin. But the school year started three weeks ago. Would your other teacher allow you to just stop coming to her class because you wanted to join mine?”

Justin answered, “I don’t think it would be a problem. I have my computer programming lesson at the same time as your music lesson. But the computer class is too easy for me. I’ve taught myself a lot about computers at home. Learning about computers is one of my favourite hobbies. So I think my teacher would understand if I told her that I wanted to transfer to a different class.”

Übung 11: Ordne den passenden zweiten Teil jedes Wortes zu! Trage die richtige Nummer in das Kästchen ein!

1. girl-	☐ -one
2. class-	☐ -end
3. head-	☐ -friend
4. week-	☐ -board
5. skate-	☐ -room
6. some-	☐ -nail
7. finger-	☐ -master

Mr Sharp looked at Justin carefully. "Well, if your computer teacher says it's okay, then it's okay with me too."

Justin held his *fist* up in the air and shouted, "Yes!" Then he realized how excited he was and said in a quieter voice, "I mean, thanks, Mr Sharp. This means a lot to me." At that moment the school bell rang. Justin said goodbye and walked away.

In the corridor he saw his friend, Joe. Joe had *auditioned* to be in the band too. He had wanted to be the band's guitarist.

"I'm glad you got chosen to be in the band, Justin," Joe said. "But tell me – why did Mr Sharp want to make the band? "

Justin smiled and said, "Well, we're not really sure yet."

"Come on, you can tell me," Joe said. But Justin was quiet. "Fine. I understand. You can't tell your old friend Joe your big secret. Fine. See you later." He walked away.

After school that day the five members of The Sneakers met in room 363 for their first band *rehearsal*. Mr Sharp was waiting for them.

"Hi everyone. You're all probably very excited about playing music and working on our song."

"You know I am," said Sarah with a lot of enthusiasm. "Where are my drums? I'm ready to rock!"

Kevin added, “Me too. I have some great ideas for the song.”
Mr Sharp *interrupted*, “I’m happy to hear that. But before you start *rehearsing*, I think you *guys* should do some *research*.”
“What do you mean?” asked Justin.
“I think you should go to the music shop on Wood Street,” said Mr Sharp. “*Check out* some of the CDs they’ve got there. Experiment. Try listening to music you don’t normally listen to. For example, Julia could show Sarah some of her favourite jazz albums. Simon, you could help Justin listen to some good rock ‘n’ roll music. And Sarah, you could introduce Kevin to the world of punk rock. What do you think?”
Simon said, “I would prefer playing my guitar. But shopping for CDs is fun too. Let’s go, *guys*. See you later, Mr Sharp.”

Übung 12: Schreibe die Wörter in Großbuchstaben um!

! ÜBUNG 12

1. Change a letter in PEG to make a word for a body part. ______
2. Change a letter in SHOE to make a word for a place where you buy things. ______
3. Change a letter in WOOL to make a word for what a tree is made of. ______
4. Change a letter in THING to make a word for what you do to find an answer. ______
5. Change a letter in SELL to make a word for something that rings. ______
6. Change a letter in ROSE to make a word for a part of your face. ______

The pupils left the school and started walking down the street in the direction of Wood Street. Kevin jumped onto his skateboard and did some tricks on the *pavement* as the group walked. His *shaggy* brown hair hung in front of his eyes and the others wondered how he could see what he was doing. It was a beautiful, sunny afternoon. No one said much as they walked.

When the group walked into Music 4 U, the music shop on Wood Street, the *guy* who worked there looked up from his computer and looked at them. He was two or three years older than they were. He had black hair and very white skin and wore a long leather jacket, although it was quite warm inside the shop. He was wearing a big pair of *headphones*, but took them off when the five teenagers entered the shop. They could hear loud heavy metal music coming from the *headphones*.

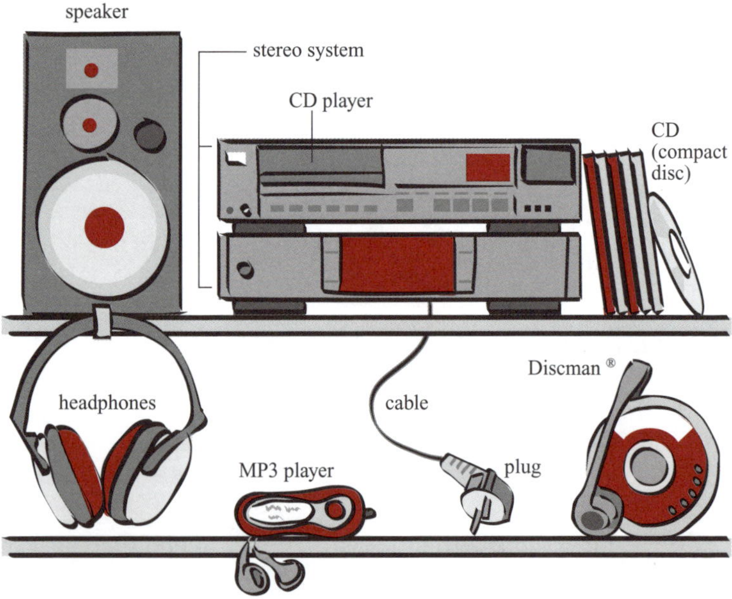

"Can I help you?" he asked them.
"No, thanks. We just want to look around for a while," said Simon.
Justin took an album from the punk section. Kevin chose a jazz CD. Julia asked Sarah which punk album she should listen to. Simon took a CD from the surf rock section, which Kevin had *recommended*. Finally, Sarah had to choose an album.
"What should I buy? There aren't any types of music left," she said.
"I could *recommend* something," said Justin.
"Oh, no," Sarah said. "I don't want to listen to classical piano music. No one can make me believe that that is good, fun music."
"Well, I really wanted to tell you about a great hip-hop group I like," Justin said.
"Did you just say hip-hop?" said Kevin. "A computer *freak* who likes hip-hop? I can't believe it. This is a big surprise."
"You shouldn't be surprised," said Justin. "There are a lot of things about me you don't know. I have a lot of different interests." He smiled. After looking around for a few more minutes, the *youngsters* went to the front of the store to pay for their CDs.
"This is a lot of music," said the *guy* working there, in his strange, deep voice. "Are you all in a band or something?"
The band members looked at each other nervously. Mr Sharp had told them to keep information about the band a secret.
"We're … um … just interested in music," Simon said. They quickly paid and left the shop.
During the weekend each of the band members listened to their new music. Simon played his guitar for a while and thought about what The Sneakers' song should be about. Sarah made her parents crazy by playing her drums all weekend long. Julia spent her weekend doing the same thing she usually did. She played her saxophone, read books, and wrote some *poetry*. Kevin played his bass at home and tried to add some jazz sounds to the things he played.

ÜBUNG 13 !

Übung 13: Vervollständige die Sätze mit ***their, there*** *oder* ***they're****!*

1. The teenagers like music. ______________ in a band!

2. ______________ are some really cool CDs here.

3. I want to go ______________ at the weekend.

4. They talked about ______________ favourite music styles.

Chapter 3: The First Rehearsal

On Tuesday afternoon The Sneakers had their first band *rehearsal*. After their school lessons were finished, Justin, Simon, Kevin, Julia and Sarah met in Mr Sharp's room.

"I hope you all enjoyed experimenting with different kinds of music over the weekend," said Mr Sharp. "I think that will help you understand each other better. And it should help you to work together."

"Yeah," said Kevin. "I'd like to show you all some ideas for a song that I was thinking about."

"I'd love to hear about it."

Mr Sharp and the pupils looked around the room, wondering who had spoken. They wanted to find out where that girl's voice had come from. Then they all saw a short girl with black hair standing at the door. She smiled and took a few steps into the room.

"What's she doing here?!" shouted Sarah. "You're not allowed in here. This is a private meeting."

"Be nice, Sarah," said Mr Sharp. Then he said to the girl, "Hi Susie. Can I help you with something?"

"Well," Susie said in a nice, sweet voice, "I think I left my pen in here during the *auditions*." She walked to the desk where Kevin was

sitting. She looked at Kevin and smiled sweetly. “Have you seen my pen, Kevin?”
Kevin’s eyes opened wide with surprise. Was Susie flirting with him? He had talked to her last week while they were waiting to *audition* for the band. She wanted to be the band’s keyboard player, but Mr Sharp didn’t choose her.
He smiled back at Susie and said, “Um … I … no. I mean, I don’t know where your pen is. But you can have one of mine, if you want to.” He reached down into his rucksack and tried to find a pen to give to her. He found one and stood up to give it to her.
Susie stepped close to Kevin and *whispered* into his ear, “Thanks, Kevin.” Kevin gave her a big, silly smile.

Übung 14: Finde die gesuchten Begriffe heraus und trage sie ins Kreuzworträtsel ein!

1. something loud that you hear
2. someone who learns in school
3. the thing in the sky that gives light
4. something you use to write
5. what you do when you’re happy

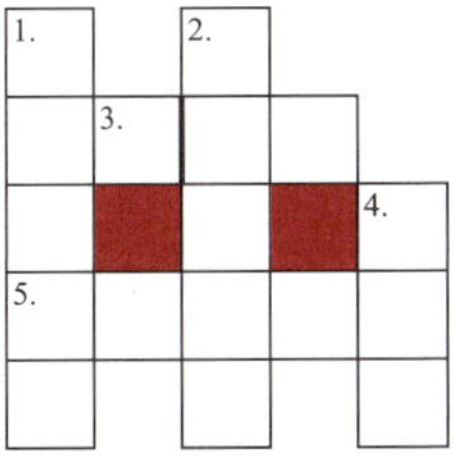

Justin *coughed*. “I don’t want to break up this lovely scene,” he said. “But we have a lot to do. I don’t want to be impolite, Susie, but that’s the way it is. So please leave now.”
Susie laughed, “Sorry. I’ll let you all return to your ‘private meeting’ – whatever that is.” She looked at Kevin again and then walked out of the room.
“What a *freak*,” Sarah said after Susie closed the door.

"Let's not worry about her," said Simon seriously. "We have a lot of work to do. Kevin, let's hear what you've done so far."
Kevin put his hands on his face. He could feel that his face was still warm – and probably red too. "Oh," he said, "maybe someone else wants to go first. Justin?"
Justin jumped up happily. He was glad that Kevin and the other band members were starting to accept him. "Sure," he said. "I've got something I'd like you all to hear." Justin opened his rucksack and pulled out a small laptop computer. He turned the computer on and started pressing *buttons* on the *keyboard*. He explained, "I have a program on my computer that lets me mix different songs together." Justin pressed another *button* and the room filled with music. Everyone listened to the sounds for several seconds. Sarah started hitting a desk with her hands, as though she were playing the drums. "I like it!" she said.
Soon the music stopped. "I didn't have time to do more," Justin said.
"That's really interesting, Justin," said Mr Sharp.
"It sounded a little too fast," Simon said. "I think our song should have more emotion. I can't sing something if it doesn't make me feel something."

ÜBUNG 15 !

Übung 15: In diesen Sätzen sind die Wörter durcheinander gekommen. Wie lauten die Sätze richtig? Trage sie mit Satzzeichen und richtiger Groß- und Kleinschreibung ein!

1. lot has Sarah energy a of

Sarah has a lot of energy.

2. this do song like you?

....

3. with likes computers playing Justin

4. secret everything a is why?

5. Janet not band is the in

"Don't be such a baby, Simon," said Sarah. Her voice sounded sarcastic. "The only thing I need to feel when I'm playing is energy!"
"I agree with Simon," said Julia. "People need to feel something emotional when they listen to a song. That's what makes music great." She picked up her saxophone and *licked* her lips. She *raised* the instrument to her mouth and started playing a beautiful, slow, sad song. Everyone else stood or sat quietly and listened to the music coming from Julia's sax. It seemed like she was putting all of her emotions into the song. Love and hate, happiness and sadness. Two minutes later she stopped playing.
"Wow," said Simon.
"That was fantastic," Justin agreed.
Mr Sharp stood up and walked to the front of the room. "This is a really exciting mix of styles and ideas. Let's try to bring some of them together. Get your instruments, everyone. Let's start writing a song!"
Two hours later Mr Sharp looked at his watch. It was getting late.
"All right, *guys*. I think that's enough for today," he said.
"But Mr Sharp," said Simon, "we were just getting started! There's still so much to do!"
"Don't worry, Simon," Mr Sharp's voice was friendly and understanding. "We still have a few more weeks to *rehearse*. And after

that we will have enough time to *record* the song too. Today was your first *rehearsal*. No band is perfect after only one *rehearsal*!" Simon smiled because he realized that Mr Sharp was right.

! ÜBUNG 16

Übung 16: Wähle das passende Wort für jeden Satz aus und unterstreiche es!

1. There were fewer/less people at the audition than they expected.
2. Sorry, I haven't got some/any money.
3. If they win the competition, they'll get a nice price/prize.
4. She wanted to tell/say him a secret.
5. I put on/wore my jacket before I left the house.
6. His father learned/taught him how to read.
7. I had to work until/for five o'clock.
8. Don't worry on/about her.

Julia was excited too. As she put her sax into its case, she thought about standing on a stage and playing in front of hundreds of people. But she was a bit nervous too. She didn't even know that she had a good singing voice till Mr Sharp chose her to be one of the band's singers. What would the others think?
As Sarah left room 363, she started biting her fingernails again. She did that whenever she was excited about something. She was filled with nervous energy. It was especially difficult for her to keep the band's work a secret. She had never been very good at keeping secrets. But she knew that she had to do the right thing. She wanted to become a famous rock star. So she decided at that moment to put all her energy into her drumming. People would find out the band's secret plans when they won the *competition*, Sarah thought. Till then, she would keep her mouth closed.

Übung 17: Bilde Sätze mit dem Komparativ!

1. village/town (small)

A village is smaller than a town.

2. car/bicycle (expensive)

3. ocean/lake (deep)

4. hip-hop music/classical music (cool)

5. tree/bush (tall)

Chapter 4: The Secret

Every day for the next two weeks, The Sneakers met in room 363 after school for *rehearsals*. They wrote the song *bit by bit*. Each of the band members had a chance to add something special and personal to the song. After the song was finished, they were all surprised by the crazy mix of musical styles it had. But the song was good! They knew it. And Mr Sharp thought so too.

"I have to say I was worried for a while at the beginning," Mr Sharp said at the beginning of the third week of *rehearsals*. "You all like different things, and I wasn't sure if you could combine them all in one song. But it's *mega*." He was quiet for a minute. Then he said, "But there's something missing."

"What?" asked Sarah. "This song rocks!"
"Yes, it does," said Mr Sharp. "But you still need to write the words for the song."
The pupils looked at each other. What should they sing about?
"I've been working on something," Julia said quietly. Everyone turned to look at her. "I write *poetry* sometimes. I think I have a poem that would fit with the music we've written."
"What's it called?" asked Justin.
"It's called 'Secret'. I was thinking about our band and about this secret project. Then I thought about how people react when they have to keep a special secret. So I wrote the poem about someone who tells a secret to other people. It's about friendship, *trust*, anger and *revenge*. But you might think it's silly," Julia said.
"Silly? Anything that's about *revenge* is cool," said Simon. "Let's hear it."
Julia read the poem. She almost sang it, using the melody from the song The Sneakers had written. When she finished, everyone *clapped*.

ÜBUNG 18 !

Übung 18: Unterstreiche die sechs Sätze, die inhaltlich nicht zum Text passen!

The Sneakers spent their third week of *rehearsals* adding Julia's text to the song. They jumped when the balloon exploded. The *rehearsals* were long. Kevin didn't have much time for skateboarding. Justin had to miss many of his piano lessons. But the five teenagers all believed that this project was more important than anything else. They were tired and stressed. Kevin loved to eat chicken and potatoes. But they knew they had to work hard till the song was perfect. It's nice when the weather is sunny.

After two more weeks of hard work, the song was ready. Not many people are on holiday. In only a month and a half the five teenagers had been changed from a group of normal pupils into a real band. And more than that, they had written a song that could win them £5,000. She works in a factory.

At the end of The Sneakers' last *rehearsal* on Friday afternoon, Mr Sharp asked the group, "Will you all have time to *record* the song tomorrow? We have to send in the song for the *competition* on Wednesday. I went to the cinema yesterday."

All the band members said yes.

"Then we'll meet tomorrow morning at 10 o'clock."

"Will we *record* the song here, in room 363?" asked Julia.

"No," Mr Sharp answered. "I've got a surprise for you all. We'll meet here in the morning. But then I'll take you to the place where we'll *record* the song."

Suddenly Simon turned around and looked at the door. "Did you hear that?" he asked. "I thought I heard a noise. I think someone is standing outside the classroom." No one said anything. Simon ran to the door and pulled it open. The corridor was empty.

"Stop worrying so much, Simon," Kevin said. "Just *chill out*. No one is listening to our conversations."

Übung 19: Ordne die Buchstaben zu einem sinnvollen Wort!

ÜBUNG 19 !

On Saturday morning the (1. twerahe) ____________ was sunny and nice. Kevin walked down the (2. resett) ____________ in a white T-shirt, a pair of baggy (3. jsena) ____________ and an old pair of blue *trainers*. He carried his skateboard in his right (4. dnha) ____________. He wore a baseball cap to keep the hair out of his (5. syee) ____________. He didn't want his hair to get in the way when he played the bass (6. arelt) ____________ in the day. Kevin was enjoying feeling the sun on his (7. afec) ____________ while he walked down the street. Suddenly he heard someone calling his (8. eman) ____________.

"Kevin! Kevin! Wait!"
He turned around and saw Janet running towards him. "Where are you going, Kevin?" she asked with a smile.
"Oh, I'm just going to meet … I mean, I'm going skateboarding. I'm meeting some skateboarding friends at the school building," Kevin answered nervously. He was so excited that Janet was interested in him. But he didn't want to tell Janet that the band planned to *record* their song today.
"Skateboarding? So early in the morning? That's strange," she said. Kevin didn't want to tell her anything about the band's plans. So he answered, "No. I don't want you to see me fall down if I make a mistake." He tried to laugh.
Janet *frowned*, "Oh, that's a pity. At least let me walk with you, okay?" When they reached the school, Janet said goodbye. Kevin was happy that he didn't have to tell her the truth. He met the rest of the band in room 363. Then they all went out the back door of the school with Mr Sharp.
"Get in my *van*, everyone," Mr Sharp said. He led them to a big white *van* with flames on its side. The excited teenagers got into the *van*.

When they got out again fifteen minutes later they were in the next town, standing in front of a building. On the building was a sign that said 'Sam's Studios'.

"Wow, that's a professional recording studio! This is great, Mr Sharp!" Sarah said. "But isn't it expensive to *record* a song in a real studio?"

Mr Sharp smiled. "I have another secret for you all – I own this studio. Before I started teaching, I bought this place to help some friends who are in bands. Now I work here at the weekend sometimes. My business partner, Al, works here during the week. But this weekend I'm helping a fantastic young band to *record* their first single!"

The pupils laughed. "Thanks Mr Sharp!" they said together.

ÜBUNG 20 !

Übung 20: Sind die folgenden Aussagen richtig? Markiere mit richtig ✔ oder falsch –!

1. Simon thought someone was listening outside room 363. ☐
2. Kevin wanted to tell Janet about the band's plans. ☐
3. Janet will help The Sneakers record their song. ☐
4. The Sneakers are recording their song in room 363. ☐
5. The Sneakers rode on Mr Sharp's motorcycle. ☐
6. Mr Sharp works at his studio at the weekend. ☐

They went inside and found their instruments in the studio. As the band was getting ready to start *recording*, Simon saw something black move past the window.

"What was that?" Simon asked. He moved towards the window.

"You're crazy," said Kevin. "This is the second time you've seen or heard something that wasn't there."

Simon didn't get a chance to explain what he had seen. Maybe he was crazy, he thought. But he decided to forget about it for a while.

For two hours The Sneakers played and played. Justin's hands hurt from playing the keyboard. Julia's fingers were tired from playing her sax. Kevin thought he would scream if he had to play the song one more time. Finally, Mr Sharp said, "Okay. I think we've got it!"

"Yes, you've really got it," said another man's voice. At the door stood a big, fat man with grey hair. He was smiling and *rubbing* his hands together. "Where did you find these kids, Sam? They're great."

Mr Sharp said to the man, "Hi, Al. These are my pupils – Kevin, Sarah, Simon, Julia and Justin. I'm helping them *record* a song for a national *competition*." Then he looked at the band and said, "This is my business partner, Al."

"Nice to meet you," Al said. "Why don't you all forget about that *competition*? I could help you *record* a whole album. I've got a lot of *connections*. I know a *guy* at a big record company. He would pay a lot of money for this kind of music."

The Sneakers didn't know what to say. Mr Sharp answered for them.

"No, thanks, Al," he said. "They're not professionals. At least not yet. Let us do this *competition*. You have other projects."

Al said, "But I'd really like to help this band. They're good. This is a good chance for me … I mean, for us to make a lot of money."

"These kids are talented enough," Mr Sharp smiled. "I don't think The Sneakers will need help to become famous." Then he said to the band, "You can all go home now and enjoy the rest of the weekend."

The pupils returned to school the next week after a nice, relaxing weekend. On Tuesday after school Mr Sharp told the band that the song was ready. He stood in front of them holding one CD in his left hand and five CDs in his right hand. He *raised* his left hand.

"Here is the master copy of the song. I'll take it to the post office when I leave here today. And I'll send it to the people who are organizing the *competition*."

Übung 21: Wähle das passende Wort für jeden Satz aus und unterstreiche es!

ÜBUNG 21 !

1. The band members will see each other again bald/soon.
2. You finished all your homework! You are so good/brave.
3. They hope they will get/become a recording contract.
4. Who is the chef/boss of that company?
5. Julia is intelligent and gets perfect marks/notes at school.
6. I just finished reading a fantastic roman/novel!

Then Mr Sharp *raised* his right hand. "Here are five copies of the song. Each of you gets one. You have to put your CDs in a VERY safe place. If anyone outside the band gets a copy of the song, your chances of winning could be destroyed."
The five pupils understood. Each of them took a copy of the song.

After school Sarah met her best friend, Karen. Karen was a tall girl with long, black hair. While they were talking, Sarah dropped the books she was holding. Her CD, which was inside one of the books, fell out onto the ground.
"What's that?" Karen asked.
"Nothing, nothing," Sarah said quickly.
"Is that what you and your little band have been working on?" asked Karen. "You've been spending all your time with them – I feel like I've lost my best friend. At least let me hear the song, please. You would let me, your BEST friend, hear your first hit song, wouldn't you?"
"I can't," Sarah said.
"Oh, come on. I'm the first person who should know how famous you're going to become. I'm sure it's really good. Can't I just listen to a little bit?" Karen said hopefully.
"Not yet. You'll get a chance to hear it soon," Sarah said and put the CD in her pocket.
When she got home later, she looked through her CD collection in her bedroom. She picked up a Michael Jackson CD. "No one I know listens to this any more," Sarah said to herself. She took the Michael Jackson CD out of its case. Then she put the CD with The Sneakers' song into the case. "No one will ever find it here."

When Justin arrived at home later, he closed the door behind him and ran up to his mum's room. "Mum! We've finished *recording* our song!" Of course Mr Sharp had said that no one should know about the band's project. But Justin knew his mum wouldn't tell anyone. "I'm afraid that I might lose the CD," Justin said to his mother. "Will you keep it in a safe place for me?" His mother said yes and took the CD.

Übung 22: Setze die richtigen Präpositionen ein!
(over, in, into, up, on)

At the same time, Kevin was walking 1. ___________ his bedroom. He was looking for a good place to put his copy of 'Secret'. After thinking for a few minutes, he had an idea. He picked 2. ___________ the lamp that was 3. ___________ a table next to his bed. He put the CD on the table and put the lamp 4. ___________ top of the CD. The bottom of the lamp covered the CD perfectly. Kevin wanted to be especially careful. So next, he lit a candle that was 5. ___________ his table. He let it burn for a minute. Then he picked it up and held it 6. ___________ the bottom of the lamp. He let some wax fall on the bottom of the lamp, where it touched the table. If anyone moved the lamp, the wax would break and Kevin would know that someone had been 7. ___________ the room.

Simon also looked around his bedroom for a secret place. But he couldn't find a place that was safe enough.

"I know," he thought. "I'll just bring it with me everywhere that I go." Simon remembered that he always carried his rucksack with him. He opened a small pocket inside his rucksack, put the CD into it and closed it again.
"Now it's safe," he thought. "I will always keep an eye on my rucksack from now on."

Julia shared her bedroom with her younger sister, so she knew she couldn't keep her CD in there. She couldn't find a good place anywhere in her house.
So she put the CD in a plastic bag and went outside. She walked to the centre of her family's garden and made a hole in the ground. She put the plastic-covered CD into the hole and filled the hole up again. Then she used a large stone to mark the place where she had *buried* the CD.

For the rest of the week, the members of The Sneakers were happy and relaxed. Simon celebrated by going back to the CD shop on Wood Street and buying a lot of new albums. He had a lot of fun looking through the different kinds of music and choosing five new CDs.
The only thing he didn't like was the strange man who worked there. Several times he quietly walked up behind Simon – and Simon always jumped when he realized the man was there. And every time Simon turned around to see what the strange man in the leather coat was doing behind him, he asked, "Can I help you?"
Simon also didn't like it when he walked out of the shop and saw Janet. Since the band *auditions*, Simon felt a bit *embarrassed* every time he saw Janet. He was afraid that Janet was still angry with him because he'd been chosen to be the band's singer and guitar player – but Janet hadn't been chosen for anything at all.

Übung 23: Setze das Gegenteil der Wörter in Klammern ein!

However, Janet seemed to be (1. sad) __________.

"*What's up,* Simon? How's the band?" she asked with a very (2. sour) __________ smile.

"Oh, we're okay. I was just shopping for some (3. old) __________ music."

"That's cool. I'm going to meet a friend. See you (4. earlier) __________!" Janet said and walked (5. slowly) __________ into the music shop.

"I guess that Janet has (6. less) __________ self-control than I thought she did. She doesn't seem to be angry about the band at all," Simon thought.

The other band members finally had a chance to do their other hobbies too. Kevin had time to go skateboarding again. Julia was happy that she had time to read and paint again. Justin spent a lot of time playing with his computer. And Sarah spent most of her free time sleeping. She was so tired from the long weeks of *rehearsing*. Although she normally had so much energy, now she loved being in her bed.

They had worked extremely hard for a long time. But they had sent in their song for the *competition*. Now all they had to do was wait until the winner was chosen. Almost 200 other bands from different parts of England were also taking part in the *competition*. But The Sneakers knew they had made a fantastic song.

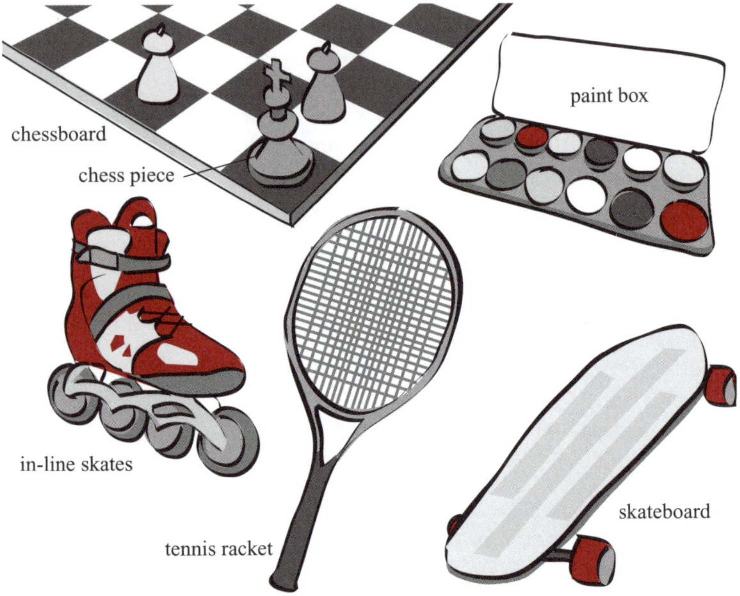

Chapter 5: The Missing CDs

But some people weren't happy that The Sneakers had such a big secret. A few other kids from school were asking questions about what the five friends were doing. People had some crazy theories about the band's plans. Everybody was very curious about their project.

One boy told people that the group was starting their own record company. Once after school Susie asked Kevin if it was true that the band members were already millionaires.

"No!" Kevin told Susie. "We've only made one song. And we will only get money if we win the …" Kevin stopped talking. He realized he shouldn't be telling Susie so much information.

"Win the what?" Susie asked.

"Uh … nothing, nothing. I have to go," Kevin said quickly and walked away.

Übung 24: Welcher Satz ist die logische Antwort auf die Frage? Kreuze die richtige Lösung an!

1. What would you like to do today?
   a) ☐ I would like a ham sandwich, please.
   b) ☐ I would like to watch a film.
   c) ☐ I would do it if I had time.

2. Where did you buy that dress?
   a) ☐ I bought it in London.
   b) ☐ I bought it on sale.
   c) ☐ I bought it last week.

3. In which direction should we walk?
   a) ☐ We should walk quickly.
   b) ☐ We should walk towards the bank.
   c) ☐ We should walk all day long.

4. What are you thinking about?
   a) ☐ I've been thinking a lot.
   b) ☐ I think so.
   c) ☐ I'm thinking about the CD.

Sarah's friend, Karen, also wanted to know what was going on. But Sarah didn't tell her anything. At first Karen just made jokes, and tried to make Sarah let her hear the song. But Sarah always said no.

Finally she started becoming angry that Sarah wouldn't share her secret.

"I can't believe you don't tell me things any more," Karen said to Sarah one afternoon.

"You've really changed."

"No I haven't," Sarah said. "I'm not allowed to say anything. I'm really sorry."

But Karen was still angry. "No, you've changed in other ways. You were a punk rocker just a few months ago. Now you're not as wild – not as crazy. I mean, you sleep all the time now. What's happening? I don't know how to say this but … you just seem so silly. And stupid."

Sarah was shocked. "Silly and stupid? You're the one who is getting angry just because you're not allowed to know a little secret. I thought you were my friend. We've known each other for years."

"Well, I WAS your friend," Karen said sarcastically.

"Come on. Don't be like that," Sarah said, trying to be nice. "Let's go to that ska concert tonight. You'll come with me, won't you?"

"Sorry, I've got other plans," Karen said angrily. "And I wouldn't want to keep you awake past your bedtime." She turned around and walked away.

Sarah didn't know what to think. She had been so happy about the band and about their song, 'Secret'. But now her best friend seemed to hate her.

Things continued like this for about two more weeks. Now it was almost the end of the calendar year, close to the winter holidays. The Sneakers were still waiting for the people from the *competition* to choose the winner. Mr Sharp said that they would probably find out the results after the New Year started.

On one especially cold winter day, Justin and Kevin were walking down the corridor at school. Their music lesson had just ended, and they were talking about their plans for the afternoon.
"I'm going to *hang out* with my friend, Joe," Justin said. "Look, there he is."
Kevin looked down the corridor and saw a good-looking boy wearing a big pair of *headphones* walking towards him. But he wasn't just walking – he was dancing too, because he was listening to music. As Joe got closer, Kevin and Justin could see that his *headphones* were *plugged into* a small MP3 player in the pocket of his jeans.

Übung 25: Unterstreiche die neun Wörter, die falsch geschrieben sind, und verbessere sie!

! ÜBUNG 25

"Hi, Joe," Justin said.
"What?!" Joe shoutid. He took off his *headphones*, and repeeted in a quieter voice, "What? Sorrie, I was just listening to this grate new song."
"I said 'hi'," Justin said. "What song is it? Let me heer."
As Joe gayve the *headphones* to Justin, Justin azked, "Who is the band?"
Joe answered, "I don't know. I've never heard of this band before. All I know is that they rock!"
Justin smild and put the *headphones* over his ears. Suddenly the smile disapeered. His face became as white as snow. His eyes opened wide.
"I told you they were good!" Joe said.
"Wait, something's wrong," Kevin said in a worried voice. "What is it, Justin? You look like you've seen a ghost. Or heard one."

ÜBUNG 26

Übung 26: Setze das passende Wort ein!
(song, word, Internet, hands, notes, eyes, day)

Justin couldn't say a 1. ______________. Instead, he took off the *headphones* and gave them to Kevin. Kevin only needed to listen to a few 2. ______________ of the song playing on Joe's *headphones*. In a second he recognized the notes he had been hearing every 3. ______________ for weeks and weeks. He tried to talk: "It's … it's … it's 'Secret'!" He looked at Justin and *whispered*, "It's our 4. ______________!"

"What do you mean it's secret?" Joe asked. "The song isn't a secret – I *downloaded* it from the 5. ______________."

"Joe!" Justin put his 6. ______________ on his friend's shoulders and looked into his 7. ______________. "Joe, where exactly did you get this song?"

Joe looked at Justin. The expression on his face showed that he thought Justin was crazy.
"You know that website where you can *download* songs, don't you? It's got a huge collection of songs. I *downloaded* the song from the site's 'New *Releases*' section. Susie told me about it."
"Susie told you? So she knows about the song too?" Justin asked.
"Sure," Joe said. "I was in an Internet chat room last night. Susie and a lot of other kids from school were in there too. And everyone was talking about this song. We all love it!"

Kevin didn't know what to think. One feeling inside him was happiness – because everyone loved the song! But the other feelings were terrible. He was angry. He was *confused*. He had to find out what was happening!

"Uh, Joe, we have to go. See you later," Kevin said quickly. He took Justin's arm and pulled him away from Joe. They started running down the corridor. "We have to tell the others!" Kevin said. He told Justin to go outside and look for anyone who was out there. Then he started looking into every classroom he passed.

"*Oops*, sorry," Kevin said when he opened a classroom door. He had surprised a group of pupils who were taking an exam. He looked inside the boys' toilet and saw Simon looking at himself in the mirror. Simon was *pretending* to play the guitar in the mirror!

"Hey superstar," he said to Simon. "Wake up from your dream. And get ready for your worst *nightmare* to begin!"

Kevin explained what he and Justin had found out.

"It can't be! Someone *released* our song?! We have to find him!" Simon exclaimed.

"Or her," Kevin added.

They left the toilet, and in the corridor they found Justin. Sarah and Julia were standing next to him.

"They both know too," Justin said.

"Okay, Sneakers, let's go to room 363," Kevin said. "Before we do anything else, we have to find Mr Sharp. Maybe he knows what's going on."

Quickly, the band walked to room 363. But when they got there, they found an empty room.

"What?" Sarah shouted in surprise. "Mr Sharp is always here during the day. He stays here until at least three o'clock!" It was *noon*.

"Forget about Mr Sharp," said Simon. "Whether he's here or not, we have to do something!"

They were all quiet for a few moments. They each tried to think of a good plan.

ÜBUNG 27

Übung 27: Finde für das Wort in Klammern ein Reimwort, das in den Zusammenhang passt!

"This is silly," Justin said. "Actually there's nothing to (1. stink) __________ about. The first thing we have to do is (2. mind) __________ our copies of 'Secret'. If one of the five CDs is missing, then we know who (3. cost) __________ it. And then we can start to find out who (4. look) __________ it – and why."

The rest of the (5. hand) __________ members agreed. Before the band left the classroom, Simon slowly opened his rucksack. He didn't want his (6. ends) __________ to see him looking for his copy of the CD. What if it wasn't there? What if HE lost the CD? He had to make (7. cure) __________ that it was there without anyone *noticing*.

"Hey, Simon! What are you doing?" Sarah had seen Simon opening his rucksack. He had a strange expression on his face, and she wanted to know why.

"Oh, um, nothing. Just looking for … something," he answered.

Sarah looked at Simon, and her eyes grew big with shock. "Oh, no. Don't tell me that you kept your CD in your rucksack. Pleeeeeease don't tell me you are such a huge idiot!"

"Well," Simon answered nervously, "I always have my rucksack with me. I thought nothing could happen to the CD."
Sarah picked up Simon's rucksack and let everything in it fall onto the floor. The CD wasn't there. She looked inside the rucksack. She opened the little pocket where Simon had put the CD.
"Empty," she said.
"Oh, no," he said. "I thought …"
"You thought wrong!" said Kevin. He sounded angry.
"Hey wait," Simon said. "Maybe it fell out in my room."
"We'll see," Justin said. Everyone seemed to be angry with Simon.
Then The Sneakers left room 363. After school, they all went to find their copies of the band's song.
When Justin got home, he looked for his mum in every room of the house. But he couldn't find her anywhere.
"She must be at work," he thought. So he went to the living room and found her telephone number at work. His mum always told him that he should use that number only if there was an *emergency*.
"If this isn't an *emergency*, I don't know what is," Justin said to himself as he picked up the phone.
"Hello?" said his mum's voice.
"Mum! I'm so glad you're there!"
"Is that you, Justin?" she asked. She sounded worried. "What's wrong? What is it?"
"Mum, where's that CD I gave you? I need it – NOW!"
His mother laughed. "Is that the problem? Oh, I was so afraid. I thought it was something serious."
"It is serious!" said Justin.
"Okay, fine. Sorry. Let me think – where did I put it?" She was quiet for a moment. "Oh, yes! I put it in the oven!"
"The OVEN? Are you crazy? I asked you to keep it safe!"
"That's the safest place I knew. I never make cakes or biscuits. I

never use the oven for anything. It's the only place in the house where no one ever looks."

ÜBUNG 28 !

Übung 28: Welche Gegenteile gehören zusammen? Trage die richtige Nummer in das Kästchen ein!

1. safe	☐ full
2. empty	☐ calm
3. rich	☐ front
4. excited	☐ seldom
5. back	☐ dangerous
6. often	☐ poor

"Thanks mum!" Justin said quickly and put down the phone. He ran to the kitchen and opened the oven. The CD wasn't there!
However, the oven wasn't empty. There was something silver at the bottom of the oven. Justin realized that the oven smelled terrible. It smelled like … burnt plastic. He suddenly understood that the silver *stuff* in the oven was his CD. But it was completely *melted*.
"There you are!" Justin heard the voice of his older sister, Anne. "Was it you who put that stupid CD in there? That's an oven, you idiot. It's not a CD player!"
"What did you do to it?" Justin asked.
"I had to make biscuits for my cookery class. It was a homework project. I started mixing things together to make the biscuits. Then I turned on the oven to heat it up. But when I opened the oven to put the biscuits inside, a huge cloud of smoke came out," Anne explained. "Now what do I do about my project?"
Justin was too excited to answer his sister.
"Should I be sad or happy?" he asked himself. His copy of the song

had been destroyed. That was terrible. But at least he could tell the others that it wasn't his fault that the CD was on the Internet now.

As Justin started cleaning the *melted* plastic from his mum's oven, Sarah was looking for Michael Jackson. She was sitting on the floor of her bedroom. All around her was chaos. There were CDs all over the floor. Some of the cases were opened. She had looked through her whole collection of CDs. But she couldn't find the CD case with the photo of Michael Jackson on it – the CD case with 'Secret' inside. Suddenly Sarah lost all her energy. She felt so tired. So she lay down in the middle of her CDs and fell asleep.

When she woke up, she saw her dad's shoes in front of her face. She looked up and saw her dad looking down at her, smiling. How long had she slept? Thirty minutes? An hour? Longer?

"I see you're tidying up your room," Sarah's dad said with a bit of sarcasm. "So, you're starting by organizing your CDs?" He laughed.

"What are you laughing about?" Sarah asked sadly.

"What's wrong? Oh – I know. You're probably sad about the *fight* you had with Karen."

"How did you know about that?" Sarah was shocked. She hadn't told her dad about her *fight* with her best friend.

"Karen told me," her dad explained.

"Karen? When did you talk to Karen?"

"Didn't I tell you? She came here yesterday evening," he said. "You were out, at that ska concert. She came here around eight o'clock. She said something about a *fight* that you two had. She told me that she didn't want to be your friend any more. And she said that she wanted to take some of her things back. I've known Karen as long as you have – almost seven years. I didn't really think she was serious about the *fight*. So I let her go into your room."

"You did what?!" Sarah shouted.

Her dad was surprised. "What's the problem? She only took her dirty old denim jacket and two CDs."

"She didn't take a Michael Jackson CD, did she?"

"Yes, she did."

Sarah sat down in a chair and covered her face with her hands.

"What? I thought you hated Michael Jackson now. Let her have that old CD. Why is it so important to you?"

ÜBUNG 29 !

Übung 29: Vervollständige die Sätze mit ***anything, nothing, anybody*** *oder* ***nobody****!*

1. The band can't tell their plans to ______________!

2. ______________ wants to come to the cinema with me.

3. I don't want ______________ to eat. I'm not hungry.

4. Sarah's not afraid of ______________.

5. There's ______________ interesting happening right now.

Sarah pushed her hands up to the top of her head and started pulling her short, pink hair. "Dad, you don't understand! That wasn't just a Michael Jackson CD. It wasn't a Michael Jackson CD at all. It was … Oh, forget it."

Sarah couldn't continue speaking. Could it be true? Had her best friend stolen their song? Had Karen put the song on the Internet to destroy the band's chances of winning the *competition*? Did she want *to get her revenge* because Sarah had been spending so much time with the band? It was all too much for Sarah to understand. She and Karen had been friends for almost seven years. Karen wouldn't destroy seven years of friendship because of one little *fight* – would she? Sarah simply didn't want to believe that Karen had done something so bad.

"Maybe it wasn't Karen at all," she thought. "Maybe it was Justin! He wasn't in our music class until he got into the band. Then he asked to transfer into the class. He's an outsider. What do we really know about Justin? All I know about him is that he loves computers. It was probably simple for him to put the song on the Internet. It's him! Tomorrow I'll tell the others that Justin must be behind all of this. It wasn't Karen."

Kevin was worried as he opened the door to his room. His bedroom was on the ground floor of his family's house. And he had a big window that was never *locked*. Kevin's family lived in a safe area, and he never thought that he had to *lock* his window. But maybe a thief had entered his room through the window. Maybe someone had found the secret place where he had put his copy of 'Secret'.

When he walked to the table with the special lamp on it, he saw that everything looked the same. He looked for the place where he had put the *melted* wax. The wax was not broken. He could see a bit of silver under the lamp. The CD was still there! Kevin picked up the lamp. The wax broke into many small pieces. That meant that no one had looked under the lamp since he put the CD there.

"Well, now we know that the thief didn't steal MY copy of the song," he thought.

Later that evening, Julia finally arrived home. While Justin, Sarah and Kevin were looking for their CDs, Julia had been sitting in a chair at the dentist's. She had asked her parents to let her miss the *appointment*. But they said no. So Julia had to spend most of the afternoon waiting to have her teeth checked by the dentist. As the dentist checked her teeth for holes, Julia was thinking about the hole in her family's garden. Was the CD still *buried* in the hole?

When Julia got home it was already quite dark outside. As soon as she got out of her parents' car, she ran behind the house to the garden. There was some snow on the ground, and she almost fell as she ran. Julia was just a few steps away from the place where she had *buried* the CD. But she could see that something was different. The snow on the ground was white with the light of the moon. But in the middle of the garden, the ground was dark. She stepped closer.

"Ouch!" Julia shouted. She had hit her toe on something hard. She looked down and saw the large stone that she had used to mark the special place in the garden. But someone had moved it.

! ÜBUNG 30

Übung 30: Unterstreiche im folgenden Textabschnitt die Synonyme für die Wörter in Klammern!
(1. found 2. place 3. created 4. part 5. perfect 6. path)

Julia got down on her hands and knees. Someone had discovered the location where the CD was! Someone had made a hole in the ground. Julia started moving the earth away with her hands. But the only thing she found was a piece of the plastic bag that the CD had been in.

"This was the ideal place!" Julia said to herself. "Who could have known that the CD was here?"

She looked around to see if she could find any *clues*. Soon she *noticed* something in the snow. There was very little light, so it was hard for Julia to see. But she thought she saw some marks in the snow. They made a *trail* that started at the hole in the middle of the garden. She followed the *trail* with her eyes and saw that they went to the garden behind the next house.

Julia stood up and walked towards the next house. She saw that the *trail* of marks went through the next garden. They ended at the back door of her *neighbour'*s house. The family who lived in that house were the Sands. There was Mr Sand, Mrs Sand – and their daughter, Susie Sand.

Susie Sand? That was the girl who had flirted with Kevin a few weeks ago. But Julia remembered something more important than that. Susie was the girl who had *auditioned* to be the band's keyboard player – but Mr Sharp hadn't chosen her.

"Why wasn't I more careful?" Julia asked herself. "Maybe Susie wanted to stop the band from winning the *competition*, because she isn't in the band. Maybe she saw me put the CD in my garden the other day. She probably knew what I was doing. And then she took the CD out of the hole and put the song on the Internet!"

Julia was shocked. Should she knock on Susie's door? No – she had to tell the others! Together they would make a plan. Suddenly Julia realized that she was very cold. And her hands were covered with dirt. She started walking back to her house.

"Aaaah!" Julia shouted. A loud noise had surprised her. She covered her mouth with her hands and looked around. What had made that noise? Was Susie watching her? She looked back at the Sands' house and saw the face of their pet dog, Hunter, in one of the windows. The dog was *barking*. Julia hoped that Hunter's *barking* hadn't made anyone *notice* that she was outside. She quickly went back inside her house.

The next day The Sneakers all arrived at school early so that they could tell Mr Sharp everything that had happened. They entered room 363 and saw their teacher sitting at his desk.

"Mr Sharp!" they all shouted at the same time. "Someone stole our song and put in on the Internet!"

ÜBUNG 31 !

Übung 31: Schreibe die Zahlen aus!

1. 32 ______________________
2. 1st ______________________
3. 13th ______________________
4. $^{1}/_{2}$ ______________________
5. 8,300 ______________________

Justin continued explaining, "A lot of kids here at school have MP3 copies of it! What are we going to do? There's no chance that we can win the national *competition* now!"
Mr Sharp became very serious. "This is terrible. How could anyone do this?" he said. He thought for a moment. "Okay, *guys* – we can't talk about this here. We have to find a safer place to discuss this. Everyone meet me after school. We'll meet at the café in town."
The Sneakers agreed.

Chapter 6: Looking for the Stolen Song

At the end of the school day, the band members met outside the school and started walking to the café. It was a sunny day and the snow on the ground was starting to *melt*.
"Where's Simon?" Kevin asked.
The others looked around. Kevin was right. Simon wasn't there.
"Well, he knows where we're meeting," Sarah said. "He's probably waiting for us at the café."
But when they arrived at the café, Simon wasn't there. But Mr Sharp was. Their teacher was sitting at the back of the café, at a

table in a dark corner. He was drinking a big cup of black coffee. Julia ordered a tea, and everyone else ordered hot chocolate. The waitress was walking away when Simon ran into the café saying, "I'd like cup of coffee, please!" Then he sat down and explained why he was late.

"I've been looking everywhere, *guys*," Simon said quickly. "I'm so sorry, but it seems that everything is my fault. I couldn't find the CD anywhere. I've looked in every room in my house. I've wandered through the streets. I've looked everywhere! I'm sorry. I understand if you all hate me now."

"Slow down, Simon," Julia said. "You're not the only person who can't find their CD. Mine is gone too."

"At least mine is okay," Kevin said.

"Mine is *melted*," Justin said.

Sarah looked at Justin angrily. "That's not true," Sarah said. "I think you're the one who put our song on the Internet." She looked at Kevin, Simon, Julia and Mr Sharp. "Listen, Justin isn't from our original music class. He's a computer *freak*. Here is my theory – he hates us for some reason and decided to make it impossible for us to win the *competition*. Maybe he's angry because we weren't friends with him until he joined the band. I don't really know why Justin did it – but he did!"

The others were shocked. Especially Justin, who almost looked like he was going to cry.

"I … I tell you I didn't do it!" he said. "Why would I do something like that? I want to win the *competition* as much as anyone else!"

"Well, you ARE the computer expert, Justin," Simon said.

"You're just saying that because you're afraid that it's all your fault!" Justin said. "You lost your CD so now you're agreeing with Sarah. It's so easy to say that the new *guy* did it!" Then he explained how his CD had *melted*.

Übung 32: Trage die fehlenden Buchstaben des beschriebenen Adjektivs in die Lücken ein!

1. no longer alive	_ e _ d
2. having a lot of power	_ tr _ _ g
3. regular or standard	n _ _ m _ _
4. not dirty	_ l _ a _
5. inexpensive	_ _ e _ p
6. prepared	r _ _ _ y

Julia *interrupted* the *argument*. “Wait a minute, Sarah. What happened to your CD? Maybe YOU put the song on the Internet.”
“That’s impossible,” Sarah said.
“Why?”
“Because … I can’t tell you.”
“That’s a good explanation,” Justin said sarcastically.
Sarah looked angry. But then her expression changed to one of sadness. “Oh no!” she said. “I can’t believe what I’ve been saying. Justin, I’m sorry.” Sarah told them about her *fight* with her best friend, Karen. She explained what had happened the night before. She said that she thought Karen had taken her copy of ‘Secret’.
“I just can’t believe that Karen would do something like this. She is – or was – my best friend. So instead of telling you all the truth, I decided to say that Justin did it. Justin, can you forgive me?”
“I understand, Sarah,” Justin answered. “But we have to stop being angry with each other.”
“Justin is right,” said Julia. “We all wanted to win this *competition*. So there’s no reason why any of us would want to destroy our chances. We’re all in this together.” Then she explained what she

had found in her garden the night before. She said that she had found a *trail* in the snow that led to Susie Sand's house.

Kevin *frowned*. "No, Susie wouldn't do something like that," he said. "She's so sweet."

"You're only saying that because she flirted with you," Simon said. "Girls can do some very strange things. One minute they're nice to you. And the next minute they steal the thing that's most important to you – and destroy your career."

"Simon is being a bit dramatic," Justin said. "It's not fair to say it's anyone's fault until we find out what really happened. But he's right – we can't trust anyone any more."

"At least we have each other," Julia said.

Mr Sharp had been listening quietly and drinking his coffee. But he had also seemed to be thinking about something else. When The

Sneakers finished talking he said, "So, let me see if I understand. One copy has been destroyed. And three copies are missing. Is that right?"

The others said yes.

"But that's not all we have to worry about," he said. "I've been thinking. There were five copies of the song. But there was also the master copy – the copy I sent to the *competition*." He was quiet for a moment. Then he continued, "All of this might really be my fault. Do you remember the day we *recorded* the song? After you all left the studio, I stayed for a while. I worked on the song because I wanted to make it absolutely perfect. When I left the studio I was quite tired. And I left the CD in the studio overnight."

"*So what*?" said Kevin. "It's your studio. You're allowed to leave things there, aren't you?"

"Yes, it's my studio. But don't forget that my business partner, Al, works there too," Mr Sharp said. "Al is a good *guy*. But he has changed a bit over the years. At the beginning he *cared about* music and about art. But now all he seems to *care about* is money. Maybe he wanted to make some extra money by putting your song on the Internet. And I also forgot to tell him the special rule for the *competition* – the rule that says the song must be brand new and can't be *released* before the *competition*."

"Oh no!" said The Sneakers.

"What should we do now?" Justin asked.

Julia answered, "We have to start finding out what really happened. I'll try to find out if Susie is the thief."

"I know that no one took my copy of the song," said Kevin. "So I'll help you, Julia."

"And I'll help you, Sarah," Justin said. "You and I will find out if Karen stole the song *to get her revenge*."

"But Karen didn't … she couldn't have …" Sarah stuttered.

"But she might have," said Justin. "We have to *investigate* every *clue*."
"What should I do?" Simon asked. "I've looked everywhere for my CD, but I can't find it. I don't know where else I should look."
"You can come with me, Simon," said Mr Sharp. "Together we can find out if Al is behind all this. And I'll also *contact* the people who own the website where the song is now. Maybe they can tell me the name of the person who put it there." Then he turned to the others and said, "Okay, everyone, you all know what you have to do. So let's go!"

Übung 33: Setze die Verben in der richtigen Zeitform ein!

ÜBUNG 33 !

Mr Sharp and The Sneakers (1. to pay) __________ for their drinks and (2. to leave) __________ the café. Julia and Kevin walked away in one direction. Sarah and Justin walked in the opposite direction. And Simon and Mr Sharp (3. to get) __________ into Mr Sharp's white van and (4. to drive) __________ away.

Julia and Kevin walked quietly for a while. Finally, Kevin asked Julia, "Where are we (5. to go) __________ now?"

"We're going to my house. I'll (6. to show) __________ you where I had *buried* the CD. And then we'll find out the facts about sweet little Susie," Julia (7. to explain) __________.

A little while later Julia and Kevin arrived at Julia's house.
"Come with me. The garden is behind the house," Julia said.

When they reached the garden, Julia *noticed* that there was no longer any snow on the ground. The sun had *melted* it all.

"So here's the hole," Kevin said. "But I don't see any *footprints* in the snow. There's no *trail* going between the hole and Susie's house. I told you that Susie had nothing to do with it."

"It was here last night!" Julia said. "I saw the marks in the moonlight. I'm sure Susie had something to do with it."

"I'm not," said Kevin. "She's a cool girl. Yes, it's true that she didn't get chosen to be the band's keyboard player. But she's too nice to do something so heartless."

"Come on, Kevin. You're in love with that girl. Naturally you think she's 'cool' and 'nice'. But we have to see things clearly. We have to get more information."

"And how do you think we should do that?" Kevin asked.

"We have to go inside Susie's house," Julia answered.

"What?! You mean you want us to break into her house?!"

"WE aren't going to do anything. YOU are going to get into her house. But you won't have to break in. If Susie is really behind this, she won't want us to realize that anything is wrong. And she won't stop flirting with you. So all you have to do is go to her house and ask her to invite you in!" Julia said.

"I can't do that," Kevin said. "You want me to ask her to let me in – and then you want me to look around her house for clues? I'm a terrible actor! She will know I'm not serious."

"But you are serious," said Julia. "You are serious about liking her, aren't you? You're attracted to her. Just be natural. You'll be fine."

Julia and Kevin argued for a few more minutes. Finally Kevin realized that this was their only chance to find out if Susie had anything to do with the missing CD. And because Kevin wanted to show that Susie was *innocent*, he agreed to try the plan. So he combed his hair and tried to look as nice as he could. Then he walked over to Susie's front door and knocked three times. Several seconds later the door opened. First Kevin saw Susie's curly black hair. Then he looked down at her face.

"Hi Kevin. What are you doing here?"

"Um, hi, Susie. I was just skateboarding along the street and I saw your bicycle outside this house. I thought it must be where you live, so I decided to knock on your door and say hi," Kevin said.

Susie looked down at Kevin's hands. They were empty. "Where's your skateboard?" she asked.

"My skateboard?" Kevin said nervously. "Oh … I … left it in a bush. It's a bit dirty and I didn't want to get any earth on the grass outside your house."

"You didn't want to get any earth on the grass? The grass grows in earth!" But Susie started smiling. "You're so silly Kevin. But I like that. Silly boys are sweet."

Übung 34: In diesem Gitternetz sind vier Pflanzenarten versteckt. Findest du sie alle?

ÜBUNG 34 !

A	M	G	T
L	E	R	R
N	K	A	E
R	O	S	E
B	U	S	H

Kevin's face turned red. He was getting more and more nervous. But he had to remember the plan.

"So, Susie, I wanted to know if you have some free time now. I think it's a pity that you weren't chosen to be in the band with me. But I wanted to know if you would play a song for me on your keyboard. I've never heard you play."

Susie was *thrilled*. "Of course! Come in!" She led Kevin into her house. After he was inside, he took off his coat. As he was hanging it up, he looked down and saw a big, black dog come running towards him. The dog jumped up and *licked* Kevin's face.

"Oh, that's *disgusting*!" Kevin said. The dog started biting Kevin's trousers and his shoes.

"Don't worry about Hunter," Susie said. "He jumps onto every new person. He likes to bite clothes, but he won't bite you. He likes to chew on anything he can find. Stop Hunter! Go!"

The dog let go of Kevin's trousers and went away.

"Let's go up to my bedroom. My keyboard is in there."

Susie and Kevin went up the stairs to Susie's bedroom. Her room had light-blue walls and a large bed. There was a white desk in the corner. In the middle of the room was a black chair and an electric keyboard. Susie led Kevin to the bed and told him to sit down.

"I'll be right back," she said and left the room. Kevin heard her walk into the bathroom and close the door. Quickly he jumped up from the bed and started looking around the room. First he looked through Susie's CD collection. There was a lot of pop music, a few hip-hop albums – but no copy of 'Secret'. Then he opened the *drawers* in the desk. Pencils, pens, paper, some old letters – but *no* CD here *either*. Where else should he look? Under the bed! Nothing.

He was looking through Susie's bookshelves when he heard the bathroom door open. He didn't have time to run back to the bed. So he just stood there, ready to tell Susie the truth. But when Susie saw Kevin standing in front of her bookshelves, she didn't get angry. She was happy!

"Oh, Kevin! You're so sweet! You're trying to find out what kind of

books I like!" she said in a happy voice. "You really do *care about* me, don't you?"
"Um, sure, I think you're a nice girl," Kevin said. He wasn't lying. He wasn't really in love with Susie – but he did find her attractive. She had a pretty face and lovely blue eyes. "Of course she likes me," he thought. "I'm in a rock band and I'm almost famous."
Susie took Kevin back to the bed. He sat down and she sat down next to him.
"Aren't you going to play a song for me?" Kevin asked.
"I'd prefer to do something else," Susie said. She moved closer to Kevin. Her clear, blue eyes were looking into Kevin's green eyes. A little voice inside Kevin's head said, "*What about* the plan? The CD!" But the little voice disappeared when Susie's lips touched his.

Übung 35: Unterstreiche die fünf Sätze, die inhaltlich nicht zum Text passen!

! ÜBUNG 35

At the same time that Susie opened her front door, Simon and Mr Sharp arrived at the building with the sign for 'Sam's Studios' on it. "Does that mean your first name is Sam, Mr Sharp?" Simon asked while *pointing to* the sign. Then his mum turned the television off. "That's right, Simon," Mr Sharp answered. "Come on, let's go inside. I think it's some kind of cat."
It was a weekday afternoon, so Mr Sharp thought his partner, Al, would be in the studios. The bank isn't open on Sundays. But when he reached the door, he found that it was *locked*.
"Hmm, that's strange," Mr Sharp said. Justin wanted to go home. He took out his keys and unlocked the door. The whole building was quiet. There was a party happening. When they entered the recording room they saw that it was empty.

"That's strange," Mr Sharp said. "I thought he would be working with one of his bands today. Maybe he's in the office." He led Simon to a door on the right side of the room. The door was unlocked and they went inside.

The office was filled with *papers* and CDs. It looked completely unorganized and Simon wondered how they would ever find any *clues* in all the chaos.

"Al isn't very good at keeping things neat," Mr Sharp said. He went to the desk and picked up a cup of coffee. "It's still warm, Al must have gone a few minutes ago. It looks like we have a little time to look around." Simon started looking through the CDs that were in short *stacks* around the room. Maybe he would find a copy of 'Secret'. Mr Sharp looked though the *papers* on Al's desk.

"All I see here are a lot of *bills*," Mr Sharp said.

After about ten minutes, Simon started to get worried. “Maybe we should go, Mr Sharp.”
“You’re right, Simon,” Mr Sharp said. “It seems that Al had nothing to do with this.”
They started to leave the room. But as Simon turned around, he saw a piece of paper hanging out of the *rubbish bin*. Was he crazy? Did he really see the letters S-N-E-A-K on the paper? He picked it up. No, he wasn’t crazy – on the piece of paper was a *drawing* of a big running shoe. And above the shoe was written ‘The Sneakers’.
“Look, Mr Sharp! What does this mean?”
“I’m not sure, Simon,” Mr Sharp answered. “It looks like a design for a CD *cover*. Could it be that Al wants to start selling The Sneakers’ song? I can’t believe it! I mean, I know that Al has become more and more interested in money. But I can’t believe he would do this. Al and I have been friends since I was at university. I can’t believe he could be a *backstabber*! However, Al does have a lot of *bills* here in his office. Maybe he needs some extra money. But we can talk about that later. Let’s get out of here.”
Simon took the *drawing* and followed Mr Sharp out of the building.

Übung 36: Welche Übersetzung der kursiv markierten Slang-Ausdrücke stimmt? Kreuze die richtige Lösung an!

! ÜBUNG 36

1. What the heck are you doing?
   a) ☐ Was zum Teufel machst du?
   b) ☐ Was ist los?

2. This band is totally wicked!
   a) ☐ Diese Band ist total furchtbar!
   b) ☐ Diese Band ist total geil!

3. She's a really cool chick.
   a) ☐ Sie ist echt ein tolles Mädel.
   b) ☐ Sie ist echt eine tolle Schauspielerin.

4. I'm completely knackered!
   a) ☐ Ich bin total besoffen!
   b) ☐ Ich bin total müde!

5. I heard that he nicked a CD and got into trouble.
   a) ☐ Ich habe gehört, dass er eine CD gekauft hat und in Schwierigkeiten geraten ist.
   b) ☐ Ich habe gehört, dass er eine CD geklaut hat und in Schwierigkeiten geraten ist.

While all this was happening, Sarah and Justin were trying to think of a way to *investigate* the role Karen might have played in all this. They were sitting in Justin's living room.

"There's no way to get into Karen's bedroom," Sarah said.

"She doesn't even let her parents go into her room. She keeps a huge lock on the door. And she keeps the key on a *necklace* that she always wears."

"But how can we find out any information, Sarah?" Justin asked. "We have to find out what she did with that CD!"

Sarah started thinking and was quiet for several minutes. Finally, she said, "I have an idea. Let's get our bikes. We're going to the *local indoor swimming pool*."

As they were riding their bikes down the street, Sarah explained that Karen was on the school's swimming team. Most evenings of the week she trained with the team between five o'clock and half past six.

"If we go there now, maybe we'll find her *locker*," Sarah continued.

"Karen takes her laptop computer with her almost everywhere she goes. If we can get her computer, you can find out if she's the person who put our song on the Internet."

"Me?!" Justin said in surprise.

"Of course you," said Sarah. "You're the computer expert. You know everything about the Internet and websites. You should be able to check her *files* and see if she's put any *files* on the Internet. Can you do that?"

"Well …," Justin began nervously. "I know how to do it. But should we do it?"

"It's our only choice, Justin. Look, we're at the pool," Sarah said. They got off their bikes and walked into the building. They passed one door and smelled *chlorine* in the air and heard the sounds of water. Then they reached a door with 'Ladies' written on it.

"Let's go," Sarah said and opened the door.

"That's the ladies' *changing room*. I can't go in there!" Justin said.

"Nobody is in there. Everyone is in the pool training now, and they'll stay there for another hour. Now let's go!" Sarah said.

Justin didn't like this plan. But he followed Sarah into the ladies' *changing room*. They walked past rows of closed *lockers*. In front of each *locker* was a pair of shoes. Finally Sarah stopped and said, "There!" She walked to a pair of black *trainers* with white stars painted on them. Then she looked up at the *locker*. There was a big, pink *combination lock* on it.

"Oh no! Now what?" Justin asked.

"What would her combination be? Let me think," Sarah said. A few moments later she said, "I know!"

Justin watched as she turned the *combination lock* to the numbers 29 – 12 – 83. The lock opened!

"I knew it! She's totally in love with the lead singer from an American band called The Stints, and 29 December 1983 is his birthday."

ÜBUNG 37 !

Übung 37: Finde für die britischen Begriffe auf der linken Seite das amerikanische Gegenstück! Trage die richtige Nummer in das Kästchen ein!

1. flat	☐ elevator
2. holiday	☐ garbage
3. lorry	☐ apartment
4. lift	☐ sneaker
5. trainer	☐ truck
6. rubbish	☐ vacation

Sarah put her hand into Karen's *locker* and pulled out a black bag. She opened the bag and pulled out a laptop computer. "Come on, let's go somewhere where no one will see you," Sarah said.
"I thought you said everyone was in the pool."
"They are. But we have to be safe. Here, you can sit on the toilet and close the door of the *cubicle*," Sarah said. Justin got inside and Sarah closed the door. "Pick up your feet!" Sarah said. "Good. I'll be right back."
"Sarah, where are you going?!" Justin asked with a worried voice. But Sarah had already left. Justin decided to try to relax and start working. He worked on the computer for about twenty minutes when he heard a door open and two girls laughing.
"Wait a second," one girl's voice said. "I've got to go to the *loo*."
Justin stopped breathing. What would he do if a girl found him sitting on a toilet in the ladies'? The *cubicle* door moved. Someone was trying to open it.
"Is someone in there?" the voice asked.
Justin was screaming on the inside. He didn't know what to do. He would get into very serious trouble if someone found him with Karen's computer – in the girls' *loo*! But instead of screaming, he

answered in a high voice, doing his best imitation of a girl, “Just a minute.”
For a moment Justin heard nothing. Did the girls outside know that they were hearing the voice of a boy?
Finally the girl’s voice said, “Come on, Liz, let’s use the *loo* in the corridor.” He heard them walking away and continued working on Karen’s computer. A little while later Sarah came back and asked if Justin was okay.
“You’re lucky that I’m okay! I almost got *caught*!” he said angrily. Then he opened the door of the toilet *cubicle* and said, “I’ve finished.”
Sarah looked excited and worried at the same time. She wanted to know if Karen was the person who put ‘Secret’ on the Internet. But she was also afraid to find out her best friend did something so bad. She closed her eyes and asked, “So, was it Karen?”
“I’ve looked through all her Internet *files*,” Justin said. “I can see that she *downloaded* the song from a website. However, I can’t find anything that shows that she put the song on the website. She only *downloaded* the song as an MP3.”
“So does that mean she’s *innocent*?” Sarah asked.
“Well, it’s possible that she gave the CD to someone else – and that person put the song on the Internet. But one thing is sure: Karen didn’t do it herself.”

Übung 38: Beantworte die Fragen zum Text!

ÜBUNG 38 !

1. Why does Mr Sharp think Al needs money?

2. Where did Justin and Sarah find Karen’s computer?

3. Where did Justin hide in the ladies' changing room?

4. Who almost found Justin where he was hiding?

5. Did Karen put The Sneakers' song on the Internet?

Sarah smiled. Of course Karen hadn't done it! Sarah felt so much better now that she knew that Karen was *innocent*.

She and Justin put the computer back into the bag in Karen's *locker*. Then they replaced the *combination lock* and left the building.

As soon as they walked outside into the cold winter air, Justin felt much better. He didn't like *sneaking* around like that. And he had never been in the ladies' *changing room* before – what an adventure! Sarah also felt better. She finally knew for sure that Karen hadn't wanted *to get her revenge* on her.

"Now what?" Justin asked as he got on his bike.

"Now nothing," Sarah answered. "We've done everything we could do. When we see the others tomorrow morning, we'll tell them what we've found out. And I'll have to talk to Karen soon. I have to get that CD back to make sure that it doesn't fall into the wrong hands. See you tomorrow, Justin."

"Okay, see you then. Bye!"

Justin and Sarah *rode* away into the darkness.

At about the same time, Julia saw Kevin walk out of Susie Sand's house. Julia had been sitting in the living room of her house for more than an hour. Through the living room window she could see the front door of Susie's house. She had been sitting on the sofa, drinking from a bottle of Coke, waiting nervously for Kevin. Several times she'd asked herself why Kevin was staying in there so long. Did Susie know why he was there? He should have finished searching for the CD after about fifteen minutes, Julia thought. When she looked out the window and finally saw his head covered with *shaggy* brown hair, she jumped up from the sofa and ran to her own front door. Normally Julia was quiet and relaxed – but now she felt like she was going crazy. When Kevin reached Julia's door, she looked at him with wild eyes.

"So? What? Was it her? Did Susie want to hurt the band because she wasn't chosen to be in it? Come on, tell me!" Julia said.

"What? Susie wouldn't hurt a fly," Kevin said.

Julia *noticed* that his voice sounded strange. And what was that strange light in his eyes? And what was that on his cheek? Was he *bleeding*? Had Susie hit him? Julia moved closer to Kevin and looked at his cheek. Lipstick?!

Übung 39: Wähle das passende Wort für jeden Satz aus und unterstreiche es!

ÜBUNG 39 !

1. They must find out witch/which person stole their song.
2. That's the place where/were they first met.
3. I don't know if its/it's such a good idea.
4. Julia waited four/for a very long time.
5. Julia was very surprising/surprised when she saw Kevin.

"*What the heck* were you doing over there?" Julia shouted. Kevin didn't seem to react.

"We have to be detectives, Kevin! Objective detectives," Julia said. "We have to look for *clues* and find out who stole our song –

remember? Or did you forget that someone stole our song and put it on the Internet – and probably destroyed our chances of winning FIVE THOUSAND pounds?!"

"You don't understand, Julia. Susie had nothing to do with it," he said.

"How do you know that? Did you even look for the CD while you were in there? Or did you two just *snog* the whole time?" Julia asked. There was anger and shock in her voice.

"Well, um … I did look in her room," Kevin said defensively. "But I couldn't find the CD anywhere. I started looking through the things on her bookshelves when she came back into the room. And after that … well … I stopped looking."

Julia couldn't believe what she was hearing.

"So you looked around her bedroom for, what, five minutes? And then what? Did you play cards? Did you help her with her homework?" Julia asked sarcastically.

Kevin's face turned red. He finally realized what he had really done. How could he tell the others what had happened? Would he tell them that he couldn't look for *clues* because he was too busy falling in love? But he really was in love! Kevin couldn't understand why he hadn't *noticed* Susie earlier. There had been a time when he liked other girls – Janet, for example. But he'd never spoken to Susie before the day of the band *auditions*.

ÜBUNG 40 !

Übung 40: Welches Wort ist das „schwarze Schaf"?

1. juice, Coke, lemon, water
2. taste, chew, lick, smell
3. butter, bitter, sour, sweet
4. cup, plate, glass, oven
5. sausage, egg, beef, ham

Chapter 7: The Band's Investigations

"Julia, something wonderful has happened," Kevin started to explain. "I think I've fallen in love."

Julia was so shocked that she couldn't speak for a few moments. She couldn't believe it. Finally, her sweet, sentimental side broke through her shock.

"That's really great, Kevin," she said with a smile. But then, more seriously, "But maybe she's just *pretending* to like you so that you won't think she put our song on the Internet. Maybe she's just acting. We need to find out what happened to our song. Susie's got a copy of it, I know it. We have to find out why – and what she's done with it."

They were both quiet for a minute. Kevin was quiet because he felt bad about *letting his friends down*. Julia was quiet because she was trying to think of a new plan.

"It seems that you're going to be pretty useless for finding out information about Susie," Julia began. "Well, you might be able to find out whether she's a good kisser or not – but not whether she's a thief or not. So I'll have to do things myself."

"What's your plan?" Kevin asked.

"It's too late for me to go over there now. I'll have to try it tomorrow afternoon, after school. But I probably shouldn't tell you more. Maybe you'll see Susie again tonight and tell your new love everything."

"Hey, that's not fair," Kevin said.

But he didn't keep arguing because he knew very well he had *messed up* their original plan.

"Okay, I'll see you tomorrow morning at school," Kevin said sadly as he left Julia's house.

"Yeah. See you then," Julia said and closed the door behind him.

The next day The Sneakers met during the lunch break to discuss the results of their *investigations*.

Sarah and Justin went first.

"We don't have to worry about Karen any more. We know for sure that she didn't put 'Secret' on the Internet," Sarah explained.

"How do you know that? Why are you so sure?" Simon asked.

Sarah and Justin looked at each other, but didn't answer the question. They didn't really want to tell the others how they had found out their information. They both knew that what they did was very risky – and a bit wrong too.

After several moments of nervous silence, Sarah and Justin started explaining what they had done. They made clear that they knew they had put themselves in danger. And they knew it was bad to take something that belongs to someone else – even if you're doing it to *prove* that the person is *innocent*.

ÜBUNG 41 !

Übung 41: Setze die richtigen Präpositionen ein!
(of, out, on, in, away, up)

1. No one wants to give _________ any information.
2. Maybe Sarah will let her short hair grow _________.
3. If The Sneakers win the competition, they could go _________ tour.
4. Will all this make Karen and Sarah split _________ as friends?
5. All the band members have a lot _______ stories to tell the others.
6. The teenagers explained what happened _________ their investigations.

"But you have to understand," Sarah said. "This band means so much to us. We'd do anything to find out who did this terrible thing to us. Karen is my best friend. It broke my heart to think that she might have done this to me. And I feel terrible now that I know she really had nothing to do with it. But I had to find out. I had to!"

"Maybe we shouldn't tell Mr Sharp what we've done," Justin said. "He might be really angry that we didn't tell him about our plan before we did it. But although it was bad, we were ready to do anything to find out the truth. We're sorry that it had to be this way. But at least we have one *suspect* fewer."

No one said anything, but the others seemed to agree.

Then Simon said, "Well, what Mr Sharp and I did wasn't exactly *ethical* either. We went to the studio he shares with Al and looked around in Al's office."

"Oh, so Mr Sharp has been *sneaking* around too. I feel a little bit better now," Sarah said.

"What did you find out?" Justin asked.

"This Al *guy* is definitely still a *suspect*," Simon began. He continued to tell the others about the *drawing* that he and Mr Sharp found in Al's *rubbish bin*. He explained that Al might be trying to sell The Sneakers' song himself.

"But Mr Sharp is his friend!" Kevin said. "He wouldn't steal our song just to make some extra money ... would he?"

"Well, he had a lot of *bills* in his office," Simon said. "Maybe he's got money problems. Maybe he thought he could secretly make some money with our song."

"How do you plan to find out whether it was really him or not?" Julia asked.

"Mr Sharp invited Al to come to the school after lessons are over. He told Al that he had to talk to him about something, but didn't have time to go to the studio. That's when Mr Sharp will show Al what we found and make him *confess*," Simon said. "Will you all be here this afternoon? We should all be here together."

"I won't be here," Julia said.

"Why not?" Sarah asked.

"Because I have to finish what Kevin started. I have to finish our plan because mister lover-boy here *messed* everything *up*."

"What do you mean?" Justin asked.

Kevin was trying not to look at the other band members. He was extremely *embarrassed*. Yes, he liked Susie. But he didn't want the others to know that that had stopped him from learning the truth.

"Can't we talk about this later?" Kevin asked quietly.

"I think the others should know what happened, Kevin," Julia said. Then she told the others what happened between Kevin and Susie.

"We still don't know whether Susie is *innocent*," Julia added. "Kevin didn't get a chance to check other rooms of the house. So I have to go there this afternoon and search through the house myself."

"Whoo, Kevin," Simon *teased*. "It looks like you've found yourself a little girlfriend. I hope your heart doesn't get broken if you find out that she's the person that made us lose five thousand pounds and a *recording contract*."

"Come on, Simon. She's really nice. I don't believe that she did it," Kevin said.

After her last lesson ended, Julia left the school quickly. She wanted to see when Susie arrived at her house.

While Julia was walking home, the rest of The Sneakers came together in room 363. They found Mr Sharp waiting for them there.

"Al will be here in a few minutes," Mr Sharp said. "But when he gets here, let me do the talking first, okay?"

The teenagers agreed.

"Oh, I also wanted to tell you that I called the people that own the website that *released* 'Secret'. They said that the person who put it there used the name Ice123 – and there's no way to find out what the real name is. But at least I made them remove the song from their website," Mr Sharp added.

Übung 42: In diesem Textabschnitt sind die Verben durcheinander gekommen. Finde heraus, wohin sie tatsächlich gehören!

ÜBUNG 42 !

Several minutes later they (1. talk) ______________ a head covered with grey hair come through the door. The head was (2. belonged) ______________ by a big, round belly. The head and the belly (3. saw) ______________ to Al.

"Hey Sam, how are you (4. let) ______________?" Al said. "Oh, look – you've got your *pint-sized* punk rockers with you too. How are you doing, kids? How's the band?"

"(5. followed) ______________ in, Al," Mr Sharp said. "There's something that I … that we would like to (6. doing) ______________ to you about."

"Good. There's something I'd like to say to you too," Al said. "But I'll (7. come) ______________ you go first. What I have to say is a bit of a surprise."

"We've got a surprise for him too," Simon said quietly to Kevin. Kevin smiled.
"*What's up*?" Al asked.

"I don't know how to say this to you, Al. This is what's up," Mr Sharp said as he reached into his pocket. He pulled out the *drawing* he and Simon found in Al's office and unfolded the piece of paper. As he did so, The Sneakers watched Al's face carefully to see if his expression changed. And it did change. The friendly smile on Al's face slowly turned into a look of surprise. Then he looked sad. And finally, the expression on Al's face showed that he was angry.

"How did you get that?" Al asked. "What's happening here? Have you been *sneaking* around in my office? I thought we were business partners! I thought we were friends!"

"Yes, Al. But I don't think a friend would try to *ruin* another friend's project. I don't think my friend would try to steal something from a group of good, hard-working, talented young people."

It seemed that Al didn't know what to say for a moment.

"I don't know what you mean. I was trying to help you," Al said.

"That may be true, Al," Mr Sharp said. "But you should have asked me before you put The Sneakers' song on the Internet. I would have told you not to do it because the band wanted to take part in a *competition*. But one of the rules of the *competition* was that their song couldn't be *released* until after the *competition* was over. And not only that. It also seems that you wanted to try to sell their song yourself. You even designed a CD *cover*. You can't wait to make some money with these kids, can you?"

ÜBUNG 43 !

Übung 43: Formuliere die Sätze in indirekter Rede!

1. "I hate potatoes." Julia said *she hated potatoes.*
2. "I don't want to." Justin said ______________________.
3. "Where is it?" Sarah asked ______________________.

4. "Come in, Al." Mr Sharp told ________________.

5. "What is Al doing?" Mr Sharp asked ________________.

6. "He is a strange guy." Kevin said ________________.

7. "I think Al did it." Simon said ________________.

Al looked as though someone had hit him in the face. His eyes and his mouth were wide open.

"Internet? I wanted to sell the song? What on earth are you talking about, Sam? What have these kids been telling you?" Al asked.

"We didn't have to tell him anything," Simon said. "We found the *drawing* in your office. And we saw all the *bills* you've got there too. Tell the truth. You wanted to get *publicity* for the band by putting the song on the Internet – and then you wanted to start selling it!"

"I still don't know what you're talking about with this Internet thing," Al said. "Sam, I'd never try to make money through a band that you've been working with. I never have and I never will. You said you were helping the kids with a *competition*. And I could hear that they've got talent. So I wanted to help. Yes, I designed a CD *cover*. But it was going to be a surprise. That's what I wanted to tell you today. I wanted to say that if you win the *competition*, I've already got a great design for your first CD!"

Then Al reached into his *briefcase* and pulled out a large piece of paper. On it was a cool *drawing* of two burning *sneakers*. Above the flames was written 'The Sneakers'. It looked fantastic!

"I didn't know what the name of your song was, so I left that out," Al said. But now there wasn't much enthusiasm in his voice. He just sounded sad and tired.

"But I guess you don't want my help. You just think I'm a poor old *dope* who only cares about money, don't you?"

Mr Sharp and the band members were *embarrassed*.

"You mean you had nothing to do with the song being put on the Internet?" Sarah asked.

"I really don't know anything about it. Does that mean there's no way that you can win the *competition* now?" Al asked.

"I'm not sure," answered Mr Sharp. "But the most important thing right now is to find out who really did it."

"Do you have any other *suspects*?" Al asked.

"Well, Julia is *investigating* something at this moment," Justin said. "And Simon still hasn't found his copy of the song. But we don't know where it might be or who might have taken it."

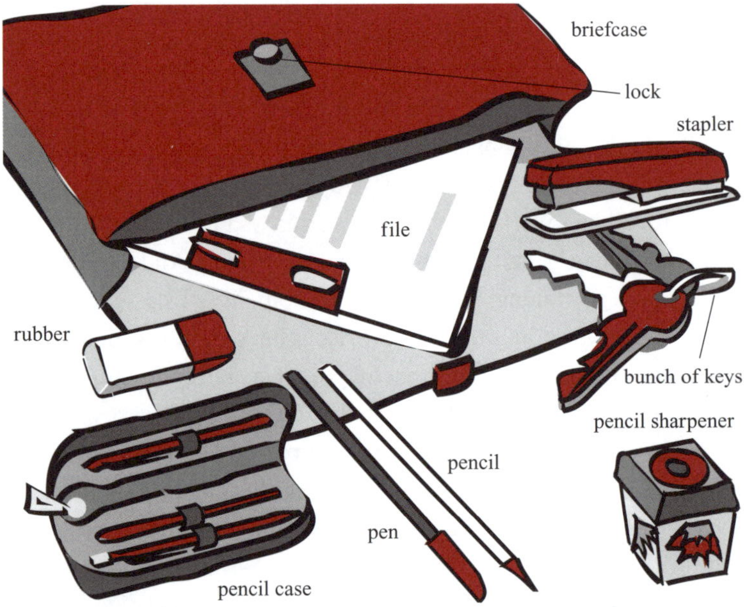

Mr Sharp was right. At that moment, Julia was watching Susie arrive at her house. After Susie went inside, Julia waited a few minutes. Then she went outside and walked over to Susie's front door. She knocked three times. Moments later the door opened.

"Hi, Julia," Susie said. "*What's up*?"
"Hi, Susie. I wanted to know if I could *borrow* something from you.
"Of course. Come in," Susie said.
Julia stepped into the house. She could hear Susie's dog *barking* somewhere in the house. As soon as she got inside, she looked around quickly. On the small table next to the door she saw some keys, a pen, a pencil, and a small black *pencil sharpener*. As Susie was closing the door and looking in the other direction, Julia took the *pencil sharpener* from the table and put it in her pocket. When Susie turned around, Julia smiled at her. Julia was quite nervous, but she didn't want to show it.
"What do you need to *borrow*?" Susie asked. She seemed to be friendly. But she could just be acting, Julia thought.
"I have to finish an art project. But I just realized that I left my *pencil sharpener* at school. Do you have one that I could *borrow*?"
"Certainly," Susie said. She moved to the small table next to the door. But when she looked at the table she *frowned*.
"That's strange," Susie said. "I got home a few minutes ago – and I'm sure that I put my *pencil sharpener* right here. I must have put it somewhere else. Let me look for it. I'll be right back."
"I'll come and look with you," Julia said quickly. "If that's okay."
"Yeah. Come on. Maybe it's in the living room."

Übung 44: Schreibe die Wörter in Großbuchstaben um!

ÜBUNG 44 !

1. Take a letter away from STRANGLE to make a word that means 'unusual'. ____________

2. Add a letter to PAL to make a word that describes something white or light-coloured. ____________

3. Change a letter in FLAKE to make a word for the fire you see on a candle. ________

4. Change a letter in TIMED to make a word that describes someone who has no energy. ________

5. Change a letter in PAIL to make a word for two of something. ________

6. Add a letter to PEAK to make a word for what you do when you say something. ________

Julia followed Susie through the living room. As they walked around the room, Susie looked for her *pencil sharpener*. Julia, however, spent the time looking for her copy of The Sneakers' song. She looked in *drawers* and under the sofa.

"Why would my *pencil sharpener* be under the sofa, Julia? You have some strange ideas," Susie said.

Soon Susie *gave up* on looking in the living room.

"Let's try my bedroom. I was up there a second ago," Susie said.

The two girls started going up the stairs.

"Now I can search her room objectively," Julia thought. "Silly Kevin. But I'll make sure that I search every corner of her room."

But about halfway up the stairs Susie stopped.

"Wait! It's probably in the kitchen. I think I put it there!"

She turned around and went back down the stairs. Julia didn't know what to do. She couldn't go up to Susie's room alone. She looked up to the top of the stairs one last time. Then she *sighed* and followed Susie to the kitchen.

In the kitchen Susie continued searching. But Julia wasn't interested in looking any more. She was sure that if Susie had the CD, it

was probably in her room. Susie wouldn't keep the CD in the kitchen. Instead of searching with Susie, Julia said hello to the dog, Hunter, who was lying on a big pillow near the oven.
"Hi there, Hunter," Julia said as she *rubbed* the dog's head. "Hunter is really quiet today, isn't he?"
"Yeah," Susie said. "He's been lying there all day. I think he's got something under his pillow. Some secret little thing he found a few days ago. He won't let anyone see it. I'm just afraid that it's a dead animal. How *disgusting*!"
Julia laughed and said to the dog, "You've got something special under there? What is it? Susie doesn't want you to keep *disgusting* things under there. What have you got?"
She tried to move the dog off the pillow. But he didn't want to move. Then she saw a ham sandwich on the kitchen table. It must have been Susie's after-school *snack*. Julia took a small piece of ham from the sandwich. Then she held the meat in front of the dog's nose.
"Come here, Hunter. I've got something for you," she said.

Übung 45: Übersetze die Wörter und trage sie ins Kreuzworträtsel ein!

ÜBUNG 45 !

1. Haut
2. seltsam
3. Suche
4. Küche
5. verärgert
6. Bleistift

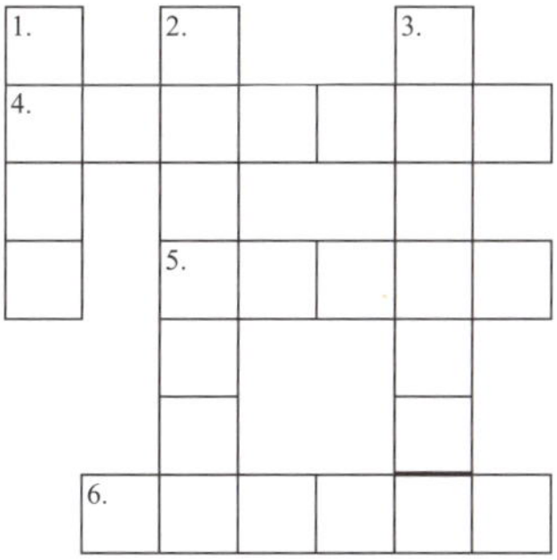

The dog stood up and followed Julia's hand that was holding the ham. As soon as the dog moved away from the pillow, Julia dropped the meat and let Hunter eat it. Then she picked up the pillow.

On the floor was something flat, round and silver. It was a CD! Julia looked closer. She saw handwriting on the CD. She read the letters 'The Sne', and under that she read 'Secr'. The rest of the text was gone. It looked as though Hunter had been playing with and scratching the CD. It was Julia's copy of The Sneakers' song!

"What does Hunter have under there? Did you find something?" Susie asked. She was on the other side of the room and couldn't see what Julia was doing.

As fast as she could, Julia put the CD in her pocket. Then she took the small black *pencil sharpener* out of her pocket and put it on the floor. She stood up.

"Look!" Julia said. "I've found your *pencil sharpener*!"

"What's it doing there? Hunter, you're a bad dog. Don't steal my things!" Susie picked up the sharpener and gave it to Julia.

"Here you go," Susie said.

"Oh, right. Thanks," Julia said. She was so excited about finding the CD that she had forgotten that she asked to *borrow* the sharpener from Susie.

"I've got to go now, Susie," Julia said and left the house quickly. Kevin was right! Susie didn't steal the CD from the hole in Julia's garden. Hunter must have found it and thought it was a toy.

When Julia arrived at room 363 a little while later, she found the other four band members and Mr Sharp in there. But she didn't see Al anywhere.

"What happened to our main *suspect*?" Julia asked. "Where's Al?"

"Al isn't our main *suspect* any more – Susie is. Did you find the CD there?" Justin asked.

"Susie didn't do it. Her dog took the CD from my garden. Here it is," Julia said and pulled out the dirty, scratched CD.

Übung 46: In jedem Satz steht ein Wort an der falschen Stelle. Verschiebe es mit einem Pfeil an die richtige Stelle!

1. I you will give a present for your birthday.
2. I want to go to the concert, but I'm not sure where is it.
3. Why you did decide to do that?
4. There were other no people on the empty street.
5. I'll tell you what do you should.
6. Susie didn't from steal the CD the hole.

"What? But Al is *innocent* too," Simon said. "He was trying to help us by making a design for a CD *cover* for us. He knew nothing about the song being on the Internet. He didn't do it."
"That's just great," Sarah said sadly. "That means we have no *suspects* left. What do we do now?"
"I'll tell you what you should do," Mr Sharp said. "You should all go home and get some rest. All of us have had several very hectic days. Why don't we relax for a while and think about our next step tomorrow?"
Although The Sneakers wanted to find out who was really behind all this, they all agreed. "Hey, I know a great way that we can relax and forget about all this for a while. Why don't we go down to the music shop on Wood Street?" Julia said. "Looking through all those great albums always relaxes me. And it helps to remember that so many other bands have become successful. It gives me hope that we might do it too."
The other band members agreed with Julia's idea.

"Okay, see you all tomorrow, then," Mr Sharp said. "Bye!"
The Sneakers left the school and started walking down the street together. When they walked around a corner, the band members saw Sarah's friend – or ex-friend – Karen.
"Um, I'll see you *guys* later. I've got to talk to Karen," Sarah said.
"Okay, you know where we'll be if you want to meet us later," Simon said.
Sarah didn't know exactly what she wanted to say to Karen. Should she tell Karen the truth? Should she tell her that she took Karen's computer while Karen was swimming? Or should she just tell Karen that she was sorry about everything and wanted to be friends again?
"Hi," Sarah said quietly to Karen.
"Hey," Karen answered.
"Listen, I have to tell you something. I'm really very sorry about the way I've been *behaving*. You've always been a really good friend to me. And I know that I've been spending more time with the band than I have with you. I also understand why you were angry that I wouldn't tell you anything about the band."
"I'm glad to hear that," Karen said.

ÜBUNG 47 !

Übung 47: Unterstreiche die sieben Adjektive, die nicht in den Text passen!

"I had to keep everything about the band a stupid secret. But it seems that I don't have to do that any more. Our hungry chance of becoming successful and famous is gone now. So I guess now I can tell you about what I've been doing." Sarah then told Karen all about the boring *competition*, the *competition*'s special rules, the website where someone had put the song, the missing CDs, and the futuristic *investigations*. However, Sarah didn't yet tell her that she and Justin had broken into Karen's wet *locker* and searched through her lonely computer for *clues*.

Before Sarah got a chance to explain about that, Karen said, "*Speaking of* missing CDs, you can have this back." As she said this, Karen reached into her empty rucksack and pulled out a CD case.

It was the Michael Jackson CD case! But what was inside?

"I've been carrying it around in my rucksack since the day I took it from your room. I know it's really mine, but I don't think I'll ever listen to this kind of music again. Do you want to keep it, Sarah?"

"Yes, yes, yes!" Sarah was almost jumping with happiness.

"Wow, I didn't know you liked Michael Jackson so much," Karen said. "Playing with your band really has changed you, hasn't it?"

Sarah tried to control herself and said, "Oh, I … I'm just happy because this is like a sign that we're friends again. Don't you agree?"

"Hmm … let me think," Karen said. "Yeah, I think I can forgive you. At least you'll have more time for me again."

"Great," Sarah said. But she was starting to feel very *curious*. Was The Sneakers' CD still inside the case? She opened the case slowly, trying not to let Karen see what she was doing.

The CD was still there!

"Hey, that's not my Michael Jackson CD!" Karen said. She had seen the CD inside the case. "What is that? Let me see!" Karen took the CD from Sarah.

Sarah let Karen have it. Sarah *sighed*, and thought that now she would have to tell Karen the whole truth. She'd have to explain that Karen had been a *suspect* for a while. But before she had a chance to begin explaining, Karen said something very surprising.

"Wait a second. The CD says 'The Sneakers'. I've seen a CD exactly like this before. Where did I see it?"
"Yes, tell me – where did you see it?!" Sarah asked excitedly. Karen thought for a moment.
"I know! I saw it in the CD shop on Wood Street. You know, the shop called Music 4 U," Karen said.
"What? They were selling this CD at the shop?" Sarah asked.
"No, it wasn't for sale. I saw it near the *cash register*. I think the *guy* who works there was listening to it. Have you ever seen that *guy* before? I think he's in a heavy metal rock band. He's totally *bizarre*. He wears a long, black leather coat all the time – when it's cold, when it's hot … always. And what a strange-looking face he has."
"Oh my God! That *guy*?" Sarah shouted in shock. "Karen, I'm really sorry, but I've got to go." Karen looked sad.
"Okay, I see." she said, "You have to go back to your 'real' friends now. See you whenever." Karen started walking away, but Sarah stopped her.

ÜBUNG 48 !

Übung 48: Wofür stehen die Slang-Kürzel?

1. 4 U ....
2. R U OK? ....
3. thx ....
4. 2day ....
5. b4 ....
6. pls ....

"Listen, Karen, I promise I'll explain everything soon. I'll tell you the whole truth. You might not like it, because I've done something bad to you. But if we're going to stay friends, I have to tell you – only not now. Please believe me. There's something I have to do now. It can't wait. I'll call you tonight!" Sarah *hugged* Karen and started running down the street in the direction that the other band members had gone.

Sarah ran as fast as she could. She ran down the street but couldn't find them. She turned onto River Avenue, but The Sneakers weren't there. As she ran, she tried to understand why the strange *guy* took their song and put it on the Internet.

"Karen said he's in a heavy metal rock band," Sarah thought. "Maybe his band took part in the *competition* too. And when he found out that we were also in the *competition*, he made it impossible for us to win!"

Then Sarah ran down Wood Street. Finally she reached the music shop, Music 4 U. Through the window she saw Simon, Justin, Julia and Kevin inside the shop.

She also saw the strange *guy* with the black leather coat. He was standing near the window. He was behind the *cash register*, at the front of the shop. A man was standing next to him – probably the shop manager. The *guy*'s back was facing the window. Sarah looked over the *guy*'s shoulder through the window and saw a CD on the table next to him.

It was The Sneakers' CD!

Sarah threw open the door to the shop and ran inside. First she went over to her friends. Before she started talking, she looked back at the *guy* in the leather coat. He seemed surprised and a bit worried. It looked as though he were counting the number of people in their group.

"*Guys*, I have to tell you something," Sarah *whispered*. "I think I know who put our song on the Internet!"
"Who?" the others asked at the same time.

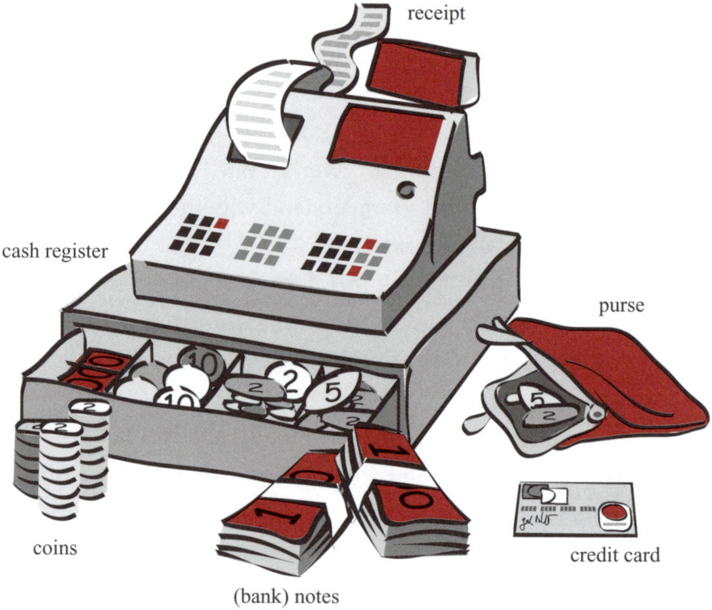

"He did it!" Sarah said and *pointed to* the strange *guy*. When the *guy* saw Sarah *pointing to* him, he jumped. He turned to the man next to him and said something quickly and quietly. Then he picked up the CD on the table and ran out of the shop.
"See! I told you he did it!" Sarah said. "Now he's trying to get away! Let's get him!"
The five band members ran out of the shop. They looked to the left and saw the *guy* running down the street. Luckily he wasn't too far away. But then he got onto a bike that was standing at the next corner.

Übung 49: In diesen Sätzen sind die Wörter durcheinander gekommen. Wie lauten die Sätze richtig?

1. found the *suspect* Sarah the has in shop

Sarah has found the suspect in the shop.

2. do what Sarah's you would in situation?

---

3. you tell would something I like to

---

4. going the how to is guy react?

---

5. Karen Sarah information told some important

Chapter 8: Surprise, Surprise!

"Oh, no! Now we'll never be able to *catch* him!" Simon said.
"Maybe you can't – but I can," Kevin said and *pointed to* his skateboard. He put the skateboard on the ground and jumped onto it.
"You've got your *mobile*, haven't you Simon?" Kevin asked.
"Yeah."
"Good, I've got mine too. As soon as I find out where he's going, I'll call you and you can meet me there. Wish me luck!" Kevin said as he *zoomed* away on his skateboard.
Kevin followed the strange *guy* down the street. He followed him when he turned right. The *guy* started riding up a big hill. It was

extremely difficult for Kevin to stay close to him. The distance between them grew larger and larger. When Kevin finally reached the top, he looked down and saw the *guy* at the bottom of the other side of the hill.

"Oh no! This hill is huge," Kevin said to himself. "Well, here we go ..." He pushed off the ground with his foot and started flying down the hill. Kevin had never *ridden* his skateboard down this hill before because it was so dangerous. He was worried that he would lose control and get hurt. Faster and faster he went. Luckily there weren't any cars on the street.

But then Kevin saw a small stone on the street ahead of him. If he hit a stone going this fast, he'd fly off his skateboard and break every bone in his body! At the last second, Kevin moved his feet a little to the right and *avoided* the stone. Finally he reached the bottom of the hill and started slowing down.

"Thank God I'm still alive!" he said to himself. Then he looked up and saw that the *guy* was quite far away now. The *guy* turned right onto Bridge Street. Kevin went as fast as he could. But when he reached the corner where the *guy* turned, the *guy* was gone!

Slowly Kevin *rode* his skateboard down Bridge Street. The *guy* was probably in one of the houses or shops in this street. Then Kevin saw a bicycle between a house and an Italian restaurant. The windows of the house were all dark. Kevin looked through the window of the restaurant carefully. A waiter was standing near the door. There were many tables and *booths* inside. But there didn't seem to be any customers.

Kevin was ready to walk away and accept that he had lost the *guy*. But then he saw something move in one of the *booths* in the restaurant. He saw a piece of black leather. The *guy* was there!

Kevin moved away from the restaurant. He called Simon and told him where he was.

Übung 50: Welches Verb gehört zu welchem Objekt? Trage die richtige Nummer in das Kästchen ein!

1. to invite	☐ a bone
2. to take	☐ a guest
3. to cut	☐ a bike
4. to tell	☐ hair
5. to break	☐ a meal
6. to order	☐ a photo
7. to ride	☐ a secret

Ten minutes later The Sneakers were standing next to Kevin.
"Let's get him!" Kevin said. The Sneakers went into the restaurant. They ran to the *booth* where the *guy* was sitting and formed a wall so that he couldn't get out.
"Now we've got you," Justin said.
"You can't get away now. You have to tell us everything!" Simon said.
The strange *guy* answered, "Fine, I'll tell you. But it *was supposed to be* a surprise."
"Oh, you surprised us!" Sarah said. "You wanted your band to win the *competition*, so you made it impossible for us to win!"
"What are you talking about?" the *guy* asked.
"Don't *pretend* you don't know what I mean," Sarah said. "If it's not true, why did you run away when we entered the shop?
"She told me that five of her *classmates* might come into the shop together," the *guy* said. "She said they might want to talk to me. If that happened, I should take the CD and go away. I don't know what the big problem is. She was just trying to help the other people in her band."
"What a minute," Justin said. "Who is 'she'?"

"She's this girl who's been so nice to me. Most girls think I'm too strange. I guess I *scare* them *away* with my clothes and the music I listen to. But she's different. Her name is Julia."

Sarah, Kevin, Simon and Justin turned to look at Julia. They were all shocked.

"What?! You?" Kevin said. "You were angry with ME for *messing* things *up* at Susie's house. But all the time you were the one who was behind it all!"

"I can't believe this," Justin said. "How could you do this to us? Why did you do it, Julia?"

Julia looked like she was going to cry.

"What are you people talking about?" the *guy interrupted*. "That's not Julia."

"Yes I am," Julia said.

"Tell us more about the Julia you know. And tell us your name," Simon said.

"I'm Rick. I met Julia about a week ago. She came into the shop and saw me using my computer. I was writing some text for my website. She started asking me what I knew about computers. I could see that she liked me. She was flirting a lot. You know girls don't normally flirt with me. They see that I look a little unusual, and they don't like that. But I'll tell you the truth. The only reason why I wear these clothes and listen to heavy metal music is because I thought no one would ever be interested in me anyway. I thought if I just *scared* girls *away*, no one would ever be able to break my heart. But Julia is different. She could see right through my dark, hard *shell*. Julia is …"

"Enough about how wonderful this 'Julia' is. Why do you have our CD – and what did she tell you to do with it?" Julia asked.

"She told me that she was in a band, but she didn't tell me the band's name. She said her band *recorded* a song. She wanted to give the other band members a nice surprise by giving the song some extra *publicity* on the Internet," Rick explained.

Übung 51: Sind die folgenden Aussagen richtig? Markiere mit richtig ✔ oder falsch –!

ÜBUNG 51 !

1. The Sneakers found Rick in an Italian restaurant. ☐
2. Susie told Rick to put the song on the Internet. ☐
3. Rick is angry with a girl called Julia. ☐
4. Rick is good-looking and many girls want to be his girlfriend. ☐
5. Rick has a website. ☐
6. The things Rick said made Julia upset. ☐

"So she told you to steal a CD, and you did it without asking any questions?" Sarah asked sarcastically. "What kind of idiot are you?"

"She said it wasn't stealing because it was her song too. She told me she saw that *guy*," Rick *pointed to* Simon, "put his copy of the song in his rucksack. So she said if I saw him in the shop, I should try to get the CD from his rucksack."

"I see! So that's why you kept *sneaking* up behind me on that day that I was buying CDs in your shop," Simon said. "I had no idea what you were doing. But I knew I didn't like it."

"After I had the CD, everything else was easy. I just put the song on a website where people can *download* songs," Rick continued. "So you must be the other members of her band. You're called The Sneakers, aren't you? I saw the name on the CD."

"Yes, we are The Sneakers. But there's only one Julia in our band – and she's standing right here," Kevin said and *pointed to* Julia.

"That's not Julia," Rick said. "Julia has long, blonde hair. And she always wears dresses. This girl here is wearing trousers. Julia never wears trousers. And this girl here seems a bit *shy*. Julia isn't *shy* at all. She's always saying that she was born to be a star. You know, it's strange – I never thought I would *fall for* a blonde girl who wears dresses. But I guess she really touched my heart. She made me want to be different."

ÜBUNG 52 !

Übung 52: Setze die richtigen Präpositionen ein!
(on, for, out, of, to, at)

The Sneakers were quiet 1. _______ a moment. They were trying to think 2. _______ who that could be.

"How could we be so stupid? I know who it must be!" Simon said.

All the band members said the name 3. _______ the same time: "Janet!"

Janet had long, blonde hair and always wore skirts and dresses. And Janet loved to say, "I was born 4. _______ be a star!"

"It's unbelievable," Kevin said. "She seemed to disappear after she found 5. _______ that she wasn't in the band. But all that time she's been working 6. _______ a plan *to get her revenge* on us!"

"And she even used my name! What if things had happened differently? I could have got into so much trouble," Julia said.
"I saw her one day outside the music shop," Simon said. "She

seemed so happy and friendly. What a big *liar*! She probably wanted extra *revenge* on me because I never reacted when she flirted with me. And I was chosen to be a singer, not her. That's probably why she decided to steal my copy of the song. I *bet* she used Julia's name because Julia was also chosen to be a singer in the band."
"Wait, you mean she's not in a band?" Rick asked. "And her name is Janet? This is horrible. I was planning to ask her to be my girlfriend. Now I don't even know who she is!"
"Janet lied to all of us. She only wanted *revenge*. She's so *evil*," Justin said.

*Übung 53: Vervollständige die Sätze mit **been, gone** oder **went**!*

ÜBUNG 53 !

1. "Where's the guy?" "He's ____________ into the restaurant."
2. Where have you ____________? I've been waiting here for hours!
3. I can't find my money anywhere – it's ____________!
4. "Do you want to go to the music shop?" "No, I've already ____________."
5. I ____________ to school yesterday, but I didn't go today.
6. He ____________ with them to the concert.
7. We've never ____________ to London, but we'd like to go.

Rick started to look worried.
"Hey, I didn't mean to do anything bad, you know," he said. "I just thought I was helping a *cute* girl. I thought she saw the real me – not just my long hair and my leather jacket. She was so nice to me. I hope I didn't make any problems for you."

"Yes, we've got some very big problems because of you and your little friend 'Julia'. But now you're coming with us, Rick. We have to find Janet and make her pay for what she's done," Sarah said.
"We should tell Mr Sharp too," Kevin said. "Does anyone know his *mobile* number?"
No one did. So instead of finding Janet *right away*, they decided to wait until the next day, at school. They told Rick to meet them at their school at *noon*.

The next morning, Simon found Janet in the corridor at school. He told her to meet him in room 363. He *pretended* to flirt with her and said, "I've got an exciting surprise for you."
Janet loved surprises. She also loved it when Simon showed interest in her. So when the bell rang at *noon*, she went directly to room 363.
The Sneakers were waiting for her. They had told Mr Sharp what happened earlier that morning. So he was with The Sneakers when Janet arrived.
As she opened the door she said, "I'm ready for my surprise, Si…"
She wasn't able to finish saying Simon's name. She was too shocked.
"What's going on here? Is this some kind of class *reunion*?" she asked. She tried to bring a smile to her face. But The Sneakers could see that she was nervous.
"No, Janet. It's a special surprise for you," Sarah said. "We," she *pointed to* the rest of the band, "are part one of the surprise. And here is part two."
Sarah *pointed to* Mr Sharp's desk. From behind the desk Rick stood up.
"Hello Julia. Or should I say Janet?" Rick said.
"What are you doing here, *sweetie*?" Janet asked in a false, friendly voice. She went to Rick and put her arms around him.

"Get your hands off me, you *liar*," Rick said angrily. "You used me. You played with my feelings. You made me believe that you liked me, but you only wanted to do something bad to these people here." He *pointed to* The Sneakers.

"What are you talking about, *darling*?" Janet asked. But everyone could hear the worry in her voice.

"That's not all," Kevin said. "You also made it impossible for us to win the band *competition* that we took part in. You stopped us from winning five thousand pounds and a *recording contract* with a big English record company."

"How did you find out that it was against the rules to *release* the song before the *competition* ended?" Justin asked.

Übung 54: Welcher Satz enthält die richtige Zeitform? Kreuze die richtige Lösung an!

ÜBUNG 54 !

1. Ihre Augen zeigten, dass sie nervös war.
   a) ☐ Her eyes have shown that she has been nervous.
   b) ☐ Her eyes showed that she was nervous.
   c) ☐ Her eyes show that she was nervous.

2. Ich freue mich darauf, die Wahrheit herauszufinden.
   a) ☐ I'm looking forward to discovering the truth.
   b) ☐ I'm being looking forward to discovering the truth.
   c) ☐ I will look forward to discovering the truth.

3. Janet wird die Wahrheit nicht länger verbergen können.
   a) ☐ Janet wouldn't be able to hide the truth any longer.
   b) ☐ Janet wouldn't have been able to hide the truth any longer.
   c) ☐ Janet won't be able to hide the truth any longer.

4. Er hat eine gute Idee gehabt.
   a) ☐ He had had a good idea.
   b) ☐ He has had a good idea.
   c) ☐ He have had a good idea.

5. Sie würde es machen, wenn sie es machen könnte.
   a) ☐ She would do it of she could have done it.
   b) ☐ She would do it if she could do it.
   c) ☐ She would have done it if she could do it.

Finally Janet *gave up*. She stepped away from Rick, and her smile turned into a *sneer*. The friendliness went out of her eyes, and only hate was left.

"You're all such idiots. You thought you were keeping things so secret. But all I had to do was put my ear to the door of room 363 a few times. You *guys* talk loudly – I heard everything. It was simple."

"I remember the day that I heard a noise at the door," Simon said. "You all said I was crazy – but I was right!"

"*What about* me?" Rick asked.

"*What about* you? Nothing. You were an easy *target*. Look at you. You're a *freak*. But I knew you would do anything I told you to do. So I told you to take the CD and put the song on the Internet. How could I really like you? The only boy I've ever liked has been Simon. But when he was chosen to be in the band, he left me behind. He let me fall into a forgotten world while he went on to become rich and famous. But I was born to be a star!" Janet said all of this very dramatically, as though she were acting on a stage.

The Sneakers looked at Mr Sharp.

"What happens now, Mr Sharp? We can make her pay for what she's done, can't we?" Justin asked.

Mr Sharp thought for a moment.

"I'm not really sure, *guys*," he said. "She didn't really break the law. She didn't even steal the CD – she made Rick do it for her. And it's legal to put a song on the Internet."
"But not if the song doesn't belong to you!" Julia said.
"That's true, Julia. But Rick did that for her too," Mr Sharp said. "I'll have to talk to the headmaster. I'll let him decide whether we need to go to the police or not."
The word 'police' made Janet's eyes open wide.
"P-p-police?" she asked nervously. "I can't go to prison! I'm going to be a star. I can't do that from a prison cell."
"You might not go to prison, Janet. But there's going to be trouble for you," Mr Sharp said. "Come with me. We have to talk to Headmaster Jones."

Übung 55: Übersetze die Wörter und enträtsele das Lösungswort!

1. Polizei _ _ _ _ ☐ _
2. Gesetz _ ☐ _
3. Gefängnis _ ☐ _ _ _ _
4. zerstören _ ☐ _ _ _ _ _
5. Rache _ _ _ ☐ _ _ _
6. Sarkasmus _ _ ☐ _ _ _ _

Lösung: _ _ _ _ _ _

Mr Sharp led Janet out of the room. But before she walked out, Janet looked back at Rick and The Sneakers and sneered.
"See," she said, "you can't become famous without me."
The door closed behind them. The room was quiet for a while.
Finally Sarah said, "That crazy *witch*."

"I only wish there was some way to make her pay for everything that she's done. She *admitted* everything. She said she wanted to hurt us, and she wanted to use Rick to do it," Kevin said.
"Maybe there is a way," Justin said. He reached under a desk and pulled out his high-tech laptop computer.

On the *screen* the teenagers could see a row of *buttons* that looked like those on a CD player. The *button* that said '*Record*' was lighter than the others. Justin clicked on the *button* and it turned dark.
"You didn't!" Sarah said happily.
"Oh yes, I did," Justin said with a huge smile. "I *recorded* every word she just said. Listen." He clicked on the 'Play' *button*.
"You're a *freak*. But I knew you would do anything I told you to do. So I told you to take the CD," Janet's voice said. It was coming from the *speakers* on the laptop computer.

Übung 56: Welche Wörter gehören zusammen? Trage die richtige Nummer in das Kästchen ein!

1. money	☐ computer
2. leather	☐ partner
3. business	☐ sandwich
4. CD	☐ coat
5. pencil	☐ problems
6. ham	☐ band
7. rock	☐ button
8. laptop	☐ cover
9. 'Play'	☐ sharpener

The next day was the last day of school before the winter holidays. After this day the pupils would have two weeks without lessons. The bell rang, which marked the beginning of the day's first lesson. But instead of going to their classrooms, The Sneakers went to Headmaster Jones's office. His secretary, Mrs Miller, was sitting outside the office. On the desk in front of her were a lot of *papers*. There was also a microphone. The microphone was *connected* to *speakers* in every classroom in the school. Mrs Miller used the microphone to make important *announcements* to all the teachers and pupils. But today the microphone would be used to make a different kind of *announcement*.

Simon, Sarah, Kevin and Julia ran up to Mrs Miller's desk.

"Mrs Miller, Mrs Miller! Come quickly!" they shouted. "Someone is smoking in the girls' toilet."

Mrs Miller's face darkened. She was an angry old woman, and the thing she hated the most was smoking. Every time she saw a pupil smoking cigarettes, she looked like she wanted to kill them.

"Well, we'll have to stop that right now," she said furiously. "Headmaster Jones is in a meeting, so I'll have to stop it myself. Let's go, children."

The four teenagers led Mrs Miller down the corridor, and away from her desk. Justin, who had been watching everything, went to the desk as soon as he saw the others leave. He opened his laptop computer and turned it on. He put the computer on the desk. He pressed the 'On' *button* on the microphone. He heard a noise come from the *speaker* on the wall of the office. Then he clicked the 'Play' *button* that was on his computer *screen*.

"You're a *freak*. But I knew you would do anything I told you to do. So I told you to take the CD and put the song on the Internet. I can't go to prison! I'm going to be a star. I can't do that from a prison cell. You can't become famous without me!"

! ÜBUNG 57

Übung 57: Unterstreiche im folgenden Textausschnitt die Gegenteile der vorgegebenen Wörter!
(1. quietly, 2. whispering, 3. normal, 4. start, 5. up, 6. worst, 7. smallest, 8. slowly, 9. poor, 10. positive)

Justin could hear Janet's voice loudly through the *speaker* on the wall. When she said those things yesterday, she was almost screaming. Her voice sounded crazy!

When the recording was finished, Justin clicked 'Stop'. Then he turned off the microphone and ran out of the room with his computer. As he ran down the corridor, he could hear loud laughter coming from every classroom.

It worked! Everyone was laughing at Janet. That was the best way to *punish* Janet for what she'd done. Janet believed that she was a star. But The Sneakers turned her into the school's biggest joke!

As Justin ran past the girls' toilet, he heard the door open. Quickly

he ran into the boys' toilet. He could hear Mrs Miller's voice coming from the corridor.
"Who did that? What's happening?!" she shouted as she ran towards the headmaster's office.
Justin put his head out into the corridor. There were Kevin, Simon, Julia and Sarah.
"Great work, Justin!" Julia said.
"Yes, that was perfect," Simon said. "People will be laughing at Janet for a long, long time!"
They all came together for a big group hug.
When they *separated*, Julia said, "But that still doesn't change the fact that we can no longer win the *competition*. We broke one of the rules."
"I guess our dreams of becoming rich and famous are over," Kevin said.
"Hey, don't be so negative. You never know what's going to happen," Simon said.

The winter holidays were fun and relaxing for all the band members. Julia, Simon, Justin, Kevin and Sarah enjoyed the two weeks without lessons. Although they were all very sad that they could no longer take part in the national band *competition*, they were happy that they had found out who put their song on the Internet.
When they returned to school, they felt fresh and ready to make a new start. When it was time for their music lesson with Mr Sharp, the pupils met again in room 363.
"Welcome back, everyone," Mr Sharp said. "I hope you enjoyed the holidays. It's good to see you all again. But before we start, there's something I'd like to tell you …"
Before Mr Sharp had a chance to continue, the door opened and Headmaster Jones walked in.

"Sorry for *interrupting*," the headmaster said, "but I'd like to make a short *announcement*. Janet Starr will not be returning to this school. She was so *embarrassed* by what happened last month that she asked her parents to transfer her to another school. I only wish we knew who did that."
The pupils smiled nervously.

ÜBUNG 58

Übung 58: Finde für das Wort in Klammern ein Reimwort, das in den Zusammenhang passt!

"I'll let you get back to (1. perk) ____________ now. Have a nice (2. way) ____________," Headmaster Jones said and left.
"I don't know for (3. pure) ____________ what happened that day either," said Mr Sharp. "And I don't think I want to (4. though) ____________. So I won't ask. Let's just leave all that behind us. But now I'd like you to (5. play) ____________ hello to a special guest for our first lesson of the (6. beer) ____________. Let me introduce a man who has a lot of experience in the music business. He works with all sorts of (7. hands) ____________ at a recording studio. Everyone, say hello to Al!"
The (8. bore) ____________ opened and in walked Mr Sharp's partner, Al. The pupils clapped.

"Hi, Al!" Sarah said. "It's good to see you again."
"It's great to see you too," Al said.

"Al is here today to give you a few tips about becoming famous in the music world," Mr Sharp said.
"That's right," Al said. "You might not know it, but I've helped several bands get *recording contracts* with important record companies. So here's tip number one for making your band rich and famous. You should always have two managers. That way you can be sure that one person isn't controlling everything. Take, for example, Sam – I mean, Mr Sharp – and me. We'd be perfect together. We work well together and we'd never try to steal money from each other." Al smiled.
"Tip number two. You need a cool, fun name," Al said and picked up a piece of *chalk*. He wrote on the *blackboard* 'T-H-E S-N-E-A-K-E-R-S'.

"Here's a really good example of a fantastic band name," he said.
The band members smiled.

"Tip number three. You need a great song." He pulled a CD out of his pocket. It was Simon's copy of The Sneakers' song, 'Secret'. The copy that Janet had stolen.

"Number four – a sensational CD *cover* design. I hate to give myself compliments, but I must say that this is a good example," Al said and took a CD case out of his bag. The picture on the *cover* of the case was Al's design – the one with the burning *sneakers* and the band's name on it.

Übung 59: Ergänze die Begriffe!

1. p _ _ c _ of chalk
2. _ _ c _ e _ of crisps
3. g _ _ _ s of water
4. _ u _ of coffee
5. _ _ t _ _ e of wine
6. _ _ _ y of The Sneakers' song
7. g _ _ u _ of pupils

"After that it gets a little more complicated," he said. "Some bands would take that one song and try to get a whole *recording contract* from a company. But that's not a very realistic plan. And because you are all quite young, a businessman from a record company might not take you seriously. You could try using your song to take part in a *competition*."

"What's your point, Al?" Simon asked.

"We've already tried to do that. But because Janet and Rick

released our song on the Internet, we're no longer allowed to win the *competition*. There's no hope for us now."

"Wait a minute, Simon. That was not the only band *competition* that exists. Another important thing to remember is that you should always think positively. Try not to be so negative," Al said. "I've got a friend at a record company. He says he likes your song a lot and says he would agree to officially *release* the song 'Secret' as a single."

"Yes!" Kevin shouted and jumped up from his seat. "How much money do we get for that?"

"Slow down, Kevin. Because you're a new band, you won't get any money for it," Al said. "But there's still a way to use the *released* single to become more successful. Mr Sharp and I have been collecting information about other band *competitions*. And we've found one that allows bands to take part using songs that have already been *released*."

"Hooray!" The Sneakers said at the same time.

"It's not going to be easy to win," Al continued. "This isn't just a national *competition* – it's a worldwide *competition*. That means you'll be compared with bands from the USA, Japan, Germany, France – everywhere! But the top three bands in the *competition* will all win a chance to get a *recording contract*."

Übung 60: Übersetze!

1. Österreich ....
2. Schweiz ....
3. Irland ....
4. Großbritannien ....

ÜBUNG 60 !

5. Kanada ....

6. Frankreich ....

7. Italien ....

"That's great, Al!" Justin said. "Thank you so much for helping us to get another chance to *make it big*!"

"It's my pleasure, Justin," Al said. "And here's my last tip of the day as your guest speaker. Never *give up*. Never accept that your chance for success has been destroyed. Think positively, fight for your dreams – and one day your dreams might become a reality!"

That day, Mr Sharp's pupils were more *obedient* than they had ever been before. They followed every last one of the tips Al gave them. They knew that they had the talent and the enthusiasm to turn their dreams to reality.

THE END

Abschlusstest

Übung 1: Welches Wort ist das „schwarze Schaf“?

1. worries, troubles, interests, problems
2. hope, friend, dream, wish
3. skirt, dress, trousers, hair
4. scream, shout, yell, whisper
5. blackboard, teacher, desk, sofa
6. table, kitchen, bathroom, cellar
7. mouse, screen, keyboard, piano
8. animal, cat, dog, hamster

Übung 2: In diesem Gitternetz sind acht Getränke versteckt. Findest du sie alle?

S	O	K	J	U	I	C	E
M	C	O	K	E	E	R	Y
U	O	L	W	I	N	E	J
R	F	T	A	K	P	C	N
T	F	E	T	M	I	L	K
W	E	A	E	H	G	B	O
B	E	E	R	D	Y	I	R
E	W	A	T	E	R	B	O

Übung 3: Wähle das passende Wort für jeden Satz aus und unterstreiche es!

1. Is there some/any information about Mr Sharp's friend, Al?
2. I spent most of my money – I haven't got much/many left.
3. Simon has been taking guitar lessons since/for five years.
4. I want to buy a CD. Could you borrow/lend me five pounds?
5. Goodbye! We will see us/each other tomorrow.
6. That was so/such a good concert!
7. I don't know whether their/they're coming.
8. Susie remembered/reminded Kevin to call her.
9. That's Susie's pet dog. It's/Its name is Hunter.

Übung 4: Welche Übersetzung der kursiv markierten Slang-Ausdrücke stimmt? Kreuze die richtige Lösung an!

1. Come on, you've got to chill out!
   a) ☐ Komm – du musst dich aufwärmen!
   b) ☐ Komm – du musst dich entspannen!

2. Susie likes Kevin. She thinks he's really fit.
   a) ☐ Susie mag Kevin. Sie meint, dass er wirklich gut aussieht.
   b) ☐ Susie mag Kevin. Sie meint, dass er durchtrainiert ist.

3. What's up, man?
   a) ☐ Was tut sich so, Alter?
   b) ☐ Was geht nach oben, Typ?

4. They snogged in her bedroom.
   a) ☐ Sie haben in ihrem Schlafzimmer geschnarcht.
   b) ☐ Sie haben in ihrem Schlafzimmer geknutscht.

Übung 5: Ordne die Buchstaben zu einem sinnvollen Wort!

1. Julia, Simon, Kevin, Justin and Sarah are members of a (dhan) __________.
2. Rick listened to music on his (eahdpnhoes) __________.
3. The Sneakers made their CD in Mr Sharp's (oustdi) __________.
4. If they write more songs, they can make an (bmalu) __________.
5. Justin had a CD (pyrlae) __________ in his laptop computer.
6. They tried to win a contract with a (drrceo) __________ company.
7. In a concert, the singer sings into a (imcroepnho) __________.

Übung 6: Übersetze die Wörter und trage sie in das Kreuzworträtsel ein!

HORIZONTAL
1. Verdächtigte(r)
6. Hinweis

VERTIKAL
1. klauen
2. erschrecken
3. böse
4. Dieb
5. umarmen

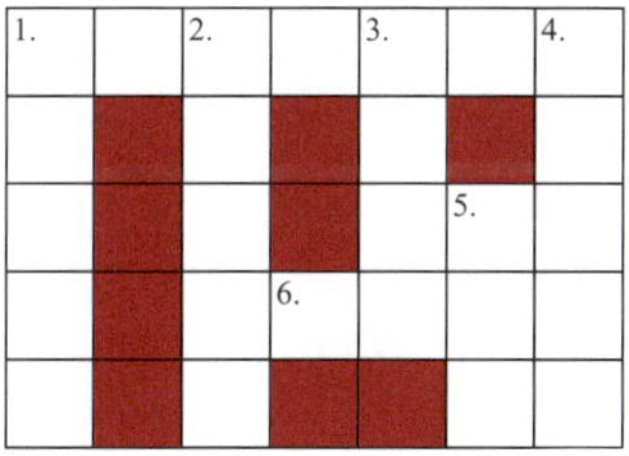

Übung 7: In diesen Sätzen werden „False Friends“ verwendet. Finde das richtige Wort und trage die entsprechende Nummer in das Kästchen ein!

1. Everyone likes Julia – she's very **sympathetic**.	☐	boss
2. I **will** a brand new bicycle for Christmas.	☐	save
3. Al is the **chef** of the company.	☐	think
4. I **became** a pet dog for my birthday!	☐	bright
5. I'm trying to **spare** money to buy a CD player.	☐	poison
6. I got perfect **notes** in my last English test.	☐	marks
7. We bought some **gift** to kill the rat.	☐	nice
8. Turn off the lamp. This room is too **hell**.	☐	got
9. I think Karen did it – what do you **mean**?	☐	want

Übung 8: Schreibe die Wörter in Großbuchstaben um!

1. Take away a letter from SECRETE to make something you're not allowed to tell anyone. ______________
2. Change a letter in REACHER to make the word for someone who works in a school. ______________
3. Change a letter in PINK to make the word for the kind of music Sarah likes. ______________
4. Change a letter in MOUSE to make the word for a place where people live. ______________
5. Add a letter to PORT to make the word for what football and tennis are. ______________

Übung 9: Vervollständige die Gegensätze!

1. lost _ _ _ n _
2. adult _ h _ l _
3. allowed _ _ r _ i _ d _ _
4. asleep _ _ ak _
5. relaxed _ x _ _ t _ d
6. black _ h _ _ e
7. up d _ _ _
8. future _ a _ t
9. work p _ _ y
10. possible _ m _ _ _ _ i _ _ _
11. guilty _ _ n _ _ _ _ t

Übung 10: Setze die richtigen Präpositionen ein!

1. The Sneakers looked __________ the person who stole the song.
2. Sarah and Justin broke __________ Karen's locker.
3. It didn't take them long to find __________ who the real thief was.
4. They had many problems – but they never gave __________.
5. The band got some important information __________ Rick.
6. __________ the end of the story, The Sneakers were happy.

Gemeinsamer Abschlusstest

Übung 1: Wofür stehen die SMS-Kürzel?

1. 2moro ______________________
2. gr8 ______________________
3. c u l8r ______________________
4. no1 ______________________
5. w8 ______________________
6. thx ______________________
7. u r ______________________
8. c u ______________________

Übung 2: Übersetze!

1. Medaillon ______________________
2. Torwart ______________________
3. Taschengeld ______________________
4. Schließfach ______________________
5. Mut ______________________
6. Probe ______________________
7. Plattenvertag ______________________
8. Rache ______________________

Übung 3: Ordne die Buchstaben zu einem sinnvollen Wort!

1. Susan was shaking from (okchs) ______________.
2. Kevin and Simon had seen a boy trying to break into a (ockrel) ______________ with a (crsewrdivre) ______________.
3. The band with the best (nsgo) ______________ would win £5,000 and a chance to get a (ceroringd ocntrcta) ______________ with a famous English record company.
4. Tracey loved her (ombiel hpoen) ______________ and was always (extnitg) ______________ her friends.
5. Simon opened his (awellt) ______________ and it was empty.
6. The three friends went up the (selactasro) ______________ to the top floor of the shopping centre.
7. She picked up her mobile phone and pressed the (eyk apd) ______________ to type in a message.

Übung 4: Setze die Verben ins Simple Past!

1. She (to go) ______________ to the pool, even though she (not like) ______________ the sun very much.
2. Julia (to become) ______________ angry with Kevin.
3. The lifeguards (to collect) ______________ money at the pool entrance.

4. They (to swim) ______________, (to talk) ______________ and (to lie) ______________ in the sun.

5. Julia (to walk) ______________ out and the three (to leave) ______________ for a café.

6. Someone (to steal) ______________ the CD player from Kevin.

7. Simon almost (to make) ______________ a joke about Kevin.

Übung 5: Sind die folgenden Aussagen richtig? Markiere mit richtig ✔ oder falsch – !

1. Simon and Kevin knew most of the lifeguards. ☐
2. Boris came from Bulgaria. ☐
3. Zoltan drove a blue van. ☐
4. Sarah likes punk rock. ☐
5. Mick is a policeman. ☐
6. Sarah and Simon are a couple. ☐
7. Kevin is a very good swimmer. ☐
8. Sarah plays the flute. ☐

Übung 6: Bilde die passenden Fragen zu den unterstrichenen Satzteilen!

1. Mick works <u>as a lifeguard</u>.

What does Mick work?

2. Rob is the manager at a pool.

....

3. Sarah listens to punk rock music.

....

4. They are spending their summer at the pool.

....

5. Kevin thought the maintenance men had stolen his CD player.

....

6. The maintenance men had access to a pass key.

....

Übung 7: Setze die richtigen Präpositionen ein!

1. Susan was the captain of the senior hockey team ______ St. Mary's High School.
2. Heather and Tracey helped Susan ______ her school uniform.
3. She emptied the contents of all the drawers ______ her bed.
4. Arthur was worried ______ the others.
5. They wanted to take Susan ______ the hospital.
6. Amanda and Giles had been going out together ______ six months, but later Giles had split up ______ Amanda.

7. Susan left her locket ________ her blazer.

8. They jumped out ________ their hiding place.

Übung 8: Setze das richtige Fragewort ein!

1. ____________ stole the CD player from Kevin?
2. ____________ side are you on?
3. ____________ boys helped Susan and her friends?
4. ____________ long are the summer holidays?
5. ____________ was the locket stolen?
6. ____________ did the thief want from Susan?
7. ____________ did the three girls go to the shopping centre?
8. ____________ lends Tracey twenty pounds

Übung 9: Übersetze die Wörter und enträtsele das Lösungswort!

1. vergessen _ _ _ □ _ _
2. Tür _ □ _ _
3. einfach _ □ _ _
4. Schließfach □ _ _ _ _ _
5. Liegestuhl _ _ _ □ _ _ _ _ _
6. beweisen _ _ _ _ □
7. Zeuge _ _ _ _ □ _ _
8. verdächtigen _ _ _ □ _ _ _
9. Erbstück _ □ _ _ _ _ _ _

10. Eingang _ _ _ ☐ _ _ _ _

Lösung: _ _ _ _ _ _ _ _ _ _

Übung 10: Wie lauten die Wörter in der richtigen Reihenfolge? Bilde sinnvolle Sätze!

1. girls spent the time of lot a out hanging park in the

____

2. looked Susan the in hair long her at blonde mirror

____

3. swam ladder he climbed of out the over a to pool walked and the to back deckchairs

____

4. school they after rehearsal band their first had

____

5. and Heather Tracey Susan into helped uniform school her

____

Übung 11: Welche Wörter gehören in die Lücken?
(record company, headphones, collection, auditions, competition)

1. There was a national teen band ______________.

2. The ____________________ are open to anyone in the school.
3. The competition is being organized by a famous English ____________________.
4. Sarah looked through her CD ____________________ in her bedroom.
5. Justin smiled and put the ____________________ over his ears.

Übung 12: Finde das gesuchte Wort!

1. the opposite of quiet ____________________
2. the season after the spring ____________________
3. the restaurant at school ____________________
4. a school jacket is called a ____________________
5. the top of a room ____________________
6. the day after today ____________________
7. the meal before you go to bed ____________________

Lösungen

Crime Scene: Locker Room

Übung 1: 1. (fredom) freedom 2. (pritty) pretty 3. (noise) nose 4. (whering) wearing 5. (moar) more 6. (thay) they 7. (cupple) couple 8. (werth) worth 9. (stuppid) stupid 10. (boared) bored
Übung 2: 1. answered 2. said 3. suggested 4. set 5. skated 6. looked 7. was
Übung 3: 1. What 2. Where 3. Why/When 4. Who 5. How 6. What 7. Which 8. Who 9. When
Übung 4: 1. a 2. The 3. the 4. a 5. a 6. The 7. an, a 8. the
Übung 5: 1. swim 2. jump 3. meet 4. climb 5. dive 6. run Lösung: summer
Übung 6: 1. closed 2. long 3. hot 4. yelled/shouted 5. followed 6. good
Übung 7: 1. study 2. room 3. cough 4. great 5. broken 6. train 7. happy 8. dive
Übung 8: 1. walked 2. waited 3. was 4. took 5. ate 6. waited 7. worked 8. got
Übung 9: 1. Simon is a shy young man. 2. Sarah has pink hair. 3. Kevin rides his skateboard everywhere. 4. It was a very hot day at the pool. 5. The pool was crowded with running children. 6. Do you want to go to a café?
Übung 10: 1. About 6 weeks – from the end of July until the beginning of September. 2. The story begins in July. 3. Sarah's hair is pink. 4. Simon and Kevin are best friends. 5. No, they don't.
Übung 11: 1. b 2. a 3. b 4. b 5. b
Übung 12: 1. swimsuit 2. deckchair 3. sunscreen 4. headphones 5. skateboard 6. lifeguards 7. freestyle
Übung 13: 1. back 2. while 3. swim 4. hear 5. asked 6. news 7. know
Übung 14: 1. A bicycle has fewer wheels than a skateboard. 2. July is hotter than April. 3. A desert is dryer than a pool. 4. Children's swimsuits are smaller than men's swimsuits. 5. Chinese is more difficult than English. 6. Ice cream is colder than water. 7. A pool is bigger than a bathtub. 8. Hip-hop is funkier than punk rock.
Übung 15: 1. affects 2. hear 3. their 4. looks like 5. sweat 6. think 7. off 8. space
Übung 16: 1. his 2. her 3. their 4. my 5. their 6. your 7. our 8. our
Übung 17: 1. blows 2. shines 3. falls 4. shines 5. blows 6. falls
Übung 18: 1. know 2. ballet 3. break 4. row (a fight) 5. wind (weather) 6. tear (crying) 7. here
Übung 19: 1. pool 2. sweat 3. tall 4. book 5. crime 6. sell
Übung 20: 1. Yes (at least most of them). 2. They keep them in the lockers. 3. He always has his skateboard with him. 4. He says it cost over £200. 5. No, they didn't. 6. His name is Rob. 7. He thinks (one or both of) the maintenance men took it. 8. The thief may have used a pass key.
Übung 21: 1. a 2. b 3. a 4. b 5. b

Übung 22: 1. from 2. in/from 3. to 4. from 5. from 6. for
Übung 23: 1. back 2. knee 3. neck 4. elbow 5. wrist 6. ankle 7. head
Übung 24: Spanish, Dutch, English, Russian, French, German

S P A N I S H G
F A B T L E F E
R D U T C H A R
E N G L I S H M
N F K M L D E A
C P Z L B A R N
H R U S S I A N

Übung 25: 1. richtig 2. richtig 3. falsch 4. falsch 5. richtig 6. falsch
Übung 26: 1. mean 2. friends 3. mad 4. stole 5. intelligent 6. answer
Übung 27: 1. b 2. b 3. a 4. b 5. a
Übung 28: 1. walked 2. nothing 3. bright 4. black 5. quickly 6. in
Übung 29: 1. looking 2. door 3. see 4. key 5. knew 6. lock 7. very 8. tanks 9. wall
Übung 30: 1. him 2. her 3. his 4. she 5. him, his
Übung 31: 1. closed 2. heard 3. came 4. pressed 5. hear 6. put 7. tried 8. looked 9. felt 10. have got
Übung 32: 1. dirty 2. good 3. perfect 4. safe 5. secure 6. best
Übung 33: 1. seventeen 2. seventy-five 3. second 4. one quarter 5. one thousand four hundred/fourteen hundred. 6. one million 7. twenty-fifth
Übung 34: 1. learn 2. follow 3. thought 4. stole 5. quietly 6. friendly
Übung 35: 1. wants 2. their 3. stolen 4. get 5. boss 6. dived 7. have 8. off 9. lost
Übung 36: 1. a 2. b 3. b 4. a 5. a
Übung 37: 1 In the air was the smell of perfume. 2. Clouds crossed the sky, blocking the sun completely. 3. It was dry everywhere. 4. There was lots of money inside.
Übung 38: 1. of 2. on 3. in 4. to 5. of 6. to 7. on 8. on
Übung 39: 1. tall/short 2. difficult/simple 3. large/tiny 4. wide/narrow 5. sweaty/dry 6. dangerous/safe
Übung 40: 1. (tryed) tried 2. (darknesse) darkness 3. (flur) floor 4. (to) too 5. (smell) small 6. (systum) system 7. (hed) head 8. (sing) song 9. (answurd) answered 10. (frunt) front
Übung 41: 1. stood 2. took 3. rubbed 4. went 5. studied 6. gave 7. stole 8. flew
Übung 42: 1. umbrella 2. swimsuit 3. ice cream 4. bottle 5. towel 6. sunscreen 7. locker
Übung 43: 1. autumn/fall 2. biscuit/cookie 3. dustbin/trashcan 4. pavement/sidewalk 5. queue/line 6 petrol/gasoline

Übung 44: 1. Kevin holds onto Boris's van and rides his skateboard. 2. Kevin looks in the storage area at the pool. 3. Simon lets Kevin out of the locked room in the storage area. 4. Boris works in a hip-hop club.
Übung 45: 1. table 2. neighbourhood 3. chair 4. efficient 5. van 6. color
Übung 46: 1. The van was driven by Boris. 2. The CD player was not stolen by Simon. 3. Kevin was freed from the room by Simon. 4. Sarah was disappointed by Simon. 5. I was driven to the airport by my parents. 6. One of the lifeguards was suspected by Simon and Sarah.
Übung 47: 1. difficult 2. less 3. quickly 4. Luckily 5. everywhere 6. shut 7. towards
Übung 48: 1. suit 2. hour 3. beans 4. cry 5. clock 6. money 7. shirt
Übung 49: (Yesterday) Kevin saw where Boris works (yesterday). 2. Sarah spoke to Simon about the problem. 3. Why did Kevin go into the storage area? 4. Who moved the deckchairs? 5. Julia said, "I'll never help you again."
Übung 50: 1. entrance 2. collecting 3. desk 4. wallet 5. reason 6. broke 7. tomorrow
Übung 51: HORIZONTAL: 1. safe 5. locker 6. ceiling, VERTIKAL: 1. storage 2. wallet 3. money 4. steal
Übung 52: 1. to make a mistake 2. to ride a bike 3. to drive a van 4. to do homework 5. to catch a cold 6. to get an idea 7. to break a promise 8. to take a picture
Übung 53: 1. falsch 2. falsch 3. richtig 4. falsch 5. falsch 6. richtig 7. falsch 8. richtig
Übung 54: 1. a 2. b 3. a 4. b 5. a 6. a
Übung 55: 1. noticed 2. didn't/did not look 3. had seen 4. held 5. followed 6. saw 7. was 8. is going 9. don't/do not know 10. expect
Übung 56: 1. at 2. to 3. on 4. in 5. for 6. to 7. at 8. at 9. at 10. at
Übung 57: 1. there 2. seven 3. rest 4. back 5. side 6. please 7. Good
Übung 58: 1. walking 2. stood back 3. pulled 4. shouted 5. silent 6. nothing 7. bigger
Übung 59: 1. Sarah had a great idea. 2. The two were very hot in the locker room. 3. What are you doing in the ceiling? 4. Mick was very angry with the police. 5. Did Kevin admit his mistake? 6. Mick, Rob and Lori were the thieves.
Übung 60: 1. to take a walk 2. Check it out! 3. Ride my bike! 4. to drive a car 5. to catch a thief 6. Come with me!

Lösungen Abschlusstest

Übung 1: 1. policeman 2. board 3. daft 4. house 5. sunbathe 6. song
Übung 2: 1. to 2. from 3. about 4. with 5. to 6. at 7. to
Übung 3: 1. swim 2. safe 3. sunbathing 4. locker 5. entry fee 6. towel
Übung 4: 1. listen to 2. wants 3. space 4. looks like 5. think 6. get 7. boss 8. their
Übung 5: 1. swam 2. ran 3. took 4. answered 5. met 6. were 7. went
Übung 6: 1. Kevin takes his skateboard almost everywhere. 2. Sarah listens to punk rock music. 3. Simon enjoys riding his bicycle. 4. Who stole Kevin's CD player? 5. Boris speaks Russian and English. 6. Julia jumped into the water.
Übung 7: 1. jump 2. dive 3. note 4. running 5. crawl 6. suntan 7. swimsuit 8. locker
Übung 8: 1. thought 2. did not/didn't know 3. was enjoying, stole 4. had been friends 5. has/had 6. was

Ultimatum by SMS

Übung 1: 1. gole (goal) 2. aut (out) 3. rite (right) 4. paine (pain) 5. fellt (felt) 6. teers (tears)
Übung 2: 1. the 2. make 3. have 4. felt 5. leg 6. pain 7. water
Übung 3: 1. hold 2. play 3. help 4. appear 5. try Lösung: happy
Übung 4: 1. apple 2. win 3. anger 4. left 5. terrible 6. shoe 7. new
Übung 5: 1. sat 2. cried 3. put 4. tried 5. said 6. helped 7. were
Übung 6: 1. She goes to St. Mary's High School. 2. Her best friends are Heather and Tracey. 3. He is caring. 4. Her grandmother gave her the locket. 5. She blew the whistle.
Übung 7: 1. my 2. their 3. my 4. her 5. his 6. our 7. her 8. his
Übung 8: 1. falls 2. sings 3. runs 4. runs 5. falls 6. sings
Übung 9: 1. June is hotter than January. 2. Running is faster than walking. 3. Russian is more difficult than English. 4. A hockey stick is longer than a tennis racquet. 5. A house is bigger than a flat. 6. A grandmother is older than a mother.
Übung 10: 1. hurt 2. thinks 3. mobile 4. blew 5. looked 6. much
Übung 11: 1. match 2. arms 3. want 4. leg 5. under 6. door 7. come 8. said
Übung 12: 1. c 2. d 3. f 4. e 5. a 6. b
Übung 13: 1. b 2. b 3. c 4. a 5. c
Übung 14: 1. falsch 2. falsch 3. richtig 4. falsch 5. richtig 6. falsch 7. richtig
Übung 15: 1. to 2. out 3. to 4. out 5. for 6. to 7. for
Übung 16: 1. She kept it on her bedside table. 2. They went to the shopping centre to investigate the first suspect Giles. 3. She pounded them with her fists. 4. She rubbed ointment on Susan's leg. 5. Susan's hair is blonde. 6. No, she finished with him.
Übung 17: 1. thing 2. feet 3. time 4. explode 5. locket
Übung 18: 1. slowly 2. difficult 3. closer/nearer 4. small/little 5. long
Übung 19: 1. laughed 2. was 3. felt 4. continued 5. was 6. rose 7. lost
Übung 20: 1. of 2. to 3. out 4. on 5. over
Übung 21: 1. blazer 2. substitute 3. exhausted 4. precious 5. anxious 6. split 7. yawn
Übung 22: 1. d 2. e 3. c 4. b 5. f 6. a
Übung 23: 1. thaught (thought) 2. runing (running) 3. fin (fine) 4. kno (know) 5. shure (sure) 6. tim (time)
Übung 24: 1. The team beat us every time. 2. The sun shone. 3. He was suspicious. 4. They were annoyed. 5. He came to the park every week. 6. We had a message. 7. They won the match.
Übung 25: 1. sat 2. thought 3. spoke 4. sent 5. came 6. grabbed
Übung 26: 1. a 2. An 3. a 4. the 5. a 6. the 7. an 8. the 9. the

Übung 27: 1. She fell into the arms of her mum. 2. The mobile was by her bedside. 3. You can come in now. 4. Who sent the message? 5. I need a bit of space now. 6. Do not tell anyone! 7. She was starting to get annoyed.
Übung 28: 1. d 2. a 3. c 4. b 5. f 6. e 7. h 8. i 9. g
Übung 29: 1. would-be 2. hot 3. big 4. traditional 5. great 6. small 7. round 8. good
Übung 30: 1. sixteen 2. sixty-nine 3. one third 4. one thousand five hundred 5. two million 6. fourth 7. one hundred and ten 8. eighty 9. fifty-three 10. forty-six
Übung 31: 1. noticed 2. cried out 3. definitely 4. normally 5. got up 6. find out
Übung 32: 1. b 2. a 3. b 4. a 5. b
Übung 33: 1. She did nothing because fear kept her from moving. 2. She was hurt on her head and face. 3. They wanted to take her to the hospital. 4. Amanda is Beverly's friend. 5. No, she doesn't want them to know.
Übung 34: 1. f 2. d 3. a 4. g 5. c 6. b 7. e
Übung 35: 1. tolking (talking) 2. to (too) 3. wos (was) 4. stealed (stolen) 5. sad (said) 6. sware (swear) 7. beleive (believe) 8. where (were)
Übung 36: 1. went 2. found 3. saw 4. told 5. lost 6. did 7. said 8. knew
Übung 37: 1. Heather is a good friend of Susan's. 2. Someone has stolen the locket. 3. Susan scored a goal. 4. Susan felt hope rise. 5. The toffees fell on the floor. 6. Who is Tracey? 7. There has to be an explanation. 8. She sent a text message.
Übung 38: 1. a 2. b 3. a 4. b
Übung 39: 1. cook 2. park 3. locket 4. night 5. pound 6. bed
Übung 40: 1. richtig 2. richtig 3. falsch 4. richtig 5. falsch 6. falsch
Übung 41: 1. hockey 2. crowd 3. shoulder 4. blackmailed 5. present 6. uniform 7. anonymous 8. yawned
Übung 42: 1. her 2. his 3. she 4. him 5. her
Übung 43: 1. Has she found the money? 2. Have you tried another jeweller? 3. Have they been to the billiard café? 4. Have I seen the locket before? 5. Has it disappeared from your bag? 6. Have we met the boy? 7. Has she told her parents? 8. Has he received a message? 9. Have you bought a new pair of hockey boots?
Übung 44: 1. How 2. Who 3. Which 4. How 5. When 6. Where 7. What 8. Who
Übung 45: 1. He wanted two hundred pounds. 2. The locket was stolen during the hockey match. 3. Arthur and George helped them. 4. Giles is Susan's ex-boyfriend. 5. Tracey's dad lends her twenty pounds.
Übung 46: 1. alternative 2. nightmare 3. tiptoe 4. duvet 5. magazine 6. purse 7. torch 8. snore
Übung 47: 1. A text message was sent by the blackmailer. 2. The money was stolen by Heather. 3. The goal was scored by Susan. 4. She was hated by

someone. 5. They were looked after by her parents. 6. Giles was suspected by the girls.
Übung 48: 1. clock 2. car 3. desk 4. drawers 5. pitch 6. teacher 7. swing
Übung 49: 1. desk 2. goalkeeper 3. breakfast 4. hospital 5. yesterday 6. boring
Übung 50: 1. chess 2. loser 3. food 4. three 5. shop 6. lips
Übung 51: 1. forget 2. strong 3. bring 4. from 5. went
Übung 52: 1. loud 2. table 3. mopeds 4. braked 5. figures 6. impos-sible 7. towards 8. run
Übung 53: 1. c 2. f 3. d 4. a 5. b 6. g 7. h 8. e
Übung 54: 1. afraid 2. wise 3. injured 4. internal 5. broken 6. muddy 7. clear
Übung 55: 1. stayed 2. rode 3. wanted 4. said 5. gave 6. drove 7. sat 8. held
Übung 56: 1. hid 2. demanded 3. rang 4. helped 5. fought 6. quiet 7. agreed 8. carried 9. fault 10. knew
Übung 57: 1. she 2. Her 3. she 4. her 5. them 6. They 7. them 8. She 9. them
Übung 58: 1. try 2. be 3. had 4. other 5. took 6. told 7. did
Übung 59: 1. blushed 2. enjoyed 3. go 4. check 5. murmured 6. stay 7. wounded 8. made
Übung 60: 1. Later 2. stopped 3. down 4. good 5. long 6. shouted

Lösungen Abschlusstest

Übung 1: 1. went 2. get 3. Where 4. Our 5. There 6. sweet
Übung 2: 1. rang 2. brought 3. twisted 4. slept 5. caught 6. rode
Übung 3: 1. ball 2. paramedic 3. trap 4. hear 5. fall 6. locket
Übung 4: 1. lied 2. shops 3. Maths 4. snored 5. burst 6. canteen 7. blazer
Übung 5: 1. in 2. of 3. to 4. about 5. for 6. on 7. at
Übung 6: 1. broke 2. constable 3. wardrobe 4. pouch 5. visor
Übung 7: 1. took 2. cooks 3. hid 4. Can 5. name 6. Drink 7. Well
Übung 8: 1. falsch 2. falsch 3. richtig 4. falsch 5. richtig 6. richtig
Übung 9: 1. goal 2. Escalators 3. savings 4. park 5. mind
Übung 10: 1. pain 2. score 3. more 4. fat 5. scare 6. her 7. said 8. foot
Übung 11: 1. Susan had stretched out her leg too far and torn a muscle. 2. The tears were now streaming down Susan's cheeks. 3. She opened her desk and took out her savings book. 4. Arthur stared at Susan with a blank expression on his face. 5. Giles had been working together with a band of

Cold Revenge

Übung 1: 1. quickly 2. Slowly (or Quietly) 3. quietly (or slowly) 4. immediately 5. loudly
Übung 2: 1. told 2. said 3. heard 4. asked 5. stepped 6. came 7. smiled
Übung 3: 1. trumpet 2. guitar 3. saxophone 4. violin 5. organ Lösung: piano
Übung 4: 1. the 2. an 3. the 4. a 5. a 6. an
Übung 5: 1. 10.15 am 2. 8.55 pm 3. 3.27 pm 4. 11.10 am 5. 12.00 6. 1.30 pm 7. 8.43 am
Übung 6: 1. blue 2. red 3. orange 4. green 5. white
Übung 7: 1. room 2. music 3. class 4. thin 5. radio 6. lesson 7. flu 8. glad
Übung 8: 1. What 2. Which 3. When 4. Who 5. How
Übung 9: 1. a 2. a 3. b 4. b 5. b
Übung 10: 1. Mr Sharp teaches music. 2. Kevin plays the bass guitar. 3. The band could win £5,000. 4. Julia likes jazz music. 5. Justin likes the name The *Fabulous* Five.
Übung 11: 1. girlfriend 2. classroom 3. headmaster 4. weekend 5. skateboard 6. someone 7. fingernail
Übung 12: 1. leg 2. shop 3. wood 4. think 5. bell 6. nose
Übung 13: 1. They're 2. There 3. there 4. their
Übung 14: 1. noise 2. pupil 3. sun 4. pen 5. smile
Übung 15: 1. Sarah has a lot of energy. 2. Do you like this song? 3. Justin likes playing with computers. 4. Why is everything a secret? 5. Janet is not in the band.
Übung 16: 1. fewer 2. any 3. prize 4. tell 5. put on 6. taught 7. until 8. about
Übung 17: 1. A village is smaller than a town. 2. A car is more expensive than a bicycle. 3. An ocean is deeper than a lake. 4. Hip-hop music is cooler than classical music. 5. A tree is taller than a bush.
Übung 18: 1. They jumped when the balloon exploded. 2. Kevin loved to eat chicken and potatoes. 3. It's nice when the weather is sunny. 4. Not many people are on holiday. 5. She works in a factory. 6. I went to the cinema yesterday.
Übung 19: 1. weather 2. street 3. jeans 4. hand 5. eyes 6. later 7. face 8. name
Übung 20: 1. richtig 2. falsch 3. falsch 4. falsch 5. falsch 6. richtig
Übung 21: 1. soon 2. good 3. get 4. boss 5. marks 6. novel
Übung 22: 1. into 2. up 3. on 4. on 5. on 6. over 7. in
Übung 23: 1. happy 2. sweet 3. new 4. later 5. quickly 6. more
Übung 24: 1. b 2. a 3. b 4. c 5. c
Übung 25: 1. (shoutid) shouted 2. (repeeted) repeated 3. (Sorrie) Sorry 4. (grate) great 5. (heer) hear 6. (gayve) gave 7. (azked) asked 8. (smild) smiled 9. (disapeered) disappeared

Übung 26: 1. word 2. notes 3. day 4. song 5. Internet 6. hands 7. eyes
Übung 27: 1. think 2. find 3. lost 4. took 5. band 6. friends 7. sure
Übung 28: 1. safe/dangerous 2. empty/full 3. rich/poor 4. excited/ calm 5. back/front 6. often/seldom
Übung 29: 1. anybody 2. Nobody 3. anything 4. anything/anybody 5. nothing
Übung 30: 1. found/discovered 2. place/location 3. created/made 4. part/ piece 5. perfect/ideal 6. path/*trail*
Übung 31: 1. thirty-two 2. first 3. thirteenth 4. half 5. eight thousand three hundred
Übung 32: 1. dead 2. strong 3. normal 4. clean 5. cheap 6. ready
Übung 33: 1. paid 2. left 3. got 4. drove 5. going 6. show 7. explained
Übung 34: 1. grass 2. tree 3. rose 4. bush
Übung 35: 1. Then his mum turned the television off. 2. I think it's some kind of cat. 3. The bank isn't open on Sundays. 4. Justin wanted to go home. 5. There was a party happening.
Übung 36: 1. a 2. b 3. a 4. b 5. b
Übung 37: 1. flat/apartment 2. holiday/vacation 3. lorry/truck 4. lift/ elevator 5. *trainer*/*sneaker* 6. rubbish/garbage
Übung 38: 1. Because there are a lot of *bills* in Al's office. 2. They found it in her *locker*. 3. He hid in the toilet *cubicle*. 4. Two girls almost found him. 5. No, she didn't.
Übung 39: 1. which 2. where 3. it's 4. for 5. surprised
Übung 40: 1. lemon 2. smell 3. butter 4. oven 5. egg
Übung 41:1. away 2. out 3. on 4. up 5. of 6. in
Übung 42: 1. saw 2. followed 3. belonged 4. doing 5. Come 6. talk 7. let
Übung 43: 1. Julia said she hated potatoes. 2. Justin said he didn't want to. 3. Sarah asked where it was. 4. Mr Sharp told Al to come in. 5. Mr Sharp asked what Al was doing. 6. Kevin said he was a strange *guy*. 7. Simon said he thought Al did it.
Übung 44: 1. strange 2. pale 3. flame 4. tired 5. pair 6. speak
Übung 45: 1. skin 2. strange 3. search 4. kitchen 5. angry 6. pencil
Übung 46: 1. I will give you a present for your birthday. 2. I want to go to the concert, but I'm not sure where it is. 3. Why did you decide to do that? 4. There were no other people on the empty street. 5. I'll tell you what you should do. 6. Susie didn't steal the CD from the hole.
Übung 47: 1. stupid 2. hungry 3. boring 4. futuristic 5. wet 6. lonely 7. empty
Übung 48: 1. for you 2. Are you okay? 3. thanks 4. today 5. before 6. please
Übung 49: 1. Sarah has found the *suspect* in the shop. 2. What would you do in Sarah's situation? 3. I would like to tell you something. 4. How is the *guy* going to react? 5. Karen told Sarah some important information.
Übung 50: 1. to invite a guest 2. to take a photo 3. to cut hair 4. to tell a secret 5. to break a bone 6. to order a meal 7. to ride a bike

Übung 51: 1. richtig 2. falsch 3. falsch 4. falsch 5. richtig 6. richtig
Übung 52: 1. for 2. of 3. at 4. to 5. out 6. on
Übung 53: 1. gone 2. been 3. gone 4. been 5. went 6. went 7. been
Übung 54: 1. b 2. a 3. c 4. b 5. b
Übung 55: 1. police 2. law 3. prison 4. destroy 5. *revenge* 6. sarcasm Lösung: career
Übung 56: 1. money problems 2. leather coat 3. business partner 4. CD cover 5. pencil sharpener 6. ham sandwich 7. rock band 8. laptop computer 9. 'Play' button
Übung 57: 1. quietly/loudly 2. *whispering*/screaming 3. normal/crazy 4. start/ stop 5. up/down 6. worst/best 7. smallest/biggest 8. slowly/ quickly 9. poor/rich 10. positive/negative
Übung 58: 1. work 2. day 3. sure 4. know 5. say 6. year 7. bands 8. door
Übung 59: 1. piece 2. packet 3. glass 4. cup 5. bottle 6. copy 7. group
Übung 60: 1. Austria 2. Switzerland 3. Ireland 4. Great Britain 5. Canada 6. France 7. Italy

Lösungen Abschlusstest

Übung 1: 1. interests 2. friend 3. hair 4. *whisper* 5. sofa 6. table 7. piano 8. animal
Übung 2: 1. juice 2. Coke 3. wine 4. milk 5. beer 6. coffee 7. tea 8. water
Übung 3: 1. any 2. much 3. for 4. lend 5. each other 6. such 7. they're 8. reminded 9. Its
Übung 4: 1. b 2. a 3. a 4. b
Übung 5: 1. band 2. *headphones* 3. studio 4. album 5. player 6. record 7. microphone
Übung 6: HORIZONTAL: 1. *suspect* 6. *clue*, VERTIKAL: 1. steal 2. scare 3. *evil* 4. thief 5. hug
Übung 7: 1. nice 2. want 3. boss 4. got 5. save 6. marks 7. poison 8. bright 9. think
Übung 8: 1. secret 2. teacher 3. punk 4. house 5. sport
Übung 9: 1. found 2. child 3. forbidden 4. awake 5. excited 6. white 7. down 8. past 9. play 10. impossible 11. innocent
Übung 10: 1. for 2. into 3. out 4. up 5. from 6. At

Lösungen gemeinsamer Abschlusstest

Übung 1: 1. tomorrow 2. great 3. see you later 4. no one 5. wait 6. thanks 7. you are 8. see you
Übung 2: 1. locket 2. goalkeeper 3. pocket money 4. locker 5. courage 6. rehearsal 7. recording contract 8. revenge
Übung 3: 1. shock 2. locker, screwdriver 3. song, recording contract 4. mobile phone, texting 5. wallet 6. escalators 7. key pad
Übung 4: 1. went, did not/didn' t like 2. became 3. collected 4. swam, talked, lay 5. walked, left 6. stole 7. made
Übung 5: 1. richtig 2. falsch 3. falsch 4. richtig 5. falsch 6. falsch 7. falsch 8. falsch
Übung 6: 1. What does Mick work? 2. Who is Rob? 3. What kind of music does Sarah listen to? 4. Where are they spending their summer? 5. Who did Kevin think had stolen his CD player? 6. What did the maintenance men have access to?
Übung 7: 1. at 2. into 3. onto 4. about 5. to 6. for, with 7. in 8. from
Übung 8: 1. Who 2. Whose 3. Which 4. How 5. When 6. What 7. Why 8. Who
Übung 9: 1. forget 2. door 3. easy 4. locker 5. deckchair 6. prove 7. witness 8. suspect 9. heirloom 10. entrance Lösung: goalkeeper
Übung 10: 1. The girls spent a lot of time hanging out in the park. 2. Susan looked in the mirror at her long blonde hair. 3. After school they had their first band rehearsal. 4. After school they had their first band rehearsal. 5. Heather and Tracey helped Susan into her school uniform.
Übung 11: 1. competition 2. auditions 3. record company 4. collection 5. headphones
Übung 12: 1. loud 2. summer 3. canteen 4. blazer 5. ceiling 6. tomorrow 7. dinner

Glossar

Abkürzungen im Glossar

AE	*American English*
fam	*umgangssprachlich*
pl	*Plural*
v	*Verb*

abandon *v*	hier: im Stich lassen; verlassen; zurücklassen; aufgeben
accuse *v*	anklagen, beschuldigen
acquaintance	Bekannte(r)
addicted to	abhängig von
admit *v*	zugeben, gestehen
advise *v*	raten, empfehlen
amazement	Erstaunen
amazing	fantastisch, unglaublich
ambush *v*	überfallen
ambush	Hinterhalt, Überfall
ankle	Knöchel
announcement	Ankündigung
appointment	hier: Termin; Verabredung; Ernennung
approach *v*	herankommen, näher kommen
approach	hier: Vorstoß; Nähern; Zugang
appropriate	passend
apron	Schürze
argument	hier: Streit; Argument
arouse *v* **suspicion**	Verdacht erwecken
ashtray	Aschenbecher
ask *v* **sb. out**	jmd. um ein Date bitten
assume *v*	annehmen, unterstellen, voraussetzen
at all costs	um jeden Preis
attention	Aufmerksamkeit
attitude	Haltung

audition *v*	vorspielen, vorsingen
audition	Vorspielen, Vorsingen
avoid *v*	vermeiden, meiden
avoid *v* **suspicion**	Verdacht von sich ablenken
awesome	großartig
awkward	unangenehm
back *v* **down**	einen Rückzieher machen
background check	Hintergrundüberprüfung
backing singer	Backgroundsänger
backstabber *fam*	falscher Fuffziger *fam*
backstroke	Rückenschwimmen
bark *v*	bellen
battered	abgenutzt, ramponiert *fam*
be (was, been) *v* **a match for sb.**	jmd. gewachsen sein
be (was, been) *v* **attached to sth.**	an etw. hängen
be (was, been) *v* **cheesed off** *fam*	die Nase voll haben *fam*
be (was, been) *v* **fed up**	die Schnauze voll haben *fam*
be (was, been) *v* **fond of sb.**	jmd. mögen
be (was, been) *v* **out to get sb.**	es auf jmd. abgesehen haben
be (was, been) *v* **outnumbered**	in der Minderheit sein
be (was, been) *v* **overcome with tears**	von Tränen überwältigt werden
be (was, been) *v* **running late**	spät dran sein
be (was, been) *v* **supposed to be**	sein sollen
be (was, been) *v* **sweet on sb.**	auf jmd. stehen
beady eyes	glänzende Knopfaugen
bedside cabinet	Nachtschrank
behave *v*	sich benehmen
belongings	Eigentum, persönliche Sachen
bench	Bank
bet (bet, bet) *v*	wetten
better-off	besser dran, wohlhabender
big mouth *fam*	großes Mundwerk *fam*

bill	Rechnung
bit by bit	Stück für Stück, nach und nach
bitch *fam*	Schlampe *fam*
bizarre	seltsam
blackboard	Tafel
blackmail *v*	erpressen
blackmail	Erpressung
blackmailer	Erpresser(in)
blame *v*	beschuldigen
blasting *fam*	mit voller Lautstärke
bleed (bled, bled) *v*	bluten
blooming *fam*	verdammt *fam*
blow (blew, blown) *v* **sth.** *fam*	hier: etw. vermasseln *fam*
blush *v*	erröten
bold	kühn
boombox *fam*	Ghettoblaster
booth	hier: Sitzecke; Bude, Stand; Kabine
borrow *v*	ausleihen
bother *v*	ärgern, quälen
bound *v*	springen
brand	Marke
break-up	Trennung
briefcase	Aktentasche
brilliant	hier: genial, hervorragend; leuchtend
broke *fam*	hier: pleite *fam*
bruised	verletzt, verschrammt
bully *v*	einschüchtern, tyrannisieren
burglary	Einbruch
burgle *v*	einbrechen
burst (burst, burst) *v*	hier: (hinein)platzen; bersten, brechen
burst (burst, burst) *v* **into tears**	in Tränen ausbrechen
bury (buried, buried) *v*	begraben, vergraben
button	Taste; Knopf

calf, calves *pl*	hier: Wade
care about sth./sb.	sich aus etwas etwas machen/ sich für jemanden interessieren
cash register	Registrierkasse
catch (caught, caught) *v*	fangen, erwischen
catch (caught, caught) *v* **the bus**	den Bus nehmen
catch (caught, caught) *v* **up with sb.**	jmd. einholen
ceiling	Decke
chalk	Kreide
changing room	Umkleidekabine
chase *v* **sb.**	jmd. nachlaufen
check out *fam*	ansehen, auschecken *fam*
Check this out!	Schau hier!
check *v* **on sb.**	jmd. abchecken *fam*, überprüfen
cheer *v* **sb. up**	jmd. aufmuntern
cheer *v*	jubeln
chest of drawers	Kommode
chest	Brust
chick *fam*	Mädel *fam*, Kleine *fam*
chill *v* **(out)**	sich entspannen, langsam machen *fam*
chlorine	Chlor
claim *v*	behaupten
clap *v*	klatschen
classmate	Klassenkamerad(in)
clay	Ton
clench *v* **one's fists**	die Fäuste ballen
clench *v* **one's teeth together**	die Zähne zusammenbeißen
clout *v*	schlagen
clue	Hinweis
coin	Münze
comb	Kamm
combination lock	Zahlenschloss
comfort *v*	beruhigen
compassionate	mitfühlend, voller Mitgefühl

competition	Wettbewerb
conclusion	(Ab-)Schluss
concrete	Beton
confess *v*	beichten, gestehen, bekennen
confidently	sicher
confuse *v*	verwirren
connect *v*	verbinden
connection	Verbindung, Beziehung
constable	Polizist(in)
contact *v* **sb.**	sich mit jmd. in Verbindung setzen
convince *v*	überzeugen
convinced	überzeugt
cope *v* **with sth.**	etw. verkraften, mit etw. klarkommen
cord	Schnur, Leitung, Kabel
cost (cost, cost) *v* **sb. a fortune**	jmd. ein Vermögen kosten
cough *v*	husten
courage	Mut
courtyard	Hof
cover	hier: Cover; Abdeckung; Hülle; Decke
crawl *v*	krabbeln, kriechen
crawl space	Zwischendecke
creak *v*	knarren
creep (crept, crept) *v*	sich hineinschleichen
creepy	grus(e)lig
cross	verärgert
crowd	Menge
cubicle	hier: (Einzel)toilette; Kabine
cupboard	Schrank
curious	neugierig
cute	süß
daft	doof
damn *fam*	verdammt *fam*
dare *v*	wagen
darling	Liebling

date *v* **sb.**	mit jmd. gehen
dawn *v*	dämmern
deckchair	Liegestuhl
deep end	Schwimmerbecken
defender	Verteidiger(in)
deny *v*	abstreiten
despite	trotz
disgusting	empörend, widerlich
dismiss *v* **sb.**	jmd. entlassen
dive *v*	springen, Kopfsprung machen; sich stürzen
divert *v* **attention**	Aufmerksamkeit ablenken
diving board	Sprungbrett
do (did, done) *v* **the dirty work**	die Drecksarbeit machen *fam*
done in	erschöpft, fix und fertig
doorknob	Türgriff
dope *fam*	Trottel *fam*, Idiot *fam*
download	herunterladen
down-to-earth	bodenständig
drawer	Schublade
drawing	Zeichnung
drown *v*	ertränken
due to	wegen
dumb *fam*	dumm
dumb luck *AE*	Glücksfall
dump *v* **sth.**	etw. wegwerfen
dunk *v*	(ein)tunken; (ein)tauchen
dustbin	Mülltonne
duvet	Bettdecke
dye *v*	färben
earplugs *pl*	Ohrenstöpsel
ease *v* **the pain**	den Schmerz lindern
edge	Kante, Rand
elbow pads	Ellbogenschützer
embarrass *v*	in Verlegenheit bringen, blamieren

embarrassed	verlegen
embarrassing	peinlich
emergency	Notfall
entrance/entry fee	Eintrittsgeld
eternal	ewig
ethical	hier: moralisch einwandfrei; ethisch
evaporate *v*	verdunsten
evil	böse, schlecht
evil	Übel
exhausted	erschöpft
expectantly	erwartungsvoll
extension cord	Verlängerungsschnur
eyeball to eyeball	Auge in Auge
fabric	hier: Stoff; Gefüge, Struktur
fabulous	fantastisch
face *v* **sth./sb.**	sich etw./jmd. stellen
fair-skinned	hellhäutig
fan	hier: Lüfter; Fan; Fächer
fancy (fancied, fancied) *v* **sb.**	auf jmd. stehen
fellow students	Mitschüler
fight	Kampf, Streit
fight (fought, fought) *v* **off**	abwehren, ankämpfen gegen
figure *v* **sth. out**	etwas kapieren, herausfinden
file	Datei
find (found, found) *v* **favour with sb.**	jmd. gefallen
fist	Faust
fit *fam*	geil *fam*
fling (flung, flung) *v*	werfen
flush *v* **(a toilet)**	spülen
fool *v* **sb.**	jmd. täuschen
foolish	dumm, albern
footprint	Fußabdruck
forgers *pl*	Geldfälscher(innen)
freak	Fanatiker(in), Irre(r); Computerfreak

freestyle	Freistil
frown finster	schauen
frown *v*	die Stirn runzeln
furniture	Möbel
gap	(Tür-)Spalt
gather *v*	(sich ver)sammeln
gaze *v*	angaffen, starren
GCSEs *pl*	brit. Schulabschlussprüfung (mittlere Reife)
geek *fam*	Außenseiter
genius	Genie
genuine	authentisch, aufrichtig
get (got, got) *v* **at sb.**	jmd. angreifen
get (got, got) *v* **one's revenge**	sich rächen
get (got, got) *v* **on sb.'s nerves**	jmd. nerven
get (got, got) *v* **rid of**	loswerden
get (got, got) *v* **struck by lightning**	vom Blitz getroffen werden
give (gave, given) *v* **sb. a hug**	jmd. umarmen
give (gave, given) *v* **sb. the creeps**	jmd. gruseln, Gänsehaut machen
give (gave, given) *v* **up**	aufgeben
Give it up! *fam*	Gib's auf!
glance	blicken, mit Blicken streifen
glimmer of hope	ein Fünkchen Hoffnung
glorious	glorreich
go (went, gone) *v* **out with sb.**	mit jmd. gehen
goalkeeper	Torwart
grab *v* **sth.**	sich etwas schnappen
grab *v* **hold of**	festhalten
grate	Gitter, Rost
grating	Gitter
gravy	Bratensoße
groan *v*	stöhnen
grumpy	schlecht gelaunt
guy *fam*	Kerl, Typ

guys *fam*	Leute *fam*
hallway	Flur
handover	Übergabe
handsome	gut aussehend, attraktiv
hang (hung, hung) *v* **around**	rumhängen
hang (hung, hung) *v* **out**	rumhängen
hate *v* **sb.'s guts**	jmd. nicht ausstehen können
have (had, had) *v* **a crush on sb.**	in jmd. verknallt sein
have (had, had) *v* **a fit**	einen Wutanfall haben
have (had, had) *v* **a nerve**	frech sein
have (had, had) *v* **a point**	Recht haben
have (had, had) *v* **a soft spot for sb.**	eine Schwäche für jmd. haben
have (had, had) *v* **it in for sb.**	es auf jmd. abgesehen haben
head *v* **(back)**	(zurück)steuern
headphones	Kopfhörer
heirloom	Erbstück
help *v* **sb. to his/her feet**	jmd. hochhelfen
hesitate *v*	zögern
hire *v*	einstellen
hug *v* **sb.**	jmd. umarmen
humiliated	erniedrigt
I'm gonna be	ich werde … sein
indoor swimming pool	Hallenbad
innocent	unschuldig
insecure	unsicher
insistent	hier: schrill; beharrlich; nachdrücklich; wiederholt
internal injuries *pl*	innere Verletzungen
interrupt *v*	unterbrechen
investigate *v*	untersuchen, nachgehen
investigation	Nachforschung
jam (jammed, jammed) *v*	(hinein)zwängen
jerk	Trottel
keen	hier: wach, scharf

keep (kept, kept) *v* **sb. in the dark** — jmd. im Ungewissen lassen
keyboard — Tastatur; Keyboard
knackered *fam* — kaputt *fam*, geschlaucht *fam*
kneel (knelt, knelt) *v* — knien
kneepads — Knieschützer
lad — Kerl
laid-back — ruhig, gelassen
lane line — Bahnseil
leave (left, left) *v* **sb. in the dark** — jmd. im Ungewissen lassen
let (let, let) *v* **sb. down** — jmd. im Stich lassen
let (let, let) *v* **sb. in on sth.** — jmd. Bescheid sagen
liar — Lügner(in)
lick *v* — (ab)lecken
life goes on — das Leben geht weiter
lifeguard — Bademeister(in)
like pulling teeth — mühsam
limp *v* — hinken
loads of — viel
loan — Darlehen
lobster — Hummer
local — örtlich
lock *v* — abschließen, verschließen, schließen
locker room — Umkleideraum
locker — Schließfach, Spind
locket — Medaillon
loo *fam* — Klo *fam*
lousy — lausig, übel
mad — verrückt; böse, wütend, fies
maintenance man — Wartungsmonteur
make (made, made) *v* **head or tail of sth.** — aus etwas schlau werden
manage *v* — hier: schaffen; leiten, führen
manage *v* **a smile** — ein Lächeln zustande bringen
mansion — Herrenhaus, Villa

mate	Kumpel
mean	gemein, mies
mega *fam*	spitze *fam*, super *fam*
melt *v*	schmelzen
mess *v* **up** *fam*	vermasseln *fam*
mobile (phone)	Handy
mood	Stimmung
moustache	Schnurrbart
muddy	schlammig
mumble *v*	grummeln
narrow *v*	zusammenkneifen (Augen)
nasty	böse
native speaker	Muttersprachler(in)
necklace	Halskette
neighbour	Nachbar
neighbourhood	Nachbarschaft
nick *fam*	klauen, mitgehen lassen
nightmare	Albtraum
no ... either	auch nicht, auch kein
no point in doing sth.	es hat keinen Sinn, etw. zu tun
noon	Mittag
nosy	neugierig
notice *v*	merken, bemerken
nuisance	Ärgernis, Plage
obedient	gehorsam
ointment	Salbe
onlookers *pl*	Zuschauer
oops *fam*	hoppla *fam*
outgoing	aufgeschlossen
outrageous(ly)	abscheulich
over the top	übertrieben
overcrowded	überfüllt
ox, oxen *pl*	Ochse
pace	Schritt
palm	Handfläche
papers	Papiere

paramedic	Sanitäter(in)
pass key	Generalschlüssel
pavement	Bürgersteig
pawn *v*	verpfänden
pawnshop	Pfandhaus
pencil sharpener	Bleistiftspitzer
pile *v* **on the pressure**	jmd. unter Druck setzen
pillar	Säule
pinch *v*	klauen; zusammendrücken
pint-sized	winzig, knirpsig
pipe	Rohr
pitch	Spielfeld
plaster	hier: Putz; Gips; Pflaster
playground	Spielplatz
plug *v* **into**	einstecken, anschließen an
pocket money	Taschengeld
poetry	Poesie, Gedicht(e)
point *v* **to/towards**	deuten auf, zeigen auf
ponytail	Pferdeschwanz
positive	hier: überzeugt; sicher; positiv
pouch	Beutel
pound *v*	schlagen, hämmern
prank	Streich
prawn	Garnele
pressure *v* **sb.**	jmd. drängen
pretend *v*	vorgeben, so tun als ob
pride	Stolz; stolz
prime suspect	Hauptverdächtige(r)
profession	Beruf
protect *v*	schützen, beschützen
prove *v*	beweisen
publicity	Werbung
puddle	Pfütze
pulse *v*	pulsieren, pochen
punch-up *v*	Prügelei
punish *v*	bestrafen

purchase *v*	kaufen
purse	Geldbeutel
put (put, put) *v* **the blame on sb.**	den Verdacht auf jmd. lenken
put (put, put) *v* **up a brave front**	sich nichts anmerken lassen
Put a sock in it!	Du hast jetzt Sendepause! *fam*
puzzled	verblüfft, verwirrt
quid *fam*	Pfund (britische Währung)
rack *v* **one's brain**	sich den Kopf zerbrechen
radio *v*	funken
raise *v*	heben; aufbringen, besorgen
real nice	toll, super
reassure *v* **sb.**	jmd. beschwichtigen, beruhigen
receipt	Quittung
recently	vor Kurzem
reckon *v*	glauben, meinen
recommend *v*	empfehlen
record *v*	aufnehmen
recording contract	Plattenvertrag
recover *v*	wiederfinden; sich erholen
referee	Schiedsrichter(in)
regain *v* **consciousness**	das Bewusstsein wieder erlangen
rehearsal	Probe
rehearse *v*	proben
release *v*	herausbringen, veröffentlichen
release	Neuerscheinung
relief	Erleichterung
relieved	erleichtert
reluctantly	widerstrebend
rely *v* **on sb.**	sich auf jmd. verlassen
require *v*	erfordern
research	(Nach)forschung
rest	hier: Pause, Ruhe
retrieve *v*	hier: holen gehen; wieder-erlangen; zurückbekommen

reunion	hier: Treffen; Versöhnung, Wiedervereinigung
revenge	Rache
ride (rode, ridden) *v*	fahren (Fahrrad)
right away	sofort, auf der Stelle
ringleader	Bandenführer
rise (rose, risen) *v* **(up)**	hier: aufsteigen
rob *v*	rauben
robbery	Raub
rub *v* **(in)**	(ein)reiben
rubbish bin	Abfalleimer
ruin *v*	ruinieren, zerstören
rush *v*	eilen, rasen, stürzen
sail *v*	segeln, hier: fliegen
savings book	Sparbuch
scare *v* **away**	verschrecken
scare *v* **off**	verschrecken
scatter *v*	verstreuen
score *v* **(a goal)**	punkten, (ein Tor) erzielen
scorn	Hohn, Verachtung
scornfully	höhnisch, verächtlich
scratch *v*	zerkratzen
screen	hier: Bildschirm; Leinwand
screwdriver	Schraubenzieher
search warrant	Durchsuchungsbefehl
see (saw, seen) *v* **sb.'s point**	jmd. verstehen
see (saw, seen) *v* **the back of sb.**	jmd. los werden
separate *v*	(sich) trennen
serving hatch	Küchendurchreiche
set (set, set) *v* **off**	sich auf den Weg machen
shaggy	zottelig, zerzaust
shake (shook, shaken) *v*	schütteln
shelf, shelves *pl*	hier: Wandbrett; Bord; Regal
shell	Schale
show (showed, shown) *v* **up**	erscheinen, auftauchen
showdown	Auseinandersetzung
shut up *fam*	halt die Klappe *fam*

shy	schüchtern
sick note	Krankmeldung
sickening thud	scheußlicher dumpfer Aufschlag
sigh *v*	seufzen
skin cancer	Hautkrebs
sleeve	Ärmel
sneak *v*	schleichen
sneaker *AE*	Turnschuh
sneer	spöttisches Lächeln
snob	Snob
snog (snogged, snogged) *v*	(rum)knutschen *fam*
snore *v*	schnarchen
so what? *fam*	na und? *fam*
sob *v*	schluchzen
somersault	Salto
sort *v* **sth. out**	etw. regeln; etw. aussortieren
space	(Frei-)Raum, Platz
spare me	verschone mich
speaker	hier: Lautsprecher, Sprecher
speaking of	da wir gerade von … sprechen
split (split, split) *v* **up (with sb.)**	sich von jmd. trennen
sponge	Schwamm
spot *v* **sth./sb.**	etw./jmd. sehen, bemerken
sprain	Verstauchung
spring cleaning	Frühjahrsputz
spy (spied, spied)*v* **(on sb.)**	(jmd. nach)spionieren
squat (squatted, squatted) *v*	hocken
squeeze *v*	ausdrücken
stack *v*	aufstapeln, sammeln
stack	Stapel, Stoß
stare *v* **sb. in the face**	jmd. deutlich vor Augen stehen
stare *v*	starren
stationery	Schreibwaren
steep	steil
steer *v*	etw. lenken, steuern
stern	ernst, streng

stick (stuck, stuck) *v*	hier: ankleben; kleben; feststecken
stick (stuck, stuck) *v* **together**	zusammenhalten
still	hier: trotzdem; noch
storage area	Lager
stretcher	Tragbahre
stroke *v*	streicheln
stroke	hier: Schwimmstil; Schlag
struggle *v*	kämpfen
stub (stubbed, stubbed) *v* **a toe**	die Zehe anstoßen
stubbornly	stur *fam*
stuck-up	hochnäsig
stuff	Zeug, Kram *fam*
substitute	Ersatzspieler(in)
substitutes' bench	Ersatzbank
suffer *v*	leiden
sunscreen	Sonnenschutzmittel
suntan	Sonnenbräune
suspect *v*	verdächtigen
suspect	Verdächtige(r)
suspicious	verdächtig; misstrauisch
swallow *v*	(runter)schlucken
sweat *v*	schwitzen
sweat	Schweiß
sweep *v*	fegen, kehren
sweetie	Schatz, Süße(r) *fam*
swerve *v*	ausweichen
swing	Schaukel
swot	Streber(in)
tackle *v* **sb.**	mit jmd. fertig werden
take (took, taken) *v* **a risk**	ein Risiko eingehen
tambourine	flache Handtrommel
target	Ziel
team mate	Mitspieler(in)
tear (torn, torn) *v* **a muscle**	einen Muskel zerren
tease *v* **sb.**	jmd. aufziehen, necken
tell (told, told) *v* **sb. off**	jmd. ermahnen, zurechtweisen

telly *fam*	Fernseher
text *v* **sb.**	jmd. eine SMS schreiben
that certain something	das gewisse Etwas
theft	Diebstahl
thick *fam*	dumm
thrilled	begeistert
throw (threw, thrown) *v* **sb. out**	jemanden hinauswerfen
tie *v* **around**	umbinden
tight	fest
tiptoe *v*	auf Zehenspitzen gehen
top secret	streng geheim
torch	Taschenlampe
trail	hier: Spur; Weg, Pfad
trainer	Turnschuh
trap *v* **sb.**	jmd. fangen, in die Falle locken
trust	Vertrauen
turn *v* **on one's heel**	auf dem Absatz kehrtmachen
twist *v* **sb. around one's little finger**	jmd. um den Finger wickeln
unbearable	unerträglich
uncomfortable	unangenehm
unconscious	bewusstlos
upset	bestürzt, verärgert, aufgebracht
vacuum cleaner	Staubsauger
valuable	Wertgegenstand; wertvoll
van	Lieferwagen, Wagen
vending machine	Automat
ventilator shafts	Lüftungsschächte
visor	Visier
vocals	Gesang
wallet	Geldbeutel
wardrobe	Kleiderschrank
weep (wept, wept) *v*	weinen
well up	sehr wohl
well-off	vermögend
whack	schlagend
What a cheek! *fam*	Was für eine Frechheit!

what about ...?	wie wäre es mit ...? was ist mit ...?
what the heck ...? *fam*	was zum Teufel ...? *fam*
What's up?	Was ist los?
whinge *v fam*	meckern *fam*
whisper *v*	flüstern
whistle	hier: Pfeife; Flöte
wicked *fam*	geil *fam*
wind (wound, wound) *v* **sb. up**	jmd. ärgern
wipe *v*	wischen
witch	Hexe
withdraw (withdrew, withdrawn) *v*	abheben (Geld)
witness	Zeuge
would-be	vermeintlich
wrist	Handgelenk
yawn *v*	gähnen
yell *v* **(at)**	(an)schreien
yob	Halbstarker, Rowdy
You're all heart.	Du bist zu liebenswürdig. (ironisch)
youngster	Jugendliche(r)
zoom *v*	hier: sausen; zoomen

Teenage-Talk-Glossar

ask *v* **sb. out**	jmd. um ein Date bitten
awesome	großartig
backstabber	falscher Fuffziger
be (was, been) *v* **cheesed off**	die Nase voll haben
be (was, been) *v* **fed up**	die Schnauze voll haben
be (was, been) *v* **sweet on sb.**	auf jmd. stehen
bitch	Schlampe
blow (blew, blown) *v* **sth.**	hier: etw. vermasseln
broke	hier: pleite
chick	Mädel, Kleine
chill *v*	sich entspannen

daft	doof
done in	erschöpft, fix und fertig
dope	Trottel, Idiot
fancy *v* **sb.**	auf jmd. stehen
geek	Außenseiter
get (got, got) *v* **at sb.**	jmd. angreifen
get (got, got) *v* **on sb.'s nerves**	jmd. nerven
Give it up!	Gib's auf!
give (gave, given) *v* **sb. the creeps**	jmd. gruseln, Gänsehaut machen
go (went, gone) *v* **out with sb.**	mit jmd. gehen
grumpy	schlecht gelaunt
guy	Kerl, Typ
hang (hung, hung) *v* **around**	rumhängen
hang (hung, hung) *v* **out**	rumhängen
have (had, had) *v* **a crush on sb.**	in jmd. verknallt sein
jerk	Trottel
knackered	kaputt, geschlaucht
lad	Kerl
loo	Klo
lousy	lausig, übel
mate	Kumpel
mess *v* **up**	vermasseln
nick	klauen, mitgehen lassen
nosy	neugierig
quid	Pfund (britische Währung)
real nice	toll
shut up	halt die Klappe
snob	Snob
snog (snogged, snogged) *v*	(rum)knutschen
so what?	na und?
split (split, split) *v* **up**	sich von jmd. trennen
stuck-up	hochnäsig
stuff	Zeug, Kram
swot	Streber
telly	Fernseher

text *v* **sb.**	jmd. eine SMS schreiben
What a cheek!	Was für eine Frechheit!
What's up?	Was ist los?
what the heck ...?	was zum Teufel ...?
wicked	geil
wind (wound, wound) *v* **sb. up**	jmd. ärgern
yob	Halbstarker, Rowdy

SMS-Glossar

@ (at)	um, bei, an
2 (to/too)	zu; auch
2day (today)	heute
2l8 (too late)	zu spät
2moro (tomorrow)	morgen
2nite (tonight)	heute Abend
4e (for ever)	für immer
4u (for you)	für dich
b4 (before)	vorher
c u 2moro (see you tomorrow)	wir sehen uns morgen
c u l8r (see you later)	bis später
gr8 (great)	toll
l8 (late)	spät
lol (lots of love)	viele liebe Grüße
c yr (see your)	siehe dein
no1 (no-one)	niemand
pls (please)	bitte
prob (problem)	Problem
r u (are you)	bist du
thx (thanks)	danke
txt bk (text back)	zurückschreiben (SMS)
u (you)	du
u r (you are)	du bist
u want 2 (you want to)	willst du
w8 (wait)	warten
yr (your)	dein/ihr

Schüler-Lernkrimis ab der 5. Klasse

Schüler-Lernkrimi
Mathematik

Schüler-Lernkrimi
Naturwissenschaften

Schüler-Lernkrimi
Deutsch

Schrecken hoch drei ISBN 978-3-8174-9027-1 ab 5. Klasse **Der geheimnisvolle Rivale** ISBN 978-3-8174-7720-3 ab 5. Klasse **Schatten in der Einsteinallee** ISBN 978-3-8174-7454-7 ab 5. Klasse	**<u>Physik</u>** **Der geheimnisvolle Code** ISBN 978-3-8174-7671-8 ab 5. Klasse	**Angst auf Amrum** ISBN 978-3-8174-7499-8 ab 5. Klasse **Das Präsent aus Panama** ISBN 978-3-8174-7455-4 ab 5. Klasse
	<u>Chemie</u> **Panik im Labor** ISBN 978-3-8174-7721-0 ab 5. Klasse	

Schüler-Lernkrimis ab dem 3. Lernjahr

Schüler-Lernkrimi
Latein

Schüler-Lernkrimi
Englisch

Schüler-Lernkrimi
Französisch u. Spanisch

Der Feuerteufel von Rom
ISBN 978-3-8174-7448-6
ab 3. Lernjahr

Der Münzfälscher von Rom
ISBN 978-3-8174-7672-5
ab 3. Lernjahr

Eiskalte Rache
ISBN 978-3-8174-7612-1
ab 3. Lernjahr

Tatort Schließfach
ISBN 978-3-8174-7611-4
ab 3. Lernjahr

Ultimatum per SMS
ISBN 978-3-8174-7823-1
ab 3. Lernjahr

<u>Französisch</u>
Stadt im Dunkel
ISBN 978-3-8174-7613-8
ab 3. Lernjahr

Diebstahl in der Rue St. Jacques
ISBN 978-3-8174-7877-4
ab 3. Lernjahr

<u>Kurzkrimis</u>
Giftmord im Kolosseum
ISBN 978-3-8174-7859-0
ab 3. Lernjahr

<u>Sammelband</u>
Teen Crime Club
ISBN 978-3-8174-7899-6
ab 3. Lernjahr

<u>Spanisch</u>
Heiße Spur auf Ibiza
ISBN 978-3-8174-7622-0
ab 3. Lernjahr